– Sojourner's Truth –

by

Katherine D. Bennett

authorHOUSE

1663 LIBERTY DRIVE, SUITE 200
BLOOMINGTON, INDIANA 47403
(800) 839-8640
WWW.AUTHORHOUSE.COM

© 2005 Katherine D. Bennett. All Rights Reserved.

No part of this book may be reproduced, stored in a retrieval system, or transmitted by any means without the written permission of the author.

First published by AuthorHouse 08/10/05

ISBN: 1-4208-5543-3 (sc)

Library of Congress Control Number: 2005904025

Printed in the United States of America
Bloomington, Indiana

This book is printed on acid-free paper.

⸺ Dedication ⸺

To my children, Lydia and Benjamin;
my partners in dreams.

— Acknowledgements —

For guidance and encouragement,
I gratefully acknowledge my friends:
Pat Kibby, Kay DeMoss, Rodney Delmont,
Pat and John Pettersen, Angie and Eric Mayel,
and Eric Knickerbocker

~ Prologue ~

The load of shield sticks weighed very little, but Elfin and Josilyn bent their backs as if it were a heavy load. Elfin walked in front of his wife, and murmured out quiet instructions about where to step so she would not trip on the hem of her skirt. She never had become used to the flowing garment and the opaque eyeholes, even though they had been here for several long years. Tripping would be a very bad thing. If she tripped, then the patrols would be there in an instant, making certain that a proper wife was not being abused. That would not do, especially since she was not a proper wife. As it was, the patrols ignored them and their odd habits, believing them to be a crazed old man and a wife humoring him out of loyalty.

They must be just as they had been for all these years. Silent, unnoticed. Ahhh! This was the place. He and Josilyn lowered their loads gingerly to the ground. It would not do to break the shield sticks, though they had plenty of them; it was just a bother to have to reprogram them. Carefully, he took out one of the long, thin sticks and inserted it with soft, sure, skill into the ground. Sometimes he had to dig around a rock, but today the soil was mostly sandy, so the shield sticks went in smoothly. Whenever a curious patrol member or citizen would ask him what he was doing, he would answer that he was planting hope for the future. Three steps over, and another stick. Planting the future. Just a crazy old man and his loyal wife.

― Chapter 1 ―

The breeze smelled sweet. Captain Jarvo noticed it momentarily, and then impatiently dismissed the thought. He would notice sweet smelling breezes and golden butter-melting sunshine, when this place was fully occupied and these heathens were properly ordered. He would not be seduced by all of this. He was afraid some of his men were being affected by all of the nonsense of these people, and he was glad that this part of the Conquest would soon be over. Then they would be safe from all these strange ideas. They would receive honor. They had accomplished much in a year.

He glanced at his men in their positions on either side of the road entering the village. Private Ritsi's Camo-loop was not functioning properly, but he would soon have it adjusted. A minor problem; his squad was exemplary. If you weren't looking right at them, you would never be able to see them positioned on the embankments that rose up on either side of the road, not even Ritsi with his malfunctioning camo-loop. The other enlisted men, Lant, Para, and Ninta were on the hills that surrounded the tiny village in the secluded valley, monitoring the village and its inhabitant's activities as they scurried about preparing for the evening's festivities. Lieutenants Bosson and Simon were in their secondary command positions monitoring the road for the arrival of the barbarian queen, Sojourner.

She should be here within the hour. That is, unless she stopped for some foolish self- indulgence. She was an unnatural woman, and ridding the world of her influence would make it a better place. No doubt she would be late arriving because she had stopped to roll in the grass like a beast or, he pressed his eyes shut tightly against the memory, she might be swimming naked in a pool or stream outside where she was exposed to all. It was no wonder these simpletons had not progressed beyond living in holes in the ground if their queen behaved like an elderly wood rat.

Still, these people had some capabilities that were puzzling, and that is why the Empire had not simply exterminated them when they were discovered. Jarvo was certain that what he saw was simply left over technology from the Dark Nation that had somehow managed to survive the thousand years since it was defeated. He did not see very much evidence of great machinery beyond the little floating scooter devices called Hover-bikes the inhabitants rode when they were going any long distance. The clever farming machinery that was used in the fields was also a wonder. Beyond that he did not see any evidence of great technology or architecture.

He felt a pang of homesickness for the Empire. He longed for the grandeur of his homeland but he would not give in to his homesickness. Soon, this would be over, and he would sail back across the vast water to the awe-inspiring towers and mighty industries of the Empire of Righteousness. He would perform thanksgiving rituals in the Contemplation Centers and go to the Palace of the Emperor and rededicate himself to Service straightaway even after being Purified, even before going home to his wife. He would be glad to be home. He would rededicate himself and then he would go home to his proper wife, and tend to his own needs. He might even look at her face and speak her name tenderly out of gratitude for her propriety. Ah! Sky and Earth! He did want to be home! A movement in the village recaptured his attention, and Lt. Simon's voice whispered in his earpiece, "She is coming!"

Captain Jarvo focused. In the village, or Burrow, as the inhabitants called it, the work stopped and a shout went up. "She comes!" A few fleet-footed children scampered off down the curving stone-paved roadway, and the villagers all stopped their bustling preparations to hurry down the road as well, jostling and laughing like children themselves. From their vantage points in the wooded hillsides, the progress of the queen was obvious. Jarvo was disgusted. When these people were aligned within the Order, and the Emperor Kalig came among them, they would show proper respect and decorum. These people were mad to act so like children. Their world cried out for the order of the Empire.

The queen came into Jarvo's view. She was sitting astride her Hover-bike, and as usual she was dressed in the most scandalous fashion. Her head was bare and her face uncovered, and she was dressed in a vivid blue outfit that exposed her arms and her lower legs to everyone that cared to look at her. The fabric was light and when the breeze caught it, it curved against her so that the shape of her breasts, the curve of her waist, the lines of her thighs could be discerned. Unnatural! Jarvo thought for a fleeting moment of his own wife, silent, solemn, modest. When he took his pleasure with her, she kept her eyes tightly shut and her face turned from him. She was not like these bold women in this wild place. She was worthy of protection and respect. This old creature in her outlandish clothes was an affront to any proper woman.

The Hover-bike glided silently over the roadway, and Queen Sojourner slowed it to a bare creeping pace. She dismounted and let an eager boy guide it for her as she walked the last hundred yards or so to the outskirts of the little village, her hand resting on the handle. The village was built into the sides of the hills surrounding the common, the doors and windows looking out of the hillsides like surprised sleepy faces. Almost all of the Burrows in this strange land are built like this. How people could live in holes in the ground was a mystery to Captain Jarvo. His own home was an apartment in a majestic building that housed a thousand families in the service of the Empire. From his vantage point on the hillside, Jarvo could see the village commons and the dais that had been raised for the queen to stand on when she told her ghastly stories of heresy and corruption. She was not a natural woman.

Privately, in his own thoughts, Jarvo called her the Harlot, and he sometimes referred to her as such when planning strategies with his men. He worried that his men might be affected by her rambling tales, but so far their fidelity was firm. At least they were all adhering to the Codes. Still, the Harlot spun out her heresies like the confectioner at festival time spun out his sugar fluffs. She had no conscience about her people's life force. Not like the Emperor Kalig. Kalig guarded his people's life force like his most important treasure, even at the expense of his own. He was a righteous man, proven by Trials and Blood. The past strengthened the future. There was purpose.

The people crowded around the barbarian queen until she was at the edge of the commons, then they stopped and she approached the dais by herself. The Chief Elder of the village came out of one of the hole-doors and approached her. He was dressed in a ceremonial robe and carried the usual wooden staff. He was followed by what must be the Head Woman of this Burrow. They stood as still as carved stone. The queen approached and then stopped. Jarvo adjusted his headset so that he could listen to their conversation. It would be the usual dull exchange, but he knew his duty.

The queen put her hand over her heart and said solemnly, "I am one of the many. I come as a sister to you. I am Sojourner."

Then the Chief replied, "This is one place among many. We are your brothers and sisters. We are Deep

Burrow and we are complete when you are here. We welcome you!"

The Chief extended the staff, and Sojourner reached out her hand and touched the metal tip. After she touched the tip, the paltry ritual was over, and the three embraced. Jarvo always felt sick at this point of the queen's greeting ceremony. How could any man touch such an unclean woman in a public place? There was no outcry from the people at this behavior, and obviously no kinsman to defend the queen against unlawful touching. When these people were exposed to a real emperor, they would undoubtedly fall on their knees in front of him in wonder and repent of their animal ways.

The villagers, chattering in their inane way, turned away from their queen and continued with their festival preparations. Disrespectful louts! The Head Woman started giving out instructions like a pompous underlord. Jarvo adjusted his monitor to filter out their talk, and concentrated on the conversation that the Harlot was having with the Chief as they stood on the dais observing the preparations. He felt his leg burn with the sting of a biting bug. Of course, even the insects were annoying here.

"Are the crops good this year, Joseph?"

"Excellent, my Lady! The corn is growing very well, and it looks like we may have a bumper crop of apples!"

"Superb! If there is a surplus, we may be able to supply Far Burrow. Their apples have failed this year. A late freeze."

"A terrible pity!"

The conversation droned on, until the Head Woman escorted the queen into one of the hole-doors. Jarvo yawned. It would be good to have this over with. He would never listen to another conversation about apples or root rot again. Soon, he would be home. He would be among honored peers, men of dignity and worth. He would be in a place of order and tradition. He would be proud to be a servant of the Empire. He was a proud man of the Empire.

He scratched at the itching bite.

— Chapter 2 —

Sojourner stood on the dais with Joseph. Her nerves were frayed, and she thought for just a moment of calling it all off and going home like Stephan wanted. She was becoming very tired, and sometimes she was very frightened. Her legs ached and her arms felt like lead. She must have her implants adjusted before the Empire abducted her. Her palms were sweating.

"So, Joseph, are our visitors still spying on us?" she asked, without looking at the hillsides. She didn't have to look. She knew that Captain Jarvo was in the blackberry bushes on the top of that rise over there, no doubt crushing good berries with his big, stupid feet. She hoped he got thoroughly scratched. How ignorant to hide in thorny blackberry bushes. The Lieutenants were down the road and the enlisted men were surrounding the village commons, monitoring her behavior like there was no tomorrow. They were all so serious and self-important. Foolish men. She thought about swimming naked one more time, just to make them nervous. There was a lovely stream about a mile down the road...

Joseph nodded his head casually. "Oh yes. I'll show you the recording if you like. They surrounded the village with great stealth about an hour before you arrived. Right now they are recording every word they think we are saying. I believe we are talking about crops right now. Apples and the like. Shall we keep it up all evening?"

"Silly boys. No, let them hear the story tonight. It may make them better people. Though, as far as I can tell it hasn't caused any of them to seek redemption yet."

"Sojourner, this is a terrible risk you are taking. We have the means to end this before it begins. You can go home and be with your family. Reconcile with Stephan and live out your days. You have done so very much for our nation already. This does not have to be on your shoulders."

Sojourner smiled sadly. " I know we are prepared to end this, but I can't face that alternative. So many others have been lost to the Empire...well, if this foolish ruse will preserve some lives we have to try it. The Plan is a good one, it has been in the making for years. Even though we were surprised and haven't all the information we need, it will work. I know this new possibility is a desperate move, but if this works then lives will be saved. They are an easily led people or else they would not have come to this pass, isn't that right? The soldiers have done every predictable thing. They still don't have any idea?"

Joseph shook his head slightly. "They still think we are simple farmers, and that they will enjoy ruling us."

Sojourner breathed in deeply. The air was sweet, and the sunshine lay across the commons like transparent gold. It was a beautiful world they had made. Her people had labored for generations to cure the land of the Great Destruction. The thought of it being invaded was more than she could bear. She wished this had not happened in her lifetime. She began to feel the telltale ache in her legs and the tingling in her fingers. She was too tired.

"Are Sala and Jakma here?" Sojourner asked, knowing her daughters were staying close to their father. This was too painful. What did it matter that far away despots would die?

Joseph looked at his feet. "No. I'm sorry."

"I would have liked to say good-bye. I just wish that I could kiss my girls and the grandbabies once more. Well, we all knew the risks, didn't we? You kiss them for me." She paused. "I don't suppose Stephen has sent word...he was so angry at me for consenting to this."

Joseph turned to her and spoke with barely concealed pain in his voice. "You don't have to go through with this."

"I know. But this is a great opportunity to save lives. Foreign lives. Believe me, I think about this. Maybe there are children that will not suffer." Sojourner knew she was trying to convince herself again to allow herself to be taken.

Joseph looked at her with fondness and regret. "You always were too brave for your own good. My wife is furious with me for voting against her. She thinks we should just entrap them all and choose out the Candidates without any further thought. She thinks that a government as brutal as the Empire should be ended. You know Cloe. She has written several very funny poems at my expense, and I can't say I am happy about it."

Sojourner smiled wryly, "Yes, Cloe always had a way with words. You knew the risk when you married her all those years ago. If I remember correctly, you were the subject of a pretty sharp limerick or two before you were a couple. You should be used to it by now!"

"The good side of her wit is that when she chooses, her words are rather sweet. I guess I can manage!" He chuckled and waved to Cloe, the "Head Woman" as the invaders referred to her. She walked over to the dais, stopping to give an occasional instruction. She mounted the dais, glowered at Joseph first and then smiled at Sojourner.

"Sojourner, you must be exhausted. Don't tell me that my husband has been talking strategy with you already, and you with the dust of the road still on your feet." She turned to her husband indignantly, "Shame on you." Then back to Sojourner, "Would you like to freshen up before the celebration? I have a nice room prepared for you. I have also notified the Healers that you will need Clarifying...at your convenience, of course. You need to be resting a bit, not talking strategy."

"Thank you, Cloe. I could use a shower and a few minutes of rest. Especially the shower. Yesterday, I found a still pool to bathe in, and just for meanness, I swam as naked as a new baby. I hope I gave at least one of the soldiers a fright. Anyway, I still feel the mud between my toes. A nice hot shower is just what I need."

"Sojourner, you didn't! You were born to scandalize repressed nations." Cloe laughed, and turned to her husband. "I hope you didn't watch. I will have to write another poem for you if you did."

Joseph raised his eyebrows and turned toward his wife indignantly. "I would do no such thing." he sputtered.

Cloe smiled, satisfied with Joseph's discomfort. "You make this too easy." She smiled coyly. "I know who you looked at last night."

Joseph blushed, but he smiled ruefully. "Cloe, mind you manners for just this once."

"Why should I change now? If you wanted a sweet, submissive woman you would have gone to the Empire as a young man and gotten one of those poor souls to marry. You like the challenge I bring you. Admit it!"

"Aren't you supposed to be showing your dear friend to her room? I imagine you have much to talk about."

"Yes. We do have much to talk about. I may have to tell her the poem I started about you just this instant. Let's see. Beware weary traveler, if you take a nude swim....The leaders of our country will watch you jump in!....I'll be working on it if you need me."

Joseph turned to Sojourner with a resigned shrug. "Let's send Cloe instead of you. She'll teach the Empire a lesson."

Sojourner smiled and held up her hands, "You two have been at this for twenty years. I stayed out of it when we were at the University, and I'll stay out of it now. I think that shower sounds like a safe place to be."

Cloe and Joseph laughed good-naturedly and Sojourner followed Cloe off the dais and to one of the doors embedded it the side of the hill. The soldiers of the Empire called them slug holes. Of course they couldn't know. Cloe opened the door for Sojourner like she was deferring to her, though they both knew that, especially for Cloe, it was all for the benefit of the watching soldiers. All this deceit and for what? She hoped it was worth it.

Together they entered a small homey looking dwelling. The soldiers had gone so far as to sneak into one of these little "dwellings" to write a report about the simple lifestyles of the heathens in this country. Foolish boys. Cloe led Sojourner to the far wall and placed her palm against the DNA Board disguised to look like a plaque of proverbs. Sojourner heard the whirr from deep within, and the inner door opened.

Sojourner caught her breath. Deep Burrow always made her breathe in deeply. This was the first Burrow created after the destruction of the Great Nation. It honeycombed deeply into the earth, and far. The vast terraces and pillars were festooned with growing things, each plant treasured and tended by the Gardeners. The Gardeners were an elite group, both those on the topside and those that kept the light and balance of the Burrows. They had kept the people alive with their diligence throughout the years, and they would save the Empire when it was contained. Stephen was a Master Gardener. She had been so proud on his Ascension Day, as he had been proud of her on her Ascension Day to Master Storyteller. Now he would not speak to her. Always this sorrow followed her. He was probably right about this. How could she face the Empire with this weight on her? The Empire had healthy people. There were strong babies there. She forced herself to think of something else. Her temples began to throb with the old familiar ache. Not now...

She must remember to visit the Safe Cavern before she left Deep Burrow, and pay her respects to the brave souls that endured the New Beginnings. There the survivors of the destruction gathered and began to heal the terrible ravaging of the earth. All of civilization had been burnt to cinders, and the topside was full of poison. It was here that humanity rebuilt itself and discovered ways to heal the ruin. Through the generations, this had become a mighty place. Through the generations, the people had planned, delved carefully, and managed; and this vast, beautiful city was the result. That was not to say that Far Burrow wasn't magnificent, or that Sand Burrow didn't have a sweet charm to it. No, indeed! But they did not equal Deep Burrow for its sense of history and grandeur.

Cloe hailed a hovercab and gave the driver their destination. The driver, a young man with the pale features of one who rarely went topside, smiled fondly at Sojourner as she got in.

"Hail, Storyteller!" He turned to Cloe. "Hail Leader! I am honored to have you both in my humble craft! Master Storyteller! I look forward to your performance this evening. Might I be so bold as to request a story?"

"Certainly! But only if you tell me your story. I am always looking for new material!"

The young man lit up with pleasure. "There is not much to tell you about myself. I am Bura, son of Jostle and Mem of Under Burrow," he explained as he eased the hovercab out into the stream of silent, soaring vehicles.

"My goodness! You are a long way from home! What brings you to Deep Burrow?"

"Two things, ma'am. Music and a pretty girl!"

Cloe and Sojourner looked at each other and smiled.

Cloe leaned forward, "Well, young Bura, how have you fared?"

Bura smiled, "Well, Leader, the pretty girl is now my Intended, we will be joined next month! The music, well, I guess I was not so talented as my mother told me! I have found that I am a better hover cab driver than singer of ballads, though I am good enough to have won my Gin's heart! It is all well and good!"

Sojourner watched her friend fondly. Cloe was always the one interested in progress. That is probably why she was chosen as one of the Leaders of the Councils. Cloe and Joseph both had been incredible, and well matched. It was a rare thing that two such powerful personalities were allowed to Join. For them, though, it seemed to work out well. Still, they only qualified for one child because it was felt that they would not be able to provide proper parenting for more. They were both very healthy, and their bodies could have made many strong children. Not like Sojourner. Her body was riddled with flaws, and if it weren't for her implants she would be a complete invalid. She had still qualified for a child based on her temperament and thought skills. If she had been healthy she would have been able to have more. Stephen had qualified for five children. She had always felt badly that he did not get to fill his potential because he had joined himself to her. She was always giving thanks that her one child had had the goodness to become twins, at least Stephan had not had to give up so much to be her husband. He never brought it up; not even now when she had broken his heart and alienated him so. Enough! She could not think of him right now. It would only make the fissures in her heart break and crumble. She had to be strong to face the invaders.

It was puzzling that the soldiers had misinterpreted their culture so thoroughly, and had mistaken a Storyteller for a queen. She would have travelled by the Undertube if she had known the idiots had never seen someone tell a story before and avoided all of this. It was so nice to travel topside, though, and feel the new breezes and see the wonderful world that was growing. She loved entering the quaint little villages that had been built to disguise the Burrows, and she loved telling her stories with the stars floating above her in the velvety night sky. She loved being a Storyteller; that is until the invaders came and decided she was the queen of the Burrows. Idiots!

"Storyteller?"

Sojourner forced her thoughts back into the cab. The young man was glancing over his shoulder, his face eager.

"May I tell you my story request?"

"Yes, of course." replied Sojourner.

"Would you tell the story of Comet and Terra? My mother loves that story, and she will burst with happiness if I tell her I asked you to tell it."

Sojourner smiled sadly and thought of Stephan, far away, and probably resolved to his innermost parts not to watch the holo-cast of her stories tonight. She missed him. The stubborn.... She took control of her scattering thoughts and nodded to the young driver. He grinned happily, and descended deeper into the vast city and then turned into an opening carved out of the deep rock. He pulled up smoothly into a portal, and stopped, then helped Sojourner and Cloe out of the hovercab.

"If you wouldn't mind, Bura, I would like for you to wait for me. I will be several minutes, but I have a number of other errands to do and will need your services for a span. You will be on duty for a while?"

"I am at your service, Leader." The young man was obviously pleased at the prospect of being connected to important events. He would have much to tell his sweetheart and mother this evening.

Cloe led Sojourner through the modest doorway with *Traveler's Place* inscribed on a simple plaque beside the door. The outer portal was deceptive, though. The doorway opened into a huge, elegant lobby, softly lighted, with plants and comfortable deep chairs arranged in tasteful intimate groupings. An attendant greeted them discreetly and after Cloe gave him several whispered instructions, ushered them down a deeply carpeted corridor. Cloe and Sojourner followed him silently. Sojourner felt her body beginning to list to her left, and Cloe discreetly took her arm and supported her.

"Perhaps I will see the Healers before that hot shower," she breathed to Cloe.

"Yes, I think that is a good idea, my friend." Cloe replied softly, silent tears filling her eyes and spilling unchecked down her cheek. "I have already sent for them."

— Chapter 3 —

She mounted the dais with sure steps. Ahh! This was wonderful. There was a fragrant breeze filled with the scent of honeysuckle and newly bloomed roses. She found herself wishing for a moment that she were a spirit, so that she could swim in the swirling, wonderful smelling air. Silly old woman! She chided herself for being too fanciful. Even Storytellers had to be a bit realistic. That was one of the tenets of Storytelling. "Be certain there is truth in your tale." Truth.

The dais was lit with a dozen or so torches, a whimsical touch for the benefit of the soldiers hidden in the brush. Joseph had ordered some ticks and chiggers released into the thickets earlier, so she was certain they were all very uncomfortable. Joseph assured her that the birds would enjoy the parasites, and it was a legitimate exercise, but Sojourner suspected he took a secret pleasure in the itchy bites the soldiers were suffering. She had to admit that she was happy they were all suffering a bit, too. Invaders.

She walked across the dais confidently. She was glad she had arrived early in the day, because it had taken the Healers hours to replace and recaliber her implants. Apparently, her implant status had been upgraded. That was not good news. She had known for a very long time that her cells were degrading, and she had always known that she was close to the limits of her upgrades. The implants were not meant to prolong life, just improve the quality of life during the projected lifespan of the recipient. Her natural flaws were profound. It was common to be flawed, but Sojourner's maladies were troubling even by Burrow standards. Still, it was rare to find someone without at least one implant, the weakness of their bodies were still a troubling occurrence in the Burrows, even after nearly a thousand years of battling the decaying radiation from the Great Destruction. Ionizing radiation had been the bane of the world for hundreds of years. The Gardeners had found a way to cleanse the Earth, but they had not been able to purge the gene pool. They needed fresh genes to do that. Do not think of this. She scolded herself. Even as an old lady, her thoughts were as undisciplined as a whirlwind. She breathed in deeply. Such sweet smelling air.

She looked out over the "villagers" in the commons. They had built long benches and tables for the occasion and had enjoyed a special feast. Of course, this was the tradition, though they had made it seem much more rustic for the sake of the soldiers hiding in the thickets on the embankments. She hoped the soldiers were drooling over the savory dishes they had consumed. The cooks had outdone themselves this evening. Of course, most everyone knew that this was the final evening before Sojourner was to be taken by the soldiers, so there had been extra effort to make it wonderful. Someone had made certain there were fresh strawberries and melon. Sojourner loved strawberries and melon, and she could still taste them on her lips. She wondered if the Empire had strawberries.

The villagers quieted and watched her with eager silence. Deep in the Burrow the people gathered around the special holo-platforms set up in public places to watch and listen as well. When all was still, and the air about her had that feeling of expectancy and suspense, Sojourner turned her thoughts inward, uncluttering herself and centering her thoughts. She was the only Master Storyteller in the Burrows, she captured her listeners with her tales....she looked up at the deep night sky and breathed in deeply again. Honeysuckle and roses, and the taste of strawberries still on her lips.....This was perfect. She began.

"Hear now! Listen! Do you hear the wind sighing through the trees? Watch how it scampers across the grasses, and whirls around in a dervish dance. See there! Look! Do you see the trees stretching their arms towards the sky? Do you know why the mountains and the grasses and the forests all seem to strain to reach the heavens? Do you know why the winds whirl and moan, whisper and sigh, tear and shriek?

"Listen! Sit quietly and hear the tale.

"At the beginning, the Maker spun this orb out among His cosmos. He spent much time on this world, making it lovely and pleasing. He made it a vast, sweeping land with deep, still pools and endless meadows. It was a serene, calm place, made to rest the eye and calm the restless spirit.

"He chose as a caregiver a great and valiant spirit called Terra. Terra had labored for the Maker in the harshest places in the universe, and deserved peace. Terra longed for serenity, and the Maker wove Terra's need into the fabric of the earth. Terra was willingly bound to this world, and his need for peace was met.

"For long ages, Terra tended the sweeping plains and calm waters of the planet, and he was content. But, after the fashion of spiritual beings, he eventually grew lonely and desired a companion. The Maker, who understands this desire, cast His voice out among the far reaches of space, calling for a companion to step forward to be a mate for Terra.

"Deep in space, among the stars, there was a lively, carefree spirit called Comet. She spent her time dancing with her sisters, and decorating the great hallways of Heaven's temples. For countless ages, she had admired Terra's bravery and noble qualities. Her heart leapt with excitement at the thought of being a companion to such a fine spirit. Eagerly, she stepped forward.

""Now, Comet," cautioned the Maker, "Once you are joined to Terra, you must remain with him on this planet for the span of this creation. He has bound himself to this orb, and his need is woven into its fabric. He cannot leave it, and he requires the serenity of solitude to heal his tired spirit. No more will you dance among the stars, or play tag with your sisters deep in space. You will be bound to Terra, and Terra has bound himself to his world."

"Oh! Maker!" exclaimed sparkling Comet, "I am filled with joy and pleasure at the thought of an age of eternity bound to Terra! I will be proud to be mated with him, even if it be in the farthest reaches of the heavens!"

"So the Maker made the arrangements. Terra was well pleased Comet would be his mate, for long had he admired her dances, and he remembered her laughter and sweet conversations with pleasure.

"Comet came to Terra's world in a grand procession. The heavens joined in the festivities, and even the spirits in the farthest reaches of the universe joined in the celebration. Terra and Comet were married in the midst of feasting and celebration, and there was great joy in Heaven. Comet and Terra were happy.

"Their union was filled with shared gladness; ages came and went without even a thought of discontentment. Sometimes, though, Comet would wander out on the vast, endless stretches of empty grasslands, and she would watch the faraway dances of her sisters as they pranced among the stars. Occasionally, her sisters would turn their attention to Earth, and they would wave and pantomime silliness for her amusement. At first, Terra watched with her and they would join together in their enjoyment of their games. After an eon, though, Terra lost interest in their gamboling games, and would not accompany his wife to watch them, preferring to tend to the needs of his planet.

"Once in a very great while, her sisters would come to visit Comet. They were happy for the love Comet shared with Terra, but they missed her lively chatter and happy games. They would regale her with the events of Heaven, elaborating on even the smallest details to make their stories more interesting. At first, Comet found comfort in their visits, and she watched them leave with no regrets. After eons, though, her restless spirit began to regret their leaving her behind. It became harder and harder for her to watch them bound into space and resume their dancing and games. She could hear their far off voices singing and glimpse their joyful twirling, and her heart would feel torn. Although her love for Terra was deep in her being, and her holy promises to be faithful were strong in her intentions, she secretly missed being with her sisters out among the stars. Eventually, the division of her heart caused her to become discontent, and her promises became burdensome to her. Her former life became perfect in its appeal.

"Terra began to realize that all was not well with his wife, and he tried to understand her discontentment, but could not. His need for serenity was so deep that it was painful for him to realize his precious Comet did not share his need for silence. Even so, he tried hard to please his mate, causing all manner of exotic plants to grow, and making all manner of animals for her amusement. This helped some, but Comet's discontent grew continually. Terra began to lose patience.

"Finally, a day came when Terra's patience snapped and Comet's fidelity collapsed. They began to argue, and as they did the first wind was stirred and began to swirl madly and lash the Earth with its first violence. Their argument grew in frenzy until the Earth cracked and formed deep gorges and canyons. Deep waters stirred and they divided and trembled. Waves began to surge and pound the shorelines for the first time. The Earth, which had been smooth and calm, became convulsed with movement.

"Comet and Terra were furious, and they hurled meaningless accusations at each other. In angry defiance, Comet leapt towards the heavens to join her sisters in their far away dances. Just before she left Earth's breath, Terra caught the end of her robe and cried out, "Don't go! Stay with me!" But, Comet pulled loose and faced towards the deep places of space. She ran away.

"Terra was disconsolate, and stood long days with his arms stretched towards the retreating Comet. So great was his desire for her, that even the Earth began to reach towards the sky, calling for Comet to come back. Terra was so deeply bound to the fabric of Earth that he could not follow her, though for the first time since his binding, he longed to leave.

"As Comet neared the edge of the solar system, her heart grew heavy with guilt, and she remembered her promises. She remembered Terra's pain, and her heart was pierced with compassion for him. She remembered the joys of love and the sweetness of Terra's embrace. Her eagerness began to fail her, and she desired to be reconciled to Terra. She turned around.

"As she neared the Earth, she heard Terra's sad lament and she, too, began to weep. The new formed mountains reached towards her, and the trees lifted their arms. The grasses and flowers searched the skies for her return.

"As she neared the earth, Comet began to think about why she had left. She remembered Terra's angry words, and her pride rose up in her. She felt her anger and discontent rise up in her afresh. She turned toward space......

"Now hear this! Do you see the mountains? See how they stand as sentinels watching for Comet's return to Terra and Earth? See how the trees and grasses search the sky? They watch vainly.

"Comet has not yet rejoined her sisters. No! She nears the edge of Pluto's cold orbit, and then she turns back. She cannot bring herself to leave her husband, and yet, she cannot forget her sisters. And so, she circles endlessly, unable to leave and unwilling to stay.

"Hear now! Do you hear the wind? Do you hear it sigh and moan and roar? Listen to the wind and in it you will hear Terra's lament for Comet. It is a song of love and lost love."

The commons was silent, and Sojourner stood as still as a sentinel, waiting for the moment when her listeners would breathe in deeply. Sometimes, they remained silent, and she would walk away silently, leaving them with the story swirling about them. Sometimes they would erupt in movement and clapping, then she would smile and reach out to them. Either way, the story was told. Then it happened, the people breathed in deeply and someone began to clap, and a moment later, everyone was clapping. Sojourner liked these moments better than the silent, captured moments. She wanted the people to release and surge up, renewed. When they were silent, she felt as if they carried her story away with them like a heavy stone. Sometimes that is what she wanted, but tonight she wanted them to press around her and look into her face. She wanted them to beg for another story, and another until her voice was hoarse and her legs trembled from standing. How else would she sleep tonight? Tomorrow she would be leaving her home for a hope, and she was not certain if it was the right thing to do or not. She wanted to be exhausted.

"Another!" shouted a voice from the commons.

"Yes! Please!"

Sojourner smiled. Ah, yes. This is how she had hoped it would be. She looked at the velvet night sky. The moon floated above her like a shining cymbal, and the stars scattered about like the imprints of its sound. She turned her thoughts inward.

~ Chapter 4 ~

Sojourner stretched and turned over. The pillow was soft under her head, and this was a very fine, warm bed. She did not want to open her eyes and find she had been dreaming, so instead, she cautiously moved her foot over to the other side of the bed to see if he was really there. Ah, yes. The familiar hairy leg of her husband was still there...Stephan. She opened her eyes just a little. Stephan. She smiled and moved closer. He slept soundly, like he always did. He never snored, but he snorted like a bull when he woke up. He always had. When he woke up, he would wheeze and bellow as he stumbled up, bleary eyed and incoherent and crash his way into the bathroom. What was left of his hair would be standing on end and he would be so groggy from slumber that he wouldn't be certain where he was for several minutes.

When they had first been joined, she had envisioned them waking up wrapped in each other's arms and cuddling. But that was not the way Stephan woke up.

He woke up in a crashing, snorting, incoherent way. At first, she had been disappointed, but then she had grown accustomed to his ways. In the months since they had disagreed about the Empire she had found it very terrible to wake up to such silence. She had not known what to do at first. Having Stephan in her bed this morning was almost as good as finding him here last night.

She did not get back to her rooms until late. She had told another story, and then another. She felt the stories flowing in her and she needed to tell them. She wanted to tell every story she knew, and all the stories she had thought, and all the stories that could be. Here in the flickering torchlight, surrounded by those who wished her well, the taste of strawberries fading from her lips, she was happy. She was a Master Storyteller, and that is all she had ever wanted be, except for being Stephen's wife and mother to her children.

When she was a very little girl, before she was entitled to her implants, when she was locked inside her invalid body, her thoughts had been full of stories. Her mother would come to the Compassion Center at every convenience and rock her and stroke her and croon to her, soft little rhymes and sweet little stories. She would sometimes bring Joran, her older brother, and he would sing to her, too. That was how they discovered she was not one of the Lost Ones that would forever be locked inside herself. She would strain toward her mother and Joran making little sounds in her throat. Happiness would envelop her every time they were near. Her mother could see the happiness in her and it made her hope.

At first, the attendants thought it was not an anomaly. Most children so handicapped would interact with the familiar in some way; it was a human thing to do. Sojourner's mother did not believe that was all it was, though, and began the Teaching Patterns, even though most, even her father at first, thought it was a waste of time. Her mother could tell Sojourner wanted to know, to understand, though, and she trusted herself. Soon her father was convinced that she was not a Lost One, as well. Her parents took turns administering the Teaching Patterns. Her father would also hold her and stroke her hair and whisper to her that she had to show everyone that she was thinking so that she could be Implanted. He told her stories about brave people in history that overcame great obstacles, and how she must be like them.

That was when they named her Sojourner, after a brave woman who had once been enslaved and found freedom. "Find your freedom, Sweet." her father crooned to her. "Find your freedom." The attendants thought it an indulgence to name her when she was so broken, but she was glad, even as a tiny child that they called her a name when the other Lost Ones were usually not named. They were tenderly cared for by the attendants, but never beloved. It was a harsh reality that they would all be salvaged when they were big enough. Sojourner knew that she had to make others believe she was awake in her unresponsive body. She would squirm whenever an attendant came near, and struggle for long hours to make her unresponsive lips move and form words. Finally, when she was almost eight, she managed her first word.

"Hello there little one," the attendant had spoken softly, out of habit mostly. None of these Lost Ones could understand, but a soothing voice was a kindness to everyone. Her name was Betta, and she loved these little helpless ones, kept alive and as healthy as possible. She hated when they were large enough to become donors, but that was how they fulfilled a purpose. All humans must live useful lives. It was how their society had survived. She reached out and caressed the little girl's hands. So soft she was, because she didn't have the opportunity to become rough. This one was a tough case because the parents believed she was thinking. "What do you need today? Do you need a change?"

"Yes."

Betta stopped, surprised. "Whaaaa...?"

"Poop."

The little girl, who had been straining and tensed, relaxed, exhausted but obviously happy. Betta had pushed the call button, summoning the Chief Healer of the Compassion Center. Quickly she explained what she had observed. A Master Teacher was called in to consult and they all went together to Sojourners crib. She was weeping miserably.

"Hush, little one. Don't be afraid." the Master Teacher crooned soothingly. "We just want to know you."

"Poop," sobbed Sojourner, uncomfortably.

Sojourner remembered how they laughed and whooped. At the time, she was outraged that the Healer and attendant and the Master Teacher all seemed so pleased that she was soiled. Of course, they were not celebrating that, and eventually she understood. Soon she was moved to the Healing Center, and she received her first implant in her occtipatal lobe, helping her to see better. Once she adapted to that, she received her next one in her parietal lobe, correcting her sense of balance, and one in her frontal lobe to aid her speech. Finally, she received an implant in her motor cortex and a variety of secondary implants throughout her endocrine system and on and on. No one had ever received so many, complicated implants, and there were some among the Healers that questioned the procedures, but they soon lost their skepticism when they observed her remarkable progress.

It was like she was a new type of human, unfettered and curious about everything. She was still very frail, but her spirit was strong. First she inched about the Healing Center, and then she walked, and then she ran, slowly, awkwardly, but it was still running. Her parents were thrilled, and she flew beyond everyone's expectations. It was obvious from the beginning of her Healing that she was a budding Storyteller, that her thoughts were full of her own fancies. A Storyteller was called in to begin training her even before she left the Healing Center.

Finally, shortly after she turned eleven, she went home to her parent's house. Sojourner knew her family well, and had been visiting as soon as she was able. Still, she did not know anyone in her Community, and she did not know how the others her age would feel about a newcomer. Her parents were both Growers, and worked with the newly healed earth after the Gardeners had cleansed it and established growing things. They loved their work topside, and Sojourner would go to the greenhouses and fields with them whenever she was home. Now, though, since she was going to be living at home she would attend the Learning Center, and there she would study her Craft. She had never been to a Learning Center, and she was very afraid that her frail body would make her strange to the other students.

Of course, the Learning Center was within Field Burrow, where she lived. The Burrows' leaders had learned about the Empire centuries earlier, and had decided then to keep all of the Burrows hidden from any possible detection by the satellites the Empire had put into space. They did not want to be invaded, and intelligence had shown that the Empire still thought of the lands as deserted and sterile despite the returning vegetation. The Empire was busy conquering the rest of the world and continued to consider the Blasted Wastelands a good object lesson for any who chose to defy the Righteous People.

The people of the Burrows did not want to wage war, or to lose the precious earth they restored, so the Plan was developed and was constantly being refined by the Leaders and the Strategists. Until the time came to regain the planet and restore all of the rest of the ruin brought about by the Great Devastation, the Leaders decided to remain a mostly hidden society. Most people spent most of their lives inside the Burrows, and all Learning Centers were carefully protected deep inside the Burrows. The technicians monitered the Empire's sattelites carefully, and when they were trained on the Land of the Burrows for the periodic examination, the technicians of the Burros would simply relay false information to the sattelites. It was important to be left alone until it was time to move forward. Even the smallest child understood this. Sojourner knew of this even before she could speak. Her knowledge of the Plan was engrained into her as deeply as her Storytelling.

Sojourner remembered the first day she started to school that she had cried to go to the fields with her parents instead. She had wanted to see the sun blazing in the autumn sky, and feel the warmth glowing off of her skin. Joran had to take her by the hand and compel her forward to the hoverbus waiting outside their portal.

"Sojourner," he had groused at her, "This is what you have dreamed of. Why are you so stupid now? Come on."

She stood at the portal door, too afraid to move forward. Joran was strong, and used to being outside with his parents, so it was a small matter to make her move forward. When they got to the waiting hoverbus, he simply picked her up and put her in. Sojourner was mortified.

The other students had been informed that Sojourner would be starting to the Learning Center that day, and most tried to look at her with encouraging smiles. She was too shy to look at them, though she was blinded by the tears that filled her eyes, and couldn't have seen them anyway. Joran sat down in his assigned seat, and he pulled Sojourner into the seat beside him. Awkwardly, he patted her and tried to calm her, but she was miserable, ashamed of the spectacle she had made of herself and frightened of the unknown place she was going. She sat huddled next to him, her hands trembled in her lap.

The hover bus stopped again, and a boy got on. "Hey there, Joran! Is this your little sister?"

"Yes, Stephan. This is Sojourner." Joran said reservedly, scowling.

A big hand thrust into her tear-blurred vision and confidently picked her clenched hands up from her lap. The boy vigorously shook her still clasped hands, ignoring that she did not release them. She looked up at him. He was robust and sun-browned with unruly curls haloing his head. He was smiling and his eyes were smiling. Sojourner felt her heart jump in her chest. She was afraid that an implant had failed, and she felt her face growing hot. This was not good.

"Sit down, Stephan," the bus driver barked at him. "We need to get this girl to school without you ruining her first day, you little Romeo."

He grinned impishly, and sauntered to his seat. Sojourner looked at her brother in confusion. He was frowning.

"That creep," he hissed. "Don't go near him. He is my age and he thinks all the girls love him. Like he is so great. He's too old for you."

Sojourner huddled closer to her brother, not certain as to what had just happened. Her heart was still pounding in her chest, and she could not even think of a simple story to calm herself. She did not know boys were so nice to look at. She did not know that smiling eyes could send her implants into failure. Her parents would be so disappointed that her systems failed the first day of school. She hoped the end would come swiftly, and that they would all go on bravely. Her heart was pounding so!

The hoverbus pulled up in front of the Learning Center, and Joran took her hand and led her firmly to her classroom. She could barely walk, she was in so much turmoil. Even though she had met her teacher earlier, but she was too frightened to return her greeting when she entered the room.

"Why, Sojourner," Mistress Patta exclaimed, "You are not so frightened of school are you?"

Sojourner burst into tears. "I think my implants are failing. My heart is pounding so. My knees are so weak I can barely stand and my face is burning."

Concerned, her teacher hurried to get Sojourners monitoring kit that had been provided for the classroom. Hummmm. The stressors seemed normal under the circumstances. The endorphine level was high. Endorphines? Mistress Patta questioned her about when her symptoms had begun. Ahhh. It was Stephan again. He was quite the heart breaker. She would talk to him about this one, though. Her heart could truly break, so he needed to save his smiles for the sturdier girls.

Sojourner had been terribly embarrassed when she learned that she was not dying, and that sometimes boys made girls feel very confused. Sometimes they made a girl's heart beat hard and fast. Sometimes a girl made a boy feel the same confusion. Sojourner felt foolish. She barely stumbled through the day, and on the hoverbus ride home, she did not look up when that heartbreaker Stephan passed. She hated him. She loved him.

Somehow, Sojourner made it through the days that followed, and gradually, she found her place among her classmates. Because it was clear she was a Storyteller, she was allowed to begin her training early, and her days passed in a busy blur. Joran confided in her that the terrible Stephan had stolen the affections of a certain girl, Lora, away from him, and that he couldn't be trusted. Out of loyalty, Sojourner decided to hate Stephan a little more everyday.

Of course, after the first day, Stephan never seemed to take notice of her at all. She was three whole years younger than he was, and frail, too. Besides, she was going to be a Storyteller. Boring. He was going to be a Master Technician or a Pilot. He had other interests. The year passed, and Sojourner only rarely thought of the brash, handsome boy, and the brash handsome boy did not think of her at all. Then it happened.

At the end of each year, before the summer holidays began, the students had to pass their Provings. As required, Sojourner had prepared stories to tell to the students in the school. Everyone had to go listen. Stephan was annoyed that he was forced to listen to that little scrawny misfit's ramblings. Most Storytellers were misfits that couldn't find something more productive to do. This particular little misfit was supposed to be very good at Storytelling, so she must be entirely useless. He dreaded having to sit still for so long and listen to some ridiculous story about something stupid. Gag.

He swaggered into the theater, jostling his friends and eyeing the pretty girls. There was

Lora. She was sitting with Joran again. Joran was stupid to be so crazy about one girl. There were so many pretty girls, why be tied to just one? Joran and he had been friends until Lora had decided to see Stephan's new hoverbike. It had only been one kiss. Now, Joran hated him. It wasn't like he had intended to keep Lora. He just wanted to try her out a little. Sometimes he missed Joran's friendship. Joran was stupid to end a friendship over a girl.

Stephan sat down just as the lights dimmed. There was old Mistress Patta. The old busybody. He still couldn't believe she had lectured him about Joran's little misfit sister. He was just being nice. How was he to know the little weakling would have a collapse if someone were nice to her? He could just imagine what would happen when she came out to tell her stories. She would probably be so nervous all her implants would explode. Mistress Patta was saying how honored the school was to have such a gifted storyteller blossoming in their midst, and that she had written the story she was going to tell herself and that it showed a maturity beyond her years. Blah, blah, blah. Then little scrawny herself walked out on stage. Well, they fixed her up cute. She sure had a lot of hair. It was very shiny. She stood very still, looking at her feet...how could anyone stand so still? Everyone grew very still, as well. She looked up, breathing in deeply as if she would inhale everyone's breath.

"Not today. I am too busy to be bothered with telling tales today. I need to work in this stubborn garden. It is so full of rocks that I despair of ever having the soil prepared for planting. Every year, this plot of ground sprouts rocks like other gardens grow flowers. It is the Fire Tenders and their constant bickering that causes me this grief. I keep hoping that someday they'll grow reconciled to their fate. They deserve it, you know, their fate.....

"Eh? What's that? Who are the fire Tenders? Where have you been? How is it that you do not know of them?

"I'll tell you, but only if you help me move these confounded rocks from my garden....

"Long ago, there was a brilliant spirit named Geo who lived in Heaven just inside the Great Gates. He was a marvelous inventor. The Maker often gave him tasks that seemed impossible to perform, and then Geo would labor with great energy and succeed where others had failed. The Maker trusted him with many important events, and He was rarely displeased with the inventions that Geo made. However, Geo was a difficult, taciturn spirit, and this did not please the Maker. In a place of joy and fellowship, Geo often chose to secret himself away in his workshop and keep his own company. He was gruff and short-tempered, and he had little sense of humor. Often the Maker would urge him to rest from his labors and join in the playful moments of Heaven. Other spirits would invite him to join in their fellowship, but Geo felt awkward in play, and he would refuse.

"There also lived in Heaven a mischievous spirit named Seism. He was always playing some kind of practical joke on someone. Often, the Maker would have to reprove him for his pranks, as Seism was not always sensible and did not understand when his pranks were tasteless. Even though he was an ornery spirit, he did have good qualities, and these caused him to be loved by many in Heaven. He was, among Heaven's host, the most able at taking the most ordinary stone and making it beautiful. Still, this is not what redeemed him in Heaven, no. Seism's very finest quality was his great love for his lovely wife, Gold. Most of Heaven's host tolerated Seism's exuberant personality and naughtiness because they valued what he did well. Some of them even thought he was refreshing and funny.

"Geo did not. In fact, Geo found Seism almost intolerable. He felt that Heaven should be a quiet, reflective place and that Seism did not have a true understanding of the dignity of Heaven. Secretly, Geo felt that Seism should be sent away, that he did not deserve his place in Heaven and that his only redeeming quality was his love for his wife. Seism sensed that Geo did not approve of him, and it rankled him. He began to single Geo out for his pranks more than the other spirits. He would hide Geo's tools and cause sudden winds to scatter Geo's scholarly papers. He would trail behind Geo, mocking his mannerisms. Geo grew increasingly more angry with the frivolous behavior of Seism, and he began to lash out at him. He also began to criticize Seism privately to his intellectual friends, and then publicity. He began to belittle Seism at every opportunity. Of course, this only made Seism more persistent. They began to bicker constantly, and the unity of Heaven was disturbed. The Maker became angry, and warned them each that they needed to be reconciled to each other. However, they ignored the Maker, and their arguings and retaliations continued. The Maker lost patience with them, and called them

Sojourner's Truth

to Heaven's Court to sit in judgement of them for their disobedience.

"Now understand, the Maker is usually benign. He loves to tend his garden, and he laughs at the antics of the young. Heaven's host was accustomed to His joy and humor. They remembered with fear and sorrow the few times that they witnessed the Maker's anger. All of Heaven trembled when they heard there was to be a judgement passed on Geo and Seism.

"The Maker was great and terrible to behold. His eyes flashed with deep fire and there seemed to be a fearsome wind blowing his hair and robes. His voice, which usually sounded like deep, moving water and music and hope, was like thunder and ice and echoed shouts. His anger and disappointment filled Heaven's Court, and the spirits wept when they saw Him like this.

"Geo and Seism," the Maker's voice echoed sternly throughout Heaven. "Come and be judged!"

"Geo and Seism crept forward, their heads bowed and their hands covering their faces. They were both overwhelmed with shame. The spirits of Heaven looked on them with pity and sorrow.

"Geo and Seism," the Maker's voiced knifed through their hearts, "Here is your judgement. Since you have fueled the fires of your disagreement with so much energy and consistency, you have prepared yourself to tend the deep fires of Earth. I sentence you to become the Fire Tenders of that place. You will remain bound to the fires of earth until you are truly reconciled to each other. Until you can prove that you value each other, you are bound to each other and to

Earth's fiery core. Tend the inferno well. This is my judgement."

"All of Heaven was silent and solemn. Then a weeping voice spoke quietly and humbly from the midst of the assembly.

"Oh, Maker," Gold wept. "What will become of me? How can my heart bear a separation from my beloved husband? Oh, Maker, mercy."

"Gold," the Maker spoke gently, "I will not punish you for the indiscretions of your husband. I am truly sorry, but you will have your joy compromised by all of this though I will not keep you from your husband. You may see him whenever your tasks are completed here. You may come and go as you need. Still, your husband must learn to control himself."

"Geo stood as if carved from stone. Geo's heart was pierced with guilt. He never meant for an innocent spirit like Gold to be punished because of his actions. Even as a solitary spirit, he understood how Seism and Gold treasured their marriage.

Seism and Gold wept in each other's arms. Their weeping was the only sound in Heaven.

"And so, Geo and Seism were sent to Earth's burning core to tend to the fires. They have not made peace with each other; they have not forgiven each other. The still do not value the differences between them. Geo rumbles and complains, and the ground shifts. Seism rages and the ground moves. They spitefully pelt each other with stones that scatter and litter the soil. They argue, and rifts widen. They come to blows and great earthquakes ravage the Earth. They wrestle and volcanoes spew forth burning, angry lava.

"They always regret the pain they cause, and they spend much of their time trying to atone for the hurt they cause Earth's children. Seism leaves beautiful, shining rocks in hidden places so children can find them and exclaim over their beauty. Geo invents wondrous caves and rare minerals that clever humans use in many ways.

"And what happened to Gold, you ask? She is faithful to her husband, and she comes to see him whenever she has finished her tasks in Heaven. When Gold is here, the Earth is quiet. When she goes back to Heaven, she leaves behind a trail of tears. She turns and blows kisses to Seism that scatter throughout the Earth. Earth's inhabitants search for the kisses and tears and fashion lovely things out of them. See? See the ring my beloved gave me? It is golden, and sparkles with a shining jewel. Love is full of kisses and tears, eh?

"Now, we are running out of light, yet my garden is still full of rocks. I am going inside to sit by the fire now. The rocks in my garden will have to wait."

Sojourner lowered her arms and stood as still as stones again. Then she moved and relaxed. The students all were silent for many long moments. Sojourner looked concerned, as if she were afraid her story had failed. Then someone from near to where Joran was sitting began to clap and then in a wave everyone clapped and shouted. Everyone but Stephan.

He sat, silent and unmoving. How could such a tiny, frail girl hold such a great idea in her head? Her voice had washed over him like cool water and warm sun, both. She was beautiful beyond words. He wanted to stand close to her and touch her hair. Joran would break his teeth out if Stephan came near his little sister. Joran hated him. Why had he kissed Lora? It was a wasted kiss. He wanted to kiss Sojourner, but she was just a little girl. She glided off the stage, and walked up the aisle, passing right by him. Her eyes were clear and bright. Her hair was shiny. He smiled at her, but she didn't look at him. He felt his insides collapsing. He loved her, and she just walked by him. His heart pounded in his chest.

— Chapter 5 —

Stephan woke, snorting like a bull, and exploded out of the bed like a groggy beast. He stumbled into the bathroom, mechanically going through all of his morning ablutions. He relieved himself and then washed his hands and splashed water all over his face and head. There wasn't any other way to get fully awake. How Sojourner managed to wake up so sweetly was beyond him. She always woke up like some fairytale princess. Her eyes would blink open, then she would stretch and turn over like a soft feather, or something like that. Sojourner was the one good at making up similes. Look at his hair, what there was of it. He was glad Sojourner had married him when he was young and still had hair, ...that she could share that particular memory with him always made him happy. Why weren't there implants for hair growth? Ahh, well, there were implants for the dire needs, like the ones his Sojourner had to deal with. Sojourner. He smiled, remembering her surprise and confusion when she discovered him in her room last evening.

She had been compelled to tell stories until late. He knew she dreaded coming to an empty room, so she would tell stories until she tired. He could wait. He had waited for her before, and he would wait for her again. Somehow, he would find it in himself to wait for her to return to his arms if he had to wait until the sun burned out and the stars fell. He smiled to himself. He had been joined to a Storyteller too long; he was thinking such fanciful thoughts.

He turned to go back to the bed. He hoped Sojourner would still be asleep because he loved to watch her wake up, all soft and sleepy warm. She would turn and see him already awake, and slide into his arms like warm silk. She was soft to touch. He ached with the thought that they had been apart, and they would be apart again.

Quietly, he opened the door to the bathroom, and peeked his head around the corner. His wife raised herself up on one elbow and smiled at him. Ahh. She was awake then. That was good, too. She lifted up the corner of the blanket, inviting him back to bed. He smiled. Even after all this time, he still felt like an eager bridegroom when she smiled at him like that. When she smiled at just him, and no one else.........

After her first Proving, Sojourner had felt for the first time, a slight rise in her status. No longer was she someone to pity because of her poor health, but she was someone to admire because of her strong thoughts and talent. The students had always been kind to her, but

Sojourner's Truth

now it seemed they liked her. Even that awful Stephan showed her some courtesy. It was a triumphant way to end the school year. Even better, she would be allowed to join her family in the fields, caring for the golden grain and the orchards of laden fruit trees.

Sojourner was eager for a chance to tend the growing plants. Almost everyone in Field Burrow was involved with some aspect of tending the plants, even those that did not come outside cared for the huge nurseries inside the Burrow. It wasn't just the food plants that needed tending. There were the wildflowers and the field grasses. Everything had to be cared for until it could grow on its own. Field Burrow was located on isolated plains, and the land stretched out for endless miles. The Master Gardener had done a brilliant job with the cleansing, and the land in this quadrant was fully productive, though there were still hundreds of species of plants that needed to be reintroduced to the area. The Master Gardener hoped that within another ten years the land would be able to support species of wildlife that had been indigenous to the area at one time. Still, to have a thousand square miles of productive land was a mighty achievement, especially since it had only been cleansed within the past twenty years. Still, there were millions of blasted acres that needed to be cleansed. The Burrows were protected from the virulent ionic radiation and the other poisons by the shield. Even now, a thousand years since the Destruction, it was death to go beyond the shield's boundary. The Great Devastation had been a deliberate, thorough attack on the Great Nation, and the scope of the ruin had almost destroyed the entire world. It was a miracle that anyone survived anywhere. There were survivors, though. They were scattered and few. Still, some of them had managed to live through a year, and they gathered together in a rude shelter, and then they lived another year, and another. The survivors had gradually gathered the scattered few they could find in hidden places and far-flung isolation. A new society was formed and the first Burrow was built. It had been a long struggle.

Every spring, the citizens of the Burrows observed a Day of Remembrance, a solemn day of reflection and dignified ceremonies. All those that were healthy and children that were old enough would don the necessary protection and go to the boundaries of the cleansed ground and cross over into the Blasted Lands. It was always a profound experience.

This would be Sojourners first time, the spring that she turned twelve. It was the first time she was healthy enough and old enough to cross the shield's boundary. She stood close to her father and he put his arm around her, comforting her as they climbed out of the hover bus and walked the last few yards to the edge of the Blasted Lands. Sojourner had never seen them before, and she gasped with horror when she saw them for the first time.

The land was mostly bare with a few scraggly plants twisted about its surface. Flung about the landscape like grey corpses were the remains of ancient buildings, their shattered visages staring out at the ruin like sad eyes. There was little movement, although Sojourner could tell there was a breeze blowing beyond the shield. Occasionally, a huge cockroach would scuttle from one place to another. Sojourner felt sick. She knew that stepping through the shield without her protective clothing would expose her to the deadly alpha and beta particles emitting from the toxic soil. The alpha particles were slow moving, and even a piece of paper could protect her from them, though if one managed to get inside an uncovered scrape, it would blast through her cells, ripping through her DNA and poison her already weakened system. The Beta particles were even worse, as far as Sojourner was concerned. They could pass through most things and her clothing had to be lined with lead to keep them out. It was the exposure to these deadly ions that had caused the terrible mutations to the DNA of the Burrow's inhabitants' ancestors. Even now, the people were compromised. Sojourner was proof of that. It didn't turn anyone into terrible monstrosities, it just made them incomplete. Completely healthy people were a treasure.

Sojourner glanced over to where that creep Stephan stood with his family. He was a completely healthy person, and it was said that he had already qualified to have as many as five children when he was Joined. How in the world he would ever find a girl to marry would be beyond her. Five children! Like anyone would have him for a husband. He was a heartbreaker. He would probably break his crazy neck long before he finished growing up. Beyond him, standing with his family, was a much nicer boy, Lepton. He was smart and had the dreamiest eyes. He wanted to be a Master Gardener when he grew up, and Sojourner thought he was very noble and good for that. Only the bravest and best became Master Gardeners. Lepton looked over at her, smiled gravely and raised his hand in a solemn greeting. Sojourner returned his greeting. Stephan watched the exchange and scowled. What made that show-off all righteous and proper all of the sudden? Sojourner hated him.

Her father squeezed her shoulder, so she lowered her hood and turned on her oxygen. Her father checked her suit just to be certain that she was wearing it correctly, and then he took her gloved hand in his. The citizens began to walk, slowly, passing through the shield. It was important to move slowly, or else the shield would absorb you. It was designed to keep the ions and the vermin that managed to survive out, and they all tended to move quickly. The secret was to move very slowly, so the ever-shifting electrons would flow around you. Sojourner was thankful for her father's steadying hand on her shoulder.

The Master Gardener was waiting for them. Silently, he waited until all of the people had passed, and then, silently he turned and walked away from them. Behind him, the Gardeners fell in rank behind him, and then the Master Growers, and then the Growers. Behind them, row upon row of citizens followed the Master Gardener. He walked solemnly for what seemed a very long time. Everyone followed him quietly. The only sound Sojourner could hear was her own breath. She felt like weeping.

Finally, the Master Gardener stopped and turned to the people. The other Gardeners lined up on either side of him, also facing the people. They all carried sub-shield sticks, and the Master Gardener had the activating device in his hands. They would bury the shield sticks in the blasted soil, and then the Master Gardener would say the ceremonial words and they would be turned on. The sticks would create a weaker shield outside the primary shield that would grow in strength as the soil was cleansed. This was the way that new land was reclaimed. During the next year land between the old shield and the new would be the focus of the Gardeners as they prepared it for replanting. Then, when it was safe, they would reseed it with some of the things designated for this strip of land. Sojourner heard that this would all be used as a place for a belt of trees and grasses, and the river that once flowed through here would be encouraged to flow again. She could not imagine all that would be accomplished in the next year. She could not picture the desolate town being removed and the materials cleansed and recycled. She could not picture this soil healthy, and clear water bubbling up from the ground. She felt very small.

The Master Gardener raised his arms ceremoniously and began to speak. His voice was transmitted into her hood, and she listened to him carefully.

"Here is land. The land was good, and the land can be good again. We will cleanse the soil from the evil poured out on it. We pledge our labor, our hope, our lives if they are needed, to do the work that we are called to do. With the help of our Maker, we will strive to undo the harm that man has brought to this place." He closed his eyes and prayed. "Accept our humble efforts. Forgive the folly of your poorest creatures. We ask for Your mercy. Bless us we pray. Amen."

The people all echoed him, "Amen"

Then the Gardeners pushed their sticks into the soil. The Master Gardener waited until all of the sub-shield sticks were in place and then he turned on the activator. There was a momentary hissing and the sharp smell of ozone as they crackled to life. A great grey mist seemed to grow upward and arc above them. The shield grew in strength, Sojourner knew, by the weakening of one side's nuclear decay. It had something to do with polarities and balance, but she did not fully understand. Within a year, she would be safe if she came up and sat on the ground right beside the shield. Today it would kill her.

The ceremony was over, and they all turned around and walked slowly back to the cleansed ground that they called home. There they would all plant a wheatfield that had been prepared, as a reminder of the timelessness of the growing cycle. Then there would be a great meal eaten outside on the ground. Safe ground.

As she walked with her family, she noticed that that ridiculous Stephan had meandered away from his family, and was walking parallel to her about thirty yards away, then closer, and then within arm's reach. She was a much more sophisticated twelve-year-old now, and it hardly made her heart skip a beat at all to have him so close. He had way too much hair; he needed to get it cut. He was very tall. Almost as tall as a grown man. He was so shallow. Today's events probably meant nothing to him.

They got to the shield, and slowly they passed through the pulsing light. Sojourner took off her hood and breathed in deeply. She smiled up at her parents and her brother, then turned to make certain that the beast Stephan had observed her behaving properly. He could learn something today from watching her. He was taking off his hood, she noticed. He was wiping his eyes as if he had been weeping. His mother came over to him and he leaned his head on her shoulder. She brushed back his hair and spoke soothingly to him.

"I know this troubles you, son...I know...Someday it will all be whole."

Stephan's shoulder's shook as he sobbed into his mother's arms. Sojourner's parents looked on sympathetically.

"That boy will be a Gardener, yet," her father said.

"He will figure it out soon," her mother agreed.

Stephan drew in a shaky breath and struggled to calm himself. Roughly he wiped the tears off his face. His hands were as big as a grown man's hands already. He smiled shakily at his mother and turned toward Sojourner. She quickly looked away because she didn't want to embarrass him. He was a worthless heartbreaker and a disloyal friend, but he didn't need to be stared at. He was so nice to look at. She peeked her eyes at him again, and he was looking at her; his face looked pure, his eyes were wide and it seemed that his soul was leaping out of them. She could not look away. She felt a great soaring inside of her, and she was afraid and she knew she was a little girl and she knew she was a woman-child, and she was fragile and she was as strong as a great beast. She looked into the terrible Stephan's eyes, and she saw he loved her, and she didn't know how that could have happened. She hated him....she loved him.....Without knowing why she did it, she smiled at him......

— Chapter 6 —

Sojourner lifted the corner of the blanket and smiled at Stephan. He was so funny. He grinned and did that silly happy naked dance he did, and he hurried over to the bed and quickly slipped between the covers. He was so alive. He was more alive than a dozen other men. He was like a great strong wind. He was like a deep mountain. He was here, and she was in his arms.

Last evening, she had told her stories until her legs began to shake with weariness and her voice began to grow hoarse. She wanted to tell stories until she was entirely spent. She wanted to disappear into the stories and float off into the deep, soft night sky. She was a Storyteller; that was all she was. How could the soldiers mistake her for anything else?

Finally, she tired, and the torches were extinguished. Joseph stood before the villagers and motioned for them to stand for the evening song. It was the custom to end gatherings this way, and most families sang the song before going to bed. "We have labored through

Sojourner's Truth

the day.." There were some fine singers in the village. Sojourner wondered if there were some true Singers, some from the choirs brought out for this evening. She would feel humbled if that were true. "For our Maker's blessings we all pray." Such a lovely melody, ancient and sweet. "Guide our dreams all through this night. We will rejoice in the morning's light."

Sojourner felt her heart swell with love and pride for her people. The villagers surged around her, speaking to her and pressing her hands gently. Everyone knew she was fragile. She looked into each face and tried to memorize them. They were all descended from just a few thousand original survivors. Did all of her people look similar? She couldn't tell...they all looked separate and distinct to her. Would the people in the Empire look strange? Their intelligence reports were so incomplete. No one had ever gotten close enough to the Emperor to see him clearly, though they did have an operative among his women and another among his servants. Their culture sounded so brutal. So dead. She should just go home and forget all of this. She could not leave with Stephan being so angry at her. It made her doubt her purpose. He was right. They should just contain the Empire as the Plan stated and evaluate the inhabitants for suitability. They were a harsh people, and they deserved no better. Look at all of these precious faces. The dozens here that she could see, and the millions that she could only imagine tucked away in the Burrows. Her people.

Cloe shouldered her way past the well-wishers and linked her arm with Sojourner's. "I think you need to come with me right away. There is something that needs your attention, O Queen!"

Sojourner smiled at Cloe. Oh, queen! That is right. The filters were off tonight, and the soldiers were listening to every word she spoke. She wondered what they thought about the ancient story she told about the naked emperor that thought he was dressed in finery. It was a grand old story. She hoped it would go in their report tonight. Nakedness seemed to be a problem for the Empire. She would have to remember that.

Together, she and Cloe left the commons and again, Cloe escorted her into the doorway that led to the interior of Deep Burrow. Young Bura was waiting inside the Burrow with his hovercab. Standing beside him was a sweet-faced young lady.

"Bura, you are as punctual a young man as I ever have met." Cloe smiled at him. "And I suppose this is your intended, Gin, correct?"

Sojourner smiled to herself. Cloe would no doubt be the Head of the Council come next choosing, and it would not be entirely based on her credentials. She had a bit of the politician in her, just like an ancient senator or congressman. Campaigning, they called it. It was hard to imagine the ancient Great Nation had managed on politics alone, but it had. Politics had been its undoing, too. Still, Cloe seemed to know how to mend situations and lead others to resolutions. Well, except with her own husband, but Sojourner guessed they thrived on their conflicts. ...

"Yes, Leader! She was very excited that I actually met our Master Storyteller, and asked if she could come along this evening." He looked embarrassed, "I hope I am not presuming."

Sojourner stepped forward and shook Gin's hand. "Hello, Gin. Congratulations on your upcoming marriage."

Gin smiled shyly. "Thank you. I have always wanted to be a Storyteller, but I get too nervous in front of big groups. How ever do you do it?"

Sojourner smiled kindly, "I guess it helps not to be too sensible. When I return from this trip I am scheduled to make, I will be scheduling some instruction time at the Learning Centers. Please feel free to come observe as my guest."

Gin's eyes lighted. "Really? Oh, Bura! Did you hear that? The Master Storyteller has invited me to her class." She and Bura hugged each other happily. Sojourner watched them, her emotions a tangle. She was still amazed that her storytelling was so treasured by the citizens of the Burrows. It was strange thing to her. People treated her like she was above them sometimes, and it was a terrible feeling. Part of her training was to keep the adulation in balance, to be humbled. In the distant past, when the Great Nation was at its grandest, it venerated and rewarded its musicians and actors in an out of proportion way. It even had teams of physically fit people, usually men, that played pointless games that were venerated and rewarded to excess as well. Some historians claim it was evidence of a cultural insanity, and others contend it was evidence of the imbalance of technology and tradition. The essays were endless. It was a cultural flaw, to that everyone agreed. Too often, the talented were made icons because they possessed an ability. Too often, the icons were terribly flawed individuals. The rest of the world saw these flawed icons, and believed that the citizens of the Great Nation were all immoral. The rest of the world did not know that most of the Great Nation was made of farmers and teachers and hard working people. Corruption was assumed. Sojourner felt the gratification that came with being one of her culture's icons, but she also knew her responsibility.

"Yes, well it will be very hard work, so don't celebrate yet," Sojourner said, trying to sound light hearted. "Bura, I am tired, and would like to go to my room now."

"Oh, yes! Right away." Bura, still smiling happily, helped Cloe and Sojourner into his hovercab. Because it was late, there were very few vehicles in the designated traffic ways, and Bura was able to glide very quickly through the twisting passageways. It seemed just a few moments, and they pulled into the portal of the Traveler's Place.

"Sojourner, I have a need to confess something before you go to your room. I hope you are not angry with me." Cloe looked nervous.

"Cloe, I have never seen you anxious. What did you do?"

"I have sent for Stephan. I have been in contact with him for several weeks, and I have convinced him to come here tonight."

Sojourner went very still. It was a Storyteller's technique. Be very still to control your emotions, to channel them. "Is he here to wage war, or to mend fences?"

"Mend fences, it seems."

"I have not seen him since this has all started... months and months. Am I to be angry or excited? I don't know how to feel."

Cloe smiled. "Be excited my friend."

"Well, then, how do I look?"

— Chapter 7 —

Captain Jarvo and his men silently gathered around the fire. Their rations had long since run short, and they had been living off of the bounteous land. It was a puzzle to him how this land had healed. After the victory over the Dark Nation, its ruins were to lie for a billion years. It was the Law of Nature's punishment for the iniquities of its corrupt people. Then, about one hundred years ago, sattelite images had begun to show some very isolated areas of regrowth. Empire scientists had speculated that it was probably the first growth of some diseased mutations. It was decided to not waste time traveling to the wastelands to investigate.

Around twenty years ago, out of curiosity, another group of scientists decided to look at fresh images, and were astonished to recognized tiny islands of growth scattered in widely isolated spots. The emperor had been notified that there seemed to be new areas of vegetation growing in the cursed lands. After much debate, it was decided that the areas were probably places where the poisons were dissipating, and that perhaps in another thousand years there might be some land worth looking into for settlement purposes. The Empire had other things to accomplish.

Last fall, a University student again looked at the ruined places through the satellite images, planning to calculate the time it would take for the continent to be useful. To his astonishment, most of the continent seemed to be covered with new growth. Only about a third of the land lacked any growth . He had to spend some effort to convince his professors to look at the images, but they finally were convinced by his frantic persistance. When they saw the verdant growth, they had immediately taken the information to the palace. The excitement at court was quickly tempered with caution. A surveillance flight was arranged, at great cost, to fly over portions of the continent to visually confirm the reports. Then a team of scientists was shuttled to the surface to run some preliminary tests to see how toxic the environment was still. The environment was pure where there was growth.

There was jubilation at the court of the Emperor. The lands of the Empire were stretched to their collective limits trying to provide for its burgeoning population. Pure lands to harvest! It would be a great relief to the empire. Many noble families were eager to establish estates on the far away continent, and the Emperor had begun to make his plans to reward his most loyal followers.

The jubilation of the Empire was short lived, though. Within a few days of their discovery that the land was pure, they also discovered it was inhabited.

First the aerial surveillance teams reported what were apparently cultivated fields. The satellites were trained in on the location and sure enough, there were cultivated fields, and even worse, there were farmers out in the fields working. It was a troubling discovery because the people of the blasted land had some puzzling technologies. They apparently had some method of making their small farm machines and scooters float. There was no evidence of refineries or any industry to support this type of technology that could be seen from the satellite images. It was decided to proceed with caution.

The scientists were able to conceal their presence and were evacuated quietly. Then a special squad of highly trained surveillance soldiers were sent to scout the land and determine the population base and type of government. That is how Jarvo and his team had come to be here, arriving at harvest time, surviving through the bitter, long winter. Now, it was late spring, and it was time to act.

Jarvo had done a thorough job. The total population of the Burrows was minimal. Perhaps there were a half million inhabitants scattered throughout this vast, apparently productive land. They lived in tiny villages, and without exception, their dwellings were underground, either built into sides of hills, or slightly mounded heaps in the areas that were geographically flat. The dwellings were simple, comfortable and the technology was functional. The various settlements were connected by an ancient computer network, with one terminal in each Burrow. The terminal was located in the Chief's residence, and all business was conducted in the Commons, a public area located outside at each Burrow. During inclement weather, they would simply conduct their business inside their houses. There were no meeting halls. No public buildings. No schools. No universities.

The people seemed fairly healthy. Simple, but healthy. They all vagulely resembled each other, being tall and thin, without strong racial differences. It was as though they all shared a similar ancestor. Even in the farthest outposts, the people all looked similar. They did not seem to travel to Burrows in other areas. The main person the soldiers had observed on the narrow tracks the inhabitants considered roads, was their version of royalty, their perverse queen, Sojourner.

It was a bizarre society. How could any culture allow such an affront to nature? The people of this land had to be addled to accept this insane creature as their leader. In the Empire, all women were properly dressed and protected. In the Empire, all women, with the exception of the Chosen, were honored by being married and being made useful. It was almost a sacrilege to allow an old woman to be exposed like this. Although she was always greeted with adulation and celebration, it was shameful that no one had taken responsibility for her. She was completely without discipline. At every Burrow, she had embraced the inhabitants, men and women alike. Men that could not possibly be a relative or a husband embraced her in public. Jarvo would never be so disrespectful to his wife. She was a worthy woman. Sometimes, he would come quietly into her quarters, and watch her tend to their children. She would smile at them and play gentle little games with them; she deserved his protection. When he returned to her, he would speak her name tenderly. In just a few more days, he would be home.

He turned his thoughts to the task at hand. Lieutenant Simon had apparently had some luck with his hunting. He was the son of Lord Rigel Simon, and had been raised on his father's vast estates with plenty of opportunity to hunt. He was quite skillful at it, though it appeared that what he had managed to kill tonight was a domestic cat. It was not his favorite thing to eat. Still, it would nourish them. Cats had a way of wandering off, and perhaps it would not be missed for several days. The people of the Burrows certainly were attached to their pets. He was glad, though, for the meat.

He and his men had done an admirable job at keeping themselves fed and surviving the brutal caprices of the wilds. They had brought provisions, but the mission had lasted much longer than anyone had anticipated. Simon had proven essential in hunting, and by secretly observing the farmers, they had discovered many plant foods growing wild. Occasionally, they would reconnoiter provisions from careless inhabitants. With skill and luck, they had survived. It had been very challenging to achieve all of the objectives set forth by the strategists of the Empire, but they had fulfilled all of them but one.

They had not been able to discover the power source for the floating machinery, and the inhabitants treated the machinery with great care, bordering on religious awe; it had been impossible to discover the source covertly. The analysts from the Empire speculated that the machines were remnants of the Dark Nation that had been preserved, and that the technology had become a mystical thing to the farmers that used the machines. The queen had a floating device she straddled in a scandalous manner and rode about to the various Burrows, exerting her strange hold over the people. Perhaps her strange hold was due to an understanding of how the machinery worked. They were to bring the device back to the Empire when the queen was taken into custody. Empire scientists would have the device figured out within a few days. Even if the queen were not cooperative it would not matter. The Empire was always victorious.

Aside from not understanding the intriguing machines, the land exceeded expectation. Jarvo and his men had discovered a ripe plum, ready to be plucked and savored. Tomorrow it would begin. They would create a subterfuge with Private Para, the youngest member of the team. He was an engaging young man, skillful at acting parts. He was the only one trained to conceal his identity and feelings. He had been training himself for days to overcome his aversion to speaking to an unrelated woman. He would engage her in conversation, giving the rest of them opportunity to surround her and sedate her. They would then travel to the military air transport that would rendezvous in a designated place, then on to the aircraft carrier, the pride of the Empire and home. They would all have to purify themselves as soon as they returned to the Empire. The Examiners had sanctified their mission, but they also made it clear that they would be Purified as soon as they were back on Empire soil. It would be a painful few days, but worth it for the rewards and honor. He wondered if he would recognize any of his children; they grew so fast when they were small, and he did not see them up close anyway until they were past the baby stage. He would not ever truly see his daughters, but soon his oldest son would be moved to the man side of the apartment, and his training would begin. He was eager to be home.

Tonight, though, he would try to enjoy a bit of this roasted cat and the weeds that had been collected to accompany it. Weeds and cat tonight. Tomorrow, glory.

— Chapter 8 —

Sojourner and Stephan joined Joseph and Cloe in the monitoring room in the Governing Center for the final briefing before the day began. Sojourner held Stephan's hand and they walked slowly, in the way they had years ago when they had finally became sweethearts, their fingers interlaced, and their sides pressed next to each other when they walked. They had lingered over breakfast, talking about incidentals. The latest antic of Sala's little boy, and the impending birth of Jakma's first child, a girl; the latest news from home. Anything to stretch out the morning.

Then the attendant at the Traveler's Place had quietly informed them that a hovercab was waiting to take them to the Governing Center. They gathered their things together reluctantly. They did not speak in the hovercab, they just sat quietly together. Sojourner felt her insides clench as they pulled into the portal of the Governing Center. She felt her resolve crumbling. She was not brave or strong. How did she come to this place? It was all a mistake. Perhaps she would tell Joseph she had changed her mind. What was it to her that the Plan might cost the Empire many lives? At least the land would be safe and her own people would not be jeopardized. The operatives were already in place. The shield sticks were in place around the capital city of the Empire. The pilots were on stand by. She did not have to negotiate a diplomatic solution to the coming invasion. She was a Storyteller. She would let it be known to the soldiers they had been duped. It was not up to her to save lives. She was a Storyteller.

She glanced at Stephan and he smiled encouragingly at her. She should go home with him. She should spend her last years in her own home, surrounded by her loved ones. She knew that her implants were at their limits, and there would be very few upgrades possible. She should go home and spend her ending days with dignity. She should enjoy the last of her strength. It was not her concern if the Empire lost lives.

An upright solemn young woman wearing the crisp uniform of a Guardian met them at the entrance of the Governing Center. "There is a slight problem with a citizen family, Storyteller, but the Leaders will be settling the matter very quickly. Would you follow me?"

Sojourner and Stephan trailed behind the straight-backed young woman. It always amazed Sojourner that the Guardians were taught to stand so straight. It made her shoulders ache to stand that rigidly. Perhaps if she practiced. The Guardian opened the doorway into a monitoring room, and indicated that they should sit in one of the observation chairs. There were several technicians sitting at large consoles but they were dividing their attention between their monitors and the confrontation going on at the far end of the observation area. Joseph and Cloe were there with an angry couple and a hysterical girl about ten years old.

"This situation is impossible!" the man was saying. "Those animals have eaten every molecule of Demeter. They even sucked the marrow out of her bones and burned the bones on their fire. How can we hope to negotiate with such unbalanced people?"

"They are ignorant of how to live in harmony with the land, we understand that," the woman added. "But a domestic cat! We have made certain they have had plenty to eat. We have gone before them adding abundant eatables to the environment. We have made it possible for them to obtain foods by pretending to be careless with food we were preparing out in the open. Like we would be careless with anything. We even prepared places for them to take shelter in the winter. Our people have bent over backward to provide for these inept barbarians. Then they eat our child's pet cat. A cat! Our poor pet."

"There were plenty of other things for them to eat. And I understand this is not the first pet they have eaten. Last month they ate a puppy near Far Burrow, didn't they? What kind of monsters are we proposing to mingle with?" The man pulled his daughter closer. "We realize we need their strength, but it is becoming evident that we have little in common with them if they eat a sweet, friendly cat."

Joseph held up his hands, trying to quiet and calm the angry family. "I know it is a terrible loss for you. You have to remember they do not know we are providing for them. They think they are hidden from us, and they think they are living off the land. It has been very unfortunate they do not know more about the earth and growing things. There have been many times during history that cultures have become ignorant of the value of growing things. Our own society struggled to discover how to grow things and preserve environments. The archives are full of accounts of the great struggle. The Empire is far from here, both geographically and culturally. Perhaps once we make contact with them, though, we will find that our differences are not so great."

Cloe stepped forward. "As a matter of fact, we have great hopes that we will be able to contact the Empire without any loss of human life. There will certainly be difficulties, but we have to remember that we have been hidden from the soldiers, and they do not know that we have been supporting them."

Sojourner sighed. Poor Cloe and Joseph. They were very good at administrating, but they did not know how to soothe people very well. The man and woman were still angry and the child still sobbed into her father's stomach. She glanced at Stephan. He watched her expectantly, knowing her training and skill would not allow her to sit quietly for too long. She smiled at him and he gave her hand a squeeze. Quietly she got out of her seat and walked toward the distressed group.

"Greetings. Hello Leaders. Is there something I might help you with today?"

The man and woman looked at Sojourner recognition dawning on their faces, their anger was replaced by surprise and confusion. This was the Master Storyteller. She was here.

"P..p..pardon us, Mistress Sojourner." The man stepped closer to her. "We realize we are keeping the Leaders from the important business at hand, but this is our only child, and we have waited for several years for a cat to become available for our household. As you know, cats may be plentiful enough to eat in the Empire, but they are not easy to come by here in the Burrows."

"Our pet scampered out of our compartments last evening, and before we could catch her she managed to get out one of the doorways leading into the Commons. From there she lost herself in the undergrowth. Our daughter was able to monitor her, and we notified the topside personnel, but they could not locate her right away. The soldier they call Simon shot her with a projectile and the spies roasted and ate her. They didn't seem to notice it was a poor sweet cat they were gobbling up. Our daughter saw them shoot Demeter on her monitor. It is shameful."

Sojourner turned her attention to the sobbing girl. It would be important to pitch her voice carefully. She needed to move the child's impulses from the brain stem into the cerebral cortex. She was only reacting to her pain, there was no purpose to her sobbing. She needed to mourn in truth, not in agony. There needed to be purpose in her pain. Her tears needed to cleanse her. There were so many kinds of tears.

"Is this true?" she asked the little girl, using concern and shock carefully in her inflections. "You saw them shoot your cat? You must be angry!" Anger was better than fear, it could be reasoned with if approached carefully. She adjusted her voice, softening it, adding a bit of breath, drawing the girl into her confidence. She looked directly at the child. She must see sympathy and strength in Sojourner's face. "It is hard to watch terrible things." Thought and grief, it was a trick to balance them. The girl raised her eyes at Sojourner briefly and nodded her head curtly. Ahhhh, yes. Just right.

Now to change the focus. "What is your name? I know your cat's name was Demeter. That is an ancient name. How did you decide on such an ancient name? Is your name Persephone? Those names go together you know. Demeter was Persephone's mother. Is your name Persephone? No? Then what is your name?"

"Loma," the girl snuffled.

Sojourner deepened her voice, changing the inflection slightly, balancing between authority and tenderness. It was a skillful inflection, hard to master on command, though loving parents and intuitive teachers often managed it when needed. She must use straight-forward language without being hurtful. Honest words. "Do you understand what is happening? Do you know why the soldiers were hunted and why they consumed your cat?" It was important for the girl to speak completely. She must respond to the situation, not react. The difference was important.

"The soldiers do not understand the land and they didn't recognize the food that was put into the environment for them." Loma ventured, her voice thick with tears.

"Why don't we just invite them in and let them know we know they are here? We could just feed them and send them home, couldn't we?"

"No." Loma shook her head. "We can't do that."

"Can you tell me why? It is important that I know you understand why." Sojourner's voice was pitched in her middle range, her tones were clear and she added the slightest touch of urgency to her voice so the girl would respond from her knowledge base. She did not want her to speculate and add opinions she may have developed or heard from the authority figures in her life.

"If we reveal ourselves while the soldiers are here, they will have time to inform the Empire and they will be able to mobilize their forces before we can activate the containment shields around the Empire. Even though we can protect our Burrows, the Empire may damage large portions of the environment before they are contained. We must wait, being certain they are unaware of our strength before we activate the shields around the Empire. If possible, we need to negotiate." Loma quoted the facts like a mantra. Even the smallest children understood the importance of remaining hidden. There were only twenty million inhabitants in the Burrows. There were over a billion people in the Empire. Their military alone had twenty million soldiers. The numbers were staggering.

"Why do we need to have peace with the Empire?"

"Our people come from a limited gene pool. We need the health of the Empire, but we need it on our terms or our culture will be lost." Again Loma chanted the facts without thinking. Good.

Sojourner again pitched her voice a shade lower, and she spoke with a lesser intensity. "Many of our people are physically weak. I myself could not move about without the implants in my body. Do you have implants?"

Loma shook her head. "No, but my dad does. He has to have them changed once a year."

"Yes. It is a problem for us. If the Empire knows how weak so many of us are, they will not want to send people to live with us, they will just want to take what we have built. Their people are very healthy. As far as we can tell, no one in the whole Empire uses implants. There are plenty of people there. A billion people. I would imagine they have a billion cats as well. Healthy cats that prowl about yowling at the moon and upsetting trash cans. Perhaps we will ask them to send us some cats, too."

Loma smiled tentatively. "I bet those cats would love to live here."

It was time to reintroduce the painful part of their conversation, diminished by a shade of humor and irony. The girl was old enough to comprehend irony, though she would not yet be formal operational. Her comment had to be almost blunt without being cruel. "Cats will never be in danger of being eaten here in the Burrows, that is certain." Then a touch of indignation and a shade of anger. "I hope those soldiers got a bellyache. Don't you?"

Loma was no longer crying. Her eyes flashed and she looked defiant. "Yeah, I hope their bellys ache forever. Someday, I will fly over to the Empire and take all their cats."

"Perhaps you will. Until then, what can we do?"

"I don't know." Loma looked thoughtful and sad.

"Here is the nice part, Loma, you don't have to take care of the problem. All of our Leaders, all of our Gardeners, all of our adult citizens, we are all going to do our best to make this problem work out. If we are very careful and if the Maker smiles on us, we will find a way to make this all good. For all of us, ...and for cats." Sojourner softened her voice. "Perhaps there will be another pet for you soon."

Loma's eyes filled with tears. She was remembering her pet. "I will like to have another cat. Are there many cats in the Empire, truly?"

"There are many cats and dogs and people. The Empire is very full. Perhaps we can be friends with them. What do you think?"

Loma looked thoughtful for a moment. "Well, I will be friends with the children and their parents, but I will not be friends with their soldiers. I don't think I want to know their Emperor, either. Just the kids." Loma looked seriously at Sojourner. "I hope you can make friends with Emperor Kalig. You are very brave."

Sojourner smiled tensely at the girl. Very brave. Oh, Maker. She was not brave and she did not want to leave her home and go to the Empire. A billion people. How did it happen that the other side of the world could have so many people? How did they feed them and clothe them? How could that many people live in dignity? So much of the world was still not usable. The Burrows did not want a billion people, the environment was still too fragile to support that many people. Just two hundred thousand people. Enough to shore up the gene pool and to cautiously expand the Burrow system to the damaged lands that had not seen any attention. Just a bit of the Empire's strength.

"Yes, well, that is why we are sending a gentle old lady. Maybe he has a soft spot in his heart for gentle old ladies." Sojourner smiled at Loma, carefully masking her doubts with her Storyteller's craft.

Joseph stepped forward, "We all hope that there will be little difficulty. Please accept our deepest sympathies about the loss of your pet. I will personally speak to the Master Breeder of cats and see if you may be given the next available kitten. Would that bring you some comfort?"

"Yes!" Loma's looked at Joseph hopefully. "And perhaps when we have Empire cats I can have one of those, too."

"Two cats," exclaimed her mother. "What would we do with such good luck?" She smiled at her daughter, the crisis past.

Joseph smiled at Loma and her parents. "Until then, my wife and I have a very old lazy cat that loves to have his chin scratched. I will make arrangements for you to come by after school to play with the lazy old rascal, if you want. Perhaps tomorrow, as we are all terribly busy today." Joseph looked meaningfully at Loma's parents, and they nodded, understanding.

"Come now, Loma. It is time to go home and get ready for school. I guess I will have to take you in since we have spent so much time here this morning," her father said. "My thanks for your indulgence, Leaders.

Mistress Storyteller, it is an honor to meet you, especially during this troubled time. I will never forget that at the moment of your greatest trial, you took the time to soothe our daughter. You are not just a Master Storyteller, you are a great soul. Accept the thanks of our family. Go with the peace and hope of our Maker. We are all one people."

Sojourner felt her insides twist and rage inside of her like a terrible storm. Still, she kept her face serene. This was only her conflict. "I thank you for your kind words. I hope I can live up to your hopes for me." She glanced at Stephan. His eyes were shining with pride and respect. She felt a sudden flush of understanding. He believed she would succeed in this. That is why he had come. He believed.....

"As you know, I will be leaving soon, and we have plans to finalize. Perhaps things will go so well that I can return with the strength we need and a cat or two as well." The gathering chuckled at the gentle joke, and the family left the monitoring room, mollified.

Cloe crossed over to Sojourner and gave her a brief hug. "You have got to teach me how you do that with your voice. Imagine what I could accomplish in the government with the skill to captivate as you do. You know that I would rather not risk you to this task, but if anyone can convince the Empire to negotiate with us and spare us all the terrible choices we might have to make, it is you. Who would have thought such a skinny little girl could use her voice to persuade others?"

"Oh, please. Don't think that it is so much. Remember, my first word was 'poop'. Live with that, and you will be humbled all your life."

Cloe laughed, and turned her attention to the monitors. The technicians had been paying only cursory attention to their screens, and they snapped their focus back to their tasks. Some were smiling, though others were trying to act as though they had not been listening. Joseph and Stephan concentrated on the monitors as well. Sojourner felt relieved that the attention was elsewhere. She breathed in deeply, focusing her thoughts inward. She must appear calm, though the torrent inside of her was like a dervish whirling out of control. She felt that her choice to stay had been taken from her. The matter had been settled without her noticing. Stephan believed she could do this, the plans were in motion. A young girl hoped for a cat.

She lifted her eyes and watched the monitor. Joseph and Cloe were busy giving instructions to the technicians, and Stephan was intrigued by their maneuvers. She stepped up to the railing and tried to keep her hands from clenching the bar too hard. The Empire killed men. They hid their women behind walls and veils. There must be a cultural bias against killing women. That is why it was determined to send a woman to negotiate. The fact that the Empire thought she was the Queen of the Burrows was an advantage. The training a Storyteller received was specialized and its secrets carefully guarded. Leaders were not allowed to learn the skills because they were too compelling; no one but official Storyteller's were taught to Control. Those with the natural ability were few and far between, and Master Storytellers were truly rare. Sojourner was the first to attain the rank of Master Storyteller in more than seventy years. She was the only one with the skill and understanding of the nuances of language to be convincing to the strangers. But, what if she was convincing to the citizens of the Burrows because they wanted her to convince them? The mindset of the Emperor would be very different.

She had to stop fretting about the mission. She had to think only of the good things that could come from her attempt to reason with the Emperor. If she was successful, the Burrows could add ten percent to their population, and in coming years, allow a population growth of up to eighty percent. Not only that, the Gardeners could begin reclamation on a tremendous scale. They had made some amazing gains since the discovery of how to create and control the gravity holes. The Gardeners were eager to cleanse the rest of this continent, and begin work on the collateral damage done to the environment in the southern continent which held promising sections of life. Preliminary reports from Empire lands indicated that much of the soil was not reaching potential because of carry over poisons and poor management. Sojourner laughed at herself, she had been joined to a Gardener too long... she was beginning to think like Stephan now.

She must be as confident in herself as the Leaders were. She must believe in herself. The Emperor was only human. He would respond, and he would see reason. He would accept the help and technology of the Burrows, and he would respect their boundaries. Surly, he would.

She looked at the soldiers on the monitors. Let's see, Captain Jarvo was the one with the tawny colored hair and the sensuous lips. He often seemed to let his mind wander, and he had mentioned that he had children once. When he slept, he talked in his sleep about Jenta, sweet Jenta. He must miss his family. Lieutenant Bosson was the fundamentalist in the group, fiercely dedicated to their religious practices, and patriotic. He was dark and spare, and he only smiled when he felt someone had received a just punishment. The other Lieutenant, Lieutenant Simon, was altogether different. He was kind of a jokester, and apparently was related to someone wealthy and powerful back in the Empire. He was the one that shot all of the animals. Then there was the cranky Corporal Ritsi, the one that looked so handsome, but was so unpleasant and rude, and Corporal Ninta. He was the oldest, next to the Captain and he clearly didn't like Ritsi always trying to boss him around. The Captain kept order, but there was always tension between them. The two remaining were called Lant and Para. They were privates. Lant was a thin dreamer and Para was talkative and cute. Many of the girls in the Burrows had taken to watching the evening briefing because they like to watch Private Para at the campfires. Many mothers had complained that the briefing needed to edit him out of the picture whenever he took his shirt off because the girls were too distracted by his good looks. He was the one chosen to distract her during the "capture of the Queen". Silly boy.

    The soldiers were carefully gathering their things and trying to disguise the fact they had camped out beside the river. Clumsily, they scattered the remains of their fire. They did not understand the land at all.

Wasn't it obvious that the sedimentary rocks they had lined their fire pit with were different in composition from the natural sedimentary rocks of the area? They had been left there, knowing the soldiers would choose that spot to camp. They were a better rock for containing fires then the ones occurring naturally in this area. This area had many tiny stones, and to find larger pieces they would have had to dig deeply to collect enough to line a fire pit. Didn't they think it was odd to happen across hickory scraps just the right size to make a fire when they were in a grove of post oaks, mulberry and cottonwood trees? No. They never noticed. As usual, Growers and the area Gardener would have to spend a good bit of time restoring the trampled area. Still, they were trying to be careful. They were all scratching their bug bites. The Breeders had released quite a few parasites into the environment for the birds to eat. The soldiers must all have many itchy bites. Well, good.

They were beginning to clear out of the area. That would mean they were going to their positions about three miles down the road. There was a crossroads there, and Para would act like he encountered her there by coincidence. He would talk to her, distracting her for about another mile, then she would be ambushed and subdued by the rest of the squad. It was a silly subterfuge, and useless. There would be no interference. After that, they would travel cross-country another three miles, carrying her and the hoverbike, where they would be met by their noisy version of a flyer. She and the hoverbike were to be transported to a huge transport ship that the hover flyer could land on, and then she would be taken to the Empire. It would take three days with their impossible, huge machines. Sojourner was not in a hurry to begin.

A Healer came in to recalibrate her implants one last time. She was fitted with a visual scanner and micro-cams, so the Leaders could see the events as they unfolded from her perspective. She was also given a small pill to take just before she was captured, to help counteract the nausea that would be caused by the sedative she would be given. All of her clothing was replaced with a bright set of clothing loaded with things she might need. In the hem of her pants, for instance, there were nutrition pills in case the food was unsuitable. There were a variety of microchips installed in the tips of her fingernails to establish dampening fields if she needed to have a private conversation with someone. Her earrings were filled with medicines. There were thin filaments added to her hair to help her evade the clumsy monitoring devices used by the Empire. She felt like she was a walking display of Burrow technology, though no one but the very well trained would ever suspect. In five days, the Guardians would come and retrieve her, regardless of the outcome of the interviews with the Emperor. She hoped they went very well, or in five days the shields would go up, and the mighty Empire would suffer.

Finally, by mid-morning, she was ready to go to the Commons, as was her custom, and tell a final, lighthearted story. This morning, Stephan had asked her to tell the story about her ancestor, a tomato stealing little girl. Sojourner loved to tell the story, and in a way it fit the events of the morning. She was lucky to have the ancient story preserved in the archives. Apparently,

Sojourner had a storywriter in her distant lineage, and as luck would have it, many of her stories were preserved, and had given the Burrows many insights into the way the world was before the Devastation. The storywriter's daughter and son were among some of those that survived the crushing upheaval and cruel poisoning of the environment. Apparently, the storywriter had been a sickly woman, and had not lived very long after the first attacks, but her children were very hardy, and they preserved her life's work out of love and devotion to her. Some historians felt it was more for the hope when they could emerge from the hidden Burrow, that they would have a commodity to sell, as their mother was quite well known. Sojourner did not like to believe that was true. Of course, most people in the Burrows could trace their lineage back to the storywriter, so it was no great mystical thing to be her descendant. Still, she loved to tell this story. The storywriter must have been a rambunctious child, and proud of her mischief to have preserved it.

They left the monitoring room, and traveled the short distance to the outer doors by hoverboards. There was no walking allowed except on carefully prepared surfaces. The interior hoverways would be worn away too soon if everyone walked on them. Sojourner did not like to use hoverboards, but Stephan loved them. He was still a show off on them, even after all these years. Perhaps she would surprise him and tell the story about how a forward boy followed a sweet young storyteller into a grove of trees and tried to kiss her. Instead of a kiss, he received a great lump on his head when she pushed him off the hover board and he landed on a tree root. Stephan still claimed that his head was dented. Of course, a great big, grown nineteen-year-old boy had no business trying to kiss a sixteen-year-old. No, she would tell that story another day.

At the doorway to the Commons, Sojourner turned and kissed her husband. They had shared their deep kisses earlier, so this was just a simple kiss, like the ones they shared every morning before they left for their tasks. Normal and everyday. Oh, Maker. Let there be a thousand more such kisses. Sojourner found herself praying from deep in her soul. A thousand more kisses to begin a thousand days. Just a thousand more.

She stepped out into the warm sunshine. The soldiers were hidden in the bushes, and they still had their monitors fixed on the Commons. They used microwaves. What an old technology. Ancient, but then, why would they have to adapt? She stepped lightly to the dais, and mounted the steps with confidence. She must appear as though the world was the same as it had always been. There were villagers gathered at the tables, waiting expectantly for her story. They were all chosen because they would be able to listen to her as if nothing was amiss. She centered her thoughts, clearing her mind. The sun felt warm on her shoulders. She heard birdsong. She lifted her head and began.

"Long, long ago, before the world was so changed, there was a little girl named Katy. She had three sisters, Vivy, Patty and Anita. Now, I would like to say these were very good little girls, but, alas, they were not. They were ornery little girls. They were ferocious little girls. They were fearsome little girls. They threw rocks at little boys and once they buried a boy named Frankie in the sandbox when he was coming home from catechism, and ruined his good suit. They were constantly in trouble, and their poor mother was often at her wits end concerning them.

"Up the street, at the corner in a neat little house, there lived a kindly old woman named Mrs. Tucker. She always kept her lawn neat, and her yard was bright with flowers and a well-tended vegetable patch. Along her fence, she planted bright green tomato plants with tiny little tomatoes dotting them like ornaments. Katy and her sister, Anita, could not resist those wonderful tomatoes. They would creep through the neighbor's yards, then they would slither on their bellies, pulling themselves forward with their elbows, then, slowly like commandos, they would pluck the sun-warmed fruit from under the leaves, and carefully fill their mouths with them. When their cheeks were full and they could not stuff another tomato in their greedy mouths, they would crawl away, as silent as shadows. When they were behind the big elm tree in their yard, out of sight from the neighbors, they would spit the tomatoes out of their bulging cheeks, and eat them one at a time. Each wonderful tomato tasted like captured sunshine. What terrible behavior!

"Then it happened. Their mother took the girls to church every Sunday, and as luck would have it, one day there was a special visitor. He stood up and in thunderous tones, he told of a terrible place called Hell, and the fate of sinners was to spend eternity in its fiery pits, tormented and abused. Liars went to Hell. Cheaters went to Hell. Thieves went to Hell.

"What was this? Katy sat up as straight as a ramrod. Thieves went to Hell? For stealing anything? Her thoughts whirled out of control. Tomatoes were part of Anything. She was going to Hell! She looked at her sister and mouthed the word "tomato". Her sister looked back at her, fear growing in her eyes. Then the preacher said that everyone must confess their sins. Then they could be forgiven. Anita and Katy looked at each other with wild hope growing in their tormented little souls.

"When the service was concluded, the two little girls joined hands and, resolve growing in their little hearts, they marched up the street to Mrs. Tucker's house. Bravely they went, never pausing, their mission was clear, their souls at stake. Katy knocked on Mrs. Tucker's door. A few agonizing moments passed, and they could hear the rustling sounds of Mrs. Tucker coming. Katherine's stomach clenched in agony. Would they have to go to jail? Would they be beaten? Anything would be worth it to save their souls from eternal torment in Hell. The door opened.

"There stood Mrs. Tucker, her white hair neat, an apron covering her Sunday dress. "Why girls. What a nice surprise. Can you come in?"

"Oh, no." The girls shook their heads. If they went in, they might be held prisoner. " Mrs. Tucker, we have come to confess." Anita began, but she was overcome with guilty tears. Katy knew she must finish the confession, and redeem their poor dirty souls.

"We have s..st...stolen...your..(sob)...tomatoes. We are so sorry." Katy gulped out between sobs.

"Are you going to call the p..p..police?" squeaked out Anita fearfully.

"Mrs. Tucker put her hands on her hips. For an eternal moment, she stood as still as a great stone monster. Her eyes seemed like an explosion was building behind them. Then....Then...THEN! Mrs. Tucker laughed.

"She threw her head back and she laughed out loud. She laughed with great joy. She laughed from her heart.

"Katy and Anita looked at her and trembled. They were afraid. Their terrible news had made Mrs. Tucker lose her mind. She had gone insane with the awful knowledge that her tomatoes had been stolen. Now their souls were lost for certain!

"Mrs Tucker wiped her eyes. She leaned forward and patted the two girls on their heads. "Oh, you sweet, silly girls. I love to watch you sneaking up on my tomatoes. All my friends come over to watch you. I have video. Why do you think I plant tomatoes along the fence? You are the funniest little girls I have ever seen.

"Mrs. Tucker, still chuckling, went into her house and closed the door. Now, what were they supposed to do? Well, there was only one thing to do. They scampered over to the tomatoes and stuffed their cheeks full, and then they crawled home to eat them behind the old elm tree out of sight of the neighbors. Each one tasted like sunshine. "

Sojourner paused, and then she smiled and looked about her. The villagers were smiling. They laughed and clapped their hands together. She smiled at them. She would be home in five days. She would tell many stories, and she would go home every night. Just five days. It could be done.

She walked down the stairs and across to Joseph and Cloe. She looked across the Commons and saw that Stephan was standing among the villagers. He had tears running down his face, but he smiled at her all the same.

"My people, it is time for me to go. Being in Deep Burrow has been like coming home. You hold my heart, you know. I leave it in your tender hands to hold until I return."

Joseph held out his staff to her and she touched it. She had a staff much like it to take with her. At the tip of every staff was a DNA scanner. Hers recorded identity and DNA samples and it injected a microscopic marker into each person that touched it. It would make them easier to find during the sorting. A nice bit of technology.

"Mistress, we are honored by your coming. Shade in heat, water for thirst. Come again soon to our place. You are one with us."

The people all echoed Joseph. "You are one with us."

Joseph stepped forward and embraced her fondly. He covertly signaled a technician to turn on a privacy field. "No one would blame you if you decided not to do this thing. Remember, we have an excellent Plan, regardless of its harsh realities. It is a noble thing to wish to save lives, and if anyone can do this, you can.

You hold us all captive when you speak the truth. Even the Emperor cannot be immune to the truth."

"We must all hope for the best outcome. Still, I did not know that parting would be so hard. I guess I have to leave this place like I have left the others."

Joseph straightened, turned off the privacy field and said formally, "Queen of our hearts, travel well, discover mercy and hospitality."

Sojourner responded with the ancient words of parting, "Bountiful harvest and warmth of hearth to Deep Burrow. Receive the blessings of the traveler."

Slowly, she made her way to her hoverbike, touching hands with those in the crowd, embracing some. When she came to Stephan, though, her feet would move no further. She did not think she could go. She wanted to go home and await the arrival of her new grandchild. She wanted to work on her new story, the one about how the Maker caused even Corruption to weep with wonder. She wanted to watch Stephan work among his vials and machines and his never-ending supply of plants. Stephan smiled at her. He believed she would succeed. He embraced her and then impulsively, he kissed her deeply. She did not want to go. He released her and then walked her the last few steps to her hoverbike. Numbly, she let him guide her.

Five days. She blinked back her tears and mounted her hoverbike. She brushed the DNA pad and it hummed and vibrated slightly, then silently hung in the air. The Empire wanted to know how it worked. They considered it a great prize. She hoped fervently that they would not manage to open the Beta Chamber. The ions were too deadly. She breathed in deeply and nudged the control stick gently. Then slowly she rode out of Deep Burrow. She forced herself not to look back.

— Chapter 9 —

Captain Jarvo had to calm Lieutenant Bosson downwith a fierce, short command. He understood Bosson's outrage, but it was too important not to lose control and break cover. It was too important to get the hoverbike from the Queen. It would spare the Empire many precious resources if they did not have to bring the war machine clear across the world to subdue the population by force. Surrender was the goal. If the Queen heard Bosson's oaths, she might flee, and they were still too close to the Burrow.

Bosson was right to be shocked and outraged by the unholy behavior of the barbarian queen. This morning, her behavior was a travesty against civilized people. First, she came out of her hole in the ground in clothing that would make any decent woman cry out in fear that her life force was too tainted to meld with the great Life Force. The colors were shocking. It was bad enough that all of the women in this forsaken place wore trousers like their men and left their heads and sometimes arms uncovered, but the queen certainly took her bizarre ensembles to an extreme. This morning, her clothing was so colorful it hurt his eyes. Stripes of every color festooned her trousers, and her blouse was a shocking, electric blue. She had decorations dangling from her ears, and a bright silver ornament in her hair, of all places. She looked like a flagpole decorated for the arrival of the Emperor. Indecent!

Next, the insane creature climbed up on the dais and gave the most incomprehensible speech about young girls left out in the open to steal food. Her notions about justice were criminal, and the outcome and advice she rendered were beyond belief. To allow girls to go uncovered in public, then to allow them to continue their misdeeds? And the old woman in the speech, laughing like a crazed monkey? How could any decent woman act like that? What was the queen trying to teach her people? Then the idiot people laughed and clapped like they had gained something from the speech. Insane!

Finally, that immoral beast had kissed a man in the crowd. Full on the lips. Jarvo would occasionally kiss his wife in the heat of his pleasure, but never on the lips. Well, once or twice in the heat of his pleasure. She almost always kept her face decently turned away. There had been times when he was tempted to go find her and embrace her for no good reason, but he knew that the best way to keep a household efficient was to maintain a level of modesty at all times. He was tempted, though, to kiss her in private. Her lips were soft and curving. Sometimes, when he called her to him, he would find her looking at him, shyly from the corner of her eyes as he undressed. It pleased him that she looked at him. Sometimes, when he moved over her in his pleasure, she would move too, and that pleased him, though he did not know why. He would be very happy to see her. He would speak her name tenderly, and he would touch her soft skin with his fingertips. She seemed to like that.

He forced his thoughts away from his wife. He would have to go through the purification rituals for a day before he could go to his home, and even then he might need to heal for several days. It would do him no good to think of her now. He must concentrate on this task. He must concentrate on capturing the ridiculous queen.

His sensors indicated that she would be in visual range in two minutes. The intersection where Private Para was to intercept the queen was just up the road, if one wanted to call the barely paved rock trail a road. Of course, with the ingenious floating machinery, paved roads would not be as necessary. Once, this continent had been crisscrossed with mighty highways, and vehicles sped down them at tremendous speeds. After the Punishment and Cleansing of this land, the roads had crumbled and turned into dusty, dead pathways. Perhaps this had once been a mighty highway. Ahh, there she was, the old hag. She floated by on her wondrous hoverbike, unaware that her degenerate reign was effectively over. She glided to the intersection, and as planned, young Para hailed her.

"Greetings, traveler. I am one of the many. I am traveling as a brother to all. I am Para."

The queen stopped her hoverbike. "Greetings. I am one of the many. I travel as a sister to all. I am Sojourner."

"Truly? You are Sojourner? Oh, no! I have missed your visit to Deep Burrow." He stopped as if stricken.. his subterfuge was brilliant. Jarvo would recommend him for a commendation for his abilities. The harlot was mesmerized. "I have forgotten my manners. This is no way for a subject to greet his queen." He bowed slightly and then he stepped forward and embraced her in the custom of the Burrows people. He did a superb job of mimicking the manner of greeting, even to the scandalous manner of embracing a strange woman. The queen briefly returned the embrace and then she took out her staff and extended it to Para. Excellent. The ruse had worked. Para reached out and touched the tip of the queen's staff.

"Para, what an unsusual name. I have never heard it before. So, tell me young Para, how is it that you are on the road during the time of hay gathering? Shouldn't you be in the fields?"

"I have been to see my sister in Bright Burrow. She has just had a baby, and our mother wanted me to take a special gift to her. I am on my way home and I thought it would do no harm to detour to Deep Burrow and see you there. I guess I am too late."

"Well, it is no great matter, young Para. You may walk with me now, and we can visit for a bit." The queen moved forward, and Para fell into step beside her. She moved at a fast enough pace that Para had to walk very quickly. Captain Jarvo was thankful he was in such good conditioning from living off of the land, else the queen might simply outdistance him.

"Where are you from, Para?"

"I am from Far Burrow, m'lady."

"Really? My father was from Far Burrow. He has been gone for many years, but he has a cousin with a daughter that still lives there. You must know Larren Botthas. She was married to a Per Johannson the year I finished regular school. They were qualified for nine children. Can you imagine that? I have often wished I could have qualified for half as many, though I am happy with my girls."

Para looked confused and disoriented. What did she mean qualified for children? Her girls? Captain Jarvo felt a moment of panic. What if this odious old woman was a mother? What if she was a married woman? They were forbidden by the deepest laws of their fathers to touch another man's wife. To hurt a woman married to another man was death to you and to all of your sons. To accidentally injure an honorable woman brought terrible consequences as well. An honorable woman was a treasure. No. It was impossible. No man would allow his wife out of doors and unsupervised. No man would allow his wife or daughter or sister or mother or aunt to be so unprotected. It was against nature, and had been so since the beginning of time. That was one of the reasons the Dark Continent had to be cleansed. The men did not value their women, and the women became feral. Society had no meaning. Surely this great sin was not still perpetrated among the Burrows. No. He wouldn't believe that the queen Sojourner was a wife or a mother. She was an unnatural woman! Evil and unnatural by her very nature.

Para was also clearly disturbed by the unlikely turn of the conversation. "Qualified for nine children?"

"Yes. Simply amazing, wouldn't you say? My Stephan was qualified for five, but he chose to be joined to me. Of course, everyone knows my story. The girls are very strong, like him, thankfully. You are a bit younger than they are, so you never met them at University, did you?"

"University?"

"Oh, my. Haven't you gone to the University? " Sojourner's voice sounded sympathetic and slightly embarrassed. She began speaking slower, like Para might be a simpleton. "So tell me, Para, do you know any of the Johannsons? A fine family."

Para looked relieved, perhaps the conversation was not going badly after all. "Well, majesty, there are so many, nine of them, it is hard not to know a Johannson."

"Nine of them? Per Johannson was killed in a harvester accident after the fifth child. My father attended the Scattering ceremony."

"I may be confused. There are so many families of Johannsons in Far Burrow, it is hard to keep them straight."

Sojourner looked alarmed. "Oh? Are there so many Johannsons? I must notify the Family Councils that an unnecessary concentration of Johannsons is building up in Far Burrow. We can't have the gene pool too thick with Johannsons, can we? And what family are you from?"

"I am from the Younger family," Para smiled tensely. Captain Jarvo prayed with all of his might that there was a family named Younger in Far Burrow.

The queen seemed to be musing to herself, softly, but loud enough for them all to hear. "Hummm, I was not aware that the Younger family had such damaged genes; how did this happen?"

Para's face was red and he tried not to look directly at the queen. She again addressed him, speaking slowly and distinctly, as if talking to one of limited intelligence. "I have to ask you where your hover bike has gone. You have a journey of many hundreds of miles ahead of you, and I can tell that you have already walked many hundreds of miles because your boots are so worn. Almost clear through."

"I left it at my sister's home. With the new baby, I felt they might need it so that her husband could go to his job and she would still have a hoverbike to go to market and such." Para looked pleased with himself at concocting such a good answer. His pleasure quickly evaporated at the outraged gasp from the queen.

"What? Are things so terribly wrong in Bright Burrow? I was only there last year, and everything seem just fine. This is an outrage."

"Majesty?" Para was alarmed at his apparent blunder.

"How could a qualified parent not have enough to care for a child? Was this child conceived out of order? Was it an accidental birth? Are they hiding it from the Family Council?"

"Accidental?"

"You poor child. To have such a scandal in your family, and to not understand. If the child were an accidental birth, it would be placed with a qualified family. Do you understand that?"

Para was desperate. "No, m'lady. The child is not accidental or hidden. It is just that my sister's second hoverbike needed repair, and I left her mine to use. Besides, I like to walk. This has been a holiday for me, walking about this beautiful land." Para paused again, hoping his blunders would not cause any delays.

Whatever hopes Para had of mending his speech faded in the next instant. The queen drew herself up in a haughty manner, and for a moment, Jarvo could see the royalty in her. Her eyes flashed and she stopped her hoverbike abruptly. "Your family is so slothful that you are not needed for the planting? It is haying time in all of the Burrows and the interior harvest is beginning. Far Burrow is still planting the late crops. How is it that you are not helping?"

"My family does not farm..." Para stammered out, "They are Healers." They do not farm." Para looked relieved at his cleverness. He smiled.

Apparently it was the wrong thing to have said or to do. The queen became enraged. "You know that is not right. If you do not grow things, you do not eat. Even I plant and harvest. My family plants and harvests. The Leaders plant and harvest. Young Para, you are making me feel very concerned about the state of things in Far Burrow. Perhaps I should change my course and pay them a surprise visit. Yes. I will hurry there right now. I am so glad I encountered you, poor child. Time is wasting. I must hurry. Run very fast, young Para, if you intend to keep up with me."

With that, the queen leaned forward and pressed the handles of her hoverbike. It took off at a very fast pace, and Para desperately ran behind her. Captain Jarvo hoped that Lant and Ritsi were in position to intercept her. Para was shouting and waving his arms.

"Majesty! Wait! Stop! Please!"

The queen slowed her hoverbike. This was a disaster. Para had better think of something to say that would hold her attention. Jarvo ground his teeth. Stupid oaf.

"Young Para, are you alright? Do you need to rest? You do not need to stay with me. I will go to your parent's house as soon as I arrive in Far Burrow and tell them you will be along in a week or so. Would you like for me to send a hoverbike back for you? I would travel slower, but if things are as you say, then I need to get to Far Burrow right away."

Para ran up to the hoverbike, gasping for air. None of the soldiers knew the device could go so fast. Jarvo and the others were moving as quickly as they could to realign their positions. He hoped that Para would be able to distract her long enough for them to regain their positions. She was an elderly woman, perhaps her hearing wasn't good, and she wouldn't hear them moving in the woods.

"Majesty," Para gulped out between breaths, "I think you should not travel alone, and I would like to offer my protection. There are many of us that feel you take too great a risk traveling alone like this."

" Protection from what, Para? Certainly not from beasts. They do not attack unless provoked. Besides, the only animals that have been released into this area are rodents and herbivores. Predators will not be released here for another year or two. I am perfectly safe."

"No, no, majesty. I mean from bandits and bad men." stammered Para.

"There are no bandits or bad men. Men are good. They do not harm women traveling alone, and have not for a thousand years. Not since implants were available for such alterations. Where do you get these ideas?" The queen looked as if she just thought of something, and then she spoke to Para gently, like a kindly person speaking to an insane person. "Are you over hot? Do you need a drink? Here, dear...I have a canteen of nice fresh water. It has a hint of strawberries in it, my favorite. Deep Burrow is famous for it's strawberries. Have you seen the growing rooms? Of course, the growing rooms in Bright Burrow have very nice fruits too, but you have to admit that the strawberries in Deep Burrow are almost profound they are so good. There dear, that is better, isn't it? Now, before we go any further, you must tell me, there are two possibilities for your strange behaviors. The first is that you are a Bent Child, and you have slipped away from your handler. If that is true, be assured that I will get you help right away. The second possibility is that you are one of the spies sent from the Empire to abduct the queen. In which case, you may stop your charade and tell your Captain Jarvo to come forward and negotiate."

Para stood as if stunned by a paralyzer. Captain Jarvo swore beneath his breath. There was always a complication when things seem easiest. How did the Harlot know? She would have to be questioned carefully and the torture would have to be well-planned. He had no stomach for such things, but that was why Lieutenant Bosson was in the squad. His righteous anger would serve them well. He signalled to the men and they stepped out into the road.

"Ahhh, Captain Jarvo, I believe? Lieutenants Bosson and Simon? Do you realize you have eaten a very precious pet when you shot poor Demeter? A little girl named Loma is terribly upset by that. Corporals Ninta and Ritsi, yes? So sorry your surveillance equipment didn't work out so well. And then there is Private Para and Lant, the cute one and the quiet one. Did you know the girls in the Burrows think you are both very handsome? They watch your every move when allowed, though I think you are both too young to be so far from home..."

"Silence!" Captain Jarvo snarled as he strode forward. How did she know? What nonsense was she spouting? He quickly crossed the distance between them as the men surrounded her, pointing their paralyzers at her. Up close, he could see she was very small, even frail looking. She didn't look as elderly up close, her face was only wrinkled around her eyes. She must seem so old from a distance because of her thin build and spindles for arms. She sat astride her hoverbike with arrogant confidence. She looked up at Jarvo, her eyes were clear, and her lips curved into a happy smile.

For a moment he could see that she was beautiful once, and still she was beautiful, though no longer young.

"Captain, do not be angry with me." Her voice was soft and it was soothing, like the warmness he felt after he had taken his pleasure with his wife. She was so small, and the fabric of her garments followed the curves of her body. She smelled clean and lightly perfumed. "We have deliberately fooled you to show you that we are not to be taken lightly. We are a strong, resilient people, and we have a need the Empire can fulfill. Take me to speak to your Emperor Kalig. If all goes well, we will have many reasons to rejoice, your people and mine. Let me show you the strength of the Burrows, and then take me to negotiate with your Emperor. I am ready. I am one of the many. I am the Storyteller, Sojourner, wife of Stephan, mother of Jakma and Sala. I speak for a great nation."

This could not be. They had watched this harlot queen for months. She was trying to create a subterfuge to confuse them. How she knew what she knew was beyond him...Bosson would soon discover the truth. He would not be swayed from his mission.

"You lie." He stepped forward, pulling out the injection to sedate her. Her hair was straying from where it was gathered at the nape of her neck. It was a soft honey color. Her eyes were brighter than he would have imagined. She was not a proper woman. "Harlot." He plunged the needle into her arm.

─ Chapter 10 ─

Sojourner still felt sick from the sedative, though the pills in her shirt sleeve certainly helped. This was a very colorful outfit, even for her, but the bright happy colors helped to cheer her in this dismal place. She looked around her cell and shuddered. Everything was grey. It would have been much easier if the ignorant beasts would have believed her. It was going to be complicated now. Still, the failure of the first part of the negotiation plan did not mean that it still wasn't worth it to make the attempt. She wanted to save lives...even Empire lives.

She checked again to make certain that all of her personal belongings were intact. It seemed the soldiers were unwilling to go through her personal things too thoroughly because of their cultural taboo against the genders mixing. It was a wonder there were so many of them if they were so bashful. It was good for her, though.

Ahhh, here were the pieces of the transmitter and the parts of the privacy field generator. The technicians were very clever, and they were easily put together. Wonderful. She made a few adjustments, and she spoke. "Hello?" Her voice sounded muffled, just as it should. Without it, her voice echoed in this grey metal cell.

"Sojourner? Beloved? This is Stephan! Are you alright!"

"Oh! Sweetness! It is good to hear your voice. I think I am fine, though I am still sickish and I have a bump on my head and some scratches. What happened? Did you see?"

"Yes, I saw it all and it was shameful. After Captain Jarvo gave you the injection, you swayed and fell to the ground. You bumped your head on the hoverbike. The imbeciles just watched you fall. Not a one of them even made the effort to catch you. It was terrible to watch..."

"Sweetness! Don't worry! I am fine. Remember, my implants are fresh, and we knew I would probably be bumped around. The Healers took this into consideration."

"Still, I will throttle that blasted Jarvo when it comes time to sort the Empire. He would make great fertilizer for cacti!"

"Stephan!" Sojourner was shocked, but she still laughed..better to defuse Stephan's anger than feed it. "Why do you suppose they let me fall?"

"Can you imagine this? None of them had ever touched a woman other than their mothers or their wives except for the hug young Para gave you. They were all too afraid to touch you. Ignorant!"

"Poor Para, shaking like a leaf! Well, apparently someone got me here. How did they manage it?"

"The Captain ordered Para to put you back on your hoverbike, thinking that they would drape you over the bike and push the bike to their rendezvous point. "

Sojourner giggled, pleased with the thought of their ignorance causing them so much trouble. "I guess they did not know that as soon as I lost consciousness, it would shut off. One must concentrate to make a hoverbike move, and one must be on the DNA database as being qualified to use one. How ever did they get it to the rendezvous point? They weigh hundreds of pounds!"

"It took all of them to lift it. You fell off several times, and so they had to take turns carrying you and then carrying the hoverbike. They were miserable and very sorry they had mistreated you!"

"I am sorry they mistreated me too," replied Sojourner with a rueful laugh. "Still, I am in one piece. I guess we had better get down to business?"

"Yes, love; here is Joseph."

"Hello, Joseph. I suppose it is time for me to begin compromising the ship?"

"Yes, the filaments you will need that hold the viruses are in the stripes of your trousers."

"What? I wondered why this outfit was so bright. Where are they?"

"Listen carefully. See the silvery threads running through the fabric?"

"Yes, the gaudy things."

"The blue stripes hold viruses that effect immediate electronic obstacles. For instance, the lock on your door is an electronic one. If you want to over-ride the lock, lay it close to the hinges, there are usually wires there, and step back. The filaments will absorb into the metal and disable the door. Hold your breath when you want to use it, it smells bad. The yellow stripes hold filaments that will infiltrate the ship's systems. We will be able to override the controls from our location. These need to be placed on the counsole of the ship's control panel. This might be trickier. If you can manage it, it would be a great advance for us. The red stripes hold filaments that will override security protocols. Put them beside any weapon firing system, they will absorb into the system and disable it, and yes, they stink, too. The pink stripe's filaments can be used to purify foods and water. When you get to the Palace of the Emperor, the green and purple stripes hold filaments that can be used there, we'll talk about them later. Do you have any questions?"

"Only a thousand, but I am going to have to end this transmission because I hear footsteps outside my cell door."

As quickly as she could, Sojourner made her adjustments and then, as the door creaked open, she sat down on the side of her cot. The door swung open on heavy hinges, groaning under its own weight. How would she ever push it herself? Captain Jarvo stood at the doorway, clearly disliking his task.

"By order of the Emperor, a servant has been provided for you," he paused and then sneered, "O Queen" as if the very words galled his mouth. "In recognition of your vaulted estate in your homeland, one of the former Emperor's Chosen has been secured to tend to your needs."

"That is all well and fine, my dear. But you misunderstand...I am a simple Storyteller, valued for my wit and glib tongue." As she was speaking, several soldiers were pushing a large heavy box forward. "I am sent as an emissary to the Emperor to negotiate..." Ignoring her, the soldiers pushed the box up to the doorway and fitted an opening over her doorway. Once the two doorways were pushed together, there was a hissing sound as they were sealed together, isolating Sojourner. The box's hatch then opened. Inside was a stinking, fetid, dank prison, reeking of human excrement and rotting food. Huddled in a corner was a dark heap of rags.

Sojourner gasped and stepped backward, the stench momentarily overwhelming her. She stumbled over to the small metal sink and retched, aching, dry heaves. She struggled to control her revulsion and disgust, and with shaking hands she washed her face and took a sip of water. She filled the metal cup, and carefully crossed over to the hatchway, covering her mouth and nose with her sleeve. She peered into the dark recesses of the box and spoke. She carefully pitched her voice to the timbre of a young woman, softer and tentative.

"Hello. I imagine you are thirsty? I have brought you a cup of water." The huddled rags raised up slightly, turning its body toward the sound of her voice. "Would you like a drink?" The dark shrouded figure nodded. Sojourner held her breath as she crossed over to the creature. She knelt down beside her and held out the drink. The figure held out a thin hand and took the cup of water from Sojourner and raised a small flap in the front of her shrouded face and drank eagerly. "Would you like some more?" The woman nodded her head uncertainly, as if she were afraid it was a joke. Sojourner rose and left the box and went to the sink, her legs felt weak, but it was important that she keep her composure. What had happened to this woman? Intelligence had shown that the women were kept cloistered, not tormented. Why was this sad creature brought to her in such a pitiable state?

"Here is some more water. Come and sit up now. Can you move about? Here, let me help you up." The woman cringed away from Sojourner's touch. "There. I won't touch you. Let me bring you a basin of water, and you can wash if you want...would you like that?" Again the shrouded figure nodded. She pulled her knees up under her chin and huddled again in her corner. Sojourner went again to the little sink and filled a small pan with water. She carried it back to the box and set it carefully inside. "I will leave you to your washing, she murmured. She went back to her cot and sat down. The basin of water sat in the doorway for several minutes, then like a silent shadow, the Chosen of the former Emperor came to the doorway and dragged the small basin into the recesses of the box.

Sojourner activated her dampening field. "What do you make of this?"

It was Cloe that answered. "We have this up on the monitor. The Healers are here, and so are the Handlers and the Psychologists. The preliminary diagnosis of the Healers is undernourishment and possible physical trauma, though we cannot tell through her clothing. The handlers agree that she has suffered extreme trauma, though the fact that she accepted water from you indicates a willingness to be reached. The fact she wants to wash indicates a sense of self preservation and the desire to be whole. Good instincts to offer her water. The psychologists hypothesize that the purpose of bringing this poor creature to you is to show you what becomes of women that do not please the Empire. It is a warning to you. Be certain to be aware that this is a threat. Joseph says to put one of the electronic disrupters on the seal, and we will be able to analyze it."

Sojourner crossed over to the hatch and pulled the first filament wire out of her pant leg. She placed it along the seal and stepped back. There was a hiss and a sharp chemical smell. Whew, another interesting scent! The Empire certainly knew how to humiliate someone, but the Burrow knew how to raise a stink as well. She paused thoughtfully and wondered how this poor woman came to this pass.

"Sojourner, initial readings show that the box can be pushed away enough for you to get out if you can convince the Chosen of the former whatever to help you. The handlers say to offer her nourishing food and medicine. Notice she has an open wound on her hand when she extends it next. Offer her more clean water until she refuses. Put some of the antibiotics from your earrings in the water. It will help her. Let her continue to wash until she feels like she is clean enough. It will be a healing process for her."

"I understand. I will remove the dampening field now."

Sojourner adjusted her disguised devises and went to the door of the box. "Dearie? Would you like some more water? Leave the basin of dirty water at the door and I will freshen it for you."

Sojourner heard scuffling in the box and the basin was pushed to the door. She carefully picked up the murky water and emptied it into the toilet; it was too filthy to be emptied in the sink. She then carefully rinsed the basin and refilled it with fresh water. Carefully, she added a few drops of the antibiotic to the fresh and carried it back to the doorway. As before, the basin was pulled into the recesses of the box. Again and again throughout the morning, Sojourner took clean water to the doorway. Again and again the water was returned, slowly loing its murky filth. Sojourner could hear the woman washing the walls of the box and the slapping sound of fabric being washed was heard. She heard murmuring and quiet crying. Slowly, the air began to freshen. Finally, the woman did not take in the basin of water. Sojourner was glad. Her arms ached from carrying the silent offerings. Sojourner looked at her timepiece and was surprised to discover it was not even noontime. She was very hungry. She wondered if the people of the Empire ate lunch. She had been too queasy to eat the hard bread and broth they brought this morning, and now she wished she had it back.

It seemed an eternity, but finally she heard footsteps outside the cell. This morning, they had opened door and the scowling Ritsi had thrust the food at her. Now, it was done differently. A narrow slot was opened near the top of the cell and a stinking trail of rotting food slithered down the wall. Sojourner again had to cover her nose with her sleeve; she felt like weeping. She activated the dampening field again.

"Oh, Maker of All! Do you see this?" she sobbed out. "They have been feeding this poor woman rotting food. What are we to do?"

Joseph spoke, "Remember the pink filaments can be used to purify food and water. It may not taste good, but it will suffice. Also, there are nutrition pills in the hem of your trousers." His voice softened with concern and sorrow. "My friend, I am so sorry this is happening to you. We are ready to send the Light planes after you this instant."

"No, I can manage this. The poor woman is coming out. She must be very hungry to want this rotten food. Tell me what to do to make this refuse eatable."

Sure enough, the woman was emerging from her box, her still damp robes hanging heavily about her. She pressed herself against the wall, her head turned in the direction of the rancid food. Sojourner pulled the filament from the pink stripe of her trousers and went over to the stinking heap.

"First you must isolate the food groups if possible."

The woman gasped at the voice coming from nowhere and pressed herself against the wall.

"I see you have done this...good...now break the filament into pieces about as long as the end joint of your thumb and mix it in to the foods. Do this quickly as the food will immediately begin to heat and a chemical will infuse itself into the food."

Sojourner began...there were three different food groups...some kind of rice, riddled with mold, a mix of vegetables, limp and brown, and some type of meat, slimy with pockmarks of green. There were no plates or eating utensils, so Sojourner had to use her hands and try to isolate the stinking food on the floor. Quickly she added a piece of the filament to the the rice and stirred it with her fingers. She jerked her fingers away as the food began to smoulder and steam. The former Chosen let out a muffled gasp. She waved the steam away, and the rice was better, less rancid and more wholesome looking. Quickly Sojourner added the filaments to the rest of the foods. They also smouldered and steamed thick billows of steam. When the steam was fanned away, there were several piles of food on the floor. It was not appetizing to look at, but Sojourner knew it would be fine. She scooped up a bit of rice on her fingers and put it in her mouth. Bland, but not terrible. She motioned for the woman to come and eat.

The woman crept toward the food and cautiously knelt within reach of the food, but out of Sojourner's reach. With trembling hands, she reached out and scooped up a bite of vegetables, lifted the flap in her veil and put the food in her mouth. "Oooh!" she breathed out quietly. She reached out for more.

~ Chapter 11 ~

Captain Jarvo had no stomach for his meal, though he knew better than to refuse it. It was a travesty to have two such women on this ship. Even worse was what was planned for them. He glanced down the table at Lieutenant Bosson. Sometimes he loathed the man. He seemed to take pleasure in breaking the will of prisoners. Oh, he kept a pious face, but even the impure did not deserve this. Swift death was better for the captive and the Forsaken than what Bosson planned for them. Captain Jarvo was appalled the disgraced Chosen was here. Bosson's instructions to the crew concerning the Forsaken Woman had made the taciturn Lieutenant Bosson smile to himself all morning.

Captain Jarvo glanced at to the big, black cube pressed up against the windowless holding cell standing exposed in the middle of the deck. He was astonished the disgraced one was still alive after all this time. Five years was a long time to live in the sewers. Her father should have known better than to offer her to an aging Emperor. He must have been in disfavor and offered her as a way to save himself from some terrible punishment. She must have been beautiful for the late Emperor Kalig to accept her so late in his rule. It was thoughtless. A moment of weakness for the aging Emperor, a lifetime of sorrow for an innocent girl. He wondered how many other Chosen were cast away into dark places because the Emperor died before they could produce a child?

He knew his thoughts were bordering on blasphemy. It was a good way to keep the Empire strong, giving the Emperor the best and most beautiful young women. He knew that the Chosen did not have easy lives, but they produced Emperors capable of ruling the world. It was a disgrace to them and yet, a great honor to them to be a Chosen. Still, he would not ever offer one of his daughters to the Emperor. He thought of his children. He had two sons and three daughters. His eldest son was eight, old enough very soon to begin his training. His other son was still an infant. He longed to see them, even though it was not proper to be close to them when they were small. Sometimes, when he stood quietly in the shadows watching them, his heart would feel like it swelled in his chest. One of his daughters, the one just bigger than the infant, especially caught his eye. She was always smiling and squealing happily. The noise in the woman's side of the apartment was wonderful to him, and he often found himself longing to go in and be a part of it all. Of course, that is not the way to maintain an orderly home. Orderly homes were the building stones of mighty empires.

It was part of the discipline of a man's life to refrain from frivolous behaviors, especially if a man was in the service of the Empire. The training was intense, but the honor of being a commoner with imperial ties was great. His family had been in service to the Empire for generations, and was well respected. It was important to maintain discipline in every aspect of life if one was in service. If he was to go home and retrieve his son into service, then he must be willing to sacrifice to insure his son would be ready.

He remembered the day his father came and retrieved him from his mother. His mother had prepared him for several weeks for the honor, but he was still frightened. He had seen his father from afar, tall and commanding in his presence, and he was very afraid of him. He was not the first son to be taken from the security of the women's side of the apartment. Two other brothers had gone before him, silently following the tall, straight, man out of the nursery without looking back. His mother would always wipe tears from her eyes and breathe in deeply. It would be strangely silent in the nursery for many days after.

When his turn arrived, he tried very hard to be brave. His mother held him most of the morning, her arms soft and tender. She had rocked him in her arms, soothing him, stroking his hair and crooning soft words to him as he cried. His brothers had cried, too. Still, they went without looking back, and he would too. The hour arrived and she put him away from her like a decision. She had told him what to expect his whole life, and he knew what he had to do. He went to his room and changed into the dark shirt and pants of a man in the service of the Empire. Then he went to the door of the nursery and he stood straight and tall. He did not look at his mother, and he did not acknowledge his sisters' farewells. He stood straight and tall, and when his father came, he followed him like a silent soldier.

He had never been to the men's side of the apartment. He knew his mother went there daily to serve food and gather dirty clothes. She went there at nighttime, too, though he did not know why his father would summon her in the middle of the night. Still, she would say nothing about the men's side of the apartment, and he had to admit he was very curious.

His father led him down a short hallway, through the locked and bolted double doors and into another hallway. There was a common room off to one side and the other side of the hallway was lined with sleeping rooms. The largest, he supposed, was his father's. His father's bed was very wide, and he wondered why his father needed such a wide bed to sleep in. His father led him into the common room. The furnishings were stark and plain. The main piece of furniture was a long dining table, simple in its construction and lined on both sides with hard stools with no backs. At the end of the table there was a heavy, plain chair. That must be where his father sat. There was a sink and cabinets along one wall, and a long couch along another. The common room had a large open doorway on one wall, and through it, Jarvo could see a large area with a gathering of men and boys in it. His father led him silently onward, through the doorway and into the gathering.

As soon as he entered the area, all of the men and boys grew silent and fell into straight rows, standing at solemn attention. Jarvo's father walked to the front of the gathering. He took Jarvo by the shoulders, his touch firm and strong. It was the first time his father had ever touched him, and his heart pounded in his chest. He guided Jarvo firmly to a place in front of the gathering.

His father spoke. It was the first time he had ever heard his father's voice; it sounded like quiet thunder to Jarvo, and he trembled. "Here is my son, Ivan, from the house of Jarvo. Accept him into our society."

"Done," the men chanted in unison.

"Here is my son Ivan, from the house of Jarvo. Prepare him to serve the Empire."

"Done," the men chanted again, their voices resounding like a fierce war drum.

"Here is my son, Ivan, from the house of Jarvo. Prepare him to rule his house."

"Done." The men's voices seemed to be a strong, alive beast, separate from the men.

Jarvo's father again took him by the shoulder and they joined the ranks of men and boys at attention. Another father came out of a doorway, propelling a trembling boy in front of him.

"Here is my son Nol, from the house of Pern. Accept him into our society."

Again, the men chorused the word "Done." The boy Nol was shaking so hard he could barely stand. Jarvo had been glad he had managed to stand mostly still, and he felt sorry for the boy, Nol, and was relieved when he could leave the front of the room. In all, seven boys were taken that morning, all frightened and one sobbing. After what seemed an eternity, Jarvo had followed his father back into their common room. He felt numb and alone. His two older brothers came into the room right behind them.

Their father pointed to the long couch against the wall and the brothers sat down. "Welcome Ivan. I must say I am proud of the way you conducted yourself this morning. So far all three of my sons have managed the crossing without too much fear. I am pleased. Burl and Rivin, I want you to take Ivan to your room and show him what he needs to know. As soon as you are done, we need to go to the market."

At this, Ivan's brothers sat up even straighter, excitement glowing in their eyes. Jarvo looked into his father's face and he saw affection and kindness in his eyes, though he kept his face stern. Jarvo felt a thrill of love for his father, and bounded up from the couch throwing his arms around him. His father looked startled. He patted Jarvo awkwardly on the back and then pried him loose with firm gentleness. "You need to know, Ivan, this is not done. You will learn the proper way to behave."

Jarvo felt his face grow hot with shame. He ducked his head and followed his brothers out of the room. His brothers were snickering at him from behind their hands. He felt sickish. He wanted his mother so badly he wanted to scream. Woodenly he followed them to their room. It was spartan and severely clean. He could see that each of his brothers had staked out a bed and had certain personal items placed on small shelves. His oldest brother, Burl, pointed to a neatly made bed on the opposite side of the room from theirs. In the nursery, there had been bright pictures and the beds were soft and colorful. He looked at his bed and nodded. It was grey. His shelf held nothing.

Burl was thirteen years old, and Ivan barely remembered him because he had only been three when Burl left. Rivin was eleven, and Ivan remembered playing with him and crying for him when he was gone. Now they both looked like strangers. His lip began to tremble and his eyes filled with tears.

"Look here, don't you be a crybaby and embarrass our father," Burl said sternly. "You knew it was time to come and begin your training. You are not much, but maybe you will become a man. Forget the past. Don't be a baby any longer."

"Yes," echoed Rivin. "Don't act like a baby."

" I for one will not aknowledge you as my brother until you improve. Stupid infant." Burl came and stood close to Ivan. He was large and hard looking. "I told father you were too young to be in our room."

"Yes, you are too young and soft to be here." Riven agreed.

Ivan stood up, he wiped the tears roughly from his eyes. "I am not crying. It is just that you are so ugly you make my eyes water."

His two brothers looked at him with amazement, then they exchanged a look that in the future, would send Ivan running for help. Ivan did not know that look, though, and he stood defiantly, his fists balled at his side. His defiance was futile, and his inexperienced fists did nothing to help him. He screamed in frustration and pain as their fists punched him in the ribs, the groin, the arms, the face. He balled himself tightly, trying to cover his head, and after long moments he was crying out in fear .

"What is this?" His father's voice washed over the room like a great wave. His brothers were whisked backward, away from him and someone was sitting him up.

"Well, Jarvo. It looks like your boy has become acquainted with his big brothers. Here boy, sit still and let me check you over. He is going to have a shiny black eye. Some bruises. Here boy, hold this against your nose until it stops bleeding. There now, don't take on. I had big brothers, too. Someday, you will be big enough to stand up to them..."

Ivan's father looked at the two older boys with angry, burning eyes. They stood very still. Rivin was shaking. "Explain this," their father's voice was low and sounded sharp like a saber.

"He was crying for his mother, and I told him to stop." stammered out Burl.

"Then he claimed he wasn't crying, but that we were so ugly we made his eyes water." added Rivin, looking accusingly at Ivan. "Our honor was compromised."

"Ho there!" laughed out the man tending to Ivan's hurts. "Your honor is not compromised. You are truly ugly enough to make a young boy's eyes water. Look at mine. See them water? And I am an old man."

The man laughed, but their father only smiled grimly. "Neither of you have any reason to scoff at your brother. You Burl. I found you by the woman's door in the middle of the night, huddled on the floor. You cried for a month. And you Rivin...You trembled like a captive bird whenever any of the men spoke to you. You also cried for your mother. As a matter of fact, when your mother brings in your evening meal, I will require that you stand at your chair and tell her what you have done to her child. For shame. A boy needs to cry for his mother for a while." He paused, "If I were to be taken from your mother, I would cry for the rest of my life."

The man that was sitting next to Ivan patted him roughly on the shoulder and stood. "Yes, Boona. I would cry for my wife, and to be honest, I cried for my mother for a very long time. Most all of the boys cry some. To leave an honorable woman is a hard thing."

"The Law Giver says: 'To every honorable man, one honorable woman, no more forever, so your soul can be preserved in future generations. Protect her, and she will give you sons for strength and daughters for honor.'" His father quoted in a dignified, quiet voice. "You boys have both been instructed in this. It is proof to me that she treats my sons with care because they all miss her. Now, get ready to go the market. Our household needs food."

With that, the snuffling Ivan got up and limped after his father. His brothers skulked behind, disgraced and angry. Ivan would have enjoyed his first trip outside the soldier's compound where he had been raised, but he did not. He suffered dozens of pinches and jabs from his brothers. It was hard not to cry out, but his instincts told him that it would only make matters worse if he cried out. He tried to stay as close to his father as possible, as he went from place to place in the market buying food.

Later, back in their own quarters, the hours dragged by with endless chores and unseen pinches from his tormentors. Finally, the hour came when Ivan knew his mother would be bringing in their evening meal. His heart raced with pleasure at the thought of seeing her. His father crossed to the door that opened into the public hallway and he slid a thin door from inside the door frame across the opening. Hurriedly, his brothers helped set the table. His father pointed to a chair, and Ivan stood next to it. His brothers and father stood next to their chairs. The woman's door pushed open, and his mother came into the hallway, pushing the cart that held their evening meal. She wore her robes that covered her, but since this was her family, she wore a sheer veil, and Ivan could see her face through it. Ivan had never seen his mother robed. In the nursery, she wore light cotton dresses made of all different colors. Her face was never veiled, and she laughed and sang happy songs. When she took the children to the learning pods, she talked and waved happily to the other mothers. Here, there was something solemn and foreign about her. She glided into the room like a soft wind, her step was light and her manner subdued. She stopped by the doorway leading into the common room.

"Our lives are blessed by an honorable woman," his father and brothers chanted. "You nourish us with your presence."

His mother quietly bowed her head toward them, accepting their benediction. She turned to the cart to retrieve a platter to put on the table. Ivan's father put out his hand and stopped her. She turned to him questioningly. "Burl and Rivin need to relate something to you that happened today." He gestured to the two elder boys to begin. Their mother stood silently, her hands folded in front of her.

"Mother," began Burl, "Today Rivin and I made a terrible error in judgement. Your youngest was sitting on his bed and he began to cry because he misses you. I told him that to cry would bring dishonor to our father and I called him a crybaby. Rivin then called him a crybaby, too. Your young son then told us his eyes were watering because we were so ugly. Then we, Rivin and I, felt our honor had been compromised and we struck your young son several times."

"He is not seriously hurt," added Rivin.

Ivan's mother gestured to his father, indicating she would like to cross over to Ivan and see him. His father nodded. Softly she came over to him, and she put her gentle hands under his chin and lifted his face up to her. His eye was swollen shut and his lip was cut, swollen and scabbed. She knelt beside him and looked at his bruised arms and then she lifted his shirt and saw the bruises on his chest. Her breath was heaving in and out through parted lips and her hands were shaking as she lowered his shirt. Burl and Rivin were looking at the floor, ashamed. Again she touched Ivan's bruised face, and although it hurt, Ivan leaned his cheek into her palm. He tried to soak her touch inside of him. He knew he would not be allowed to put his arms around her neck and bury his face in her hair and cry away his misery. This is where he lived now. He would never live with her again. Tears poured down her cheek, and she sobbed once. His brothers winced at the sound of her cry. Ivan did not want her to cry over this. He took her hand away from his cheek and held it. He wanted to soothe her.

"Momma, don't cry over this. I don't feel it much. I am a soldier, and I will defend the Empire. Don't worry about me."

"Wife, do you wish to speak?" his father's voice was commanding yet gentle.

Ivan's mother nodded and rose to her feet. She walked over to Burl and took him by the shoulder and looked into his eyes. "Be honorable. This was not honorable." Then she crossed to Rivin and took him by the shoulder and looked into his eyes. "Be honorable. This was not honorable." Rivin looked at his feet, his breath coming in and out of his clenched teeth, fighting his emotions. Burl stood as carved from stone, his fists balled at his side.

"We will eat now," his father stated. Ivan's mother crossed to the cart and again lifted the platter of food with shaking hands. His father helped steady the platter as she placed it on the table and returned to the cart for the other foods. After all of the dishes were placed on the table, she straightened and stood silently by the cart.

The others knew what to do, and Ivan watched and followed suit. Each reached over and broke off a piece of bread from the loaf Ivan's mother sat on the table. His father crossed to his mother and lifted her veil slightly and placed the bite of bread into her mouth. "Your presence nourishes me, accept my thanks." His voice was husky with a tenderness that in later years, Ivan would understand was private. Burl then crossed to his mother and fed her the piece of bread. "Your presence nourishes me, accept my thanks," he said woodenly, though when he turned his eyes flashed angrily at Ivan. Rivin then took his mother a piece of bread,... he could not look at her face when he placed the bread in her mouth, "Your presence nourishes me, accept my thanks." Then Ivan took his piece of bread to his mother, she stooped slightly so he could put the bread into her mouth. He smiled up at her through his bruises; he didn't want her to look so sad. "Your presence nourishes me, accept my thanks." His mother drew in a sudden sobbing breath and turned to go. When she was gone, they all sat down and ate in silence.

Jarvo jerked his attention back to the present. The long table where they all sat was laden with food, but Jarvo had no stomach for it. He had seen what Bosson had taken to the barbarian queen and the unfortunate Chosen. He had taken rotting food, unfit for even the feral beasts to eat. Only insects that ate refuse could stomach such filth. Bosson looked satisfied as he pushed the slimy mass into the slot at the top of the cell. He sauntered back to the mess table. "Later, I will cut off their water. I will break her spirit quickly."

— Chapter 12 —

Sojourner sat cross-legged on the floor. Across from her the Chosen crouched, scraping her finger across the floor, trying to gather the last remnants of food.

"Chosen, I realize you are undernourished. I have some nutrition pills that I am going to take. Would you like one? It will not fill your belly, but it will give your body some help. Sojourner took out two of the pills and swallowed one. She held out the other one for the Chosen. The woman held out her hand and Sojourner put the pill in her palm. Still, she did not take the pill right away; she sat quietly and watched Sojourner for many long minutes. Sojourner thought she was waiting to see if there were any ill effects. She had to stifle her impulse to do something startling like bark or jump up and dance. Those types of antics were for another day. Instead, she sat quietly. Finally, the Chosen put the pill under her flap of her veil and into her mouth.

"I couldn't help but notice that you have a wound on your arm. I have some medicines here that might help you. May I take a look?" Again, she sat silently as the Chosen struggled with her distrust. Slowly, she extended her arm.

The wound on her arm was a deep, festering, torn place. Sojourner could see that the Chosen had tried to clean it with the water, but even the antibiotic had not touched the red, angry infection.

"I am going to talk to my friends through this transmitter. They have the means to have a true Healer look at this through a scanner I have in a contact lens. The healer can tell me what to do to help you...would you like that? Would you like for your arm to heal?"

The Chosen nodded. Sojourner took her staff and placed it on the edge of the wound and bent over her arm, examining it closely. The voice of a Healer spoke. "In your pack, there is another pair of earrings. They are blue and dangle. The dangle holds a rolled up bundle of Deep Heal. The Deep Heal peels off in very thin sheets and is used in industrial accidents to heal stubborn wounds. Our analysis of this wound shows a deep staph infection. It may take several sheets, apply them one at a time and take a reading between applications. To the patient, this will be uncomfortable and might cause you some pain. Prepare yourself for the first application."

Sojourner dug around in her pack and found the earrings. Gaudy things. She held them up to her ears and turned to the Chosen and made a face. The Chosen did not laugh. Hummm...humor would not work here. Of course, the woman was still too distrusting to laugh. Sojourner unscrewed the dangle and took out the roll of Deep Heal. Carefully she peeled off a thin sheet and motioned for the Chosen to extend her arm flat. She gently pressed the Deep Heal on the wound. Immediately it began to bubble and absorb into the wound. The Chosen moaned and trembled, but she did not move her arm. Sojourner put her staff up to the wound and sent the new data back to the Healer.

"She needs another nutrition pill, and a drink of water," the Healer instructed. "Then apply another Deep Heal. The infection is affected, but it still rules the wound."

Sojourner gave the Chosen another pill and a drink. The Chosen held the cup to her lips with her other hand and lifted the flap of her veil with her wounded hand. She could barely use her hand, so Sojourner reached for the veil flap, speaking softly to the Chosen. "Here now, let me do that for you. Rest your arm."

The Chosen relaxed her wounded arm, and Sojourner lifted the veil so she could drink her water. Then she sat back quietly, waiting for the Chosen to extend her arm again. After just a few moments, the Chosen seemed to steel herself, sitting up straighter and squaring her shoulders firmly. She extended her arm again, and again Sojourner pressed a thin sheet of Deep Heal into the wound. Again, it bubbled and absorbed into the skin. This time the Chosen did not moan, though she could not keep herself from shaking with pain. Sojourner took her staff and pressed it against the side of the wound. It looked better.

"Excellent!" The Healer's voice was pleased. "You are strong to respond so quickly! Do you think you are ready for another?"

The Chosen nodded and extended her arm. Sojourner pressed another sheet of Deep Heal on the wound and again, it bubbled and absorbed into the wound, though this time, it was not as terrible to watch. The wound looked clean like a fresh cut instead of a festering wound. Sojourner pressed her staff against the wound and waited.

"We are ready to do the next procedure. Sojourner, in your bag, there is a necklace with a medallion of a swan. Pry the medallion open and you will find thin sheets of synthoskin. This is used to treat deep cuts. You will have to pull the edges of the wound together. Chosen, you can help....., and place the synthoskin over the cut, then brush over it with water. This will have a pulling sensation, Chosen. It will not be nearly as painful as the Deep Heal. Have you found everything?"

Sojourner held up another gaudy piece of jewelry. This time, when she held it up to her neck and rolled her eyes, the Chosen grunted softly with amusement. "This definitely isn't my style," Sojourner said, lacing her voice with amusement.

"I can't be responsible for the style," the Healer joked. "Now get some water ready, because you want to wet this right away."

Sojourner crossed to the sink and turned the handle. A bare trickle ran out of the faucet and into the waiting basin. The pipes wheezed and the trickle stopped. She stared at the water puddled at the bottom of the basin.

"What has happened?" she gasped.

"We are unclean women," the Chosen whispered. "We do not merit water..." Her voice was heavy with sorrow and shame, a dry rasping voice, unaccustomed to speaking. She shuffled herself into the corner and pulled her knees into her body tightly.

"Is there enough to do the job here?" Sojourner was getting irritated at the stupidity of this treatment. She had spent her life overcoming obstacles, and she was not going to be stopped by meanness.

"Yes. Actually there is plenty of water to do several procedures," answered the Healer. Just be careful with it. Later tonight, the Leader will relay the method to get you out of your confinements."

"Wonderful!"

"But now, let's tend to this poor woman's hurts. Are you ready, Chosen?"

The Chosen raised her head in an attitude of amazement. "You do not fear this? They have taken our water."

"I am a woman from the Burrow. They can't take anything from me that I can't take back. Now, let's tend to this."

The Chosen held out her arm again, and as Sojourner held the edges of the cut together, she put the thin layers of synthoskin over the wound and brushed them with water. The synthoskin did not fully absorb into the wound, but unless one was looking very closely, it could not be seen. The Healer then told them it would peel off as the wound healed. At a glance, the Chosen's arm looked whole.

"Do you have any other wounds we can treat for you?" Sojourner made her voice pleasant and unassuming. "I have plenty of medicines, and we have the attention of a fine Healer."

The Chosen seemed to struggle with her inhibitions for a moment, then she began to disrobe. First she removed her veil. Sojourner caught her breath. She was prepared for the fact that the people of the empire would have more distinct characteristics of region than the people of the Burrows. The spies all had strongly distinct features and so she had been somewhat prepared for the people of the Empire to look different than the homogenized citizens of the Burrows. It had caused endless speculation as to the appearance of the people. It was still startling to see such a white face with such brilliant hair.

Her face had been very beautiful once, but now she looked starved and haggard. She was missing several teeth and her hair was dull and thin. She tiredly removed her heavy robes and stood before Sojourner in a worn shift, tattered and stained. Following the instructions of the Healer, Sojourner started at the Chosen's head, and worked her way downward, administering the sometimes painful treatments. The Chosen would wince, but she endured the pain silently, occasionally wiping away tears that slid down her cheek. As the afternoon passed, the Chosen began to answer Sojourner's questions. Sometimes, Sojourner had to pause to wipe away her own tears.

Her name was Lyla, and she was the favored daughter of a minor lord, Lord Dertha. Although her home was a proper one, it did not strictly follow the rules given by the Lawgiver. Instead of being strictly separated, her father had often come to the woman's side of the house to play with his children and spend time with her mother. He was a happy, jolly man, given to pranks and silliness. Her mother had also been good and kind to her, though she was a bit more strict than her father. Lyla had been trained from very early to understand that her life might be very different after she married. So she was instructed in the ways of the Lawgiver, knowing the changes that might make life less pleasant after she came of age.

When she came of age, as was the custom, the Examiners came and tested her. She knew what was expected of her and answered well. It seemed she would be well mated, and she hoped that the kind of affection that her parents shared would be in her home. It was not to be because the trouble with Lord Simon started and would not go away.

Her father came home one day in a morose mood, weighted with worry about something that happened at court. Apparently, he had irked the powerful Lord Simon with some joke, and Lord Simon had taken exception to him. It was nothing to worry about, he assured them. It would be forgotten. The next day, though, he came home burdened and troubled. Apparently, the Lord Simon had decided to call in debts, and everyone owed Lord Simon. Her father owed Lord Simon... a sizable debt. He was hard pressed to liquidate enough assets to pay it off. He would have to sell the family home, he was afraid, and Lyla's dowery would be gone as well. They would have to move to a smaller house and

Lyla may not be well matched. It was all because of his stupidity.

That is when the lone Examiner returned covertly to their home. He had heard of Lord Dertha's troubles, and had come with a possible solution. Offer his daughter to the aging Emperor. He was still a randy old goat, and he favored willowy fair, women like Lyla. All she would have to do was produce a child, and she would be able to live in the palace, even after the Emperor was deposed. That did not seem to be too far in the future, as a son with fiery eyes and a sharp sword had already proven himself many times over. No one could collect debts from one connected to the Emperor by direct blood. Even the conniving Simon could not touch them.

Lyla's father did not even think about it. He said no. He said he would rather starve than have his daughter exposed to court and cloistered, bound to a concubine's shame. When Lyla had found out that the Examiner was at their home, she hid herself in a wardrobe and listened, hoping to hear news about her future husband. Her heart sang when she heard her father would not offer her to the Emperor. But all that changed.

In the next days, her father grew gloomier and more desperate. He sold the family heirlooms. He sold many of the household furnishings. He grew gaunt with worry. Lyla watched her father become diminished by his worries. She decided to tell her father she was willing to become a Chosen if it would help. After all, all she had to do was produce a child, and after the Emperor was deposed, she would live a quiet life in the palace cloister. Her father would never lose his status, regardless what happened to her. Her mother would have her home. Her brothers and sisters would grow up in peace. In a moment of desperation, her father agreed. Lyla felt a deep joy when she realized her family would be safe from the capricious Lord Simon, and she was proud of her ability to do something important to preserve them.

The next several days were tense as the Examiner was notified of the decision, and he took the offer to the Emperor. It was with mixed happiness and fear that Lyla faced the future. Within just a few days after the acceptance, she was taken to the palace to be prepared for the purification ritual. When she was taken to the cloister, the other Chosen saw her and they wept for her. One of them, Tura, the mother of the present Emperor Kalig, was especially kind to her. She told her what to expect, and how best to survive the humiliation of the purification rites the Chosen were subjected to before entering the cloister.

Emperors never married their Chosen, Lyla explained, to prevent political alliances. They were to produce at least one son before they were retired from the use of the Emperor, though if he favored her, she may have many sons, though that was cruel and most Emperors did not require so much loss from a Chosen. If they produced nothing but daughters, they were used until they could produce no more children, and the daughters were bestowed on a worthy son of a noble house. It gave them no standing in court, but it was an honor nonetheless. There were thousands of couriers, so the thirty or so daughters produced in a lifetime were a status symbol for noblemen and underlords. If no children were produced, and the emperor was deposed, the Chosen could return to her father's home, but only if she had not been enjoyed by the emperor. If she were no longer a virgin, then she would become an outcast. She would be called Forsaken. It was a terrible thing for the emperor to take another Chosen so late in his life as he would surely be deposed before the year was over. It was very important for her to conceive quickly, as soon as she was healed from her purification ritual.

The purification ritual was a terrible thing. All young men were trained on how to purify a woman and to deliver her babies because when he married, he would be the only one allowed to see any portion of his wife's body. It was rumored that some men chose not to purify their wives, but would cut themselves in order to show the requisite blood on the shift worn during the ceremony. It was a great gift to be married to such a man. Unfortunately, for the Chosen, the ceremony was public. All married men in the noble houses and officers of the military living in Empire City were to attend the ceremony. It was held in a huge ampitheater, and the cutting was displayed on an enormous screen so that there was no uncertainty as to whether or not the purification was done thoroughly. It was done to give the Chosen a small bit of their soul back since they would be having relations as unmarried women. It was a horrible experience for all of them.

On the day of her purification, Lyla recounted, she was arrayed in a dress of pure white, scandalous in the way it conformed to her body, soft to the touch and edged with pearls in an intricate design. She was veiled in a sheer white veil that did not conceal her face, and her hair was elaborately styled . Her arms glittered with close fitting bracelets around her wrists and upper arms, and she had a sparkling jewel on a chain hung about her neck. When she saw herself in the mirror, she gasped in delight at her reflection. The other Chosen smiled with her, but their smiles were tempered with sadness. A brightly colored robe was draped across her shoulders, and the other Chosen donned soft, sensuous robes and veils. There was a sounding gong and Lyla and the other Chosen filed quietly out of the cloister. They were each put into the woman's chair of a vehicle, and they were taken to the amphitheater. Unceremoniously, they were ushered into a waiting room. There were no chairs, and they had to stand a long weary hour. Furtively, the other Chosen would whisper instructions to Lyla on how to endure the viewing, the touching, the cutting. Lyla was glad she knew what to expect, but knowing also made it worse. Finally, an Examiner came to the door and told them it was time. The Chosen lined up in order of their seniority, with spaces left for those that had died in the cloister. There were fifteen women, not including Lyla, and two blank spaces. The Emperor was entiled to a new Chosen every other year except for the first five years, when he could have one a year to build up his blood quickly. That meant he had been ruling the Empire over thirty five years. A long reign.

Silently they filed out on the staging platform. There was a plain wooden table in the middle of the stage with many straps dangling from it. The table was illuminated by bright lights and there was a device Lyla knew to be a projection camera on an adjustable metal arm suspended over the table. The Chosen filed out and stood in a silent line, their beautiful colors glowing. Lyla stood at the end of the line, feeling like a gaudy trinket. She could feel the eyes of thousands of men boring upon her. Her heart pounded. Suddenly, the air was split by the explosion of drums beating out a deep, insistant rhythm. From the back of the amphitheater, a phlanx of standard bearers started a solemn, measured march down the aisle dividing the amphitheater. They were followed by high officers in the military and then by an honor guard. In the middle of the honor guard was the Emperor, and behind him and the honor guard were the musicians.

Lyla did not know why, but she strained her eyes to catch a glimpse of the Emperor Kalig as he moved forward with the procession. She realized that she would be seeing him up close very soon, but she still wanted to see him. He was taller than the others, and spare framed. He was dressed in a severe dark blue uniform, unadorned and striking in its simplicity. He had graying hair brushed back from his forehead and falling to his collar. The only ornaments he had on were a ring with his signet on it and a simple circlet of gold resting on his brow. As he drew closer, she could see his eyes were deep set and his features were handsome and strong, and although he neared sixty, there were very few lines on his face. He mounted the steps of the platform alone. The drumbeats stopped suddenly, and Lyla could hear his footsteps as he crossed the stage to the first Chosen. He spoke, and his voice was deep and rough.

"I bring greetings to my Chosen, whom I find acceptable and agreeable. First, I will greet Mara, mother of my first son and the provider of two daughters for the honor of the Empire." Mara lowered herself to her knees and prostrated herself before him. "Next I will greet Chumia, mother of twin sons and provider of two daughters for the honor of the Empire." Chumia then lowered herself to her knees and prostrated herself before him. He went down the line, one by one, greeting them and acknowledging the empty spots by stating the manner of death. Both had died in childbirth.

Finally, he came to the end of the line where Lyla was standing. He was very tall, and he smelled like soap. She did not dare raise her eyes to his face. She was very afraid. "And finally, I greet Lyla, who has come to serve the Empire by pleasing her Emperor. Step forward and become a Chosen. Come and let me purify you."

He extended his hand to her and she shyly put her trembling hand in his. His hand was hard and smooth and warm. Her hands were slick with sweat and freezing. She wanted to pull her hand from his and run until her heart burst. She forced herself to follow him, one agonizing step after another. Her family would be saved from the anger of Lord Simon. She forced herself to walk willingly. She had never touched a man's hand before. He clasped her hand firmly and led her to the center of the stage. Her family would have a place to live. Her father would not be so burdened. The emperor guided her to the center of the stage beside the table and then he stopped. With a casual, practiced motion, he removed the colorful robe from around her shoulders, and tossed it toward the Chosen who now sat on their heels with their heads bowed. Lyla winced and trembled, trying hard to control her desire to run from the stage. The men in the amphitheater murmured to each other, evaluating her body. The Emperor stood aside and let them look at her for many long monents. Then he took her by the shoulders and turned her around so the men could see her from that angle.

Beneath her veil, Lyla felt tears streaming down her cheeks. No man had ever seen her without the proper robes on. Here she stood in this terrible dress, all but naked before all of the noble houses and those in high service. He tilted her face up to his. His eyes softened when he saw her tears. Quietly he spoke to just her. "Little Lyla! This will soon be over, and I will be kind to you. Be strong!" He smiled at her kindly; his teeth were white and even. He touched her face undcrncath the veil and wiped away her tears. "This must be done," he whispered to just her as he carefully lifted the veil from her face and let it fall to the floor . He turned her again, and the men saw her face. They stared at her, some hungrily, some with polite indifference, some with curiousity, some with ashamed curiousity. There were a few that leaned forward and examined her with feral eyes that burned out of the crowd of eyes like arrows. The theater was full of men as far as she could see. She never imagined that there could be so many men with eyes to look at her and judge her without knowing the content of her heart. They became a blur. She felt she would be sick. She closed her eyes. She felt the Emperor's touch on her arm, and she opened her eyes and looked at him. He looked very serious and resolved.

"It is time, little Lyla."

Lyla tried to take a step toward the table, but her legs buckled beneath her. The Emperor caught her before she could fall, and he put his arm around her waist and supported her weight as he helped her to the table. No man had ever touched her before. Not her face to brush away tears, not her clothing to move them, not her waist to support her weight. His arm felt like a steel bar across her back and his hand was large and warm. She was afraid of the wound he would give her, and she was afraid of what would come after, when she was healing. She was afraid of what came after. All of these men had seen her, and all of these men would see her. She longed to be back in her father's house hidden behind its safe walls. Her father would still have a house after this.....Oh!

The Emperor guided her onto the table, lifted her onto its flat hard surface, and then firmly lay her on her back. Very quickly, with practiced motions, he strapped her down. Her arms, her head, her shoulders, her ribs, her waist, her hips. He strapped her ankles down separately, and then he moved a control switch and the lower part of the table split, moving her ankles far apart, spreading her legs. He moved between her legs, blocking her from the audience. He lifted her skirt, exposing her legs and genitals. He then strapped her thighs and knees down to the table, being careful not to expose her to the men in the audience.. The lights were bright in her eyes.

"Try not to scream, little Lyla! You will not bleed as much if you can remember to breathe as you have been instructed. Let us get this business over with now!" He positioned the camera over her privates, blocking any other part of her from the men. He turned it on, and her genitals were instantly displayed on the screen. He pulled out a drawer built into the table and took out a scalpel. Lyla felt herself sweating profusely and she shook uncontrollably. Her breaths came in ragged gasps. She squeezed her eyes shut. She felt something being forced gently between her lips and into her mouth, a thick piece of fabric. "Bite down, it will help..." She did not open her eyes, but she nodded. The amphitheater became very quiet.

Suddenly, she felt the sharp searing cuts invade the tender flesh between her legs. She bit the soft cloth hard and struggled to not cry out around it. Three pieces to be removed..the Emperor moved his hands between her legs with practiced confidence. No man had ever touched her in her secret places before....her family had a house...that raveger of men, Lord Simon could not touch her father... the pain washed over her like a terrible curse. She felt the Emperor stitching her up to the specifications of the Lawgiver.

The Emperor intoned, "Leave her room to provide for her needs...her wants only make her impure." He quickly unbuckled her ankles, her knees, her thighs and covered her outraged flesh with her skirts. She could not move. He loosed her from her bonds, her waist, her shoulders, her head. He took the cloth from her mouth. She could not speak.

"Open your eyes, little Lyla. Look at me! This gives me no happiness, but your desire to be in my service honors me." Lyla opend her eyes. The emperor was leaning over her, searching her face. "I am a foolish old man for this...Come, look at me! I will take care of you..."

She looked at him through her pain and she could not focus on him. She sobbed. He looked saddened, he sat her up, and gestured that her veil be brought to him. The First Chosen retrieved it and brought it to him. He covered her head and lowered the veil to conceal her face. He lifted her to her feet. She could not balance, and the Second Chosen came forward to help balance her, and another brought the colorful robe. The Emperor draped it over her. He turned and gestured to the drummers and they began their solemn booming processional. The First and Second Chosen put their arms around Lyla's waist and they helped her off the staging area. As they left, the Emperor left the dais from the other side. The rest of the Chosen left silently, and were again unceremoniously ushered into the woman's seat of waiting vehicles. Lyla was no exception. She was taken from the Chosen and was placed none too gently into the woman's seat, an isolated compartment in the back of the vehicle that had no windows. The ride back to the palace was agonizing, her tortured privates throbbed with pain. Finally, they arrived back at the palace, and she was helped out of the compartment by the Chosen and they carried her back to the cloister. Tenderly, they lay her down and undressed her. They bathed her head with cool water and they crooned kind words at her, as if she was one of their children.

Presently, a gong sounded, and the women all left her and went to stand at the entrance of the Cloister. The Emperor entered, carrying a valise. He nodded to the Chosen in greeting. He walked directly back to the room where Lyla lay.

She was naked under the sheet, and the Chosen had washed the blood off of her legs and belly. He lifted the covers from her legs and gently spread her legs apart. None of the women spoke; it was not proper to speak in his presence. Lyla did not speak. He took a container of medicine from his valise and applied it to her altered privates. It felt cool on the burning fiery spot that had once been her secret place. He carefully swabbed the area, cleaning it, and he covered it with clean, gauzy fabric. The pain subsided enormously. He then asked for a glass of water and he mixed a different medicine in the water. He slipped his arm under her shoulders and half lifted her and helped her drink the medicine.

"There little one..young chick..sweet dove...drink it all. It will help you sleep." He held her and stroked her hair, her arm, her breast. "Sleep and get well little Lyla! You are so lovely!"

— Chapter 13 —

Captain Jarvo was furious, but his rage was impotent. How could this be happening? This day had been impossible!

It had all started at morning watch. When the morning watch went to relieve the night watch, they had found all of them unconscious at their posts. Commander Po, the esteemed captain of the vessel was tied up in a supply closet. The ship was sitting dead in the water, and every single system was inoperable. There were no lights, there was no running water, no steering , nothing. It was like a vast, silent tomb. All hands were called, and the men began a frantic search for ways to repair the ship and get back on course. Apparently, they had been drifting for several hours.

There was a great commotion in the galley area, and shouting and swearing. Captain Jarvo and his squad were summoned. The Harlot was loose, and the cursed Forsaken as well. How they had gotten out was beyond him. Still, there they sat in the galley eating the choicest foods and talking like they had no concerns in the world. The former Chosen had removed her proper robes and was dressed in her shift, (and could it be?) a uniform jacket of the Empire? Scandalous! Jarvo motioned for Ritsi and Ninta to seize the women, but they could not. As they neared the women, there was a bright flashing light, and the men fell to the ground, unconscious. Shields? How could this be?

The Harlot stood up and brushed the crumbs off of her clothes. She looked at the gathered assembly. "I am one of the many. I am here as a captive. I am the Storyteller, Sojourner. There is no queen. I will not tolerate being mistreated. Lieutenant Bosson, do not try anymore of your silly tricks on me, or my friend, Lyla. I have taken all of your clothes and thrown them into the sea, and I have injected you with an implant that is being controlled by the Handlers at the Burrows. You are a bent and terrible man, and you need to be altered. Every time you try to access the parts of your brain to plan a torture, you will find yourself doing something untoward and personally embarrassing. That is part of your reconditioning technique. You have caused great discomfort to others, now it is your turn. I threw your clothes into the sea on an impulse...just because I don't like you very much."

She turned to the others. "I have implanted most of you. Your DNA is being evaluated as we speak. Now, I am going back to my little cell. I am very tired from my night's labors. I will return the control of the ship to you when my friend, Lyla, and I are back inside our rooms and comfortably settled. I will expect a sincere apology from you before I return the control of the ship to you. Further, to avoid any trouble with me, I must insist on plenty of water and good food at mealtimes. Come, Lyla."

The Harlot then walked out of the galley, followed by the unveiled Forsaken who paused only long enough to fill her arms with food. The Forsaken woman walked with her back straight, and she seemed unashamed of her bare face. Jarvo felt outraged betrayal. He had been at this creature's purification, and he knew she had been a proper woman of the Empire at one time.

He remembered the purification ceremony with a pang of pity. It was a terrible process to endure, and then to have the former Emperor deposed within months of the rite. It was a shameful thing for the Empire to cast out a woman who had no evil intent in her heart. The former Emperor had to know his time was growing short as the current Emperor Kalig cut a brutal swath toward the throne. Jarvo was certain that the poor woman was made a cruel sport by the less scrupulous members of court. He had heard rumors of some nobles hunting for her and the other Forsaken in the access tunnels where they had been sent to live out their lives. In his less guarded moments, he felt that it was a terrible thing that the Law had made such harsh provisions for the Forsaken. Surely the Emperor did not think he would live out the year, and after purifying so many women, he had to know she would not recover and bear a child within that time. It must have been a political move, a message to the young pretender that he would not have such an easy time deposing of him. That, or it was a way to protect Lyla's father, a minor lord, but loyal. It was rumored that Lyla's father was in jeopardy from the cunning Lord Simon. Then, of course, the young Lyla had been beautiful. Jarvo remembered her standing before the assembly, trembling, vulnerable, as beautiful as his own young wife.

His wife. She was lovely. He remembered the years of training in his father's house, preparing for her. At first, he was terribly embarrassed by the purification training and the birth training. Being trained to tend to the order of the home began as soon as the boy was taken from his mother and was an important part of the education of every boy. He remembered how appalled he was by the first lesson when the synthetic female body had been brought out and shown to him and his classmates. He had hidden his eyes from his mother for days afterward.

Still, it was important to understand the responsibility of maintaining the home properly. In ages past, men left most of the care of their homes to others. Women went to hospitals, and had their bodies prodded and touched by the ancient medical practitioners, many of them men. Disgusting. Women were forced to go about in public, leaving themselves open to attacks from less scrupulous men. They were forced into the workplace, where they were constantly under scrutiny from men outside their families. Their dignity and honor were treated with indifference by huge portions of the societies of the times. Women became feral. They lost respect for themselves and their sacred functions. Men lost control of themselves, using women only for carnal reasons, not for the deeper functions. When the Lawgiver came into power, he taught that each man was entitled to one woman, and only one woman. He taught that it was impossible for men and women to mingle without a woman becoming feral so it was imperative to keep the genders separate. It was imperitave to understand how to care for a family, especially how to take care of the body of the woman. It was important that only one man touch her so she would not become untamed.

The hard physical training and the challenges of preparing for his service exams were a pleasure compared to the training every man was required to complete before he could become married. A man had to be married before he could join the service of the Empire. He had to be married before he could leave training. It was shameful to be unmarried.

Jarvo remembered how afraid he was when the Examiners came to his father and informed him it was time for Ivan to be married. He had heard that some men were joined to out-of-control women that only appeared to be tamed for the Examiners. He heard that sometimes they did not survive the purification ceremony, and then a man would never have a career. So much depended on the process going well. He remembered his brother Burl's marriage. Burl had grown into a harsh man, and it was rumored he had incised his wife so thoroughly that she could barely walk. Jarvo did not want to circumcise his wife. He hated the practice sessions with the synthetic dummies. He hated the way the fake blood flowed over the knife, and it took him many many trials before he could perform the procedure without the computer on the synthetic dummy signalling death. After he finally mastered that, he had to learn how to deliver his future children, and how to tend the complicated needs of his wife's body. He was not certain through most of his life it would be worth it all.

Still, if he were going to serve the Empire, he had to be married. Even though he had been terribly frightened, he did not show it to the Examiner when it was announced that a match had been found for him. He smiled and joked with his friends about the pleasure that awaited him when the woman was healed. He acted eager when the elders and officers clapped him on the shoulder and congratulated him. It was not that he did not want the pleasure, and it was not that he did not want children of his own; it was not that he did not want to be in service to the Empire. He did not want to cut away a woman's genitals.

He went under review, the Examiners making certain he understood the Law and the procedure for purification. He demonstrated the procedure flawlessly, clean smooth strokes of the knife, certain and sure. Quick stitches so the woman would not lose too much blood. Application of medicines and clean gauze. Then he would be required to tend to her until she was healed. He would be the only person in the whole world to see or touch her; it was the only way to prevent a woman from becoming too untame to tend to the household. He had to do this...the Examiners had to see the shift she wore, covered with blood. It was impossible to avoid.

The morning came for Ivan Jarvo to purify his wife. His father came and got him out of his bed, and helped him dress for the rites. He looked into his father's face, searching for a way to ask him the questions burning in him. His father looked solemn. Ivan loved his father, but the restraints of their customs did not allow for emotional outbursts. He wanted to be a small boy again, and climb onto his mother's lap. He was not ready to be a man.

They walked down the long hallways of the Serviceman's building to the hall of Joining. He knew there would be the Examiners and the father of his intended wife waiting for him inside. In a room off to the side of the hall, his wife would be waiting, dressed in a simple white shift. He would wheel in a cart with the supplies on them to purify his wife. He did not want to do this. His steps slowed and his father slowed his steps as well. His heart was pounding and he felt sweat trickling down his sides.

"Father, this is a real woman. She is the only one ever to be offered to me. How can I do this without shaking and hurting her more than she will be hurt? What do I do?"

His father turned to him, and looked into his face. His eyes were proud. Silently, he held out his hand, looking at his palm and then at Ivan. Ivan looked at his father's palm and he noticed the old scar slicing across the hard plain of his hand. "There must be blood on her shift, and a wound must be tended. This is the Law."

Ivan did not know what to think, and the questions on his lips were silenced as the doors opened and one of the Examiners commanded him to come inside. The hall was deep and severe, and at the far end of the room was a raised dais with an unadorned conference table facing the hall. The Examiners sat at the table, their faces set and serious. The father of Ivan's intended wife was also at the table. Ivan was stunned to see his intended's father was the Commander of the forces. His eyes bored into Ivan as he tried to walk forward without showing his nerves. Ivan's father walked at his side, straight and dignified. Ivan was aware of the great honor it was to his family to be joined to such a powerful family. It would be impossible for him to reach higher without being a nobleman. His father-in-law was powerfully built and his dark eyes and ebony skin made him an imposing figure. The Commander looked grim.

The Chief Examiner rose and spoke in his strange, high voice, "Step forward, Ivan Jarvo. You have been measured and considered for all the years of your life and now it is time for a reckoning of your worth. It has been determined by examination and by honor to join you to the daughter of Perth Chammera. She is a worthy woman, tamed and prepared for the honor of the Empire. Her father offers her to you. Do you accept this?"

Ivan knew the words to speak, and he hoped to say them without stammering. "I am honored by the gift of a proper wife. I will order my house with descretion. I will protect her. I will provide for her. I will build the Empire's strength."

"Go to your intended and make her pure. Tend to the wounds inflicted, remember her honor daily."

Perth Chammera and his father led Ivan down a hallway and stopped before a windowless door. Again his father extended his hand to his son. "There must be blood on her shift, the wound must be tended. It is the Law." He took Ivan's hand and ran it across the scar in his palm. Perth Chammera also extended his hand to Ivan. He, too, had a scar running across his palm . "There must be blood on her shift, the wound must be tended. It is the Law."

Commander Chammera opened the door to his daughter's room and stood aside. Ivan firmly took hold of the purification cart and pushed it into the room. Standing beside the purification table was a black shrouded figure. The door clicked firmly closed behind him. Ivan had never been in a room with a girl since he was a tiny boy in the nursery. He had never seen any woman other than his mother's robed and veiled figure since he had joined his father in the men's quarters. He had faced great perils in his training, but he had never felt this kind of fear. He knew he had to cross the room and take her veil and robe off of her and hand them out of the special drawer built into the wall to her father. It was the Law. He took a hesitant step and then another. After what seemed an eternity, he stood beside the woman. She was shorter than he was, only coming to his shoulder. She was slightly built, and standing properly still. He stood beside her for long minutes trying to will his hands to touch her. How could such a small person cause him to fear so much? He had long since stopped fearing other men. Even his cruel brother Burl was no longer a threat to him. Ivan was an accomplished warrior. He was uncommonly strong and fearless. He would face any warrior. This was not a warrior. It was one small woman.

He cautiously raised his hand to her facial veil and carefully touched the lower edge of it. Like he was defusing a carcinogen bomb, he carefully lifted the veil upward and off of the figure standing before him. Ivan caught his breath. She was lovely. Her thick curling hair smelled sweet and clean. She shyly raised her eyes to his face and looked back down. Her eyes were green, and her skin was not as dark as her father's. Her mother must be fair. He was flooded with the desire to see more of her. He cautiously reached out his hands and undid the clasp at her throat that held the robe together. He was suprised to find that there were several connectors that held her robe closed, and he muttered to himself as he tried to discover how to undo them all. She stood silently, properly, her eyes downcast, only moving in a startled way when his hands brushed her breasts as he struggled with the impossible clasps. Finally, sweating with discomfort and a strange excitement, he managed to unfasten the robe and remove it. Again, he caught his breath. He had seen the synthetic models of women in the training classes, but he was not prepared for the sudden rush of feelings he felt when he saw his wife's unshrouded body for the first time. The white shift seemed to flow down her body, curving around her breasts, lying across her belly and thighs like water curving in a streambed. He had been taught about women, but he realized that he knew nothing about them. The synthetic model's breasts were smaller, and cold to the touch. He could feel the warmth of the woman's skin, even though he was not touching her.

She stood before him, clearly frightened, and yet she did not cry or cringe from his touch. She surely knew what he was going to do to her? Ivan took the veil and the robe and went to the door and knocked on it descreetly. A drawer emerged from the wall, and

Ivan folded the robe and veil and put them into the drawer. He then tapped on the door again. The drawer was pulled back into the wall. The next part of his task loomed in front of him like a dark evil.

He crossed to his intended again, taking her by the shoulders and guiding her to the table. She let him guide her to the table, but she did not climb up. She could not move, she was too frightened. Ivan felt like a beast as he lifted her onto the table. She was feather light in his arms, and the simple white shift clung to the curves of her body. He did not know the fabric would be so thin. She felt warm in his arms, and he looked at her, and he could see hints of her own colors through the fabric. The synthetic models did not tremble. They did not smell sweet. Their hair was not soft against his arm. He carefully sat her on the table. She did not cry out, though silent tears coursed down her cheeks and her breath was driving in and out of her in silent gasps. He held her against him. He wanted to soothe her, but he did not know how. No one prepared him for this. She was beautiful, and she was frightened of him, and he did not want her to be afraid of him. He realized he was pressing her tightly against his chest. Reluctantly he loosened his grip.

He gently laid her down on the table, and he strapped her down. He knew this would be painful, and if she were allowed to wince or fight or jerk, it would be terrible for her. He crossed over to the purification cart and took the scalpel. He had practiced this a thousand times. He did not want to cut her. He spread the legs apart and stood between her legs. He lifted the hem of her shift, exposing her genitals. This was nothing like the synthetic models. He looked at her face. It was contorted in silent sorrow, her eyes squeezed shut, braced for the searing pain. She was so afraid. "There must be blood on her shift.." He reached out and touched her tender flesh; it was his duty. Even this private part of her was beautiful to him. He did not want to change anything about her. There must be blood on her shift. His father had a scar on the palm of his hand. Her father had a scar on the palm of his hand....there were other men with scars on their hands...He took the scalpel, sweat beading on his lip. She was afraid of him...she was beautiful.....he did not know her name.

Tenderly he covered her exposed genitals, gauging mentally where blood would need to be..."There must be blood on her shift..." He positioned his hand over the places where blood would flow. He cut the palm of his hand, the sharp knife slicing through his own calloused flesh. He grunted with the pain. His intended opened her eyes and looked at him; she sobbed, but only once. "There must be blood on her shift..." He wrapped his hand as well as he could and awkwardly, he undid the straps. She rose quickly from the table, wiping the tears from her cheek with her hand. She turned to him, her eyes full of her own thoughts. He hoped she loved him someday.

"My name is Jenta," her voice whispered. "Let me tend to your wound!"

Ivan extended his hand, and Jenta tended the sliced palm. Her touch was gentle and he was aroused by her even though his hand throbbed. She cleaned the cut, and then with a practiced hand, she stitched the places that were deeply cut, and then bandaged his hand with the gauze provided for her own wounds. He watched her covertly, uncertain as to how to behave toward her. If he would have taken her flesh, she would be undressed and placed on the table and covered with a sheet.. He would descreetly move the sheet to tend to her wounds for the week to ten days it would take for her to heal. He was supposed to take her shift and put it into the drawer. He did not know what to do.

"Jenta," his voice sounded hoarse in his ears, "I, um, need your, ahhhh, shift for the, um, Examiners." He was aroused, he was terrified, he felt big and awkward, his hand hurt. Jenta looked at his face shyly, but she smiled like she knew something he didn't as she looked down properly.

"You must look away, sir. I am prepared for our honor. " Ivan nodded nervously and turned his back to her. He listened to her rustling movements, he wished he could stop sweating. He could hear Jenta moving closer to him, and then she was beside him, holding out her bloody shift. He took the shift from her, not daring to look at her. He sensed her amusement, though she did not laugh out loud. He felt the prickles of irritation. He turned to look at her...let her feel the discomfort of this impossible situation! Jenta stood quietly beside him, the sheet from the surgical table wrapped about her modestly, mimicking a dress. Ivan did not know whether to feel relieved or disappointed. He took the shift to the drawer and put it in. In ten days, they would be formally joined...he would certainly look at her then. It would be proper then. He would look for a long time, and he would touch her...

Jarvo pulled his thoughts away from the past. There was this problem to deal with that could shake the foundations of the Law. The Empire was the mightiest power on Earth. Its power was based on the Law. The Law made things clear and certain. Ivan Jarvo loved the absolute certainty of the Empire. He could not wait to be back home, where there was order and clarity and his proper warm-bodied wife. He couldn't wait to get off this cursed ship where harlots and outcasts ran amuck. The situation was unbelievable.

After the crazed Harlot had made her announcement, she and the outcast had sauntered back to the cell on deck. Somehow, they had managed to pull the outcast's containment box away from the door to the cell. They entered the cell like it was where they wanted to be and pulled the door closed behind them as if they were entering a rich palace suite. The crew watched them in horrified fascination. For most of the men, it was the first time any had seen a woman outside of his individual authority since childhood. It was confusing for them. Even battered, the Chosen was a beautiful woman.

As soon as the two women were out of sight, Captain Jarvo became aware of his duty. As a man of experience, he had to rally the crew to begin to repair the damage to the ship and to begin the cleansing process on the ship. First, he ordered that the cell be chained shut to prevent any more unfortunate escapes. Then Commandar Po and the ship's Examiners began the day long cleansing of the ship while the technician's attempted to get the ship's systems back online. It confounded them. The ship would not respond to anything they tried.

After several hours of futility, Commander Po came to Jarvo. "You were among this woman's people for a year. What does she mean we need to apologize? How do we approach her? We are going to have to do something! The commands she has implanted in our systems are very complex and the protocols are altered as soon as we decode them."

Jarvo felt his silent fury mounting. How could he have misjudged the culture of this woman so thouroghly? Could it be possible that she was telling the truth about not being queen?

"To be honest," Jarvo admitted, "this confounds me as well. I suppose we must humor her until we have the means to properly restrain her. Gather your senior officers and together we will say some meaningless thing to appease the witch."

Grudgingly, the senior officers were gathered and the crew was notified of the unusual circumstances. They seemed demoralized. It violated the Law to talk to a woman outside of the home. It made them all impure. The purification rites were unpleasant and lengthy. The Harlot did not know how many she was hurting by this ridiculous demand. The men gathered outside the cell. Jarvo stepped forward and put on the voice amplifier.

Jarvo thought of a thousand curses he would like to hurl at the Harlot in the cell, but he knew he had to serve the Empire, even if it made his soul filthy. "Mistress Sojourner, we are men of the Empire of Light and Law. We come humbly to ask for our ship back. We are sorry we treated you poorly. Please accept our apologies." He felt like he would vomit. It was bad enough that he and his men would have to have their skin scrubbed bloody in the purification rites, but now so many more would have to endure this pain. How he hated the Harlot. It was silent for a few moments, and then there was a jarring vibration deep in the bowels of the ship. The ship hummed to life, the crew seemed to sigh collectively. Some of the men clapped Jarvo on the back and some murmured thanks to him. He took no comfort in their thanks, he took no comfort in anything that was connected to the Harlot.

The ship began to move.

— Chapter 14 —

The ship surged back to life, its mighty engines pulsed, the deck vibrated with its deep powerful movements. Lyla had been sleeping peacefully, and the sudden movement woke her. She sat up and wiped the sleep from her eyes, disoriented and groggy for a few moments. Sojourner watched her grow into the awareness of movement and the deep thrumming sound. Her eyes went wide and she stiffened in fear.

"Storyteller!" Lyla hissed frantically. "What have you done? You have given them back the ship. Please, don't. Take it away from them." Tears began to course, unchecked, down her cheek.

Sojourner had been anticipating her reaction. While she slept, the Healers had briefed her on the possible reactions and they had developed a plan to deal with the Chosen's fear.

Sojourner spoke softly, but with confidence. "Hello, Lyla. I can tell you are startled. As you know, I have a mission in your Empire, and I cannot stray far from the

Plan devised by the leaders of the Burrows. With your consent, I would like to make arrangements to have you taken off this ship tonight. There is a hoverpod shadowing the ship, and it can remove you within the hour and take you directly to the Burrows."

"Hoverpod?" Lyla's voice stumbled over the word like a wounded creature. "How...?"

"We are capable of establishing a visual shield that will camoflauge our behaviors. The hoverpod will lower itself above the cell, and the crew will open the top of the cell and extract you. I have shown you many amazing things; you know we can do this. You will be taken directly to the Burrows. You will be welcomed and given acceptance and care. You can be healed of your hurts, even to the repair of your private places. You will be given the freedom to live and even worship as you please."

"Even worship?" Lyla had been listening intently, and she blinked as if she did not understand.

"Yes, the Leadership of the Burrows understands that it is very difficult to separate from your culture and your religion. We cannot accomodate all of your cultural differences, but we want you to feel free to continue worshipping as you please..."

"Religion? Do you mean the citizens of the Burrows still practice the superstition of religious belief?" Lyla stood up. She began to pace about the cell. "How can that be? The Law teaches that the reason man created the concept of a god was to try to find order in the world. Once we understood that the ritual and restrictions of religion were only our own instinct trying to guide us to the most natural way of Man, then we could build a society freed from its superstition."

Sojourner looked at Lyla curiously. "Do you mean that there is no religion in your culture, but just empty ritual?"

Lyla stopped pacing and stood proudly, her back straight and her voice firm. "Our culture has order, Mistress Storyteller. Our Lawgiver analyzed the religions of history and determined the practices that had the most relevance to culture overall. The characteristics that had strength in them were built into a system of Law, devoid of the superstition of religion. Our society is strong because it is based on the practices and rituals that bring strength to a society."

"I don't know what to say to that. Our society is strong as well, but we do practice religion. Our society is strong because our individuals are strong..."

"To depend on individuals is a risky venture. Where would your society be if your population were larger? What happens if your purpose is no longer common? How will you adjust to the diversity of a vast population?"

"Lyla, I can't tell you how it will all work out. I am just a small part of this story. What is important now is to make arrangements for you if you want to go to my country. Do you want to go?"

Lyla looked at Sojourner with sadness, the conflict clear in her. Sojourner felt pity well up in her, and she knew she did not have enough words to describe the sadness in Lyla's face. Lyla's shoulders slumped. "I don't have any choice. If I go back, I will be returned to the maintenence tunnels to try to survive as best I can. There will be the endless hiding from the nobles who would force me to relieve their passions and there will be endless hunger. There would be other babies that die as soon as I give birth to them alone in the filth."

"You have had babies die?" Sojourner felt tears well up in her eyes. To have a baby die was the deepest fear of any Burrowite. "How many?"

"I have been made sport of by many noblemen and the laborers that work the maintenence tunnels. I have given birth to three babies. The first baby was pried from my arms by an underlord and its head was crushed. The second, I was able to hide for several days after its birth until it died of the cold and hunger that the Forsaken experience. The third was born, blue and cold and shriveled. It never drew a breath. Even now, I carry a baby in me. I would like to have it live and grow, even if it has to live and grow in a superstitious, bizarre culture. I have no choice but to go to your country. The other Forsaken look to me to help them survive, but I cannot think about them now."

"There are other Forsaken? How does that happen? How does a woman become Forsaken?" Sojourner was appalled.

"There are not many of us. I do not know the exact numbers because we do not live long. Most take their own lives after a time. One must fail beyond all words to become Forsaken. The women of the Empire take great care not to fall so far. It is a great shame" Lyla's voice trailed off and she sat down wearily. When she spoke, her voice seemed to sag out of her like a tired trickle. "One of the Forsaken, Hant, did not desire children and refused her husband's summons. She desires only to be in the company of other women. Another, Krolla murdered her husband in his sleep for his rough treatment of her. There are other Forsaken hiding throughout the Empire, but they are few and scattered. It is better to follow the Law even if it is very hard. The alternative is to be poor and alone. Poor. Poor...we are all poor and alone." She drew her knees up under her chin.

Sojourner felt Lyla's words as great leaden weights. How could these things be true? She knew she should not be shocked. The Empire was a society that had an abundance of people; look at how they wasted their soldiers in their conquest of their hemisphere. In the Burrows it had been so vital that every living person have a purpose and be productive that they had developed extraordinary means to draw out potential. They had perfected surgeries and neural implants that brought life and sanity back to the most hopeless. The Healers were thorough and everyone in the Burrows was treated in a manner that would insure they would be productive. Any deviation was corrected, both physical and those deviations that were found in thought. Sojourner was grateful for her implants and the freedom they gave her, though they would not serve her forever. Technology could only spare somone a measure of his or her disability. There came a time when they were no longer effective, and then the individual was harvested for other purposes. There was no waste.

Sojourner wondered if there would be enough implants to save the Empire. A man who had a brutal nature was easily retrained. Any behaviors that were not productive could be redirected. It was hard to imagine someone living lost and forsaken. Of course, the ancient Great Nation had many problems with citizens getting lost in the vastness of its society. The strain on the society was enormous and made it vulnerable to splintering apart. When the terrible poisoning of the environment was poured out and ruin was complete, the segments could not pull together to salvage any semblance of a culture. The dying was constant, and only a handful were able to be saved. Without the power of the Great Nation, the rest of the world succumbed to poison and chaos. The survivors of that chaos must have been very strong, and the culture that grew out of the chaos was one that respected strength rather than preservation and restoration.

Sojourner understood all of this intellectually, but she was beginning to understand how vastly different the cultures had become. Her stories may not mean anything to the citizens of the Empire. How would she know if she could read their reactions? Perhaps her stories would be meaningless to a different culture, her skills of persuasion only antics to the people? She needed to see if she could connect to this woman with a story.

"Lyla, I am a Storyteller, and I do not understand your truth. All I can offer you is the chance to start over in a new place unfettered by your shame. I want you to understand a bit of our culture before you go there. The stories I tell are not how we see truth, but they reflect our attitudes. Would you like for me to tell you a story? It is not part of our religion, but it can give you an idea of our religion and how it is woven into our thoughts. May I? It may help you with this transition..."

Lyla looked at Sojourner, and she seemed to shrink into herself. Miserably she nodded, and Sojourner could tell Lyla battled a deep conviction when she consented to listen. It seemed that Lyla had spent her whole life battling her deep convictions to fit into impossible situations. She must tell her story well. She must tell this story with deep compassion, her conviction must be clear but not overpowering. The persuasion must be subtle. She sat next to Lyla as she huddled on the cot and breathed in, preparing her thoughts.

"Be still in your thoughts, and listen. It is time to tell you why we are here, and why in the furthest reaches of the Cosmos, we are known as the Maker's Hope. It is a terrible tale, and a wondrous one, too. We are a new thing in the Universe, for we are the only world inhabited by children. In all of Creation, we alone know the powerful love that binds a parent to a child. It is our blessing and our trial.

"Let the tale begin where it should begin.....

"There is a mighty spirit in the heavens, and he brings joy to no one. His name has been lost to time, and it may never be rediscovered because he has given himself a new name, Corruption. Long ages ago, this mighty spirit lived in Heaven, and he did great deeds and he was valued by the Maker as a trusted friend.

"For unmeasured eons, the Maker and his treasured friend were in harmony. Unfortunately, the friend became proud of his familiarity with the Maker, and he began to consider himself better than the other spirits of Heaven. He did not realize the value that the Maker had given him was an honor, and he began to think of himself as equal with the Creator of all. He began to question the tasks that the Maker gave him, and he began to feel contempt for the Maker.

"Why does that old fool putter around in his paltry garden when he could be making a new universe?" he thought. "If I were the Maker, I would never wear that ridiculous hat. I would always be mindful of my dignity. I would inspire awe everywhere I went. I would be magnificent."

"The Maker, who is wise beyond all others, hoped His friend would come to his senses, but he did not. The Maker even considered punishing Corruption's arrogance, but He decided instead, to hope Corruption would become wise himself. Corruption did not.

"Instead, Corruption began to conspire against the Maker, and he renounced his portion of Heaven. He declared that he would return to Heaven's perfection only when the Maker was willing to share His authority with Corruption. Some spirits agreed with Corruption and left Heaven with him. For the first time, there was discord in the universe.

"Corruption and his followers strove to disrupt all of the workings of the Maker, but they could not. The Maker and His spirits were in harmony. Corruption could only rage in his thwarted madness, and all of his terrible actions were easily put to right by Heaven's valiant spirits.

"Some spirits wondered why the Maker tolerated these troubles, and some even wondered why the Maker did not destroy Corruption. But, the Maker remembered Corruption's original name, and in His heart He felt a deep pity that his former friend had chosen to defile himself.

"Finally, after eons of struggle, Corruption came to the gates of Heaven and demanded to speak to the Maker. The Maker was tending His garden, but He came straightway when He heard who was at the gates. He, Himself threw open the gates, and with the host of Heaven, smiled a welcoming smile at the errant spirit that stood there.

"Have you come home, my old friend?" the Maker asked kindly with hope in His voice. "Are you ready to resume your life here, in peace and harmony?"

"Hah! Old Fool!" snorted Corruption derisively. "I have not come to Your gates like one of your pitiful, cringing dogs! No! I have come as a conquering hero to free the dazed, lost, weak inhabitants of this shameful place. I have come with a challenge that even You cannot master. I have come to claim my rightful place as Master of All."

"The Maker's face grew sad. His voice was heavy with sorrow. "And tell Me, then...what is your challenge? What do you need to prove?"

"Corruption leered malevolently, "It is not I who needs to prove anything. It is You, Old Jester!"

"The Maker was taken aback with surprise. "I do? Whatever do you mean?"

"Corruption put his hands on his hips and began striding back and forth in front of the Maker. "You have made the Universe to please Yourself. You win because You made the laws that govern it. You protect Your spirits, and I will admit it, You are mighty. When

You defeat me, it means nothing because You do not risk anything."

"Corruption turned suddenly and spat at the Maker's feet. "Coward! You have no honor! Risk something, and if You defeat me, I'll trouble You no more!"

"The Maker looked at Corruption sadly, remembering their long ago friendship. "What do you propose?" he asked.

"Corruption sneered, "It is a simple thing, though I doubt that any of Your stupid spirits have the backbone for the challenge. Still, I will tell You what I propose. I want for You to give me dominion over a world that I have chosen, and I want Your spirits to prove themselves there. Simple enough, eh?"

"Nothing is simple when so simply said," replied the Maker. "What exactly do you want?"

"First," stated Corruption, "I want dominion over Terra's world, Earth. It is a place of beauty and pain, deceptive in its sweetness, terrible in its conflict.

"Secondly, for those spirits that are bold enough to rise to this noble cause, they must agree to be a part of the weaving of Earth. They must gain their sustenance from it and be dependent on it. I want them to be made of weakened flesh, assuming the same fabric of the beasts of that place.

"Thirdly, they must forget Heaven, only knowing You through riddles and unclear ideas. You must leave them to struggle and understand without seeing You or hearing Your voice. You must be as a puzzle.

"Finally, I will be allowed to imbue in every spirit an evil for every good. Love will be tied to lust, valor to violence, gentleness to weakness. They must fight the darkness in their natures.

"When all of this is in place, they will have a life mission to fulfill, and none can complete their missions without the aid of another. They must overcome their own ambitions to help each other, even if there is nothing to gain personally."

"What do you gain from this?" the Maker asked quietly.

"Simple," replied Corruption slyly, "Every spirit that fails in his or her task will belong to me. Those that accomplish what they are sent to do will return to You. When the Earth has finished its allotted time, the one with the most spirits will gain Heaven."

"This is very clever," the Maker said musingly. "All that they are, you would corrupt."

"The Maker straightened, and gathered His might about Himself like a cloak. "I do not need honor from you, Corruption. I do not need to send my beloved spirits into such jeopardy. I have nothing to prove! Begone from here! I will not choose this path!"

"The Maker turned to enter Heaven, when one Heaven's inhabitants stepped forward and said, "Oh! Sweet Father of All! I would choose to do this task! If it would restore peace to the universe, and to bring Glory to You, I would choose to do this task!"

"And I!" said another.

"And I!" said another.

"One by one, spirits stepped forward and they kept coming, until a vast numberless multitude stood ready. The Maker looked at them for a long moment, His heart throbbed with pain and pride.

"Oh! My beloved!" he murmured. "This is a difficult task! You must do as you choose, I would never ask this of you!"

"The spirits of Heaven stood in silence, row upon row, ready.

"Only if you choose," whispered the Maker.

"He turned to Corruption and said, "Make this so..."

"Corruption smirked, and as he turned to go he said, "I will love being God in Your place."

"Wait!" commanded the Maker. "Is there anything else you would add? Any other restrictions?"

"What else is there?" replied Corruption, satisfied with himself.

"Very well, then." said the Maker. He smiled.

"And so, it was arranged. The first spirits were made into humans, carved out of dust and filled with the conflicts of good and evil. There was a man and a woman, they were beautiful and they loved each other.

"Corruption came again to the gates of Heaven, and again the Maker welcomed him with hope.

"Save Your sentiments, Idiot!" gloated Corruption. "You may think the love your curs share will endure, but it won't. Send the next spirit, and there will be jealously and murder. Send him, and watch infidelity and lust take control of Earth. Send him, and see if he is not torn apart by Man and Woman. I dare You! Send him!"

"Old friend," whispered the Maker in wonder, turning His eyes toward Earth. "I have sent him, and it is wondrous! Look! It will make you weep for the glory of it!"

"Corruption turned and peered at the man and the woman. There, nestled between them, was a baby.

"Beloved," breathed the woman through weary joy, "Look at his eyes! They are like your eyes! He is perfect!"

"He is perfect because he has your sweet mouth. I will teach him all I know. I will protect him from falling!"

"They continued murmuring to each other, exclaiming over their child, resolve growing in their hearts to provide their best for him. The baby suckled at his mother's breast, and drifted into a sweet sleep.

"Corruption whirled around and faced the Maker. His face was purple with rage and madness. "You tricked me!" he snarled savagely, spittle dripping down his chin like dark acid. "You tricked me with this..... this...."

"Family," offered the Maker helpfully.

"I will corrupt this, too! Don't think I will not! I will find ways to make families fail. Mothers will murder, and fathers will abandon, and these vile productions will steal from their parents! I will corrupt this. too!"

"That may be true," replied the Maker sadly. He turned His eyes toward Earth and the baby sleeping in his mother's arms. His eyes softened and filled with love and hope. "But, not today."

"And so it began. Corruption labors mightily to destroy families, and sometimes he succeeds. More often, though, he does not. Watch! See how the father takes pride in his daughter's dance when he does not dance himself? That is a reflection of the Maker's smile. Listen to the lullaby the mother sings to her tired baby. Do you hear the love? It is the Maker's voice. Remember if you can, the glory of the first kiss of true love, and the soft embrace that made your heart beat in the same rhythm with another. It is God's heartbeat. We are not so far from Heaven, are we?"

Sojourner watched Lyla. Through the story Lyla had sat, huddled, her knees drawn under her chin. Slowly she buried her face in her arms and only occasionally raised her eyes up to glance at Sojourner. Now the story was finished and Lyla still sat, huddled as if the story continued. Sojourner did not know how to interpret the silence, but she did not want to appear anxious. She sat quietly beside Lyla.

After what seemed a very long time, Lyla stirred. She raised her eyes and turned her face to Sojourner. Her eyes were clear and her expression was calm. "I do not know if I can ever believe in a God or in any superstition. But I can live in a place that thinks kindly. It will be hard to leave the order of the Empire, but kindliness will be good. I will go to your country."

Sojourner smiled, relieved. She felt a moment of peace. A mother and a child would be in the Burrows by breakfast. Two down, a million or so to go.

— Chapter 15 —

The hoverpod had gone hours ago. Sojourner felt relieved that Lyla was finally safe, but it was lonely in the cell all by herself. Lyla had gone quietly, unflinching even when being touched by the male technician; resigned to her fate. Sojourner wondered if the Healers would have the means to help her with her terrible memories. She said a prayer for her happiness and for her baby.

Her time with Lyla had left Sojourner troubled. Her story about the Maker giving children to the world usually stirred her listeners and moved them to tears and deep smiles. Her story had only seemed to skip across Lyla's consciousness like a rock skipping across water. It puzzled her. The Burrows had been observing the Empire for many years, and yet had missed the lack of belief in any deity. Everyone had assumed that the rituals and structures of their society were motivated by a religious belief. Her stories may have no meaning for the citizens of the Empire. It was hard to imagine a culture without a religious belief, though there was a nation that exisited during the height of the Great Nation's sovereignty that discouraged religion, but even still there were those that had a faith. They practiced their religions covertly and suffered for their beliefs. Their struggles to preserve their faith were inspiring, even now. It was hard to conceive of the reality of a nation with no believers. None. Anywhere. Just ritual.

Sojourner's musings were interrupted by her husband's voice slicing through the silence like a warm knife gliding through softened butter. "My sweet?"

Sojourner smiled. She loved it when Stephen called her that. It always brought back the memory of the first time Stephan tried to kiss her. Stephan had brashly followed her into a grove of trees on his hoverboard, showing off and acting like he was an ancient celebrity. He was so handsome and strong, and in truth, many girls had thrown their hearts at his feet. He only gave them a passing notice. Sojourner had heard rumors that he was smitten with a young lady, but that his feelings were unreturned. She tried not to think about it, though it was hard not to listen to the gossip. Sometimes, in her less guarded moments, she would wonder what it would be like to be the mystery girl, desired by the bold Stephan. She would chase her thoughts away from those thoughts. The girl was obviously sensible to stay away from such a reckless young man.

She could understand how any young woman would be overwhelmed by his good looks and bravado. She, however, was frightened of him. He was just barely contained, like a Beta Chamber, filled with ferocious power. She could not imagine being foolhardy enough to try to have a marriage with him. Besides, it was well known he qualified for five children. There were very few women that ever qualified for more than three children, and it would always be an issue unless he could find a very strong young woman somewhere in the Burrows. It would take a very special woman to be bound to such a fiery soul.

Because she understood her own needs and abilities, she did not allow herself to think about him very much. She was very busy with her training, and she was already making a name for herself as a storyteller. There was too much to do to concern herself with wild young men. There was a time a few years earlier, just after her first Telling that she had a bit of an crush on him. She had been stirred by his deep reaction to the Rememberance rituals. But he was a brash young man, and everything he did was large and loud. He took too many risks for her taste, and she soon forgot her feelings for him as her heart moved from one fancy to another.

On the day he tried to kiss her, Sojourner was going into a grove of peach trees to gather fallen leaves for her father. The air was thick with the smell of peaches ready to pick and there were even a few pieces of fruit on the ground where they had fallen. It was a sweet place. Sojourner carried a basket to put the leaves in, and she would take them to her father for analysis and testing. She loved these little moments alone in the trees where she could pretend that she was strong and vibrant, free from her limitations. It was deep and shaded in the peach grove, and she was happy with her task. She was happy with her task, that is, until that bothersome Stephan showed up.

She had seen him on his hoverboard careening across the meadow like a possessed arrow, showing off his prowess for any and all to see. She disdained his antics. Every time she saw him, he was doing some fantastic trick. He made her feel weak and small. Turning her back deliberately, she walked steadily toward the peach grove.

It was always a task for her to walk across the open ground because the surface was uneven and there were few things for her to touch briefly to regain her balance. Still, she stubbornly refused to use a walking device to help her unsteady limbs. She wanted to be strong. Strength was wasted on the foolish. She glanced at the frivilous Stephan. Ugh. The beast was coming her direction. Even though she distained him, her heart still beat faster, and she quickened her pace so that she would not have to speak the Greeting to him. He always made her uncomfortable. He seemed to go out of his way to appear important. She hoped he was going to pass by the grove and not be about too much. He was a distraction, and she wanted to be free to sink into her thoughts. She laboriously quickened her pace, delving deep in her will, striving to reach the peach grove and the shelter of the trees. Perhaps he hadn't seen her and it was a coincidence that he was coming her direction.

She had only been in the carefully tended orchard for a few minutes when she heard his voice. "Well, hello there, little Sojourner!" She turned, her heart beating so loudly she was certain he could hear it. He stood with the easy grace of a strong young man, one foot propped up on his hoverboard, arms akimbo. He smiled at her, "It is a beautiful day."

"I am one of the many, I am Sojourner, I greet you." Sojourner replied firmly, glaring at him indignantly.

"Oh! I see! I must observe the proprieties!" He stood up straight, "I am also one of many, I am Stephan, and I return your greetings." He nonchalantly stepped up on his hoverboard and casually shifted it side to side, his lithe body adjusting to its movement. Sojourner felt his presence swarm over her. Her stomach fluttered. "So, little Sojourner, are you going to tell stories to the trees?"

Sojourner felt hot fury in her. Was he making fun of her? It would be just like such an arrogant show-off to come all the way over here to be rude. She drew herself up as tall as she could. "It is none of your concern what I do in the peach grove. Haven't you better things to do than to bother those minding their own business?" Sojourner's voice trembled with anger. She turned as quickly as her unstable legs would allow and stepped with resolute anger deeper into the grove of trees. She heard the hum of the hover board behind her. That ridiculous Stephan was following her deeper into the peach grove. She hoped he would get knocked off his silly hover board.

"Sojourner, please stop! I didn't mean to offend you. I was just trying to make a joke."

Stephan nudged his board forward and stopped beside her. He towered over her. He would be tall enough standing on the ground, but he remained on his hoverboard, and Sojourner had to crane her neck to look up at him. He looked at her intently. She could feel his wamth, smell his scent mixed with the smell of the wind on him. He was so close. He reached out and brushed a stray strand of hair off of her brow.

"If you were going to practice a story, I would be a better audience than these silent trees." His fingers felt like sweetness and fire when they moved across her brow and left a trail of his essence behind. She fancied everyone would be able to see where he had touched her; that his touch glowed across her skin like a beacon. He looked in her face like he was trying to set her on fire with his eyes. She was transfixed by him.

"Tell me a story about how the Maker invented kisses to help men and women express their love for each other...." Slowly, seductively, he bent his head to her. Sojourner's heart was beating wildly in her chest. Stephan was going to kiss her! Suddenly, she felt anger boiling up in her like a beta chamber that was pierced. This arrogant beast was going to try to kiss her and add her name to the list of unfortunates that had fallen under the spell of his hyponotic snake eyes. She pulled away from him abruptly, flinging her leaf basket at him. Her sudden movement and the spirited blow from the basket knocked the beastly Stephan off of his hoverboard. He flailed his arms about, desparately trying to keep his balance. He fell.

He fell and he hit the ground with a wrenching thud. His head snapped forward and cracked against a shallow root. He moaned and then he lay still. His head was bloodied and his face was ashen. Sojourner's anger vanished and was replaced by fear and guilt and concern. She hurried to Stephan's side and knelt beside him. He was unconscious. Sojourner quickly pushed her med-alert, glad for once that she was required to wear the device because of her ill health. Within just a few moments, a medical team arrived, expecting to have to tend to the frail Storyteller.

The team entered the grove of trees and saw the prone young man and the wisp of a girl kneeling beside him, wringing her hands. They were unprepared for the type of injury that Stephan has sustained, but they rapidly moved into action. The Healers apprised the situation and asked Sojourner rapid, terse questions. She struggled to answer them clearly, feeling thick and wool-headed. She was embarrassed and ashamed. Quickly, Stephan was transported out of the peach grove and taken to the Healing Center. Sojourner was left alone in the suddenly silent peach grove. It was no longer a lovely place, and she did not want to sink into her thoughts, nor did she want to gather leaves.

She stumbled to the basket and woodenly gathered the spilled leaves back into it...she must finish her task... leaves should not be wasted. She felt like weeping, but she didn't know why. Stephan had harrassed her, stalked her. Her actions were entirely justified. No one would blame her for not wanting to be pawed by that arrogant show off. He had a reputation for breaking hearts. She was only defending herself. Still, her feelings were a tangle, it was only a kiss.

With her basket full, she resolutely began her difficult walk back to the Burrow. She felt her unreliable legs trembling tiredly halfway there. She did not stop, though. It would serve her right if she had an implant failure. It was foolish of her to go into the groves by herself. It was foolish to think that Stephan was intending harm. He was an arrogant fool, but he would never hurt her. It would go against the directives of the Burrows. Healers monitored aggressive traits and tendencies, and implanted those that couldn't be redirected with interventions. It was basic to the survival of the Burrows that each person be useful, sane, and productive. Every person was examined regularly and treated if there were behavioral anomalies. There were no predators in the Burrows. Stephan may have stolen a kiss, but he would not hurt her. He could break her heart, but he would not ever fail the standards of the Burrows. She had overreacted to his overtures. Why?

She went directly to the Healing Center, and was not surprised to find her parents waiting there for her. Together they went to find out how Stephan was doing. Sojourner's father put his arm around her waist, partly supporting her slight weight. She was grateful that she did not have to ask him to help her. Her legs were so tired. She had over extended her strength coming back so quickly. Her mother chided her for not calling for a hover cab. She didn't say anything. Her mother was right. What was she trying to prove?

Stephan's mother and father were in the room with Stephan. His mother looked up when they came to the door, and then looked back down at her prone, silent son. She tenderly stroked his forehead, seeming to gather her thoughts. She looked up at her husband, and their eyes met.

"Don't Palla. It isn't the time or place." Stephan's father said tiredly. "This will be sorted out another time."

"Jak, I will not be silent about this any longer. This situation is ridiculous, and all it needs to be brought out in the open," she spat. Her eyes flashed angrily.

"This is not what Stephan would want, and he will be too embarrassed to think his mother has discussed this so openly."

"I will not be silent any longer. This is getting out of control." Palla's voice was adamant. "Our son has no good sense where this is concerned. What will he have broken next? This will heal, Maker be praised, his heart may not."

Palla turned to Sojourner's mother. "You know what I intend to say, Sara. This is an old conversation for us."

"Palla, I understand why you want to spare your son some heartache, but this just can't be. He is too strong for her. He will break her like a twig."

"Have you ever seen my son among the seedings and new plants in the nursery? Twigs are perfectly safe in his hands. I can't bear to watch him wear his heart out about this."

Sojourner had been listening to them talk, growing more confused and yet understanding their talk at the same time. She stepped into the room and crossed to the bed where Stephan lay, his face pale beneath the swath of dressing around his head. She reached out her fingers and trailed them over his hand. His hands were large and strong, already crisscrossed with the tiny scars of one who worked in the earth without regard for their appearance. Sojourner looked at her own pale, spindly fingers next to them. Her hands were weak and useless looking next to his.

"This cannot be." She breathed out, her voice barely louder than a whisper. "I am the one that he loves? This is not good..." She turned to Stephn's mother. "Oh, Ma'am! I don't mean to be rude, but this can't be true. I am not right for him. He may never have children if he loves me. I can't live with that. Can't you reason with him?"

Palla sank tiredly onto the corner of Stephan's bed. "From the moment he heard you speak your first story, he has been determined to gain your attention. At first, I thought it would pass, but it didn't. He just admires you more as time passes. He has tried to leave his feelings behind, but he ends up hurting someone else's feelings. We have even thought about having him implanted, but there is no implant to guard against unrequited love. His actions today were brash and foolish. I don't know what to say to you. I wish I had some magic to make him not love you, or to make you return his feelings, but there isn't any magic to perform."

"I didn't know it was me that he loved. I would have been kinder. I thought he was just showing off," Sojourner's voice trailed into silence.

"I know that he acts the fool when you are about. He has been instructed to leave you be. We have had just about everyone we can think of speak to him about this hopeless infatuation. We have even had the Burrow Leadership involved. Stephan can see the logic of not being joined to you, but he can't accept it. So, since he can't talk to you, he breaks his neck showing off for you. Now this."

"What do you want me to do?" Sojourner looked at Stephan. He was beautiful to look at. He was perfect to look at.

"You must either break his heart or love him. I can't tell you which." Palla stood up and walked over to her husband. "Jak, I need to get some air. I have said all I need to say."

She and her husband walked out of the room. Sojourner crossed to the only chair and tried to move it close to the bed so she could sit down. It was too heavy, and her father had to help her position it next to the bed. She sat down wearily.

"If you don't mind, I will just sit here and think for a while." She smiled wanly at her parents. "I need to think about this."

"We'll be back in an hour to take you home. Don't hesitate to call us if you are getting tired." her father said. Gently he tilted her face up to look at him. "You don't have to do anything at all! You can't make yourself love someone, but you can be kind. Whatever you choose to do or not to do, we trust you."

Her parents left the room. Sojourner was alone with the Stephan. She did not know what to do. Tentitively, she reached out her hand and smoothed his hair off of his forehead. That is what his mother did, and she must know what gestures comforted him. She remembered at the long ago Rememberance when Stephan wept in his mother's arms, she had stroked his forehead. It was soft. His hair was soft, and the skin across his forehead was soft. She did not know it would be, and she was surprised. For some reason, she thought he would feel rough.

"I'm sorry you are hurt. I did not know I could hurt you. I thought you were indestructable. I imagine you are surprised I am so strong and fierce." she laughed softly at her joke, but her laughter sounded loud and strained in the silent room. "I didn't have any idea I could hurt you. Truly...I did not know I was so strong...." Her voice trailed off into silence again. Stephen stirred slightly, and Sojourner quickly stopped stroking his forehead and snatched her hand away. The monitors chimed, signalling the need for a Healer.

Stephan groaned and stirred. His eyes fluttered open briefly. "Ohhh. My sweet! You are here. Stay, please...."

A Healer hurried into the room and made adjustments to the devices releasing medicines into Stephan.

"He is a strong one. Still, it is important he be kept quiet right now. I imagine he has many things to say to you, but he needs to heal up a bit first." Sojourner winced. Everyone in the Burrows must know about Stephan's feelings.

The Healer smiled at Sojourner. "While I am here, I will scan your implants. I understand you exerted yourself today. It is important to be prudent." He quickly used a hand scanner and examined Sojourner. "There! We will need to see you before you go home and adjust your motor cortex implant. Nothing serious. Remember to keep Stephan quiet."

"Did you hear that? You must stay still and let your head heal. Next time you follow a girl into a peach grove and try to get a kiss, get off your hoverboard. It will go better for you. Then if she throws her basket at you, you may be able to duck and not end up with a bump on your head." She took his hand. The palm was hard and calloused. Her father's hands were like that. It was comforting to hold his hand. She was surprised at its weight. "I think you should know that I have tried not to think about you for as long as I have known about you. I have tried not to think about the way you look, or the way you move. I tried not to think about the way you are brave and the way you plant and cleanse the soil. I have tried not to think about the way you play with the children in the creche. That is what I especially try not to think about. I try not to think about how many children you may have and how I may not be allowed any, and I try not to think about you playing with them. I will never be able to avoid thinking about these things again.

"Now, I will think about them all of my waking moments. I will think about the way you move and the way you look and the way you are brave and the way you tend the earth. I will think long and hard about the way you play with the children. If I love you back, it will be the most selfish thing any woman has ever done to any man. I may never give you a child, and that is so important. We are so few, and you are strong. How can I live with this? I don't know you, nor do you know me. We need to talk for a long time when you are well enough. You will see that joining with me will only bring you heartache. You will see the wisdom of the Leaders and of our parents. You will be happy to be far from me once you know me well. The cure for your feelings is a good dose of me. You will see.

"Well, Stephan, it is time for me to go. Well, I am going to go, but I am going to give you a kiss first. For all the trouble you are having, I guess, you have earned it. You won't like it. I am going to kiss you right on the lips, and you won't like it, and you will be over this. Well, one kiss."

Sojourner leaned over Stephan's bed, carefully, not touching him. She bent her head close to him and she softly pressed her lips on Stephan's still lips. His lips felt strange to her. She had only ever kissed her parents, and she had felt herself too grown up to kiss them on the lips for a very long time. Stephan's lips felt like a new thing in creation. They were smooth against her lips and they were pleasant. She pulled away, her heart was thumping against her chest.

"Do you see how inexpert I am at kissing? You would have been very disappointed if you had actually managed to kiss me today in the peach grove. I hope you can hear me and that you remember."

"My sweet? Is every thing well?" Stephan's voice interrupted her thoughts.

"Yes, Stephan. I am fine. It is good to hear your voice!"

"I was thinking that when you get back we will spend a few days in Deep Burrow. Would you like that?"

"Yes. Stephan? Just in case this doesn't work, we need to talk. Something might go amiss"

"No, I can't think of that!" Stephan's voice was heavy. "I have only just accepted that you are doing this. Why would you ever think this isn't going to work?"

"I told the story about the Maker's Hope to Lyla, and she was not moved. Their culture has no god. How will I talk to them?"

"They have no god? But our people have observed rituals that are religious in nature. What is the point of their endless ritual?"

"Their cultural icon, someone called the Lawgiver, spent time analyzing history and decided that ritual was necessary for an orderly society, and that ritual removed from superstition was the most efficient way to manage a culture. It is complicated. It sounds empty. Anyway, Lyla can give you more insights when she arrives. I am afraid that I will have no common ground to begin my task. My most powerful stories all mention Heaven."

"My sweet, you may have to rely on little stories instead of big ones. You must trust your voice and your manner. You are the Master Storyteller of our entire country. You are treasured and valued for the thoughts in your head. It will be fine. You moved my thick head from one place to another."

"Well, I cracked it anyway."

Stephan chuckled. "We will get very busy, the Healers, the Leaders, the Psychologists, the Handlers, all of us. We will get very busy and think of ways to help you convince the leadership of the Empire to be at peace with us. You are not alone. If your doubts are too big though, I will tell Joseph and we will have you out of there within the hour. Oh, yes! Another thing. We can have a Guardian placed in with you as soon as we can synthesize Lyla's appearance and identification markers. It would not do to have her missing when the chamber is reopened. Besides, a friend inside would be a good thing."

"No." Sojourner said resolutely. "I want to tell them that it was the will of the Maker that she be freed from her bondage. Let them puzzle about the realities of faith. I will tell them it is God's will that she be taken from them. He uses His servants. Maybe they will wonder..."

— Part Two —

— Prologue —

Josilyn stepped on the hem of her robe again. It was an amazement to her that this stupid way of dressing had not brought down the Empire long ago. Elfin slowed his steps so that she could regain her balance. He wanted to turn and catch her and steady her, she knew, but that would attract too much attention. That and the patrols would haul him off to the Purification Center and scrub him raw for touching his wife in public. Purity above all else. Purity could be painful at times. The laws governing touching were too numerous to count. Josilyn stepped carefully.

Elfin led the way past the final shield sticks that had been implanted into the soil. It was a constant amazement to them that none of the thousands of shield sticks had been disturbed. The discipline of the Empire was complete. If it was installed, leave it alone until someone authorized arrives to remove it. Do not do anything remarkable.

It was good to be prepared in case the Master Storyteller could not convince the Emperor that it would be better to forge a bond with the Burrows rather than try to conquer them. Peace, if possible, power where necessary. It was a hard hope to hold dear.

Elfin spoke quietly to her, "We must hurry!" She nodded slightly. They must look like they were silent in each other's presence. Speaking to a wife was not necessary if both understood their place. Men and women were not compatible except for the propagation of the species. That is what the Lawgiver taught. Allow women freedom among women, but not among men. Allow men freedom among men, but never among women. Elfin hated the restrictions. Elfin needed to speak to his wife because she nourished his soul. Talking to her had always helped him find his balance. He would talk to her endlessly when they were finally home. Right now, though, they had floors in the Palace to scrub. Josilyn walked carefully and Elfin remained silent.

⁃ Chapter 16 ⁃

Minerva Provo focused on her husband's feet as he led her up the winding Path of the Nobles, the first light of a cloudy day feebly lighting the sky. She hated these trips to the Palace. The Lawgiver was a jackass, and these celebrations designed by the long dead jackass were evidence of his stupidity. Damnation! She hated these hot dragging robes. She refused to wear them at home. She wished she could resurrect the ancient jackass Lawgiver and make him go about in the awful Robes of Honor for a week. He would then have designed the Robes of Honor more thoughtfully. They would have had some color and been made out of a more comfortable fabric. Maybe they would have been more like the outfits the ancient women of the Evil Society wore. They didn't dress modestly, but they certainly looked comfortable. She tried to imagine what it would be like to feel a breeze on bare arms and legs. She imagined it would feel wonderful. She tried to imagine what it would be like to see the world without a veil covering her eyes. The only time she was allowed outside was when she was properly robed and veiled. She had always wondered what it would feel like to be outside in the wind and sunshine. She imagined it would be more wonderful than music.

Lorn hissed at her twice through his teeth. Two short hisses. That meant that they were approaching the stairs. She wanted to shout in frustration. The Woman's Stairs were poorly maintained and arduous to climb. The Men's Stairs were broad and flat and followed a gentle curving route to the top of the steep slope leading to the Noble's entrance. The Women's Stairs went straight up. The logic had been that women only came to the Palace for State Celebrations, and a direct route was the best one for a robed woman. Minerva was certain that no nobleman had ever tried to climb these stairs in heavy robes. Even though the Men's Stair was a longer route, Minerva had never gotten to the top before Lorn. He would be waiting at the top with all of the other husbands, trying to act nonchalant about her long climb. She knew he hated how she had to suffer at these horrid celebrations, and he would care for her tenderly for many days to come. It was the only thing that made the trips to the palace bearable. She wondered how the wives of the diehards survived them. She stepped off the path and paused for a moment to gather her strength.

The stairs were clogged with the wives of nobles. The noble wives struggled up the steep stairs, their black robes gathered close, backs bent into the steep climb. Once, a wife of a minor nobleman took off her robes to climb the terrible stairs, thinking that there were no patrols about since it was a woman's place. She had been mistaken. The stairs were carefully monitored. The woman was Forsaken at the top of the stairs. Minerva never climbed the stairs without thinking about the poor unfortunate woman. She thought about the woman, and she wondered why the Empire spent the resources on monitoring the stairs but never bothered repairing them. The stairs were a crumbling mess. She knew she needed to start the climb. If she waited too long then Lorn would be worried. He had enough to worry about. She took a deep breath and began the climb.

The stairs were even worse than they had been at her last trip to the Palace two years ago when the rebels in the Southern Arm had been defeated. That had been a terrible situation, and Lorn had been hard pressed to keep the other provinces from joining forces with the rebels. He had done some brilliant negotiating and had received some very nice indulgences from the young Emperor Kalig. It must never be known that it was Minerva that had written the treaties for Lorn. Lorn was a wonderful man, full of conscience and brilliant in his way, but he did not write well and his thoughts scattered about like leaves caught up in a sudden wind. Still, she loved him. She loved him enough to climb these infernal stairs and suffer through the Celebration of the Capture of the Barbarian Queen. She loved him enough to write treaties.

A woman in front of Minerva stumbled as a piece of the stairway crumbled unexpectedly. She fell hard on her knee, her breath grunting out of her in pained surprise. Minerva scrambled out of her way, fighting to keep her balance. The woman's fall had a chain reaction as the wives of noblemen all bumped into each other and fought to keep from falling also. There were a few frantic moments as the women righted their balance. The dark procession stopped for a moment, then Minerva and several others stepped up to the dark robed woman and lifted her up as best they could. She was shaking and struggling to swallow her sobs, her hands pressed against her swollen midsection. She was enormous with child. Minerva remembered how hard this climb had been when she was expecting her children. She was thankful that she had not had a baby in eight years. The woman trembled as Minerva slipped her arm around her. Carefully, Minerva and another wife supported her weight as she struggled to continue her climb. It would not do to attract the attention of the patrols, even for a simple accident. They would manage to get her to the top somehow. Hopefully her husband was a compassionate man and would tend to her in some way before the Celebration began. Perhaps this would be the last Celebration they would have to endure now that the Blasted Lands had become livable. Perhaps they would not be here for anymore Celebrations.

Minerva hoped fervently that Lorn would be chosen to represent the Empire in the Rediscovered Lands. She hoped he would be made a governor and they could move their family far across the ocean far from the prying eyes of the Examiners and the Lawyers and the Patrols. She knew these things would make an appearance in the Rediscovered Lands someday, but perhaps there would be a span of time when she could go outside and she and Lorn could talk in public instead of communicating in hisses.

"We are half way up," the woman in front of Minerva murmered.

"We are half way up!" Miverva said quietly. She listened to the message being passed to the others in turn in a quiet murmer as each woman passed the half way point. Minerva glanced at the hurt woman at her side. She was not shaking so hard, but her breaths were still heaving in and out of her. Once Minerva had been supported up the stairs when she had been swollen with child. When she finally gotten to the top, shaking and sweat drenched, Lorn had taken her in his arms. Immediately, they had been surrounded by the Patrol and several Examiners. Since she was not in labor, Lorn had been taken to be Purified for touching his wife in public. He had been scrubbed raw and bleeding, purged until he was weak and shaking. Even after all of these years, his body bore the scars of that hateful ritual.

Minerva glanced upward. Finally, she could see the top of the stairs. Mercy and damnation! Her legs felt like lead and sweat coursed down her back and slid down her arms and neck. The pregnant woman was breathing in the prescribed manner of a woman in labor. Minerva wished there were a god like the one the ancients possessed so that she could pray. She felt a gentle tug on her robe and turned toward it. A large squarely built wife reached for the pregnant woman, relieving Minerva of her burden. Gratefully, she stepped aside and let the strongly built woman take her place. She didn't pause but for an instant, though. The flow of black clad figures must not be interrupted.

Resolutely, she gathered her robes closely and forced her now heavy legs to move. She could see the top of the stairs. It drew nearer with every step. Lorn would be there with his kind eyes. She climbed.

"Fifteen steps left," the woman in front of her murmered.

Minerva took a step forward. "Fifteen steps left!" she said quietly over her shoulder.

Mentally she counted each of her steps. Twelve. Lorn would be at the top. Five. She would make it through this part again. Three...two...one.....Someday, she would discover a true god and she would pray to it for strength while climbing, and she would pray a prayer of thanksgiving when she reached the top of these terrible stairs. Wearily she ambled to the Woman's Line and waited for Lorn to approach the line and point to her. He always gave her a few moments to catch her breath after the climb. Some of the husbands were not so thoughtful. They strode up to the Woman's Line as soon as they recognized their personal emblem embroidered on the shoulder of their wives' robes. The wife would then be required to follow her husband to the Palace to begin her long day of work. Minerva watched anxiously as the heavily pregnant wife completed her climb and stumbled to the Woman's Line. Good, the woman was not immediately approached. Minerva looked out at the nobles. Lorn was watching her for their secret sign that she had caught her breath enough to follow him. A young, fresh-faced nobleman approached the Line and pointed to the pregnant woman. Minerva could see the scar across the palm of his hand, and she breathed in deeply. Perhaps this would go well for the poor young woman, then. The pregnant woman stepped forward, her breath heaving in and out of her in panting gasps. The young nobleman then spread his hands wide in the Gesture of Exceptions. His wife sank to her knees as the pain of a contraction overwhelmed her.

"As you can see," he intoned formally though his voice was edged with panic, "my one wife is in distress due to fulfilling her purpose. Her purpose is to bear me strong children, sons and daughters, and I am obligated to tend to her. She is my one wife. I claim the right of exemption, and I will remove her from this place. "

An Examiner stepped forward and looked at the woman struggling to catch her breath and then at her husband. He spoke in the strange, high-pitched voice of his calling. "Take your wife and deliver a child for your honor. Because of the circumstance, your way is made clear." The Examiner then looked intently at the young nobleman, "Trust in your skills. You are ready for this, young Trenter."

"I thank you, sir. May I tend to my wife now?"

"Yes. A medi-car will be here in just a few moments. Your wife's difficulties were observed on the stairs. Several of the other wives helped her up the stairs, and you are excused from all of your obligations today." The Examiner then turned to the gathering nobles and their wives. "Turn your faces away. The Right of Exmeption has been claimed and deemed necessary. Give this man respect. Give this honorable wife respect."

The nobles and their wives all turned their backs to the young nobleman and his wife. Minerva could hear the rapid steps of the young man as he crossed to his wife and spoke to her softly, soothingly. There was the sound of a vehicle crunching across the path and the soft grunt of the man as he lifted his wife onto the medi cart. Doors clicked shut, and then the hum of the medi-car faded. Minerva felt a wash of relief and hope as they all turned back around. This would go well, she was certain. She would pray to a god someday, regardless of what that emptyheaded Lawgiver said. She would pray to a god and say a prayer of thanksgiving for the moments of hope.

She looked up at Lorn. She shook the skirt of her robe as if shaking dust off of it. He stepped forward and pointed at her. His eyes were full of hope for the young couple, and concern for her. She wished he could see her smile. She wished she could hug him. He turned his back to her and walked down the Path of the Nobles. Minerva followed him, though she wished she walked beside him with her hand in his.

— Chapter 17 —

Minerva sank wearily to her knees. It was soon going to be over, this cursed Celebration. She longed for a good long soak in a deep, scented bath. She and the other wives had outdone themselves. "The nobility will provide nourishment for the population as a sign of victory." That blunderhead Lawgiver had no common sense. There were three thousand noble families in the Capital City, fewer in the outlying cities, and virtually none in the countryside. From the first sign of daylight, all of the wives of nobility in every province in every village had been cooking and preparing the ritual celebration meal after climbing the cursed stairs. Of course, they had been preparing for weeks, but the final touches took all of their strength.

There were twenty million people in Capitol City. With only the three thousand noble families the task was staggering. Even though the meal was a ritual meal, a tidbit only, the work was overwhelming. "Victory is a cause to nourish the common man." Minerva wished she knew some good salty curses to express her frustration, but she didn't know any. The nobilty had been working without rest for the entire day, passing out the ritual meal to every adult in the empire. The population was organized into managable groups and given specific times to approach the Palace, but even so, it was a formidable task. First the poor were fed, then the working class. Their meals were simple, bread and dried meats and fruits served to them in prepackaged containers. They were not required to fulfill any ritual, and even though there were many millions of them in the city, the passing of the ritual nourishment to them went very quickly and smoothly. Of course, the men passed the food to the men and the women passed food to the women. The Law was served first.

The aristocracy and the military were next, and they were given a larger, more elaborate meal, and they were expected to sit and eat the meal in a ritual fashion. Of course, it was very organized and the ritual meal was eaten at a certain pace and with strict protocol that had to be followed. The meal was eaten in silence and reverently, so the actual meal went very quickly, but the preparation took hours and hours for the wives to accomplish. Of course, then they had to serve the wives of the aristocracy and the military. It was exhausting... and still the day wasn't done.

Now it was time for the Palace celebration. This feast was the last to be served, and the most lavish. At least the weary wives only had to serve their own husbands, and when they were done eating, the wives would get to sit and eat as much as their growling stomachs could hold. Of course, most of them were too tired to eat too much, and they still had the long descent back down the Wives' Stair before the night was over. Thankfully, they were not expected to clean up after the feast. The process was ponderous. The Empire captured a barbarian queen and then all of this endless bothersome ritual.

Minerva was proud of the work that had been accomplished, even though she thought it was all ridiculous. Curse the Lawgiver forever. She wished there were a real hell like the one the ancients believed in, so she could hope he suffered terrible torments there. She shifted her weight slightly. It would not do to have gone through all of this today and then be Shamed for fidgeting. She must be still. Soon this would be over and she would be free from this obligation until the Emperor found another land to conquer. As soon as the nobles had filed in, and the Emperor had been served by his Chosen, Minerva would be able to serve Lorn and then she could sit in a real chair. It would feel so nice to sit. She hoped she did not go to sleep.

The nobles were all at their places. Lorn glanced back at her. She knew that he could not pick her out in this great collage of black, but it meant something to her that he glanced back. The Emperor's Approach was sounded and all of the noblemen dropped to one knee, bowed their heads and placed their hands over their hearts. The wives, already kneeling, leaned forward and put their foreheads on the floor. Minerva again hoped she didn't fall asleep as soon as her head touched the floor. She didn't dare, she must listen carefully for the cues and not stand out in any way. Order above all else. She listened for the soft click as the Chosen's door opened. That meant that the Emperor had taken his seat and his favored Chosen had entered the banquet hall to serve his meal. The fanfare abruptly stopped and the room was left in utter silence. She heard the soft swishing sounds of the Chosen's robes as she moved about preparing the Emperor's plate and then settled it in front of him. Sometimes this did not go well if the Chosen did not prepare the plate to the emperor's liking. Then the Chosen must correct her mistakes and sometimes it took a very long time to fix the plate correctly. Ahhhh! Good! It sounded like this was not a problem tonight. Minerva would thank a god if she could find one.

Minerva remained still. Damnation! Ahhh! There was an ancient curse word. No one used the word much anymore since there was no Hell. Her toes were cramping and sweat coursed down her face. Now the emperor would name the twelve that would come and sit with him during the evening. It was a great honor, and indicated favors and power to come. She strained to remain still and listen. Lorn. Please let it be Lorn this time. He deserved so much more than he received.

"Lord Simon." Of course, the rich bastard always got picked. "Lord Joban." What was he thinking. That beast would drool all over the tablecloth...Lord Doran, Lord Grall, Lord Jonta, Lord Provo. Miverva caught her breath. Did she hear correctly? Lord Provo? Lorn Provo! Minerva willed herself to be still, though her heart pounded in her chest. Lorn would sit with the Emperor. She must be still. She must listen to the cues and perform flawlessly this evening so that Lorn may gain favor in this brutal game. Lord Simon was at the table, and she must pay special attention to him because he was so treacherous. She forced her attention back to the names being announced. She had lost her concentration, and she did not know how many names had been called. "Lord Bento. Lord Ponce." Silence.

Minerva heard rustlings as the wives of the Twelve Honored rose to their feet. Cautiously she glanced up and saw through the opaque eyeslits that it was time to serve her husband his plate. As gracefully as possible, she climbed to her feet and crossed to the serving tables. She had paid close attention to the food as it had been laid out on the tables so she could go directly to the dishes she had prepared and fix Lorn's plate. She knew how he liked his food and was careful to prepare plenty of what he liked. She was well known among many of the noble families for being a very good cook, so she rarely managed to get any food from her own dishes because others usually took notice of her dish placement, too. She was pleased to see that the Chosen had taken portions of her food to put on the Emperor's plate. She was just as pleased that there was some left to give to her own husband. She wished there would be some left when the men were done eating so that she could have some of her own food instead of the vile concoctions that would be left. Tomorrow, she would soak in a tub and eat in her own kitchen.

She put some of the carefully spiced meat and the complicated vegetable dish that Lorn liked so well on his plate. She was careful to fill it but not overfill it. It was all about balance and presentation. She took in a deep breath and turned toward the Honored Table. "If there is a god in this universe," she breathed, "help me not to trip and ruin any chances Lorn has to gain what he deserves." She stepped carefully over to where her husband sat, holding the plate waist high so that she could hook her little fingers in the carefully camoflauged loops in the front of her robe and hold her robes out far enough so she would not step on the hem and stumble. She placed the plate in front of her husband, being very careful not to touch him. It would be a disaster to have Lorn hauled away from the table to be Purified. She stepped back three paces as he did the ritual approval of his plate. She noticed that Lord Simon's wife had to redo his plate. Of course. He was evil to everyone he knew and to those he met. She sneaked a quick peak at the emperor. He was beautiful to look at, but terrible in his power.

She crossed to the screened off area where the wives traditionally sat and gratefully sank into a chair. The screen was made so that the wives could see out, but were not seen by the nobles. That way a wife could rise and replenish her husband's plates if he signalled her. Of course, the nobles only did this if the Emperor had his plate replenished. Once there had been a Kalig that did not have a healthy appetite and these feasts were wretched affairs for the nobles.

Now the other wives were rising from their prostrate positions on the floor, row upon row, and crossing to the serving tables to prepare a plate for their husbands. Occasionally a husband would send his wife back for a better-prepared plate, but most accepted their food without much of a glance. Minerva figured they were all about to starve from the long fast and hard work of the day. Very soon, the husbands had been served and the Emperor signalled that it was time for them to eat. Minerva wondered if the Emperor's food was cooled off from his long wait. He didn't look hungry. She would wager that he had eaten earlier if wagering was allowed. Someday, someone should force him to do what was required of his people. No. Then someone might be forced to do what was required of the Emperor. That would be a terrible thing. No one wanted to be the Emperor or a Chosen One. It required too much sacrifice.

Minerva breathed in deeply. One more hour. She would eat only enough to give her the strength for the long descent back down the stairs. She knew the food that would be left would be poorly prepared and flavorless. The best would be taken first. She breathed in deeply again. It was time to watch. She paid close attention to what happened at these feasts, then she would tell Lorn what she observed. It had been very helpful to him in the past. It was her sharp eyes that noticed the illegal alliance of the traitor lords from the outlying provinces some fifteen years ago. Between the behaviors of the wives of the traitors and the odd behaviors of the traitors, Minerva was able to alert Lorn of the danger with their secret handtalk. He was still just an underlord at the time, and the former Emperor Kalig had not noticed Lorn's abilities despite the excellent work that Lorn had done for him. Lorn had taken the observations of his wife and had quickly been able to prove the conspiracy. He had risen to being a full lord in his own right soon afterward despite the neglect of the former Kalig. Ever since, he relied even more on her keen insights to help him in his work as the Minister of Imperial Security. If this evening went well, perhaps he would receive an appointment to the Rediscovered Lands.

She watched and listened to the softly whispered conversations surrounding her. Two wives sitting behind her were talking quietly about the Favored Chosen, Chiria. "I grew up with her. I miss her so much. She was so funny and loved the common gardens in the women's circle. She showed great promise in her work with the babies. Now she is Chosen and lost to us."

"It is a terrible life. I was offered to the former Emperor, but he preferred a girl with a tad more bosom , though they needed to be tall and slender-built and fair to please him. I will admit that I starved myself and exercised like an ancient wanton to become an unsuitable stick. When I was rejected, I was so thrilled that I ate everything I could get my hands on for two weeks. Then I heard that he had taken my friend, Lyla, the daughter of Lord Dertha. It was soon after her ritual that he was deposed. She did not even get a chance to conceive and regain her honor. She is Forsaken and lost now."

"At least this Emperor Kalig is young and will not have to face his murder any time soon. Plus, I heard that Chiria has already had a baby. A boy. Poor thing...."

"At least you may get a chance to wave at her at these celebrations..."

"Yes. I hope I can catch her eye. If not I will have to wait until the next time a barbarian queen is captured."

"I wonder if a barbarian queen looks like a regular woman. I have heard that she is unnatural and deformed."

"I wonder how? Like a tail?"

Minerva snorted to herself. Ignorant girls. Still, the idea of a woman actually having the rule of a country in her hands was appalling. She must be a brutal woman if her country were anything like the Empire. Surely it was brutal, because the Lawgiver taught that all cultures, when isolated, naturally developed into a semblance of the Real Culture of the Empire. It was natural and complete. She shifted her attention to the banquet hall.

The wine stewards were pouring wine into the glasses of the nobles and they were lifting their glasses toward the emperor. Minerva sighed miserably. Not wine. It was forbidden to consume alcohol except at these celebrations, and no one was used to it. If the occasion wasn't considered very important it wasn't served at all. This must be a very important occasion if the wine was being served this early in the meal. No telling what kind of trouble Lorn would be in by the end of the evening. He was so tired and hungry, Minerva was certain that the wine would go straight to his head. She clenched her teeth and waited for it all to become terrible.

The Emperor drained his glass, and so it was understood that the nobles were to drain theirs as well. Lorn hated wine, saying that it tasted like spoiled juice, and he strangled his down. His face flushed as the alcohol blasted through his tired system. The Emperor signalled to his Chosen to refill his plate. Minerva heard the two women behind her fall silent as Chiria glided forward. She was a slight woman, robed in the bright garments of the Chosen. She prepared a plate and carefully placed it before the Emperor. She took three paces back watching him for the ritual approval. He signalled that the plate was unacceptable and she hurried forward to take it away from in front of him. He clicked on his voice amplifier as was the law when he wanted to instruct his Chosen. His words could only be those that were prescribed by the Lawgiver.

"Chosen! This does not meet my needs. Please provide what I need!"

The Chosen hurried to the serving table to the platter that had held the food Minerva had prepared. There was very little left of the spiced meat. Chiria scraped every bit of the food that she could, but there was still much that couldn't be scooped out. She tried to tilt the heavy platter and scrape the meat out onto the plate, but it was too heavy and awkward. Minerva silently rose from her seat and crossed to the struggling young woman. It was permitted, but unusual for her to do this. This was a night when they were serving wine. All help should be given on the nights when wine was served. No one was safe.

Minerva lifted the heavy platter and the Chosen then scraped all of the remaining food onto Kalig's plate. Chiria's hands were trembling. "My thanks," she breathed quietly to Minerva. Minerva did not acknowldge her thanks, but returned quickly to her seat. Chiria carried the plate back to the Emperor. She took the required steps back and he nodded his head in approval. The Chosen turned and returned to her seat, her steps measured and controlled. She sat alone, her head bent.

Minerva could hear the slight hum of the Emperor's voice amplifier being switched on. Kalig undoubtedly was going to speak to one of the men about his wife or family. It was not proper to address a man about his family privately, all questions were to be public and in order.

"Lord Provo! I understand this dish was prepared by your wife?"

"Yes, Exalted One."

"Please have her send the recipe to the palace."

"Yes, Exalted One. You honor her."

"Your wife is a proper woman?" Kalig leaned forward and peered intently at Lorn.

Lorn was taken aback by the question. Minerva did not know what could happen, and she shifted nervously in her chair. "Yes, of course she is a proper woman. She was well trained by her mother and observes the precepts of the Lawgiver." Lorn then shrugged and smiled, "Well, I do hear her singing under her breath when she serves my meals, but I do not mind. Her voice is lovely."

Kalig became very still and stared at Lorn. Minerva felt a hot slash of panic rise in her. Oh! Lorn! Do not say any more! Say that you reprimand me and that I am a foolish, silly-minded woman. Please don't say anymore than that. Please don't say enough to have the Examiners called into our home. Behind the doors of their home, they were not proper at all. It would mean becoming Forsaken and Outcast if the liberalities of their home were discovered.

"A lovely voice? Your wife sings as she serves you?"

The banquet hall was silent and still. The men were no longer eating and behind the screen, the women were tensed and unshifting. Minerva felt her throat constricting. Oh! That there was a god to pray to and beseech for mercy and guidance.

"Well," stammered Lorn, "it is not like real music, not like the songs that men sing. It is just little unimportant ditties like the kind that mothers sing to their young. I allow a bit of it, and then I silence her. She does not presume, she just forgets herself. You must admit that she is a fine cook, and if she forgets herself occasionally, I do not discipline her for that shortcoming. I am usually too hungry to take much notice of anything beyond what is on my plate."

"Still, she sings?"

Miserably, Lorn nodded his head. Minerva felt her eyes fill with hopeless tears. Think Lorn. Think of something to say.

"Her voice is lovely?"

"Exalted One! I have rarely heard a woman's voice, so I couldn't really be trusted to judge her voice. It is as the Lawgiver intended. 'If the only women you ever see are your mother and your wife, you will not be inflamed for any woman other than the warm comfort from your mother when you are a child and the flame of fulfillment you receive from your wife. Your life will be pure.' We all know this is a truth. I have only truly heard my wife sing, so I have no comparison. Aside from a glimpse of the faces of the Chosen at Purifications, I know no other face. I do not mind her voice because when she sings, I know that my supper is being served, and she is quite a good cook."

Lorn shrugged his shoulders as if he was intending a joke. For a moment the room was entombed in silence. Then the emperor leaned his head back and laughed. The tension seemed to wash away. "You are conditioned by your hunger, eh? Well, remind her to be silent when your belly allows you to think clearly." The men in the room laughed, some too heartily, relieved that there would be no disaster at the Celebration. Even those that did not agree with Lorn all of the time could not wish for him to become an Outcast. Certain realities were too painful to watch. They all were fallible. Kalig took up his fork and began to eat the spiced meat with gusto. He raised his glass of wine and drained it. The nobles drank, too and then they began to eat their food again, cautiously. They began to talk again, their voices slowly growing confident.

Minerva sagged back into her chair. She felt a hand on her shoulder and turned toward the comfort of the hand. She recognized the insignia of her friend, Pola, on the robed figure next to her. She had shared confidences with her friend as children, and even now they remained friends through the woman's ways. She wished she could smile at her, but no doubt the Examiners were watching.

Suddenly, Kalig slammed his fork down and pushed his plate back. He switched on his amplifier again. The room fell silent.

"Lord Provo, I want to hear her sing."

Minerva felt as if someone had crushed her. No, please Lorn. Think of some way out of this.

"Exalted One," stammered Lorn, his hands clenched his fork so tightly that it began to bend. "I have an honnorable wife. I mean, how could this be possible without shaming her?"

Kalig was the emperor. 'Emperors may be mad, if they need to be!' This is what the Lawgiver taught. 'Cultures need an emperor to do the things that regular men are not inclined to do and are not allowed to do. It is how balance is maintained. They may ask for more than their shares, but they are required to sacrifice their morality to maintain balance.' Kalig was the newest in a very long line of Emperors named Kalig. He knew his rights and his capabilities. Lorn also knew his rights and capabilities. He had been required to observe the terrible Replacement Ritual. He had watched four of the six Purifications in the six years this Kalig had been in power. This Kalig was made of stone and ice.

"I know, Exalted One, I will make a voice imprint of her at our home and send it directly to you this evening. She will be very tired, so I cannot promise she will sound very good. Of course, if I hear her sing, I may get hungry!" The men at the tables laughed nervously, hoping the jest was enough to dissuade the emperor from pursuing this further. Lorn was tense, and the men surrounding him were also tensed. It was a good idea, though there were very few imprints of voices made. The Lawgiver did not prohibit them, but strongly cautioned against voice imprints being made of people singing. Apparently, during the reign of the Corrupt Nation, there had been entire industries devoted to singing raucous songs and imprinting them on a variety of devices. Perhaps this would appease the emperor enough to keep his standings among the noble houses and still not disobey the temperamental Kalig.

Kalig frowned. "I do not believe I am willing to wait to hear her. I would like for her to sing right now. Call her forward and instruct her to sing." He waved his hand diffidently, "I will instruct the Examiners that none should suffer for this." Kalig smiled benevolently at the nobles. "You will be spared the purification rituals, though you must all cover your ears. Now, call your wife forward and instruct her to sing for me. Is not the Emperor like a father to all of his subjects? Fathers are allowed to hear their daughter's voices. Tell my daughter to come and sing for her father. Come now, I want to hear her sing."

Minerva watched in numb disbelief as Lorn raised his arm in the ritual summons. Her many years of training took control of her legs and she rose and crossed to her husband's chair. She stopped the required three paces behind him. Behind the screen, there was the sound of muffled crying.

"Wife, the Father of Civilization requires you to sing. Make it so and we will all honor you." Lorn's voice was thick and the words seemed to fall from his lips like heavy stones.

Minerva stood silently behind her husband and she was trembling. She burned beneath her robes, and then she felt like ice. She could not think of a song and her voice was caught in her throat. An eternity of silence resounded throughout the room. The nobles all had their ears covered and they had all turned their backs to her. Oh! Please! Let a god appear that she might pray for deliverence.

"Wife," Lorn's voice was strained and she could see that his shoulders were tensed beneath his finery. "The Father of Civilazation requires you to sing...." And then his voice strained out like a gasp, "Make it so, and we will all honor you."

Minerva forced herself to breath in deeply. She would sing the song she knew the best, the old lullaby she made for her babies. She had sung it a million times when Bota was colicky, pacing the floor late at night singing and patting the fretful baby. She had to sing it again. She squeezed her eyes shut and concentrated on how it felt to have one of her five babies in her arms. She must not open her eyes. She began to sing.

"Close your eyes, my sweet baby," her voice was like a thin wavery thread.

"Rest your head, my lovely child." She could not find enough breath for this.

"It's time to sleep, my sweet baby," She listened to her own voice and opened her eyes.

"Love will hold you through the night." She focused her eyes on the back of her husband's head.

"I'll gather stars to guide your way," She did not want to shame her husband before the Emperor. She sank into the song.

"They'll guide your dreams to tomorrow.
And when the night-time fades away-
We will know no sorrow.
So, close your eyes, my sweet baby,
Rest your head, my lovely child.
I hold you softly, my sweet baby-
This love guards you through the night..."

Minerva ended her lullaby, and the room remained silent. She dared not move, and she willed her legs to hold her erect. She kept her eyes on her husband's back. Please Lorn. Give her the signal to return to her seat. Lorn was looking at the Emperor, waiting for a sign from him that this ordeal was over. Minerva dared not turn her head to see what the emperor was doing. After what seemed far too long, Lorn raised his hand in the signal that she was to return to her seat. Breathe. She bowed her head and turned, trying not to stumble or rush. Control. Control. She measured her steps as if she was walking in front of the Examiners. She made her way to the screen and still she measured her steps as if she was being judged by the Examiners. As she walked she felt the light touches of fingertips from those wives that knew her and those that wanted to comfort her. She wanted to weep. Please, oh god of her imaginings. Spare her from any more disaster. She sank into her chair, exhausted in body and mind. The room was still silent. Please. She breathed. Begin to talk...move past this moment. Let it be a small thing.

The Emperor spoke.

"That was not unpleasant. Of course, a woman's voice does not truly sing, not real music. Not music that stirs a man's soul to the greater heights. Still, it was affecting on some level. Tell me, truthfully, how many of you have listened to your wives sing?"

There was a thick silence. The women around Minerva seemed to tense and she could not hear any stirring. She watched through the screen as the men sat uncertainly, shifting in their seats.

"Oh, come now. You are all forgiven for your weaknesses. Surely Sir Provo is not the only man here that has heard his wife sing and has found himself enjoying the strange tones. I myself, have distant memories of my mother's voice, though I cannot remember any of the music. Now, tell me, men. How many of you have happened upon your wife when she is singing a tune. Come now."

A few of the men tentatively raised their hands, and then a few more. Lord Simon did not. Minerva mentally moaned. Lord Simon would find a way to turn this into a scandal. Please, many men raise your hands. Make this a common problem among women, to foolishly sing in the presense of their husbands. More men raised their hands...please more, enough to insulate Lorn from being singled out by Lord Simon. Please, more. No. It wasn't enough. It was many, but not enough.

"Ahh!" the Emperor said rising slightly in his seat so that he could see who all had raised his hand. "There are some honest men in my court." He sank back into his chair. "I would imagine it would be hard not to hear the voice of your woman at least once in your life." He spoke again, though not to anyone. "It is not like being here in the palace, separated by many floors and protocol from the women that are serving their emperor. They come to me in silence, and they never defy any precept of the Lawgiver. I have only distant memories of the sound of a woman's voice...."

The Emperor fell silent. He picked up his cup and drained the wine in one drink. The nobles drank. He sat in a silence that shrouded him like a deep night.

"I have to wonder if my son will remember some distant shred of his mother's voice. I have to wonder if it will feel like this for him." His whisper was amplified in his forgotten microphone. " 'The Emperor will know little comfort'. That is what the Lawgiver said. 'Little comfort so he will reach far for glory to fill the echoing silence'."

Kalig sat up straight and looked resolved, as if some conflict was solved for him.

"Chosen, I wish for you to come forward and sing for me. I need to hear the voice my son will remember. Here in the presence of many, so all will know that you have not spoken to me directly as it is decreed. Come here now." There was an edge of command and anger in his voice.

Chiria came forward, her steps halting, her tension evident even through her robes. She came forward and knelt heavily before Kalig. She placed her forehead on the floor and stretched her hands out, palm up as if in supplication. Kalig leaned forward and gazed at her as if her attitude were a puzzle.

"Chosen, you are in the position of one who wishes mercy from the Emperor. Am I to infer that you do not wish to sing for me?"

Chiria nodded without looking up.

"Nonsense! I have the right to hear the tones that my son will hear when you put him to sleep. Stand before me and sing a lullaby. That is what they are called, these little songs that are sung to babies. Lullabies. I command you to sing one for me now. A lullaby."

Chiria climbed slowly to her feet. Her shoulders drooped and she did not seem to be able to raise her head. Minerva watched her sadness and despair, and she felt her insides clench in sympathy. If there were a prayer to say, she would have prayed it. She would have prayed, "Oh! Ancient God of all Heaven and Creator of all! Help this captive find a voice and sing!" That is what she would have prayed, if there were such a thing as prayer.

Chiria seemed deflated by the command to sing. The moments of silence were thunderous. The men were silent, and most had their heads bowed. One man had put his head on the table and was silently sobbing. That must be Chiria's father. Minerva wondered who her mother was, and how she might be bearing this shameful spectacle. Chiria drew in a deep breath. She began to sing. Her voice was thin and wavering and unlovely. She did not seem to know how to change notes, and her song grated across Minerva's ears like sharp shards of stone. Minerva did not know that a voice could be so harsh. Kalig raised his hand impatiently, stopping her song. He looked annoyed.

"Chosen One, that was terrible." He spoke through his teeth. "I cannot have you singing to my son." He waved her away. "Sir Provo, how is it that your wife makes her voice so pleasant? What did she do to learn this skill?"

Lorn stiffened. "Sire, I am a follower of the Lawgiver's instructions. My wife forgets herself and sings as she busys herself with my meals. I do not know if women study singing as part of their training. Perhaps it is a talent as it is with men, though I have little understanding of music, being unskilled in the practice. I would imagine that women have their societies just as we do. I would imagine they explore their abilities together. There are many gifts available to them, just like there are gifts available to us. It would stand to reason. Perhaps my wife sings because it is a part of who she is, and your Chosen does not sing because it is not a part of her."

"That is sensible reasoning, Sir Provo. That is why I value you when it comes to negotiationg difficult matters. But, tell me this, do you think that the Chosen One can learn to sing? If they have their own societies, then they must have some method to teach their skills. Perhaps the Chosen did not have the opportunity to learn because of the nature of separated communities. Perhaps there was not a singing teacher in the Chosen's Grouping, and she did not have the opportunity to learn."

"Of course, that must be it, Sire. Women must have their own teachers and such. I would imagine that there are many special talents among them, though we are removed from them at such a young age that we do not realize what is happening among them. I do not know very much about it all. Aside from my distant memories of my mother and sisters, the only true memory of women I have are the memories I have of my own wife. Well, I have glimpsed the faces of the Chosen at their purifications, but that is all I know."

"Well then, you know more than I do. I have only the Chosen, and I do not know if they are acceptable or not based on my experiences. I am assured by the Examiners that they are the best examples of the species, but now I have my doubts. I taste your wife's cooking, and I realize there are better cooks in my Empire than my Chosen. I am not complaining, but many take notice of where your wife places her dishes at these celebrations and enjoy her offerings. I have heard your wife sing, and her voice is stirring and lovely. I wish she were still singing. Now I have to wonder if she is excellent in every way, superior to my Chosen. Perhaps she is very beautiful. Now I am curious about her."

Minerva listened to the Emperor with growing horror. She began to shake, and without knowing it, she began to moan softly. The women around her drew closer to her. "Hush," one whispered urgently in her ear. "Keep your wits, sister," said another.

"Sire, she does well because of her experience." Lorn was struggling to keep the desperation out of his voice. "Why, she has had years to learn how to cook and all that. As for her singing, it is just a thing that happened. She is just an ordinary woman, I would imagine. As for being beautiful, well, she is pleasant enough in her way. From the brief glimpses I have had of your Chosen, she is not remarkable at all in comparison. It shows the wisdom of the Lawgiver that ordinary men like myself are not given many women to look at. I am content with her, though I am certain she would not be to your liking. The Examiners did not offer her to the former Kalig, and she was Proven like every young woman."

"Well, that might be true. Still, I need to know if I am being properly served by the Chosen." He raised his arm in a summons. Chiria, still halting and shaken, rose and came forward. "Summon your wife, Sir Provo. Command her to show me her face."

"Sire, no! Please reconsider. My wife is an honorable woman."

There were murmurs of assent throughout the room.

"I will not dishonor your wife. I want to see her face. I am the father of this Empire. Fathers are allowed to see the faces of their children. Show me her face now, and I will let the matter drop. I will be content and not look at the faces of all of the children behind these screens."

The men in the room turned their faces to Lorn in almost one accord. Most of them had pleading eyes, some of the eyes looked hopeless, and some of the eyes looked furious. Lorn raised his arm in summons.

Minerva could not make herself stand. She could not. Her legs refused to move.

"Sister, save us. We will honor you. We will love you." The women around her whispered pleading encouragements and they lifted her to her feet. She sagged against them, unable to walk. Carefully, the women took her to her place behind Lorn. Two stayed with her, holding her up. Minerva kept her eyes tightly closed against the movements around her. She could hear the nobles standing, and she knew they were turning their backs to her. The women holding her up were supporting her with their backs to the approaching Emperor. They were holding her up by her arms and whispering, quiet encouragements. She felt as if she were in a fog. She heard Lorn's voice as if it were coming from a far away place.

"Honorable wife, the Emperor, the Father of Truth wishes to see the face of his child. I am going to remove your veil...Know that we honor you for your obedience to the Empire."

She felt Lorn's hands touching her veil, lifting it from her face. She felt a rush of cool air and her nostrils were suddenly filled with the smell of many foods and the smell of her husband's sweat. Yes. He would be suffering, too. He was exhausted too. He would be afraid too. She heard the steps of the Emperor as he approached her.

"Open your eyes, daughter."

Minerva forced her eyes open. Kalig was standing in front of her, his hands behind his back. He looked at her the same way she looked at vegetables from her garden. She had never had her appearance judged before. She saw in his eyes that he did not approve of her looks. She realized that she was probably disheveled and sweaty and tearstained. He looked at her as if she were a distasteful insect or some such thing. No one had ever looked at her like that before. She knew she was exhausted and that she probably had dark circles under her eyes. She hoped she looked like a demon, and that she was frightening this beast of a man into sensibilities. Kalig had turned his attention to the silent, drooping Chosen. He lifted her veil and studied her face with the same dispassionate judgement as Lorn lowered Minerva's veil. Kalig's eyes were stones. He gestured to her that she could go to her seat. Woodenly she allowed the women to lead her back to her seat. She was drained. She felt violated. She felt ugly. She had never felt ugly before.

The Emperor's voice loomed into her consciousness. "Sir Provo, I offer you my apologies for my imposition.

You are right. Your wife may have gained great worth and is honorable, but she is just a plain woman. I do believe that I prefer my Chosen's appearance. However, I would like for you to bring your plain wife to the palace this next week to teach my Chosen to sing properly. My sons will live lives of great sacrifice, and they must have the distant memory of a lullaby to comfort them in their last hours. From now on, I will require that the Examiners listen to newly Chosen sing, as an assurance that my sons will have that comfort."

"It is a wise decision, Sire. I will bring my wife when arrangements can be made." Lorn was speaking carefully. He must not betray his anger. He must be strong. Surely this ordeal was over.

Kalig looked about the room. His eyes flashed with annoyance. "Men of the Empire, this is a celebration. Why aren't you eating? Eat! Drink! We have a captured barbarian queen to educate in the ways of the Empire. It is glorious. Eat!"

The men picked up their forks and silently they ate.

— Chapter 18 —

The sun filtered in through the curtains and pierced Minerva's sleep. She moaned and turned over, her body leaden with heavy sleep and long labors. Ahh! How was it that she had slept so long? Why was she in the never-used wife's room instead of in bed with Lorn? If the sun was shining through the curtains of this room it must be afternoon....

She threw back the covers and drew herself up into a sitting position as if she were pulling a great, heavy bucket out of a well. She paused as the memories of the night before flooded back and filled her up with a new heaviness. She was in the wife's room because she had collapsed last evening and the Examiners had escorted Lorn and Minerva home. Somehow, Lorn had managed to alert the children, and the household was proper when they got home, separate and silent. Minerva only had vague impressions, but she felt certain that all was well, or else there would be bars on her door. She stood and crossed to the tiny bathroom. She needed to wash the old sweat smell off and think clearly. She had to be proper until she was certain that last evening's events were sorted out. "The whim of the Emperor must be endured to pay the price for his sacrifices." Blast that miserable Lawgiver and his miserable platitudes.

She stepped into her shower and turned on the water. She adjusted the timer for an extra five minutes and raised the temperature setting five degrees. She chose a relaxing lavender scented soap to be added to the water. Yes...that would do. She rubbed the soap into her hair, scrubbing her arms and legs, across her belly. She wanted to feel clean. She wanted to wash away the memory of the emperor's eyes looking at her as if she were an unacceptable creature. She wanted to feel the way Lorn made her feel when he looked at her, like she was precious. She wanted to find him and have him look at her a long time, until the memory of the Emperor's eyes was diminished.

The water started running clear and she knew that she only had just a few minutes left before she had to dress in her impossible clothing and step into the pretend life of a proper wife. She knew there would probably be Examiners visiting under a variety of pretexts for quite some time, even with the assurances of Kalig that there would be no problems for them for obeying his whims. The Law is greater than the ruler.

The water trickled to a halt. She stepped through the doorway and braced herself for the cyclone of air the whirled around her, drying her. She chose the most traditional robes she owned and reluctantly put them on. She saw that Lorn or one of the children had already filled her closet with the dark, proper clothing. Usually, women were allowed to wear their shifts about in the women's quarters, but Minerva decided not to chance it for a few days. She stepped through the doorway of the Wife's room. The chime sounded that indicated she was available for summons. It was a strange sound to her. Usually, she woke up with Lorn, pressed up against his back. She heard someone in the Women's Quarters stirring and her second daughter, Tooya came into the hallway where Minerva was standing. She was dressed in her robes and was semi-veiled.

"Mother! Are you back among us? I saved you some breakfast. Then I saved you some lunch. Hope you are hungry!"

"Yes, I am. What did you fix?"

" I fixed a stew. It wasn't quite right, but we all survived it."

Minerva smiled wanly at her daughter. She was a disaster in the kitchen, unlike her brother who was an excellent cook. Examiners must have been here, then, if Tooya was cooking. She imagined that Born was very unhappy about being kept out of the kitchen. She wished that there would be a place in the New Lands where Born could cook and Tooya would be forbidden to go near a kitchen. It would be better for everyone... Minerva looked at Tooya standing before her, uncertain and unhappy. She breathed in deeply. Stew. Bad stew. One more thing to survive.

"I'm sure your stew is just fine, Sweetness. I can't wait to fill up."

Tooya looked relieved and grateful at her mother's reaction. Minerva imagined that the rest of the household had not been kind. Resolutely, Minerva followed her daughter to the kitchen and at her daughter's prompting, sat and let her daughter wait on her. Quickly Tooya heated a serving of stew. Rather a stew-like substance. Oh! Tooya! Minerva groaned inwardly but she smiled at her daughter and picked up her spoon and scooped up a spoonful of the slimey goo. Could it be that Tooya had put lettuce in this? She bravely put the spoonful in her mouth. Cherries. Sausage. Minerva focused on the love she felt for her daughter and chewed. Not lettuce, spinach.

"Mother, I made some bread, too." Tooya's voice was just barely louder than a whisper. "It is a little dry."

Tooya sounded very miserable. Minerva swallowed and took a deep drink of water. Bread. By all the worlds, she loved this girl! She looked at Tooya and her heart wrenched inside her. Bread, too.

"I would love some bread...." She struggled to sound encouraging and cheerful.

"Oh, Mother, I know this is terrible!" Tooya whispered painfully, "But they were here and will be back. I am so sorry."

"Hush, it will be fine!" Miverva whispered urgently. The Examiners could have left their clever listening devices hidden and she would have to do some cleaning to find them. "I would love some bread. Is there any jam left?"

Tooya nodded and crossed to the cupboard and took out some jam and set it in front of her mother. Embarrassed, she brought out a dark, lumpy loaf with one end obviously hacked off. Tooya placed it in front of Minerva and turned away, busying herself washing an already clean countertop. Minerva lifted the heavy, dense bread and looked at it closely. Banana chips and dried beef. Boiled egg chunks. Oh. Minerva sighed.

Tooya was gifted in so many other ways. She told the most amazing stories to the younger children in the learning groups. She drew wonderful pictures and she invented small tools that were endlessly useful. None of these things would matter for her. It would matter for her to cook something edible. It seemed an impossible task because Tooya couldn't bring herself to follow recipes. She just had to try something new.

Minerva sighed and rose from her chair. "Tooya," she crossed to her daughter, "This isn't the end of the world. We will find a way to incorporate this attempt. There will be no waste." Minerva sighed deeply. The laws against waste were as strict as any. She heard that the waste of the Empire was barely enough to keep the Forsaken alive. Minerva shuddered. A Forsaken would be happy to have this. "Right now, I think I will have something else, though. We will have this turned into a delicacy before you know it, but now I need something quick and easy. I haven't the energy to chew this!" Minerva hoped her voice had the right amount of tenderness and humor in it. Tooya had to learn to control her impulses, but making her miserable wouldn't help her now. Tooya nodded tightly. Minerva opened her arms to her daughter, and Tooya sagged into her mother's arms. Minerva wished that cooking was less important to the future of daughters. It would be a kindness if there were some other way to measure their worth. Minerva patted her daughter and released her. There was much to do, but first she needed something for her growling stomach. She set some water to boil and added an egg. Boiled egg and some dried fruit for now. Simple and quick. She looked at Tooya and added an egg for her as well. Tooya looked grateful. She must be hungry, too. Everyone must be hungry, but the boys would have to wait for the proper time for eating since they would all be under scrutiny.

Soon the meager meal was prepared and they sat at the preparation table and ate the eggs and fruit. It was a good moment to be here with Tooya. In just three short years she would be married and gone like her sister. Minerva missed Jolliann, her oldest daughter, but she was glad she had recently been married to a young man from a good family. The men all had scarred hands, and Lorn said the young man now had scarred hands. Only Lorn could see Jolliann since her husband's family lived in another complex of houses and there were no common courtyards for them to cross through to see each other. It was the generation for movement and it was hard on everyone.

In the distant past, women could go wherever they wanted to go, but that changed when the Lawgiver established order. Homes were arranged into village groups and the social needs were all met within that group. That meant that children were married within the village, and it was possible for parents to keep in contact with their children. Every fourth generation, though, the children were married to those in different villages to prevent inbreeding. All of the daughters had to leave their villages and go to the villages of their husbands and live there. It was hard, but it made the Empire strong by building strong loyalties in small communities and in the city as well. Connections. Well, that was what the Lawgiver said. All Minerva knew was that she missed Jolliann, and in three years, she would miss Tooya.

Her thoughts were interrupted by the summoning gong. That would only mean that the Examiners had come. Lorn never summoned her like this unless it was necessary. She started up and hurried to her room to retrieve her heavy veil. Hastily, she arranged it as she half ran to the door leading to the men's quarters. It was stupid of her to leave it behind; she should have known to keep it at hand. She stopped at the door to regain her composure. "The honorable wife is serene, untroubled by conflict." Whoever wrote that had rat dung for brains. Oh yes. It was the Lawgiver. She forced her thoughts away from her ironies.

Breathe! Examiners were just men. They had no special powers, just uncommon authority. They had no great insight, though their alterations gave them the ability to think without sentiment. Be serene. Be silent. She pushed through the door and quickly placed her hands inside her sleeves so that none of her skin was showing. She went to the wife's place and stood silently. She was glad for once to be veiled against the stares of the Examiners. She was surprised to see there were three of them. That was a good thing. Three meant they were here for inquiry or information. If there were five she would be concerned. Five meant judgement.

"Lord Provo, we require speech with your wife." The Examiner's voice had the high, eerie quality of all of the Examiners. Minerva had read that in the very distant past, even before the Corrupt Nation, procedures had performed on young boys that could sing well so their voices would not change and they could sing the high parts in choral arrangements. In the most ancient past, men and boys were altered so they could guard the harems of wealthy men. It was ironic to her that the manhood of those boys was squandered for music or sacrificed for the breeding purity of a rich man's harem. It was as though they were sacrificed for no good reason.

Minerva had to wonder if these men, too, had sacrificed too much for the Empire, even though they were given uncommon authority. Castration was castration no matter how it was compensated. It made them so different from everyone else that Minerva wondered how they could make their judgemants. It was as though they were a different species, separated and fearsome. They were trained in the most deadly arts and they lived strange, austure lifestyles. Still, history had proven that societies functioned more smoothly when there was a cloistered portion of the population that governed morality. At least that was the rationale.

"Speak, then, to my wife," Lorn responded formally. "Speak to her in my presence as is proper."

"Wife of Lord Provo, Minerva by name, we require your obedience in the service of the Empire. First, we require that you accompany your husband to the ship that is returning in triumph with the barbarian queen. She is difficult and requires touching. The contingent is no longer willing to manage her, and it has been decided to sedate her. You and several other wives will be required to administer the sedative and accompany her to the palace cloister. Further, while you are at the palace, you will be required to teach the Chosen, Chiria, to sing. Additionally, you will be required to teach all of the Chosen to cook the dish you served at the Celebration last evening. If you know other savory dishes, it is the Emperor's wish that you cook them as well. Do this to serve and soothe the troubles of the Emperor who serves his people with dedication and perserverance. Prepare to accompany your husband!"

Minerva felt light-headed. She was going to a ship? She was going to actually see the barbarian queen? Suddenly, the walls of her house seemed wonderful and safe. She did not want to go anywhere.

"Lord Provo," the Examiner continued. "Prepare yourself and your wife to accompany us!" With that, the three Examiners turned to leave the house. At the door one of them turned and looked at Minerva steadily.

"Wife of Lord Provo, be cautioned against singing in the presence of you husband. He does not need to hear your voice. 'Only the voice of reason should be in a man's ears. Only the voice of truth. Let all other voices be silent and let the troubles of the weak be confined to the hinder places.' This is what keeps us strong and mighty! If the sound of your weakness becomes common, what will become of us? That the Emperor desires a woman to sing in the palace is no indication that it will be tolerated anywhere else. His madness is as it should be."

Minerva bowed her head as if she agreed. Inside her sleeves, her fists clenched. She tried to breathe slowly through the red wash of fury. It was a certainty then, the Examiners would be listening to their home for any unnecessary word exchanged. That would be torturous until they could find the listening devices and place them in one of the illegal loop boxes that some men with scarred hands owned. She raised her head and turned to Lorn, searching for his eyes. He was looking at her furtively, afraid the Examiners would turn suddenly and catch him with his eyes on her. She did not want him to be caught trying to consol her with his eyes. She did not want him to be Purified for something that happened in their own home. He had endured that once for loving her. She did not want him to have to endure it again.

She squared her shoulders with a purpose and prepared to follow him. Relief flooded his face and he strode to the door behind the Examiners. The last Examiner turned and glanced over his shoulder and the look of satisfaction that Lorn was following and Minerva behind him, was disgusting to Minerva. Stupid rules. One day, she would sneak out of the village and find the shrine of the Lawgiver and spit on it. She wanted to take her veil off and feel the sunshine on her face. She wanted to hold Lorn's hand. She followed him silently.

— Chapter 19 —

Sojourner felt the stillness of the ship as keenly as she had felt its movement. She did not know what they would make of Lyla's disappearance when they finally managed to pry the door of her cell open. It had been a difficult voyage for them, poor sailors. Sojourner felt a pang of remorse for them. It sounded like her escapades were going to cause all of the men to undergo Purification. What a horrible thing to endure! The Examiners must be castrated, sterile monsters. Scrubbed raw and bleeding and cleansed with stinging salt water. Purged until there was blood. How terrible! The Empire should be happy to have that custom changed and the terrible Examiners removed.

Sojourner was appalled at how incomplete the intelligence gathered on the Empire had been through the years. How could so many things have been ommitted or overlooked by the operatives? It had always been difficult to send intelligence from the Empire because the Empire monitored its airwaves. It was hard to know the extent of the Empire's technology. Apparently, it was not very evolved. It seemed that they were using only the most ancient of power sources, and it hampered the Burrow's when they tried to establish links within the vastly different systems. Of course Empire technologies were refined versions of ancient technologies, but there was little progress and the pollution and waste were appalling. How could it be the Empire inventors had not discovered the Harmonies? It was the next natural step. Well, perhaps not. The Empire had never had to survive underground for close to a thousand years. One had to live close to the earth to discover such truths. Sojourner knew the Burrows were very advanced compared to the Empire, but she had not realize how much more advanced until she rode on this polluted monster of a ship.

She heard the raking sounds of the sailors attempting to pry open the door's seal. They were half crazed in their desire to be rid of her. In the three days she had been on the ship she had caused terrible disruptions to their lives and routines. She had not only delayed them a number of times by stalling their engines, but for the past day or so, she had managed to program holo-images of herself throughout the decks telling stories day and night. The sailors were frantic. She was glad that Lyla was already safe in the Burrows. She was certain that the crew would have torn her to bits in their frustration because they knew they could not harm the Barbarian Queen.

The noises grew more intense. It was time. Stephan's voice crackled through the air.

"My sweet, we have just received word that a group of nobles' wives are being brought on board to sedate you. They will arrive within a few minutes. You may want to take a buffer so as to not be so sick when you awaken. They are also going to take all of your things and robe you so you will not have all of your supplies. Can you conceal some on your person?"

"Yes! I still have the nail covers and all of the hair strands. I have smoothed some Deep Heal on me; they may not notice it. I have listened to the orders being given on deck. Oh well. Is there an operative in the palace that will be able to help me?"

"Yes, Josilyn and Elfin are in the Empire."

" A Gardner and a Healer! Wonderful! I thought they had gone to the expansions"

"In a way they did!" Stephan chuckled. "They are drudges in the palace."

Sojourner caught her breath. A Healer and a Gardner scrubbed the floors of the palace? It was not right to waste such talent. Still, she was glad that they would be there. Maybe she would get her things back soon.

The seal around the door gave a screeching wrench, and a corner of it was pried loose.

"It is time, my heart. I love you." Sojourner suddenly wished she had left with Lyla.

"And you, my sweet. You will win them over." Stephan's voice sounded strained, full of hope and sorrow. Sojourner sighed. She knew too much of voices. To make a voice sound so full while trying to sound careful was painful to hear.

Sojourner steeled herself. There were so many things to think about. She understood the nobles' wives would be coming in to overpower her and sedate her. She needed to be prepared for that. She was relieved that she would not have to see their faces or hear their voices. They would be silent, shrouded attackers. She needed to relax and not allow herself to be hurt. The door to her cell gave another wrenching screech as it was pried further open. Sojourner smiled resignedly and deactivated the seal she had placed on her cell. The door flew open, scattering the sweaty crew members and their tools. She stepped to the doorway. Might as well make an entrance.

"Greetings wives of the nobility. I am one of the many. I am Sojourner, a Storyteller. I bring you my best thoughts."

The wives of the nobility stood in a row by the railing of the ship. Between Sojourner and the wives, the men who had been trying to pry the cell open were climbing to their feet and gathering their tools. Several of them still lay prone, unconscious from their sudden fall. Captain Jarvo and his squad stood at attention off to the side. Sojourner felt a pang of guilt. All of these men would be suffering through their Purification Rituals in the next few days. Scrubbed and purged within an inch of their lives. These extra bumps and bruises would make it more difficult for those that had fallen. It was an impossible culture.

There were five wives assembled by the railing, and off to the side there were a group of men that must be their husbands. There were also several odd looking individuals dressed in severe robes with them. They must be the Examiners that Lyla had spoken of. Their faces were smooth and had the soft, rounded look of very old boys. Still, their bodies looked lean and hard under their robes. Lyla had said they were trained from early life to be deadly fighters. Their alterations and training were intended to give them an authority and mystique among the population. They had the look of aloneness and brokenness about them. Sojourner wondered if it was possible to restore them. One of the Examiners said something to the wives, his voice high pitched and grating; the wives stepped forward toward Sojourner with measured reluctance, careful to not brush against the unconscious men on deck.

Sojourner pitched her voice to convey consolation and authority, "So, you are Examiners. I would imagine that we could find some way to fix you right up back home in the Burrows. It would take some doing, but you could be regular men in no time at all. Don't be too self-conscious about your oddities because with some effort and a good will you can be Healed. Just don't speak until you have received treatment, and most wouldn't even recognize there is something wrong."

The women stopped their careful forward stepping. Everyone fell silent and turned their eyes toward Sojourner. The Examiners stiffened almost in one accord.

Sojourner continued, adding a slight edge to her voice intended to make the listeners feel remorseful and self-conscious, "Don't be too concerned that your skewed thinking will be a hindrance either. We will, no doubt, be stretched to find Handlers for all of you, and those of you who are older may have to settle for behavioral implants for a span of time, but I am confident you will all be altered and regenerated in good time. Be patient."

"Silence Barbarian Infidel!" One of the Examiners stepped forward, his face contorting with outrage and disgust.

"Infidel? How can I be unfaithful? What am I not believing in? You use words you do not understand! My poor mangled fellow, you have much to learn about proper definitions! Your poor Lyla told me about your Lawgiver. As for being a Barbarian, when your Empire is dismantled, we will sit and speak of this. I am certain your Emperor will want a treaty with us before it comes to that. That is why I am consenting to this charade. We are prepared to contain your people and cull them for our purposes, but we would rather negotiate with you. Notify your Ambassadors. Prepare the conferences. You haven't much time. We have much to accomplish before the shields are activated!" Sojourner pitched her voice with the overtones of authority and urgency, though she smiled in a disarming way. The Examiner stopped, confused. Sojourner continued, "Ask these sailors what I have done on this ship with just my small technologies and my poor understanding of them. I would tell you to ask Lyla about our healing and other skills, but she has been freed and sent to the Burrows as our Maker wills. Her faith is small, but she will soon be whole."

The Examiner seemed to wrestle with his impulses. He glanced quickly at his comrades and then, again, stiffened. Sojourner felt her heart sink. Her voice may not be an asset here. Perhaps the training she had received was only valid with the people of the Burrows because their population was genetically narrowed by their long years of isolation. Perhaps the vocal pitches needed to stimulate the neural connecters to illicit specific reactions were dissimilar. Maybe she was useless here among this diverse population. Her stories may be useless, and her voice may be useless. The thought sent an icy tingle up her spine. She did not have many advantages. She prayed that reason would be enough.

She squared her shoulders, "So which of you ladies has the sedative? Just step forward and administer it. I understand you are compelled to do this...I just ask that a couple of you hold me up so that I don't fall. We grandmothers have brittle bones."

Sojourner was unprepared for the reaction to her words. The crew members that were still conscious fell to their knees and covered their faces. The nobles that had been standing apart also began to tremble and hide their faces. The Examiners stood with ashen faces.

"Grandmother?" squeaked one. "You are a wife?"

Captain Jarvo strode forward, his face stern and his demeanor commanding. "Hold there! No fear! This woman lies. We observed her for an entire year, and we saw no evidence of a husband or children. We saw no grandchildren. We saw her behave in unnatural ways and speak terrible lies continually. She lies! If she were not a queen of the barbarian land, she would be Forsaken. Trust my eyes and have no fear. This is not an honorable wife."

Sojourner watched the men on the deck regain their composure. They drew in shaky breaths and wiped tears and sweat from their faces. They glanced self-consciously at each other, trying to place distance between themselves and their fear. Sojourner was intrigued with their reaction. She turned her attention to Captain Jarvo. She must use her voice carefully here. She knew Captain Jarvo, though he did not understand her knowledge. Authority, intimacy, pity, kindliness must be present, a tricky mix. Fortunately, Captain Jarvo had been carefully monitored, and she did know that these vocal movements would work on him.

"You do not know much dear Captain Jarvo. You do not know that we watched you constantly and that we all know every detail of you and your adventures in our land. You are married, and you miss your wife, Jenta, I believe she is called. You would dream about her and touch her soft skin in your sleep. You have eaten seven pet cats during your time in my country, and the leaders of our Burrows are hoping that there are plenty of cats in your country that we can import to replenish the deficit. But until then, I suppose we have to play out the story, and this is part of it."

Sojourner stepped forward and extended her arm toward the small group of women. "Let's begin this."

One of the women turned to the wife holding the sedative and took it from her with a resolute set to her shoulders. She walked over to Sojourner with measured steps.

"I greet you." Sojourner spoke softly, her voice tinged with patience and motherly concern. "I am one of the many, I am Sojourner. I forgive you..."

The woman paused, and Sojourner heard her draw in a deep shaky breath. She took Sojourner's arm as the other women surrounded her to catch her and keep her from falling.

Softly the woman whispered, her breath laced with hushed tears, "I greet you, Sojourner. I am Minerva. I am sorry..."

Sojourner felt the bite of the needle in her arm and then she sank into darkness.

~ Chapter 20 ~

Ivan Jarvo's heart pounded in his chest. The harlot was impossible, even to the last! She had, admittedly, surprised them all with her ability to disrupt things aboard the ship. Now there was this new problem. The Forsaken Chosen would be torn apart when the men found her. The men were not allowed to leave the ship until she was found, and the anger that would be directed toward her would be unforgiving. It had taken all of Commander Po's and Jarvo's abilities to bring the men under control enough to begin a systematic search. It did not bode well that one of the Examiners remained to supervise the search. They had been looking for hours, the ship being meticuliously scoured with an intense sense of purpose.

Lieutenant Bosson was the only one not engaged in the search. The harlot had done something to him, and the ship's doctor had been hard pressed to determine how she had managed to place the devilish device controlling him so deep in his brain. It was impossible to remove it. Ivan had always found Bosson's appetite for punishment unsettling and had often wondered why he was not an Examiner. Still, the pitiful, huddled creature on the infirmary bed stirred his pity. Bosson was frightened and frightening. His behavior had become bizarre and self-destructive. He had spent a morning crowing on the deck like a crazed rooster, strutting and crowing and weeping because he could not stop. He had washed himself in the latrine water. He had danced like a madman on the tables during mess. Since the search began, he had been inconsolable, rocking and wailing in fear and panic. The ship's doctor had given him dose after dose of powerful seditive, and he finally slept a deep, drugged sleep. Still, he whimpered and tossed occasionally. It was terrible. And the Purification Rites were still ahead, even for Bosson. The Harlot was evil.

The men were nearing an end to their search. There were no other places to look. The Forsaken was gone. The Examiner was grim-faced and the atmosphere was thick with tension and fear. How could this have happened? There was no place for her to go except the deep brine of the ocean. Surely she did not jump over during one of their escapades? It was more likely that she was thrown overboard by the Evil One so she could build her mystique. He hoped he would be able to complete the Purification Rituals in a timely manner so that he might speak openly about the unnaturalness of this terrible creature.

An Examiner strode into the control room.

"It is complete as the Law requires." His voice had the hoarse quailty of someone that had been shouting for far too long. It made his voice sound even more eerie. "Somehow, the Forsaken has been removed from the ship. Perhaps the wretched creature is dead. Perhaps the unclean woman killed her and disposed of her. There is no consequence for manufacturing the death of an Outcast or a Forsaken. They are dead already. As long as the Forsaken is no longer on the ship, we must proceed. We have prepared additional accommodations for the large number of Purifications needed. Organize your men into groups of ten, and we will begin this task. It is unfortunate the unclean woman has compromised you all. When it is time to end her, we will be certain she remember her crimes."

Ivan did not respond. He did not realize that it was already a given that she be terminated at the end of this. Of course, it was for the best that so unnatural a woman be ended. It would demoralize her people and make the occupation of their land much easier. Of course, it was for the best. Impatiently, he pushed the thoughts of the barbarian queen from his mind. He had much to do to organize the crew into suitable groups for the Purification Rituals. He must group the men carefully, placing those that were afraid with those that were able to endure pain stoically. He was careful to scatter the members of his squad in with the ship's crew. His squad was always aware they would require Purifying, and had many months to mentally prepare for the rite. Unfortuanately for the crew of the ship, none were mentally prepared. Many were terrified and Jarvo was afraid they would be resistant. It would have been better if they had found the Forsaken and been able to vent their anger on her. Now, they had no true crime to repent of, and they felt the harsh judgement keenly.

Jarvo kept his own fear and concern tightly reined. He knew that the men would gather courage from him and face their difficult task with bravery if he faced it with great control. Still, in his deepest places, he was afraid. He was too nauseated to eat, but he choked down a meal at mess as though he was tending to a regular day instead of facing his skin being scrubbed bloody.

Although the day dragged as he organized his men into groups, his time to begin his ritual cleansing came suddenly and too soon. The Examiners came for him and his group like those who prepared animals for slaughter. Their demeanor was neutral, as if what was going to happen was commonplace and of little consequence. Of course, to an Examiner, this would be commonplace. Their lives were harsh, and they were purified numerous times a year. "Harsh requirements must be given by those that are harsher than the requirements." The Lawgiver designed the Examiners as personifications of pure Law, genderless, single-minded, self-righteous, unforgiving.

Ivan followed the Examiner to the waiting transport with stoic resolve. The men in his group followed, most trying to match his resolve. The ride to the Purification center was short, and Ivan was thankful for that. A long ride would have frayed the nerves of his men even further.

The Purification Center was a huge, sprawling building designed to resemble a sunburst, with long wings projecting off of a vast, circular center. It was beautiful and gleaming, built from carved blocks of pristine white marble. Around it, gardens and groves of fruit trees thrived. There were benches placed in contemplation gardens, though they were rarely used. Most that were purified were unwilling to spend any time in the gardens thinking. The only people ever seen on the grounds were the Examiners that tended to them. It was hard to imagine this great beauty was generated by the same harsh hands that tormented bare flesh into repentence.

Ivan Jarvo tried to show an interest in the gardens and the grandeur of the building. He paid attention to the immaculate marble and the cool rush of air when he entered the great hall. He saw, but he did not see, he attended to details, but only saw a blur. He followed the Examiner that came for him with sure steps, and he wondered that he was able to walk at all. He hoped his men faced this challenge bravely.

The Examiner led him down one of the sunburst arms past many closed doors. Ivan was astonished that it was so silent. His steps sounded like drumbeats, slightly out of beat with the rhythm of the Examiners steps. Almost at the end of the hallway, the Examiner stopped and opened a door. Ivan paused and drew in his breath deeply, gathered his strength, and entered the room. Like the rest of the Purification Center, the room was made of smooth white marble. In the center of the room, there was a broad, square, sunken tub about chest deep, and in the middle of the tub, there was a raised dais with straps on it. For a fleeting moment Ivan considered looking for scars on the Examiner's hand, and he almost laughed out loud at his absurd thought.

The Examiner silently gestured to clothing pegs on the wall and pointed to a thin strip of cloth he was to wind about himself. The Examiner then went to a control panel built into one wall and entered a code. The tub began to fill with water. Ivan stood, unable to begin until the Examiner looked at him and gestured sharply. Ivan began to undress. Surely there must be an easier way to become pure again. A thousand years ago, men would pray to a conjured god that would forgive their sins. It was all so simple that men sinned often and long. It would not be simple today.

Ivan quickly undressed and wound the thin strip of cloth about his waist. The Examiner pointed to the tub in a cursory manner and Ivan lowered himself into the water. It was cool and soothing on his skin, and if there were not so much ahead of him, he would have allowed himself to enjoy it for a moment. Instead, he sat on the dais and waited.

The Examiner turned and began the ritual chants. He stood at the edge of the tub and spread his arms wide. "We are Man! We are Man and we are responsible for the condition of our souls. Our souls belong to the collective thought. Our thoughts must be individually pure to keep the collective thought pure. We are Man."

The Examiner continued chanting the same phrases in his high keening voice, sometimes emphasizing certain words more than others. Ivan felt the water temperature change slowly, growing colder and colder until Ivan felt himself begin to shake as the chill soaked into his skin and deep inside of him. He clenched his teeth. Abruptly, the Examiner stopped his chanting, and the silence seemed enormous. The Examiner slowly began to descend into the tub. In his hand he held a small scraper. Ivan marvelled fleetingly that the Examiner did not seem to feel the frigid water. He did not wonder for very long. The Examiner stood before Ivan and without speaking gestured that he was to lie down on the platform. Ivan felt a moment of panic because he realized that most of his face would be under water. If he lay his head flat, only his nose was out of the water. If he tilted his head back so that his eyes were more deeply submerged, then his mouth was out of the water. He felt the Examiner strap him down, and although he knew he was not going to die, he felt the fear of death.

"Ivan Jarvo, you are here because of the sin in man. You will be purified from sin. I am here to examine you. Examine yourself."

The Examiner then began to gently move the scraper down the length of Ivan's body, removing the cloth as he descended Ivan's body. The sensation was not painful the first time the Examiner scraped over Ivan's body, but the second time it ached and stung. The third time it felt like his skin was crawling with stinging bugs. He felt his breath gasping in and out of his lungs, though he was afraid to breath too deeply fearing that he would suck in water. Ivan lost count of how many times his body was cleansed by the small scraper. He did not know how many times he lost control of his breathing and sucked in choking swirls of water. Still, the Examiner continued his silent scraping. After what seemed an eternity, the Examiner stopped and the water began to drain out of the tub. The Examiner handed Ivan a dry strip of cloth to wind around his middle and then motioned him out of the tub. He pointed to a small table in the corner with a small bowl of broth and a piece of bread sitting on it.

Ivan had no appetite, but he understood that it was expected for him to eat. Stiffly he climbed out of the tub and walked gingerly to the table. He was grateful that only his frontside had been scraped because the chair was hard and cold. At least there was that small mercy. He picked up the bread and moaned inwardly. It was dry and hard. Resolutely, he crumbled it in his soup. There was no spoon, so he picked up the bowl and took a drink of the thin broth. It was very salty and bitter. He put the bowl down and pushed it away.

"You must eat it all!" the Examiner looked at him steadily.

Ivan felt his stomach clench, and understood. Purging was also part of the Purification Ritual. He felt a hard burn of anger rise in him. Yes, he would drink it and submit to the cleansing. He would be scrubbed and purged, and he would no doubt weep and scream and wail in the final moments of the ritual. He would experience all of these things, and he would never forget them. When it came time to assume leadership of the barbarians, he would remember all the evil that lived in their land, and he would purify it for his people. He drank the soup.

— Chapter 21 —

Sojourner woke to strange voices singing badly. At first, she thought some animal was being hurt, but when her head began to clear, she could tell it was just an odd, off key music. She wondered if it was a ritual that captured monarchs were subjected to, in order to demoralize them. Then the wailing stopped abruptly and she heard a lilting voice speak in patient tones. What a good voice. The good voice began to sing, and though the style of music was odd to Sojourner's ears, it was beautiful and Sojourner was drawn to it.

She was lying on a cot in an enclosed room. There was a door with a barred window in the top half. Cautiously, she sat up and eased herself into a standing position. She was thankful the antidote was effective. Even though she had been sedated, she felt rested instead of groggy. She crossed to the window as quietly as she could and peeked out to see what was happening. There were a number of women dressed in the dark robes of the Empire's women, though they were all open and she could see their bright shifts. They were sitting stiffly in chairs paying close attention to an older woman standing in front of them. The older woman was singing the haunting song in a clear, sweet voice. Her range was good, and though her delivery was unschooled, her emotional stimulations were right on target. Sojourner felt the calming effects of the music. Ahhh! A lullaby! This woman had a rich natural ability. Very excellent tenderness. Any baby would find comfort in this song. The woman stopped abruptly and gestured to the young women sitting in their bright shifts.

"Can you tell what I am doing? It is important for you to open your mouths wider, though you must not have tension in your face or neck. Singing is like speaking with great range and emotion. Let's try again. Ready?"

"Your journey's long but your burden's light...."

The young women began to sing discordantly. Sojourner could see that the main problem was uncommon tension. She detected the indicators of barely controlled fear. It was hard to imagine anyone trying to sing with so much fear coursing under the surface.

"Just close your eyes and see..."

The young women were beautiful. There were six of them. The new Kalig had reigned for seven years, so these must be his Chosen.

"A thousand rainbows dancing now-
Beside a crystal sea..."

They were learning to sing. Sojourner smiled through her wince as the Chosen attempted to sing a high note.

"Hush a baby! Don't you cry!
Sleep, it's a lullaby!"

Sojourner silently moved away from the window and began to assess her situation. She was wearing a dark robe, but all of her own clothes were still on her body underneath. She guessed that the women did not suspect her clothing to be a threat. She had not had any of her hair wires or her nails removed. She was still wearing her jewelry. It amazed her that the simple scans had not been done, but then the women that were her jailers were not trained in this. It could be a great advantage.

Quietly, Sojourner pulled the necessary wires out of her clothing and placed them around the fixtures and door. There was a moment of static, and Sojourner was afraid that they had failed, but then Joseph's voice sounded.

"Sojourner? Is that really you?"

"Yes! I am here in the cloister of the palace. I am in a holding cell of some kind. Lyla never said anything about the structure of the cloister. I am not certain what to expect. A noblewoman is giving singing lessons to the Chosen in the great room. Is all well at home?"

"Yes, well, Cloe is angry at me again. She thinks I should insist that we come and get you immediately rather than wait two days. To be honest, I tend to agree with her. The shield sticks are all in position and the infrastructure is compromised. Lyla has been debriefed. The probability of you being able to convince the

Emperor to negotiate is very small. It is a strange thought they live with, that all of their answers are contained in Law and that all morality is contained in behavior. The Emperor is their outlet from the structure of their lives. He is raised to be a madman who makes sane decisions."

"How do you mean?" Sojourner was mystified.

"Did Lyla tell you how an Emperor is chosen?"

"I assumed it was by acts of war or conquest. She said some things about the old Emperor being deposed, but I was paying attention to the rest of her story and did not question her about politics. I suppose it is more important than I imagined?"

Joseph drew in a deep breath and sounded as if he were trying to find a way to say something that made him uncomfortable. "'In order for a son to ascend to the throne, he must clear his path by strength of arm and strategy. That is how a people will know their Emperor is worthy. He must love the Empire more than his own blood ' This is the quote that Lyla shared. The Lawgiver decreed that the one that gains the throne must first vanquish his brothers and then his father. Then he is crowned. He must murder his brothers and father, then he is named Kalig. The boys aren't even named, they only gain a name when they are Kalig."

"Oh, dear God in Heaven. The boy is raised to be a murderer? Why?"

"The Lawgiver wrote that there must be an element of madness in every culture, and it was best that the madness be contained in one person. He pointed to ancient, stable cultures that had insane rulers. As a matter of fact, the Emperors are named after a particularly insane Roman Emperor named Caligula. He was quite a terror. He waged war with Neptune and I believe, he married his horse. It is not a pretty story."

"So the Emperor is insane?"

"It actually doesn't sound like he is insane, though he is cruel and capricious. I imagine he is not going to be healed from the injury done to his character. The Psychologists and Healers are trying to come up with a comprehensive plan for dealing with him. Sojourner, I don't think you are equipped to deal with this. I have supreme confidence in your abilities, but we did not plan for this. If we would have had just one more year to study them, we would have known how to approach this better."

"It is a shame to have gone through all of this and not have a chance to reach the people. It is going to be a conflict one way or another, isn't it?"

"It seems so..."

"Well, then, let's try to reach as many people as we can. Let me tell some stories and stir things up anyway I have come a long way in a silly cell not to speak to anyone about truth."

"Are you sure? We can have you out of there within a few hours. The shields will be activated within days, and then we will begin the culling. It was a great idea to attempt a negotiation, but it is not likely to work out to anyone's advantage."

"I will tell stories until you arrive, then." Sojourner sighed, "At least I can introduce a new thought or two to the thinkers of the Empire. Will the operatives remove me from here, or will it be done by Guardians?"

"We will notify Josilyn to remove you this evening, and then you will be taken to a transport from there."

"That will be good. Is Stephan there with you?"

"We convinced him to sleep for a while. Shall I wake him?"

"Mercy on us all, never wake him. He is as grumpy as an old bear when he hasn't had enough sleep. Let him wake when he is rested. We will talk until our lives flee from us later."

"As you wish, Mistress Storyteller. Tell me what you plan, so we might find a way to support you."

"I think I will start by telling a story to these ladies. Based on what we know, what might be a good choice? Are there any Psychologists there with you?"

"Actually, there has been some discussion about this already. To gain the sympathies of this group, it might be good to tell them a love story. They are the Chosen, and all possibility of a loving relationship has been removed from them. They have been sacrificed to the Emperor's madness, or so they have been taught, and they have no personal happiness to look forward to in their lives. It is rumored that some Emperors are kind to their Chosen, but mostly it is a relationship of sacrifice. Do you have a love story that is not too happy, one they can relate to but also instills a longing in them?"

"Well, yes. I do have a story like that, though I don't often tell it because it is sad and bittersweet. I only tell it to small groups that are experienced listeners because it evokes large amounts of introspection. With the cultural bias here, I don't know if it will have any effect at all. Lyla did not respond to my story as

I expected." Sojourner trailed off into silence, feeling the weight of uncertainty growing in her.

"Not to worry, Sojourner. Lyla has spoken of your story often in the short time she has been here. It did not cause her to respond as we have grown to expect, but she is asking many questions. It has shaken her because it has shown her another way to think. That is also powerful. Don't expect any normal response and it will be easier for you. "

"Yes. I understand that. I will try to be patient. Of course, that is not what I am best at being, so if I get cranky, I guess I can write a poem about you and that will make me feel better."

Joseph laughed. "First Cloe, now you. It is a perilous life being a public servant."

Sojourner allowed herself a small, tight laugh, but the situation did not allow her to give herself over to her desire to laugh. She had too much to do before she was extracted. She needed to try to reach someone. She had to believe that her training was reliable, that the people of the Empire were not so different from the people of the Burrows. If they could not be reached, how would they be assimilated into Burrow culture? Surely their hearts were still human. There must be a way to reach them entirely. Perhaps the reason that Lyla responded in her limited way was because she was so hurt by her culture. Could she reach somone who was not hurt by the culture?

"Well, I will begin. Say a prayer for me, and say prayers for me always. It occurs to me that we may have been too optimistic about my skills. None of the soldiers became completed when they listened to me.

At least, we know of none. It will take mighty prayers to help me say the right things."

"Again, I have to say that you do not have to do this..."

"You are right, but it will be valuable for us to understand when we watch the reactions of the citizens. We have some very important questions to answer. Can we meld with these people? Have we grown too far apart? Do we in the Burrows work well together because our gene pool is so limited and we have adapted to it, or is our culture truly superior as we believe?"

"Yes." Joseph's voice sounded thoughtful. "If there is no connection to be made, then we are merely conquerers, just like any tyrant. It will be very helpful to understand more of them and their reactions. Still," there was resolve in his voice, "we do not want to put you in danger. We are resolved to avoid the casualties of a war. Be safe."

"Pray hard and deep, my friend." Sojourner deactivated the dampening field and straightend resolutely.

She crossed to the door and stood by the barred window. The older woman was demonstrating how to take a deep breath. She was so natural. With training, she could have been a great storyteller, perhaps another Master Storyteller. Sojourner felt her heart beat faster at the thought of another Master in her lifetime. It would be a great accomplishment for anyone to make such a discovery. The woman began to sing the same lullaby.

"A distant voice is calling you-
It dances on a breeze-

It tells a tale of emerald shores
Beside a crystal sea!
Hush a baby don't you cry
Sleep it's a lullaby!"

Sojourner was entranced by the woman's voice. It was clear, but not sharp, and she had all of the maternal elements in the timbre of her voice. There was the soft vibratto on the sustained notes, and a gentle but noticable cresendo and decrescendo, making an almost hypnotic calm grow in the listeners. Without knowing what she was doing, the woman was touching on all twelve of the basic tenets of singing. Her interpretation of the lyrics was brilliant for one unschooled in the deeper training required to become a true storyteller.

"Feel the warmth of you mothers arms" Yes. Just the right emphasis on the word 'feel', it would stimulate a soothing response in a baby...excellent!

"Listen to her breathe!" Very good, but there should have been less 'r' sounded in breathe...

"Then watch the phoenix rise and fly!" Maybe a bit more clarity on the 'fl' in fly....

Beyond the crystal sea!
Hush a baby don't you cry!
Sleep it's a lullaby!"

The woman stopped singing. Yes, excellent. She did not move for an instant, letting the final note resonate for a moment, holding her body still as if captured by the music. Brilliant. Brilliant. Sojourner felt a great welling up in her. If the women were singing such lullabies there was hope that they were not so different from the women of the Burrows. She must speak and it must make a connection to this woman because Sojourner had to believe they could be reached.

She stepped away from the door and gathered her thoughts, carefully adjusting her vocal pitch to include reflection and serenity. "That was beautiful. Your children are blessed to have such lullabies given to them to grow with..." She heard the room draw in a breath and felt it grow tense. She stepped to the door and stood before the window and looked out at the women with a calm demeanor. "You must teach it to me so that I might sing it to my grandchildren." Now she must sound more formal, as if she suddenly remembered her manners, yet still warm and inviting. "I am one of the many. I am Sojourner, Master Storyteller to the citizens of the Burrows. I come as an ambassador with hope for great friendship between our people. Let us speak of peace together."

The women turned blank faces to her. One of the young women turned back to the singer and leaned toward her. "She is lying, isn't she? How can she be a grandmother and a queen? What do we do?"

"I don't know what to do. I have been protected my whole life from the Forsaken. She is unnatural and unclean, so we must not speak to her. There is no way to purify a woman who has been contaminated. Just don't look at her."

Sojourner sighed. "When I teach this lullaby to my daughters, I will remember to use much of your interpretation. Let me see..."Your journey's long , but your burden's light.." She began to sing. She hoped she had had a chance to hear all of the verses, but she would sing what she had heard. She used her voice carefully, placing comfort and familiarity in her voice. Her training had taught her to remember songs and texts in detail, so remembering the song was not hard, but she felt like she needed to make the lullaby powerful in its possibilities. "Just close your eyes and see! A thousand rainbows dancing now, beyond a crystal sea! Hush a-baby! Don't you cry! Sleep, it's a lullaby!" Sojourner sang and the women stared at her, slack-jawed and confused. At the last note, she held the moment and then she calmly folded her hands and regarded the women through the bars of the door.

"Mistress Minerva, how did she know your lullaby?! Isn't it a song you made yourself for your children? She has sung your lullaby."

Interesting, perhaps this was the same Minerva that spoke her name in a bare whisper. The Minerva from the ship. She must be the wife of a nobleman, and a woman of some consequence.

Sojourner turned to face Minerva as directly as she could and bowed, palms up in a formal posture. "Hail Minerva, woman of the Empire. I am Sojourner, one of the many. I greet you on behalf of my people and crave a response to my questions. Answer them please, and my people will honor you upon your liberation."

"Minerva, what is she talking about?" one of the young women whispered frantically as if Sojourner could not hear.

"I am right here, and I can hear everything you are saying. Do you wonder why we speak the same language? One would think with us being on opposite sides of the world we would not have the same language, wouldn't you? Our people have been monitoring your

Empire's transmissions for several hundred years. We decided as a culture that we should all speak a common language and everyone in the Burrows can speak your language as well as our own. Unfortunately, the transmissions were all centered around battlefield maneuvers, and we have not had a very clear idea of the structure of your culture. I have to say I am relieved that you sing such lovely lullabies. We were all fairly certain that your culture had no tenderness and heart, and it has been a very sad and distressing discovery that you have no faith in God. Still, Lyla has been able to show us that we have many things in common."

One of the young women gasped and covered her face. The other women gathered around her in sympathetic shock. "She is speaking of Lyla," one whispered in a shocked hoarse whisper.

"How could she have discovered her?"

"Don't cry, Pura."

Sojourner was dismayed. The one named Pura struggled to control her tears. "I know she is Forsaken, but she is still my kin. What has become of her? How does this person know her name?"

Sojourner turned as best she could to Pura and greeted her. "Hail Pura, woman of the Empire. I am Sojourner, one of the many. I greet you and bring you news of your kinswoman, Lyla. She was placed on the ship to act as my body servant. She was covered in filth and had only been given rotting food to eat. She was wounded and sick. Over the past years, she has been hunted for sport by the depraved and she has given birth to babies, none of which have lived. She has found the strength in her to live and help other

Forsaken, but her struggles have taken their toll on her. Because of our superior technology, I was able to give medical aid to her, and my people extracted her from the ship and took her straightway to our best Healing Center. I hope she will soon be happier and healthier. The baby that she carries will be loved and given every care. She has great hope today. Lyla is safe."

"You lie," spat Pura. "I don't know how you know about Lyla, but this is not true. The Forsaken are bereft, but no man of the Empire would hunt her for sport and behave without honor toward her. Her life is a lonely one, a hungry and cold one, but not impure. Our men are above that."

Sojourner was surprised at Pura's outrage. The faces of the other women were also contorted with anger and disbelief.

"Joseph?" Sojourner did not bother activating the dampening field. "Are you listening to this? Is it possible for Lyla to speak to her kinswoman, Pura?"

"Of course. It may take a few moments to rouse her...."

"Certainly. We have all the time we need, I would imagine."

Sojourner turned her attention back to the women. They were silent and still once more, as if they were holding their breaths. Minerva seemed to gather her resolve around her, squared her shoulders, and strode over to the door. She folded her arms and glowered through the bars on the door.

"How did you do that? What trick of your voice did you use to make a man's voice sound in this cloister? If you are transmitting a signal to a distant place, how did it get past our security? Where is your device? I demand to know." Minerva's eyes blazed.

"Mistress Minerva! I understand your concern. I have said the true and obvious fact. My country is superior to yours in technology. We have become a society of scientists and growers. We do not appear strong because we keep our upper environment free from clutter. Our cities are underground and efficient. Do you think you can contain us? Do you think you can conquer us?"

"Yes! We will assume leadership of your lands, just as we have assumed leadership of all lands. How can you bluster and posture at us? You are our prisoner. I, personally, do not want to see you hurt, but the Empire will do as it needs to ensure the strength of the Empire."

"Well, it has overlooked several things in its decision to conquer us." Sojourner adjusted her voice to sound kindly with just a hint of patronage. "First, we already have leadership and we are happy with it. Secondly, the lands are not all healed and we will not tolerate interference from your country in our mission. Finally, I am not your prisoner. I am here because I want to be here."

"You say," interjected another of the women. "See where you are? You are locked in a punishment cell, and there you will stay until it is time to complete the subjugation of your pitiful nation."

Sojourner felt a moment of anger, but she held it in check. Instead she smiled calmly and without saying a word, she pushed open the door to her cell and walked out. The resulting pandemonium was worthy of a good story. The women screamed and scattered to the far corners of the room, hiding behind furniture and crouching against walls. Sojourner smiled despite herself. This would be a wonderful moment to describe. She would vividly recount the swirling flurry of black robes slashed with bright flashes of color as the women rushed for their safe corners. She would mimic the horrified screams and fearful faces. Then she would illustrate her small, frail body stepping carefully into the room. It would make a wonderful comic moment when she paused and struck the pose of a conquering warrior. She would enjoy developing this into a story, she would relish the process, though now it was not the time to be comedic. Now was the time to forge a bond or to establish fear. It would be better to create a bond.

"Don't be concerned. It is a simple matter to leave this place. As a matter of fact, I intend to leave well before the shields are activated. I want you to know that our intentions are good, and we will spare as many of your people as we can manage. I have been speaking the truth. I am not a queen. I am the Master Storyteller to the Burrows, and I greet you. I come as an ambassador to your people."

Sojourner stopped and waited, certain that someone would speak, but no one did. She would wait. The silence was thick and she tried to project calm strength. She silently exhaled a prayer of thanks when Lyla's voice crackled through the air.

"Sojourner. Is it true that you are in the cloister of the Palace? Can it be true? Are the walls still cream colored with the designs of flowers and birds etched in them? I always thought they were beautiful."

"Yes, I am just now looking at the walls of the cloister. They are beautiful! To be honest, I have been very busy talking to the Chosen and a noblewoman named Minerva. I understand that one of your near kinswomen is now a Chosen. She is right here...her name is Pura."

"Pura," Lyla's voice strangled out through new tears. "How did this happen? How is it that you are a Chosen? How did this happen?"

"Lyla? It is you. It is your voice. Where are you? Where are you at? Are you safe? How can this be?" Pura unfolded from her crouched place behind a table.

"I was placed on the ship that went to retrieve Sojourner. I was in a crate for the trip to the Blasted Lands and then I was placed into the holding cell with the Storyteller. She healed me with the wonderous medicines she has. I decided to go to the Burrows and begin a new life there, and they sent these amazing light planes to fetch me and bring me here. It is a place of wonders! I cannot begin to tell you what it is like. The land above is natural and pure and the city I am in is hidden and like a magic place. "

"So, it is true that their society is mighty? It is true that they can conquer us? The queen is not lying about her nation?"

"She is not a queen. She is a Storyteller. She is an honorable wife. She is a mother and grandmother. I have met her family and they are eager for her to return."

Sojourner started and smiled. "You met my family? How is Stephan? Are my daughters well? Jakma is expecting in three months. It will be her second. Sala has two already...were the babies there? They are so precious."

"Your family seems very well to me. Of course, I did not speak with your husband. I just can't be that forward. He is obviously concerned about you. Your daughters look like you, though they are not frail like you are. One of your grandsons hugged me. I hope my child will be happy and healthy like these children."

Pura stepped forward, her eyes blazing. "Your child? Then it is true that your are expecting a baby? You have been violated. Who did this! Who has dishonored you?"

"Pura, all of the Forsaken are made sport of by certain nobles and maintenence workers. We hide and fight, but it does little good when we are mostly starved and weak. The Examiners do nothing because we are no longer valid women. We have all had many children, though none of them live. They are hunted and killed as well. Pura, our Empire holds evil in its tunnels."

Sojourner watched the women in the cloister with fascination. They came out of their hiding places, some with dismayed eyes, and some blazing anger from every fiber of their beings. They began to talk, seemingly in one voice, some waving their hands, some pleading. They stabbed at the air and paced and gestured. Only Minerva and Sojourner watched and they listened.

"No, I can't believe this!" The young woman with the vivid green eyes began to weep.

The ebony skinned woman was slashing the air with her fists, "Deceived! The teachings are a deception! What have we sacrificed to be here in this place if there is evil in it?"

"I knew it," the woman with the cascading wheat colored hair was hissing her anger, "I knew it was a lie."

The women cried and screamed in frustration for a few moments longer, when one of them gave a cry of fear. The women fell silent and listened like the woodland birds did when a predator was stalking through the forest. There was a chime sounding like a summons. For a moment, the women looked at Sojourner with the awareness that she was a prisoner out of her cell.

"He comes! Quickly! As we should be! Please! Storyteller! Back in your cell! Pretend to be asleep! Be still!"

Sojourner understood their urgency and hurried back to her cell and closed the door behind her. She was grateful that they had apparently decided not to betray her to the Emperor. He was still a violent madman. She heard the scraping of the chairs as the women settled back into their places. Minerva quickly veiled her face and gave the Chosen a place to begin to sing. Haltingly, they began their pitiful singing.

"Hush a baby! Don't you cry! Sleep it's a lullaby!..."

Their voices trailed off as the door to the cloister opened and Kalig entered. Sojourner closed her eyes and listened with all of her strength.

— Chapter 22 —

Minerva dropped to her knees and bowed with her head to the ground. Her heart pounded in her chest and she felt her stomach clench. Kalig's boot made a resounding thump as he crossed to the cell door where the Storyteller was supposed to be pretending to sleep. She did not know why, but she did not want the Storyteller to be exposed. Maybe it was because Lyla was safe in a far away place. Maybe because she was still angry with the liberties the Emperor had taken with her life. Maybe it was because there was something more in the world than she had imagined.

"I see the wretch is still unconscious. That is well enough. I just wanted to look at her. What a pathetic specimen. The people of the Burrows must be weak beyond all measure if this creature could ascend to the heights of a ruler. I will tend to her later. Right now, I would like to hear how the singing is progressing. Wife of Provo, are my Chosen ready to sing?"

Minerva felt her heart fall. Miserably she shook her head not daring to look up.

"Ah, well, I guess it is not as easy for some to learn. Singing always came naturally to me. Sit up and listen to me."

Minerva sat up, though she kept her head down. She did not know what to do. Was the Emperor really going to sing? It was another impossible situation. What if he sounded like one of the bullfrogs in the pond in the commons at her village. Was she supposed to applaud or what? She closed her eyes and clenched her teeth. The Emperor drew in a deep breath and began to sing. His voice was deep and full and resonated from him like waves of crisp, cold water.

"For honor and for strength of days
I stand alone-
I will not let my resolve fade
To guard my home.
I love the breath and bone of all
My people.
And never will I let them fall
To evil.
Oh! Watch with me all through the night
And vow with me to hold on tight
To the reality of righteous dreams-
The Empire's strength is what is seems!"

His voice was beautiful and strong. All of the Chosen watched him with astonishment, and none of them moved or even seemed to breathe. Minerva let her breath out in a great sigh. Cautiously she extended her hands, palm up, in the gesture of a woman who wishes to speak. The Emperor Kalig looked at her expectantly, like an eager child that knows he has pleased his mother.

"Yes, wife of Provo?"

"Sire, I am honored."

"Ah, well, of course it is not the most important thing I do, but it pleases me to sing. Still, it is not proper that I should sing lullabies to the children. I think that if the children heard some music in the creche, they might have a better time of it when the singing master gets ahold of them later. Of course, I am only speaking of the true children. It will ease their burden to have music. It certainly did mine."

"Yes, Sire." Minerva could not think of anything else to say, so she bowed her head.

"Well! Chosen, isn't it time for the children to be up from their naps? I would like to see them."

Minerva stood up during the flurry of activity and went to a far corner to sit and watch. She was confused. The Emperor wanted to see his children? She could not imagine that he even knew they exisited.

In a very few minutes, the Chosen had gone into another room and had returned with an impressive number of children. Pura had three in tow. She was the first Chosen. Simiat had two, Lara brought two as well, and so did Kata. Jonta brought one, and her belly was swollen with child. Chiria, the newest Chosen, brought in a baby just a few months old. All of the children were under five years old. Some were wide awake, and others were still heavy with sleep. The Emperor watched them come in with a satisfied smile on his face. As soon as the older children saw him they let out a whoop of joy and swarmed over to him, pulling on him and trying to climb into his arms.

Minerva watched in silent wonder as Kalig scampered and played with his children. He seemed to transform into a different man before her eyes. He laughed and played like her own Lorn did with their children. His face looked like the face of a father. While he played, the Chosen busied themselves preparing a low table with snacks. They brought out small plates and child cups and placed fruit and cheese and small pieces of bread on the plates. When the table was prepared, Kalig and the children that were big enough sat in the small chairs. The Chosen, even those with babies, positioned themselves among the children and assisted the children and fed the babies what was appropriate. Kalig talked with his children, listening to them and interacting with them as they ate.

At one point, he gestured to Chiria that he wanted to hold their baby when it began to fuss. He looked deep into the baby's face and spoke soft, cooing words to it. Gently he put the baby over his shoulder and patted it rhythmically. Soon the baby let out a tremendous burp and settled down on Kalig's shoulder, drifting into a soft sleep. Minerva felt her eyes fill with tears. How could this gentle father be Kalig? How could he sit at the table with these children, knowing that his daughters would be given away for political alliances and he would spend the latter part of his life battling his sons for the right to a worn out name? How could this all be? There they sat, eating pieces of fruit and cheese together. It was not too long ago that Lorn had come back from the Rite of Ascension, white-faced and shaking. This Kalig had been a weapon, dangerous and unforgiving. He had slaughtered his father with a single-mindedness that left the nobles gasping and frightened. More than once, Lorn had come home, unable to speak of the swift and unyielding judgements passed down by this Kalig. This same Kalig. This man with the golden voice and loving father-eyes? Minerva wanted to weep and laugh. It was true that there was a madness in the Empire, but it was the madness of a Law that required a son to kill his father after killing all of his brothers.

There was the sound of a summoning chime. Kalig's face darkened and he scowled in disappointment and displeasure. The older children fell silent, and several of them looked abjectly saddened by the summons. Kalig stood, still holding Chiria's baby. He seemed to gather his persona around him, and as he did, it became more and more strange to see him holding a baby. Chiria silently glided forward and took the baby from him without speaking. Kalig turned his eyes to her, and for a moment, it was as though he did not know her.

"Chiria, I will require you tonight. I will expect you in my room one hour after the Captive's Ceremony. Wife of Provo, your husband will come and get you after the Captive's Ceremony. You are to meet him at the cloister door. The Examiners will guide you to the place. I will have the captive removed and returned by them, so be certain to be properly veiled."

Kalig turned and without speaking again, he left.

Chiria had turned pale and slowly sank into a chair. Simiat and Pura crossed to her and patted her consolingly.

"Don't fear this, Chiria." Pura put her arms around Chiria's shoulders as Simiat gently took the baby from her arms and held him close to her. "We all know how hard it is to accomodate the Emperor."

Kata stepped forward and knelt in front of Chiria. She took Chiria's hands. "We all know that he requires more from you than he has from the rest of us. He is obsessed with you and it is hard on you. Still, know that we will all be here for you when it is finished. We all will be here for you."

The prisoner had come, unnoticed, from her cell. Minerva also stepped forward. She was thankful again and would be infinely thankful for the scars on her husband's hands. She did not know what to do. She had no wisdom to share. Between the revelations of the prisoner and Lyla, and the visit of the Emperor, the women were spent.

The air crackled and Lyla's voice spoke. "It is as it always has been with the Chosen. The Chosen help the Chosen to endure. The pain of service is intense; it is the price of purity. Only those that are blessed by scarred hands are free from the price."

The prisoner turned her face upward and spoke to Lyla. "You will find it will be different for you now." Then she spoke to the rest of the women in the room. "It can be different for all of you if you choose. We are taking a million people to the Burrows to add to our numbers. We need to refresh our gene pool and are accepting one million emmigrents. We have the medical knowledge to restore your bodies and counsel you into a new life. We will be take several thousand citizens of the Empire the day that the shields are activated. We can be certain that you are taken on that day. It will protect you from the harm that will certainly follow until all is contained."

"What will become of the rest of us?" snapped Pura. "It is all well and good that you are going to conquer us, but what will you do to us as your captives?"

"We will re-order some things. We will evaluate the wishes of the people, and gradually institute changes. We will purify the environment and negotiate trade. It will be a difficult process, and it will require that the Empire be contained for a season. We will use our technologies to do this. We would like to avoid as much of this as we can by treaties. I am here as an ambassador."

"Your plan is ridiculous." Pura was furious. "Why didn't you establish your might before all of this? Why the charade?"

"We had no way to defend ourselves. We have a population of twenty million, you have twenty million in your military. Even with our technologies, we can be overwhelmed by sheer numbers. We did not realize just how difficult it would be to bridge the gap between our cultures. Our operatives have not been very successful in infiltrating all levels of society. We thought we had more in common with you. We thought that once I could tell you my stories, that it would soften your hearts and the heart of your Emperor enough, we could show you our intentions and reason with you. We know now that we cannot make a treaty with your people. I will be extracted from here soon, and the Empire will be contained."

Minerva stepped forward. Her questions burned in her. "Why would you think that you could not reason with us? Aren't we all the same species? How is it that we have so little in common?"

"The basis of our entire culture is a faith in a Deity. We believe and teach that our survival of the Great Evil was the will of the Deity we worship. Most of my stories center around the exploration of the nature of the Maker, and though they are in the form of myths, they are designed to inspire faith. We assumed that the rituals we observed were also based on the worship of a deity. Only after meeting Lyla did we understand that you have no faith, just Laws. How can we understand each other?"

"You are being foolish." Minerva retorted. "We simply ignore the question of faith. It cannot be that compelling."

"You don't understand the energy contained in faith. It is a strong force in our culture. It permeates all of our doings. When I told a story to Lyla, she did not connect to it as I have grown to expect. Did it mean anything to you, Lyla?"

"Storyteller, it is new to me. I don't know if it will mean anything to me or not. It was moving, but not life affirming as it is to your people. I need time to decide about your Maker. I don't understand all of what your people do here. It seems that your machines do not even work without the energy of the prayers of your spiritual leaders. I am stymied by the thought. Still, I hate to think that you are going to give up on my people without ever having told a single story. "

"I think you are making us too different from you, Storyteller." Minerva said, trying to sound casual. Could it be that there was a place where people could pray to a god? "So, tell us a story, and let us decide for ourselves if we have an understanding of your thinking."

The Storyteller looked around at the women. Chiria was still being held by her cloister-mates. The children were playing or sitting snuggled in a lap. She seemd to wrestle with herself for a moment, and then she nodded if resolved.

"Fine then. I will tell you a love story, one of bittersweet love and loss. It is a complicated story, but if we can understand each other in this, then there is hope."

Chapter 23

"Listen, Chosen. Listen to a love story, the story of Humor and Sorrow. It is the tale of how we think and how we feel. It is about the feelings that pour through us and wash into others. It is about laughing and crying. Laughter is caught between good and evil. So are tears. Sometimes laughter lifts us up and joins us to others. Sometimes it crushes. Sometimes tears cleanse and heal, and sometimes they rip the soul to shreds. It is a bittersweet tale, the one of Humor and Sorrow, but it is full of hope.

"Listen.

"Before this fragile orb was made, before there was division in Heaven, there were two spirits living among the hosts of Heaven that loved each other with all of their hearts. Their names were Solemn and Humor. From the moment they first saw each other, they loved each other, and they love each other still. Solemn had lovely, dark eyes, and her hair flowed about her like a shimmering, midnight cape. She was thoughtful and quiet, and she sang soothing songs that resounded like deep bells and soft winds. Humor was her opposite. He was full of laughter and he was always changing his appearance to delight those around him. He loved to be the center of attention, and he sometimes got into bits of mischief. Still, he was kind-hearted, and he never hurt anyone.

"It was an amazement to everyone, except the Maker, that Solemn and Humor were so devoted to each other. For long ages they seemed inseparable. Humor would find some gentle, sweet way to make Solemn smile and laugh, and Solemn would remind Humor to, sometimes, be sensible. In fact, they were so devoted to each other, that the Maker joined them together in marriage, and their love for each other deepened.

"One would think that this kind of happiness should last forever. Unfortunately, Corruption has caused this time of darkness and division to come upon the universe, and Humor and Solemn are estranged. It happened like this....

"The strife in Heaven was a new thing. The Maker still kept company with Corruption, and Corruption had not yet left Heaven to wage his insane war with the Maker. Corruption was not yet openly defiant, and he spent his time in endless conversations with the other inhabitants of Heaven, striving to convince them that the Maker had outlasted His usefulness. He did not move many with his pathetic arguments, but he did convince some that his ideas had merit. One of the spirits he convinced was Solemn.

"At first, Solemn did not listen to Corruption. But he perceived that her serious nature could be bent to his will. He would wait until she was by herself, thinking or singing her soft, deep songs, and he would act like he happened upon her. At first, it seemed innocent. He would talk to her about deep, serious matters, and praise her for her fine, clear thoughts. After a while, he would seek her out, asking her advice about the growing conflict between the Maker and himself. He would talk to her sympathetically about how hard it must be for someone of her serious nature to co-exist with frivolous beings. Gradually, and with great patience, he gained her trust. Slowly, and with infinite care, he won her thoughts. On the day that Corruption announced his new name and left Heaven, Solemn left, too.

"Humor pleaded with her to reconsider.

"Oh! My sweet companion! Don't go! I will never have a moment of joy if you are gone! We complete each other! Stay with me!"

"Solemn hesitated.

"Don't listen to him!" snarled Corruption. "He would make you as foolish as he. He would diminish you. You are destined for greater things. Come and discover your own greatness."

"Solemn left. She left her husband, she left her deep music, and she left her name. Her new name became Sorrow, and she hardened her heart to her past.

"For untold years, Sorrow cut a deep path of pain through the Heavens. Although she had no power to destroy, she was devious in her ways, and discovered many ways to hurt and wound.

"Humor was dismayed by Sorrow's actions. He blamed himself for neglecting Solemn and losing her to Corruption. In truth, he did not neglect her at all, but he blamed himself. For long ages, he hid himself in a far, secret place, too hurt and ashamed to join in the defense of Heaven. The Maker understood his pain, and left him alone.

"Finally, though, the Maker knew it was time for Humor to return to Heaven and take his place with the other spirits of Heaven. He, Himself, went to Humor's hiding place, a rocky, dead planet. Humor was brooding in a deep, cold cave. The Maker came to the entrance quietly, stooped and peered into the deep gloom.

"Humor," he called softly. "Humor, come out."

"No, please. Go away," replied Humor, his voice full of lonely pain.

"Humor, my friend, I have come for you. It is time for you to put this behind you and come again to Heaven." The Maker's voice was kind and strong.

"Maker, I ache all over. My mate is gone from me, and I miss her, ...and I'm ashamed of her. All that I have ever known is tangled. My wife is gone..." Humor's voice trailed off into silence.

"The Maker came into the cave like a soft, warm breeze. His eyes were full of light and compassion. He found Humor huddled in a corner. He knelt next to him.

"Humor," the Maker said, and the ground trembled and thrummed with a deep stirring. "You are the only one that can bring meaning to this."

"How can I be of help? She believes me to be insignificant. My love could not hold her in Heaven. I am but a silly jokester. Pathetic." He buried his face in his hands and wept bitterly. The Maker waited until he regained his composure.

"Humor, you have been here in this cold, hopeless place. It is interesting that you came here. Doesn't it seem like a silent tomb? Can you imagine this place alive? I will tell you, once it was alive, and it teemed with a fragile life. I made it unique and when it blooms, it is lovely. It blooms when I come to it. Come and see it. It is wondrous."

"The Maker helped the sorrowful Humor to his feet, and guided him out of the cave. With each moment, the planet that had been so bleak and desolate quivered and shook like a creature arising after a deep sleep. Life stretched up from the barren surface of the planet. Plants swirled up out of the ground like delicate dancers, scattering blossoms like a celebration. Tiny, translucent creatures lifted themselves out of the cold dirt, and bounded upward like unfettered light beams. They burst out in musical chirping and chattering. The surface of the planet was a fantasy of color and movement.

"Humor was breathless. He had never imagined that there could be such a place. In wonder, he turned his eyes to the Maker. The Maker stood silently and watched the shifting, dancing, swirling life with pleasure and delight. The Maker looked at Humor, his eyes were full of deep joy.

"Maker, I never even imagined this. How can there be such places in the Universe? It was so empty!"

"Yes! It will end when I leave it. It is how this place is made. Sometimes our presence makes all the difference between life and desolation. It is a simple thing...." The Maker looked at Humor kindly. "It is time for you to come with Me."

"Yes," agreed Humor. "It is time to face her...I can do this..." His voice trailed again into silence, but he no longer wept.

"Humor went with the Maker to the Gates of Darkness, the place where Corruption and his minions gathered to scheme and rage. They joined a host of Heaven's faithful spirits waiting for Corruption to make his next move. They did not wait long. Out of the depths, the dark hoards poured, howling in hatred and madness.

"Humor knew what he needed to do and he did not cringe away from his task. He searched the faces of Corruption's followers until he saw his wife. He stood still, like one carved from stone, his being was consumed by the sight of her. Sorrow did not notice him at first, but she felt his eyes on her and turned to find whose eyes burned her so. When she saw Humor, her heart leapt with joy and then with fear. She turned and tried to fight her way back into Chaos. Humor's whole self focused, with grim determination, he fought his way to her side. Ferociously, he battled with the other spirits of Heaven to drive Corruption back into Chaos, but he kept himself close to Sorrow. Before she could escape back into the darkness of Corruption's realm, Humor captured Sorrow in his arms and pulled her away from the Gates just before they closed.

"Frantically, Sorrow fought Humor, trying to escape, but as the Gates closed, she sagged into Humor's arms, sobbing in frustration and rage. Angrily, she shoved him away from her.

"Fool!" she spat at him. "Why are you here? You are not a warrior. You are a nonsense maker, a bit of fluff, a silly jokester. You have no place here."

"Our place is together. I have come to take you home with me. I miss you." he answered. "Come home with me."

"No, I am important here."

"Humor placed his hand over his heart. "You are important here."

"Sorrow's eyes softened. Humor opened his arms to her, and she came to him. They stood in silence, holding each other.

"Come home with me," he murmured into her soft, shimmering hair.

"Join us, here. You will be mighty." said Sorrow.

They looked into each other's eyes.

"And that is where this story ends. Humor and Sorrow still embrace on the edge of dark Chaos. They whisper lovingly to each other, trying to convince the other to change. Sometimes, Humor steps close to Darkness, and sometimes Sorrow approaches Heaven. Sometimes, Humor makes his wife laugh, and sometimes she makes him cry. They have not left each other's arms; they are bound together. Laughter and tears mingle."

Sojourner stood still, letting the moment sink in. She watched the women in the cloister, struggling to remain still and calm. She must seem serene and let the story exist in their minds for long moments. The Chosen were silent. Only Minerva and Chiria wept.

Chiria's baby began to wake and let out a cry. Simiat brough the baby to her and Chiria began to nurse him, though she still remained on the edge of tears.

The one called Simiat sat down next to Chiria. "Chiria, it was a compelling story, and I am moved in a strange way, though not to tears. Why are you crying?"

Sojourner smiled. Simiat would have made a fine Psychologist or Teacher. Perhaps someday.

"I don't know why, but the story makes me feel my own hopelessness. I have had thoughts that I am ashamed of having, and I heard my own thoughts in this story. I have not shared them because I don't want to be different from the Chosen. It is our unity that helps us survive this."

Pura crossed to her. "Whatever it is, there is nothing that can happen that will make us break our trust with you. " She would make such a good Leader, woman of great potential. Sojourner had to remind herself to be still.

Chiria took a deep breath and let her words out like a river undammed. "The story made me feel sad because I, too, feel lured away. I have listened to all that you have said when you discuss the Emperor's requirements, and at first, it was the same for me. Now it is not. It is still painful because of the price of purity, but something has happened that I have not spoken about. I am ashamed that I have not told you."

"We are as sisters. We have been sacrificed for the Empire, and our children as well. We have to be strong for each other, no matter what." Pura leaned forward, intense and seeming to blaze with her own fire. "What could you do to betray us? There is nothing. Don't be ashamed of whatever it is."

"It started after the birth of this boy..." Chiria's voice choked out. "The Emperor was in the birthing room with me, tending to the stitching. He was gentle and sure in his touch, and I was relieved that it was almost completed. I was holding the baby and my sweet little son turned his face into me and nuzzled me, looking to nurse and I was so happy that I began to cry. Kalig came up to where I was holding the baby and he guided the baby's mouth onto my nipple, helping me to feed the baby. He was gentle and his touch was sweet on my skin. He stroked my hair and watched me as I fed our baby. He kissed my forehead. I was not certain what to do. Then he began to talk to me, and my heart was stretched in a new direction.

"He spoke of his childhood, and his memory of being taken from his mother and moved to the proving school. He told me of the harsh conditions and endless lessons. Mostly, he spoke of his brothers, his only companions. They are not named, but they had nicknames for each other. He was known as Emptylegs, because his appetite was so big that his trainers complained that his legs must be empty, not just his belly. He had brothers called Jumper, and Big, and Sleepy. He had many brothers that he loved and he killed them all. It was his duty to the Empire. The first real woman he had seen since he had been taken from his mother was you, Pura, and then Simiat and Kata. He knew he frightened you and he hated that he frightened you. He asked me to not be afraid of him.

"I looked at him, and he looked so sad and alone that I could barely stand it. I reached out and touched his cheek and I spoke his boy-name, Emptylegs, and he began to cry, great terrible sobs. He eased into the bed with the baby and me, and he put his arms around us and he cried until he was asleep. His arms felt strange and wonderful around me, and I was exhausted from my ordeal, and I slept, too. When I woke, the baby was in his crib, and the Emperor was gone. He did not speak to me again until he required me to come to him after my time of rest was over.

"When I went to him that first time, he greeted me tenderly and he did not make a requirement of me. Instead, he sat with me on his lap in a big soft chair and he stroked my hair and talked about the stars and how as a boy he had dreamed about building a spaceship and escaping to them someday. He would take all of his brothers, and he would start a new world where the brothers could eat all they wanted and never fight again. I found myself relaxing in his arms, breathing in his scent. Then his voice became sad again, and he said that he would never reach the stars because he had to be the Emperor and most of his brothers were dead. He was silent for a long time, then he gently tilted my head up so that I was looking in his face and he said there were some good things about being Emperor. Then he kissed me."

"A kiss!" Simiat interrupted. "What was it like?"

"Could you breathe?" squealed Kata.

"Did he open his mouth?" teased Jonta.

Minerva stepped up and shushed the Chosen. "Girls! A kiss is a private thing. A sweet kiss is a gift."

The women looked at Minerva with amazement. "Do you mean Lord Provo kisses you? A Lord? Kisses?" Pura was sputtering and her face grew red. She sat down hard on the floor. "The whole world has gone mad." Unexpectedly, she covered her face and began to cry.

Sojourner was taken aback. These were grown women, and all of them mothers. Yet they were like young schoolgirls concerning kisses.

Minerva sputtered, "It isn't a terrible thing, Pura. Sometimes kisses happen."

"You don't understand. This just makes me feel so lost. When I was a child, there was a boy in our village who was my age, and we played together until he was taken to the men. Our parents approved of our friendship and we all secretly agreed to arrange a match for us when we were grown. When the last Kalig was disposed and our kinswoman was made Forsaken, we were grieved, but we did not think it would interfer with our plans. Unfortunately, the same Lord Simon that persecuted your father, Lyla, took it upon himself to use the situation to try to take control of my father's business concerns. I am not even sure what it was all about. All I know is that I was given to the Empire, and I have borne three children, and two of them are sons. I have clung to the belief that all of this was for a greater reason, but now I am hearing that the Empire is not the mightiest nation, and that there is a place where I might ask the questions about deity that fill my thoughts. And now this. The Emperor is not only a tender father, but his kisses his favored. I don't begrudge you your kisses, Chiria, but I regret the ones that I will never get from Bine. I cannot sacrifice my little boys now. It is all changed in a single hour. I cannot do anything about it, either. I am Chosen, who will hear me?"

"We can make arrangements for all of you that want to go to the Burrows. This is a difficult life. We had no idea." Sojourner stepped forward. "But right now, I must make arrangements to be taken out of here without causing any difficulty for you. I do not want to go through the Captive Ceremony. I have an idea it is not pleasant. Joseph? Have you been listening to all of this?"

"Yes, we can make several arrangements while we are speaking. We promise you, Chosen, whoever of you want to leave the Empire, we will take you. You will not have to watch your children die, or be given as trophies. Sojourner, Josilyn is coming. She is wearing an extra set of those robes so you can have one to disguise yourself in. We are not ready to activate the shields, but we have a safe house in the city that you can hide in until the extraction force is in place. She will be there as soon as she and Elfin can return from their home with the extra set of robes. Since they have to walk, it could be an hour or so. Do you know when the Captive's Ceremony is to be held? We certainly need to have you taken out before then."

Chiria looked at Sojourner. "Don't worry, none of us will betray you, no matter what. You are a wife and a mother. You are honorable. We have to hope now that our children will be safe, that they will live to be grown."

"Do you mean that the contender to the throne kills even the baby boys?"

"No. It is not that terrible. Once the Kalig is replaced, the boys in the creche too young to be contenders are joined to the Examiners. They are terrible and cruel, but they are alive." Minerva said. "The Lawgiver was thorough."

"It is a form of mercy to spare the boys..." Sojourner looked at the faces of the women. Without exception they looked at her blankly. "Or not." She smiled wanly at them.

There was a moment of silence, and then the women erupted into fits of giggles. For the first time since she had encountered the people of the Empire, she had made them laugh. She had not intended to make them laugh, just break the tension, but it felt wonderful to hear them laugh. They were so different, and yet, they were so much the same. They loved their children and dreamed of peace and better things for them. They longed for romance and intimacy. They cried over broken hearts and lost dreams. They wondered about God. They were people that she could learn to care about.

Minerva sobered and spoke to Sojourner seriously. "Truthfully, you have to understand that all you say does not bring any of us much hope. We understand that you will only allow a few to emmigrate to your country. But what of people like me? I have five children, and my oldest is married. How do I leave them? Will you take entire families? When I thought that we were going to conquer your country, I had no problem with the idea of leaving the Empire because I would have some authority. Now, if your people allow us in, we are not going to be nobles anymore. We will not have anything. These Chosen will be saving their children, but what of my children? If we are allowed to go to your country, what will become of them?"

"There will be many details to work out. We cannot guarantee that anything will work out perfectly. To be honest, we had not planned on this happening so soon. When your country sent its spies, we were only just beginning to put our own plans in motion. Just like in ancient times, international politics is an unpredictable business that ends up affecting the common man the most." Sojourner filled her voice with sincerity and kindliness. Then a thought hit her. "You have five children? You must have an amazing gene pool! I understand why the Emperor and his Chosen are allowed so many children, but for another to be given the opportunity to have five children is quite amazing! My Stephan qualified for five children, and it was almost an unprecedented thing at the time to be qualified for so many."

Minerva looked at Sojourner as if she had sprouted horns on her head. "What do you mean 'qualified'? My husband and I chose to stop at five children because we had two girls and this is the generation of reorganizing and we knew we would have to send them to another village once they were grown and we would never see them again. We did not think we could bear that. Two will be hard enough to say good-by to. It was our choice to stop. Actually, we have a small family by some standards."

Sojourner did not know whether to feel envy or outrage. To presume that one had a right to produce more children than the land could support was a fundamental act of foolishness. To produce children without regard to the gene pool was outrageous. To have as many children as one wished for was a dream come true. She steadied her voice and tried to sound nonchalant.

"Through our history we have been battling the effects of nuclear terrorism. Our ancestors numbered only twenty thousand people. That is a medium sized city surviving out of hundreds of millions of people. We gathered together and we made very difficult choices about survival. At first, the choices were harsh and now we can see that they were ill-advised. For instance, food was scarce and medical care was rudimentary. We culled ourselves mercilessly. Only the brightest and best were allowed to reproduce. The perfect specimens. Any genetic predispositions toward substance abuse or other aberrations were stamped out. Our population thrived for several generations, but then it became apparent the gene pool held surprises for us. Our children were effected by the decaying radiation, and our vigor was abated.

"Then a particularly brilliant young Healer discover the implants, and we have grown and prospered since then, though we all understand that it is only a solution that treats the symptom, and is not a cure. I, myself, have around ninety implants in my body. They bridge the neurological gaps that are my affliction. Without them, I am a complete invalid, only able to breathe and digest food. My heart beats. I think clearly. I am locked inside this faulty body. My implants give me a life. Still, I would never wish this weakness on another generation. Since I have been blessed with the ability to tell stories, I was granted the gift of bearing one child. To my great joy, she became identical twins, and I am thrilled about them every day. To my sorrow, my husband was qualified for five children, and he had to resign his rights to marry me. It is something I am ever mindful of, and I have to live with it as best I can."

"He must love you very much!" Chiria looked thoughtful. "He has made choices to benefit you."

"And now your daughters have children?" Simiat asked.

"Yes! They were each qualified for three! Neither of my girls have a single implant, just like their father. Sala is a teacher and Jakma is a journalist. They are named for brave sisters of the early Burrow that found a way to use recycled materials to make strong tools. Their names are reserved for twins so they are rarely used. When anyone meets them, they know the girls have the good fortune of being a twin."

Lara spoke, and Sojourner was surprised that the silent one had finally decided to join the conversation. "Do you mean that even your names are assigned to you?"

"No. Not assigned. But we are all named after historical characters or ancestor names. I am named after a great woman of ancient history, Sojourner Truth. Do you know of her?"

The women looked at their hands and a couple of them shook their heads.

"She was an amazing woman. Might I tell you about her?"

Lara looked up at Sojourner and said with a glint of humor in her eyes, "Can we stop you? You are a Storyteller."

Sojourner laughed, and it felt good to laugh. When she got home, she would laugh for days on end, just because it felt so good.

"Well, then have a seat and listen. I will tell you of Sojourner Truth, a great and determined lady. A champion of honor.

"Many, many long years ago, the Great Nation and the world had a terrible blight on its face. You see, it was a time when men and women were made into slaves because their skin was dark and their faces ethnically African. Faces like yours, Jonta, dark and full. Sojourner Truth was born a slave and was treated like a piece of property. She could not read or write and the condition of her soul was of little concern to her owners. She was of breeded stock, designed to be big and strong and work endless, long hours. She was not fed or cared for properly. When she was a young woman, she was given to another slave to breed with him and produce children. Her children were taken and sold. Her brothers and sisters were taken and sold. Her parents were taken and sold. Her life seemed hopeless. Then she had the opportunity to gain her freedom, and she worked hard and achieved it. She began to learn and to fill her great mind with the truth of a pure faith. She had been called Belle, but she changed her name to Sojourner Truth. She went about the land speaking against the horrors of slavery and the rules that stripped every woman of her freedom to make choices.

"She once gave a speech in rebuttal to a comment made by an ignorant man that suggested that women could not participate in the world of men because they were too weak. She rose up and showed her mighty arms and spoke with her compelling voice. This is what she said....."Well, Children, where there is such a racket, there must be something out of kilter....the white men will be in a fix pretty soon. But what's this about anyway? That man over there," she said pointing to a minister who had said that women were the weaker sex, "he says women need to be helped into carriages and lifted over ditches and to have the best of everywhere. Nobody ever helps me into carriages, over mud puddles, or gets me any best places. And ain't I a woman? Look at me!" She bared her muscular arm and the men and women gasped. "I have ploughed. And I have planted. And I have gathered into barns. And no man could head me. And ain't I a woman? I have borne thirteen children and seen them sold into slavery and when I cried out in a mother's grief, none heard me but Jesus. And ain't I a woman? You say Jesus was a man so that means God favors men over women. Where did your Christ come from? From God and a woman. Man had nothing to do with him. Suppose a man's mind holds a quart and a woman's don't hold but a pint, but if her pint is full, it's as good as a quart. If the first woman God ever made was strong enough to turn the world upside down all alone, these women together ought to be able to turn it back and get it rightside up again and now that they are asking to do it, the men better let them."

"The men who believed that women were weak were silenced and Sojourner went forward with her great work..."

Sojourner stopped. The women looked puzzled and somewhat horrified.

"What is ain't?" asked Jonta.

"Who is Jesus?" asked Pura.

"You know," offered Simiat, "there is no such thing as God?"

"Oh my!" said Sojourner, and she sat down heavily.

⁓ Chapter 24 ⁓

Sojourner's heart was pounding and she felt a trickle of sweat trailing down her back. Oh! Dear Maker in Heaven! Mercy! She prayed from deep in her soul. The Examiners guided her roughly, without regard for her fear or frailty. It was an understatement that things had gone terribly wrong.

The women had continued talking, learning about each other and beginning to open themselves to understanding each other. It had been almost a shock when Josilyn had arrived, breathless and frightened. She was dressed as a palace drudge, a servant to the former Kalig's Chosen. She came in like a barely contained scream, almost unable to convey the urgency of her news. The Captive's Ceremony had been moved forward in the schedule of the day. They only had bare minutes to escape. The patrols were watching everyone intently, and the safe house was not accessible. Then they heard the warning chimes, announcing the arrival of the Examiners. In a terrified flurry, Sojourner returned to the cell, understanding dawning on her that she could not betray the Chosen, that she had to protect them from the Examiners discovering their conversations.

She lay down on the cot in her cell, which she had learned was the holding cell for newly Forsaken Chosen, and pretended to sleep. She heard the Chosen rustling about, putting on their veils and fastening their robes. Josiyln was, no doubt, performing some task. Sojourner hoped she was not too distressed. Josilyn was a great Healer, and Sojourner knew that she would need her services very soon.

The Examiners came into the cloister; they did not speak to any of the Chosen, and they did not speak to Sojourner. They came into the cloister, fierce and silent, and they took possession of Sojourner. That was the only way she could think of it. They stood her on her feet and placed a metal ring around her neck that had semi-flexible poles attached to it. The Examiners then took hold of the ends of the poles and guided her out of the room as if she were a toxic beast being taken to slaughter. Sojourner felt fear thrum through her, humiliated and helpless; she was compelled along.

They guided her up a long, winding ramp and then through tightly secured doors into the vast corridors of the palace. Lining the walls, shoulder to shoulder, row on row, were men in the service of the Empire. She had never seen so many men standing so stiffly. If she had not been so frightened, if her eyes had not been so clouded by tears, if her blood had not been roaring through her veins, she would have taken delight in mentally describing them; the nobles dressed in their grandest clothing.... the military men with shining insignias of rank radiating from their somber uniforms....the musicians playing their strange rhythmic march. It would, no doubt, make a wonderful story, but only if something wonderful could happen to spare her from what was coming.

The Emperor Kalig was going to ritually hack off her fingers and send them to the Burrows to prove his intentions. That is what Emperors did to captive rulers. She must convince them she was not a barbarian queen. She had to make them understand. Slicing off portions of her body would be disastrous to the balance of her implants. The intense pain would be awful to experience, but also ruinous to her delicate system. Why had she decided to come? Why did she think her stories and persuasions would work on such a strange people?

Sojourner was marched down a narrow pathway that opened before them and closed behind them as they moved to the Hall of Judgement. Sojourner tried to look into the faces of the men as she passed, but they were filled with hatred and judgement and disgust, and so she did not look at them. Instead she stared straight in front of her and tried to step surely and steadily. She must not be a coward. These men were the enemy.

When the Examiners guided her into the imposing Hall of Judgement, Sojourner cringed. The room was as big as the commons at the Sand Burrow. What a waste to have so much unusable space. She felt lost under the vast ceiling and empty air above her. This room was less crowded. Only men of special merit would be in here. They sat in silence, rigid and stern. She knew that

Minerva's husband was in this room because he was a man of substance. She wondered fleetingly how he would feel if he knew that she had been talking about kissing techniques with his wife just a few minutes earlier. She had to repress a hysterical giggle at the thought of her shouting out how much more he would enjoy his "improper moments" with his wife.

An Examiner jerked her forward and she had to struggle to keep from falling. She looked up at the raised dais, and she saw a magnificent throne-like chair, and sitting in it was Kalig. She had watched him play with his children and she had listened to his rich lyrical song. He did not look the same now. His face was set and stern and his eyes smoldered like the feral eyes of a great predator. He seemed like a new kind of man, cruel and perfect in his strength. He was the Empire, and Sojourner understood that her stories would not touch this man at all. Her words would be noise and her face an affront. Somehow, she must find a way to talk to the man inside, the one that played with his children and sang songs like they were the most important music in the world. She needed to talk to the man who loved Chiria and missed his brothers. She hoped he was somewhere in this room and not lost in the power of the Empire

As they neared the dais, she saw the altar upon which she would be forced to kneel as her fingers were taken from her. She tried not to look at it, instead she looked at objects strewn about the floor around the throne. Her things, she realized with a shock. Her staff. Her hoverbike. Her jewelry. She realized with a shock that the leadership of the Burrow would know what was happening. Perhaps this would not be hopeless! At least they would know to be prepared to help her. These past few frantic minutes held hope as well as terror. She prayed that they were seeing everything, the vast hall, the great assembly. She hoped they would be able to prepare even better for the coming days.

Sojourner was forced up the steps and she mounted them with as much dignity as her fear would allow. Without concern for her pain, the Examiners pushed her down on her knees at the altar and strapped her arms out in front of her. They then tightly bound her to the alter so that she could not move. The broad bands were uncomfortable and pressed her tightly against the altar, making it hard to breathe.

All at once, the music stopped and the air was tense with deep silence. Kalig rose, graceful, powerful, fearsome, and approached the alter. He towered over her, and she had to crane her neck to look into his eyes. With all of her energy, she searched his face, trying to make a connection with him, trying to reach him. His face did not change.

"Captive!" he snarled, his voice amplified to fill the hall and the hallway. "The Empire requires your lands. Concede them, or face the annihilation of your people!"

"No, I cannot concede a free people to anyone. They will have to concede themselves one by one. I doubt they will be willing to do this. Additionally, you cannot annihilate us because you do not understand our technology. I would imagine you have had your best men trying to understand my little devices, and they can't even turn them on. Your words do not end my country, and they do not make you Emperor of anything other than this empty nation."

Kalig's eyes widened for a moment, then he smiled, a slow, dangerous smile. "You are right. We do not understand your technology, but we are mighty, and it will not take my subjects long to understand it and conquer it."

"That is not an issue. Untie me and I will show you how it works. It is no mystery. Even a child can make it work."

Kalig laughed. "You must think I am very stupid. Of course you will show me how it works as you try to escape on it. It is a clever little riding machine. Don't try to outwit me."

"How am I to escape from here with these poles attached to my neck and these big apes attached to the poles? Look at them. They act like a frail old grandmother is dangerous."

Sojourner knew that saying she was a grandmother would at least cause a gasp, but she did not expect the level of reaction that she received. Most of the men in the hall covered their ears and cried out in fear. Many stood and turned their backs, shouting out "Mercy!" and other such supplications. The Examiners and the Emperor seemed to expect their reaction and they calmly walked to the edge of the dais and stretched out their hands. Sojourner looked at them and realized with a shock that they all looked similar. These must be relatives of Kalig, near and more distant. They were all from similar casts, except the Examiners had all been castrated at some point in their development and had unnatural sounding voices and lean, boyish forms.

They shouted with one voice for silence. The men in the hallway gradually grew quiet, but there was a hum of murmured talk that still remained.

"Citizens, this is a crafty, unnatural, old hag of a woman! I have read every report made by our fact-finding squad, and in it, throughout it, they describe the outlandish behavior of this old woman. As a matter of fact, one who stands high among you had a son in this very squad, and he has spoken to his son. Lord Simon, come up here and tell the men of the Empire what your son has said."

A man rose from where he was sitting calmly amidst the chaos and strode to the dais with a proud, confident swagger. He was dressed very richly and his hair and beard were carefully groomed. His face was much like the face of his son, Lieutenant Simon, the cat killer, the teaser, the thief of fruit. If Soujourner had not been bound, she would have gone over and rubbed herself all over him so that he would have to be purified. That would be something to talk about in a story.

The men grew silent as Lord Simon struck a regal posture and began speaking. Pompous ass! Sojourner seethed with every word he spoke.

"Honorable men of the Empire. I have been privileged to speak with my illustrious son, an officer in the Imperial Military. What he had to tell me was so urgent that the Examiners, respect them in their sacrifice, gave him leave to speak with me before he was taken to be purified. What he told me scandalized me to my core. This unnatural creature has been swimming, unclothed, in pools of water outside in the plain sight of any passerby. This unnatural creature has embraced different men in the sight of all of her people. This ghastly creature told her people barbaric lies. As a matter of fact, she was observed telling a group of children a heinous tale about an Emperor that was so vain and ignorant that he believe in magic clothing and went about in public naked, not believing that he was naked until a child told him. What kind of madness is this?

"Never was she observed in the company of a family group. Never was she called "mother" or "wife" by any of those who interacted with her. Granted, this is a nation of unnatural people. They live in holes in the ground and frolic about like animals when they are not obsessively digging about in the soil. Harden your hearts against this woman. Harden your hearts against this strange people she represents. We do not need any of them. We may not have these specific technologies, but we are men of the Empire of Light. We will uncover the ways to work these paltry pieces of machinery. There are no mysteries that men of reason cannot unravel. We are the highest evolution of man, and there are none that can conquer us. It is our duty to remove low forms of humans, it is the great man that must survive. This is justified."

Sojourner felt outraged at the misrepresentation of her people. She breathed deep and said a calming prayer. She filled her voice with conviction and strength. "So you say, but you say much that is self-serving Lord Simon. How many in this assembly have suffered at your hands? I know a woman that has suffered at your hands, and her only crime was being Chosen late in the life of the former Kalig. Shall I say who fathered her child? She has whispered his name in my ear, and she is as afraid of him even now when she is safe as when she sacrificed her life to the service of the Empire. Shall I say his name Lord Simon? Shall I say how he made sport of her in the tunnels and maintenance passages? You speak of honor. How honorable is it to take advantage of others that struggle with finances? Is it honorable to undermine the efforts of others to forward your career? You speak of my life like you know it, but you don't. My truth is a sweet one. I am a Storyteller and a wife and mother and grandmother. I am beloved by my people because of my stories. I have deep friendships. I am a free individual. Measure my truth against yours. All those in this assembly know that your truth is a terrible one. There is no ritual that will purify you deeply enough to be beloved by anyone. Given the chance, how many men in this place would tear your heart out with their own hands and leave your carcass to be eaten by the carrion fowl? Look deeply in the faces of the men of the Empire and see if they have any loyalty to you, except out of fear. Believe this, Simon, when your Empire is contained, these men will tear you to shreds."

Lord Simon's face reddened and he raised his hand as if to strike her. He looked at the Examiner standing close by, and with great effort, he controlled his impulse. He obviously feared the Purifying ritual as much as anyone.

She turned in her bonds as best she could and she looked at Kalig. He had a surprised look on his face as if he had never heard this before, but perhaps suspected it. She softened her voice, filling every word with as much reason as she could.

"Sir, you and your people will never be able to master our technology because it is based on our DNA and other concepts that are excluded from your thinking. The DNA of our original twenty thousand survivors was used as the basis of our technology. We have extrapolated the possible combination of allels with each generation, and only those that fall within the possiblilities of that generation are able to operate our machines. We are a limited people and our genetic markers are clear. Further, our technology is based on using energies that rest in the earth. For instance, the huge magnetic field is harnessed, the rich chemical components of the atmosphere are harnessed. Even more, the toxic decay of the nuclear waste is harnessed and given a use. Finally, the intention of the user is harnessed. In ancient times this was called Ki, ch'i, the force, soul power, psychic power or some other such thing. It is the ability to reach beyond your own boundaries and explore the realm of prayer and pure thought. Philosophers have searched to understand this since man first had language. Your culture denies it, and so how will you use it? You don't believe in anything, so you are stuck here in this empty, hurting place. Alone and only barely satisfied. Sacrificed to this enormous, soul-less machine that forgets its dead children and requires you to walk through this hopeless life unloved. You may conquer us, but you cannot conquer our spirit. It will exhaust your resources trying to stay ahead of our development. Let me up from here, and let us make a treaty that will bring peace between us. Let me up from here and we will build a united world that will not demand all of your heart."

Kalig stood for a breathless moment, his face awash with indecision. He bent near to Sojourner and finally returned her deep look. For long moments, he searched her face. His eyes were full of sorrow and he looked lost and bereft. Sojourner felt a great wash of pity and she longed to hold him in her arms and rock him like she would a sad child.

"Mistress Storyteller, this is the Empire," he whispered. "It is the Law...."

With that he stood and he was the Emperor, and he commanded silence with his fierce eyes. His ferocious countenance was unreachable, devoid of mercy. With one quick savage motion, he raised a hatchet that had been on the floor out of sight, and with great and terrible force, he slammed it downward severing Sojourner's first two fingers and burying the hatchet deep in the alter. Without missing a moment and without any conscience or notice of Sojourner's screams, he reached downward again and raised a glowing hot poker and cauterized her bleeding hand. Sojourner slumped unconscious across the alter, her face pale and covered in sweat. The Examiners stepped forward and released her from her bonds, laying her down with ungentle sureness. Then they began roughly administering rudimentary first aid to her, first smearing a dark ointment across her outraged hand and then they began reviving her with an injection. They placed a breathing device over her face and waited.

While she was slowly regaining her consciousness, they casually gathered up her two severed fingers and placed them in a small vial of preservative, and then placed the vials in an ornate box.

Kalig took the box and held it high above his head. Ritually he held it out to yet another Examiner that strode upon the dais with the dark scowl of his calling branded on his face.

"Have this returned to the Burrows, to the leadership of the First Burrow, I believe it is called. Have the Captain of the expedition, Captain Jarvo, lead the delegates to the place. He will know the way, having been there before."

"Sire, the captain is in the final stages of being purified. He will not be ready to travel until noontime tomorrow. He will need to rest until morning, and we have been informed that he will need to tend to a medical issue with his wife after his ritual is complete. It is somewhat urgent."

"Are the fathers of Captain Jarvo and the Captain's honorable wife here among us? Bring them here."

There was a short wait as the fathers were escorted from the ranks of the military personnel. With stately precision, the men formally presented themselves to Kalig, stepping with measured dignity to the base of the dais and then kneeling on one knee before him, straight backed and stern faced. Each covered his heart with his fist and bent his head.

"Rise honored fathers. These are my instructions to you. General Chammera, what is the nature of your daughter's affliction?"

" A fistula, Majesty. It is obvious she suffers from a fistula."

"A fistula? Is your daughter honorable? "

"Yes, Sire. She is exemplary in every way."

"The child was conceived in a moment of weakness with my son just before he left to fulfill his glorious mission," explained Commander Jarvo.

"My daughter did not want to burden him or cause a difficulty for the Empire, so she kept the pregnancy a secret. It is their sixth child, and she did not realize it would be such a difficult pregnancy. When it came time to deliver it, she was unable to manage and developed a fistula. Her mother attended her as best she could, but it was useless. The baby was delivered dead and we tended to the disposal as the Law dictates. It was apparent that the fistula was a terrible one, and my daughter is suffering. It needs the attention of her husband as soon as possible." General Chamarra's voice was tight with concern.

"Yes, this is most unfortunate. Her husband may be gone for several weeks, and it can be a terrible thing for an honorable wife to suffer through. She has had the fistula for several months, then? Yes? This will not do. Go to the residence of your daughter and prepare an operating theater with all of the necessary provisions. Take your wife so that she might help prepare your daughter for the procedure. Afterward, both her mother and mother-in-law may tend to her needs. You may instruct them both through your wife."

"Commander Jarvo, after the procedure, you are to accompany your son on his journey to the Burrows. He will still be weakened from being Purified, and performing a fistula procedure on his wife may be taxing to his system. Tend to him well. He is a man of great honor. That all men of the Empire be honored with such accomplished sons."

Sojourner was aware enough to watch what was happening. Oh! Maker in Heaven! That these requirements were made of these people to preserve the might of a nation. She moaned as the fathers of Captain Jarvo and his silent wife, Jenta, stood and grave-faced, removed themselves with dignity from the presence of the Emperor.

The Examiners stood Sojourner on her feet and compelled her forward through ranks of men who hated her.

— Chapter 25 —

After what seemed an eternity, the purifying and purging stopped. The water drained from the scrubbing pool, slowly, pink tinged and hateful. An Examiner approached him and Ivan flinched, though he did not intend to do so. Again, without speaking, the Examiner began applying a soothing ointment, though his touch was rough as he smoothed it over Ivan's body. Ivan's chest and throat ached from screaming and his breath rasped in and out of him in painful gulps.

"You did well, Captain Jarvo!" the Examiner spoke suddenly. "Many are completely broken by this necessity. Your virtue must run deep. Now drink this. It will soothe your throat and nourish you. It also holds a sleeping agent. Soon after you drink it, you will become very drowsy, so you will need to be in a sleeping room quickly, before it takes full effect. It is important that you walk to the room because your skin is too fragile to be touched much more. Prepare yourself to walk as soon as you have drunk this."

For the first time since he was a small child, newly removed from his mother, Ivan felt tears trickle down his face for his own misery. Shakily, he drank the draught and was pleasantly surprised that it tasted like a strong beef broth. Suddenly he was hungry and thirsty enough to gulp the warm fluid, and he was surprised that it settled in his stomach and calmed it.

With his last resolve, he pulled himself out of the now empty cleansing pool and with trembling legs he stumbled after the Examiner, supporting his weight against the walls when he was near enough to reach out to one. The Examiner's back seemed to be retreating from him more quickly with every step, and he sobbed in grief and fear as he tried to make his exhausted body keep pace with the tormentor leading him. Suddenly, the Examiner stopped at a doorway and pushed open a door.

Ivan pulled himself forward, his entire being straining toward the door and sleep and peace. The opening beckoned him and he felt himself crying in frustration and pain, each step an agony of will. After what seemed like unmeasurable time, Ivan came to the door of his sleeping room. There in the corner was a thick pallet, clean and soft. Naked, exhausted and weeping for his mother, Ivan fell on the pallet and his eyes closed of their own accord.

...And then they opened after what felt like just a moment. An Examiner was shaking him awake. Ivan had to stop for a moment and remember where he was; his eyes were not easily focused and his head felt like it was full of smoke and fire.

"Captain Jarvo! You have many requirements today in the service of the Empire. In order to bolster your strength, we have taken the liberty of administering several healing treatments to your body through the night. Now here is food for you to eat. You must dress and eat very quickly."

Ivan felt a moment of nausea at the thought of Examiners touching him through the night without his knowledge. He hoped deep in his deepest places that he would never have to see another Examiner again. He nodded to let the Examiner know he had heard the instructions and understood. He stiffly dressed in his own clothing, clean and folded neatly by some Examiner. Then he walked with aching steps to the small table with a tray of food on it. He did not sit because the idea of bending his stiff body was unappealing. The Examiner looked at him sharply and indicated that he was to sit. Painfully, Ivan lowered himself into the hard chair and reached for the cover on the tray.

The food underneath was all that he had dreamed of eating during his long absence. There was a complicated dish of vegetables and rice with a thick dark sauce like the dish his mother prepared on festival days. There was a heaping plate of tender beef and pungent onions like the delicious dish his Jenta made for him on the nights when she would raise her eyes to his face as though she could not stop herself. There was hot bread and fresh fruit. Ivan felt gratitude welling up in him, and his tired, raw body and soul almost cried again, only this time with gladness. This reminded him that this day he would see his father and have knowledge of his mother's well-being. This day he would finally see his children. This day, he would see his Jenta, and tonight, he would hold her in his arms, despite any discomfort..

"This meal is a gift from the Emperor, one way he wishes to thank you for your devotion. Eat and grow strong, nourished by the strength of the Empire."

Ivan smiled, his hope and strength growing as he began to eat. He ate with relish and his heart sang in his chest. This was the best meal he had ever eaten. He was home and soon, after his obligations to the Empire were met, he would be truly home. He let his thoughts pour outward from him, imagining his family, the sturdy little boys and the sweet, laughing girls. He thought about Jenta and the sound of her voice in the woman's quarters, laughing and playing with their children. He imagined her robes curving against her body and he imagined just for a moment, her feel against him. He ate as fast as his belly and tiredness would allow. He was purified, and he was home. All was well.

"Your father has come to accompany you to your home. He has grave news to share with you. He is outside waiting for you."

The Examiner spoke matter of factly. Grave news? Ivan felt his happiness drain away, and he had to fight the fury rising in him. He felt almost compelled to attack the Examiner, but he knew that even as deadly a fighter as he was, the Examiner would kill him without thought. He swallowed the food in his mouth. It felt like lead in his stomach.

"Do you know the nature of the grave news? Is my family well?" Ivan struggled to keep his voice steady.

"It is a matter of family," the Examiner said the word as though it was heavy in his mouth. Ivan looked at him and saw that his face was like the Emperor's face. This could be one of the younger brothers. Ivan had a brief moment when he felt sorry for the Examiner because he knew he had never known his mother and would never know the comfort of a wife. The moment passed quickly, and the Examiner continued, "Your father will tell you the details and how they concern you."

Ivan nodded and stood up. He looked at the plates on the table and was surprised at how little was left on the tray. It seemed he had only eaten a few bites. "My gratitude for the fine meal, sir. The Empire is indeed mighty and gracious to its faithful!"

The Examiner nodded, pleased that Ivan had thanked him, and then he led Ivan out into the corridor. Ivan blinked his eyes, trying not to show his astonishment; he had only walked a short distance last night, though he had felt as if he had walked the longest journey of his life. He followed the Examiner through the hallway, retracing his steps from yesterday. Had it only been yesterday that he had come to these halls? Part of him could perceive that the place was beautiful, but still he walked as quickly as his stiff, sore body would allow.

He passed through the graceful entrance hall, but he paid it no mind. Through the doors, on the walkway outside, he saw the straight, strong back of his father standing in the cool brightness of the morning's first light. Without a thought as to how he might appear to anyone else, Jarvo ran as fast as his soreness would allow, to greet him. His father turned as Ivan burst through the outer doors and stood blinking in the bright glare of sunlight, laughing and crying and trying to remember his dignity. His father seemed to swell with joy and relief when he saw his son and hurried to him, holding out his arms as if to embrace him, but then stopping just out of arms reach. It would not be proper to embrace. Ivan understood, and covered his heart with his hand, a gesture usually reserved for moments of the greatest honor, and slowly lowered himself to one knee. It was not the same as an embrace, but his father would know what it represented.

"Father!" his voice cracked. "I have returned to serve the Empire!"

His father took him gently by his shoulders and raised him up, his eyes full of pride and concern. "This is a good moment, son. But right now, the Empire can wait as you tend to the needs of your wife."

"Jenta? What is wrong with her?" Ivan felt his stomach clench and his breath stop inside him as though some large hand was smothering him. "What are her needs?"

"Come, I have many things to tell you, and this is not the place to discuss them. Our transport is waiting."

They crossed the compound as quickly as Ivan's stiffness would allow. An officer's car awaited them, long and sleek. Ivan had a fleeting wish that it hovered, but it did not. He could smell its exhaust, and it was irritating to him. The driver opened the passenger door and Ivan and his father slid inside. The interior was soft and rich, but dark and somber.

As soon as the car started moving, Commander Jarvo turned to his son. "There are three things I need to tell you. The first is that your wife has developed a fistula. Your mother and I are caring for your children in our apartments, so they are not an incovenience to her in her illness."

"I didn't know that she was expecting a child, or else I wouldn't have gone! When did she deliver?"

"You have been gone a year, and she delivered almost nine months to the day after you left. Did you command her to come to you before you left?"

"Yes," Ivan lowered his head. "I knew it was imprudent, but she fills up my thoughts...."

"Your mother fills mine; don't blame yourself for being a man." His father looked out the window, as if he was embarrassed at the admission. "The child, of course, was stillborn."

"I have always had to use great care when delivering our babies. It is not possible for her to deliver without assistance." Ivan felt a pang of sadness. "Was it a boy or girl?"

"A girl. The General made the arrangements for her disposal, though it was decided to wait until you returned to enter a name in the records."

"So Jenta, er, rather my wife, has been alone and bereft for three months in this condition?"

"It is unfortunate that she has had to suffer like this. Her father petitioned the Examiners to allow him to correct the tears in her bladder and bowel, leaving the other wounds for you to repair, but they denied the claim. Jenta has been isolated because of the odor, which is a great difficulty for her. Her mother and your mother visit her daily and bring her food and supplies. Your wife had struggled to keep herself as acceptable as possible, but of course, it is impossible with the extent of the damage. She is in great need of you."

"Has she been given no help for her pain?"

"The Examiners allowed her father to run scans on her and prepare the necessities of the procedure. All is in readiness for you."

"Are you telling me that I must do the procedure on her today? I would do better if I could practice for a day or two on a simulator. I might not do well. I have not done a fistula procedure since my training days. Why does it need to be done today? One more day or so will not make her worse, and I will do a better job of it with some practice first."

"There is something else I need to tell you. It is not good news for you." He paused and watched his son gathering his resolve about him. Ivan nodded curtly, indicating he was ready to listen. The Commander felt a swell of pride. His son was honorable and strong. "Before nightfall, the Emperor has decreed that you will accompany the delegation back to the Burrows to guide them to the leadership."

Ivan turned wide eyes toward his father, and for a moment the years and discipline seemed to disappear from his face, and once more he was the frightened child that had just taken a beating from his brothers. The Commander felt his heart clench in his chest, just like it did when his little son had raised his battered face to him all those years ago. He watched his son struggle with his emotions and he longed to make the world right for him.

"Could another squad member go? What of the Lieutenants? Bosson or Simon?"

"There is a madness in Bosson. The Examiners have determined that he must be contained until he recovers his senses. Last evening, after the Captive's Ceremony, Lord Simon received an injury from the captive and his son must stay and try to help him."

"An injury from the captive? She is a frail, crazy, old woman. What could she possibly have done to Lord Simon?"

"After the ceremony, she begged for her walking stick to help her keep her balance as she was taken back to the cloister. The emperor allowed it. When she had it in her hands, she held it and caressed it like it was an old friend, then as they began to move to the stairs, she seemed to stumble, and she managed to give Lord Simon a good solid rap on the head with its tip. Of course, Lord Simon had managed to get himself on the dais, as he always does, so it is his fault for being where he ought not to have been. The blow must have been worse than was thought, because throughout the night, he behaved in the most irrational manner."

Ivan looked at his father with interest, momentarily distracted from his worries.

"What did Lord Simon do?"

"He went about the city to many residences, giving back deeds to property and divulging plots and intrigues. This morning he is all but penniless. The Examiners have collected him, and have sent his son, weak and miserable, to try to salvage his father's estates." The commander paused, and Ivan saw a glint of humor in his father's eyes. "That little, crazy, frail woman must have hit him harder than it looked. There are many in the Empire that would like to keep her for a bit, and see who else she might hit."

Ivan laughed in spite of himself. "Her staff holds implants that can be programmed to modify behaviors. He will need to be scanned carefully, as well as Bosson. It is a sinister technology that we did not know about until just days ago on the ship. Though in Bosson's case, it has improved his behavior."

"How is that?"

"Lieutenant Bosson is a cruel man, and he delights in the power of his position. He has no scars on his hand, and he uses the most force allowable in any situation. I have often wondered why he wasn't an Examiner because he has the taste for the demands of the job. After he was implanted, any cruel thought he had would cause him to exhibit bizarre behaviors that were embarrassing to him. It was troubling, but he was a kinder acting man as a result."

"I imagine we should inform the Emperor at once!" the Commander exclaimed. Then he paused and considered for a moment. "Well, we should inform him by the end of the day. Lord Simon has more restitution to make, I am certain, and it should be done by the end of the day.

"Ah! Yes! One more bit of news, the third thing I was to tell you. I will be accompanying you to the Burrows, but only as your father. The Emperor has decided you need someone to tend to your needs for a span. Is that acceptable?"

Ivan felt oddly vulnerable, but glad as well. He had a hard time imagining anyone tending to him, but the tired sadness in his bones and his heavy concerns made him realize that he would need his father. "None of the other squad members could go? None of them?"

"During purification, the other squad members confessed to having listened too closely to the speeches of the Queen. Without exception, they have all confessed to believing in a god and to questioning the Laws that make us mighty. They are all in the care of the Examiners. This was a perilous mission, it seems."

Ivan sagged against the plush seat. So much lost in this mission. His men were all lost. He felt like a failure. He should have forseen the damage a seductress could do. Frail old lady! Never! She was evil.

Ivan felt his father straighten, and he looked up. He noticed that they were in the residential complex provided for the military, and he straightened. His father looked over at him and smiled encouragingly. "We are here. Take a moment to gather your wits. Remember that your wife has been scanned and there will be a clear set of guides to help you. We will be right outside if you need us."

Ivan nodded. He was not ready to face such a challenge, but that was the nature of challenges. They came from unexpected places. The driver opened the door for him and saluted him. Ivan saluted him back distractedly and only paused a moment before he began yet another long walk. He squared his shoulders and forced his feet to walk steadily. He should be running for joy up the steps, bounding into his long-awaited homecoming. He should be greeting his wife and children and settling down for an afternoon spent with them. This is not the way for a man to come home, he caught himself thinking.

His father walked beside him in silence and together they rode the elevator up to the floor where Jenta was isolated. Halfway down the hallway he saw two robed figures standing silently with an Examiner. He must not falter in front of the Examiner. He must not falter in front of his mother. His mother! He breathed in deeply and he and his father strode with similar steps down the hallway to the trio.

"Sir, I would speak to my wife!" the Commander addressed the Examiner.

The Examiner nodded, and Commander Jarvo turned to his wife.

"Honorable one! I bring our son, Ivan to this place. He has served the Empire, and now he comes to perform his duty to his wife. Know that I am proud of him and I speak a greeting to you on his behalf."

Ivan's mother nodded and turned toward him. His heart beat faster. He had not seen his mother since his marriage, and though his father kept him appraised of her well-being, this was the first time he had actually seen her in many years. He longed to lift her veil and look into her face. He would have treasured a touch from her hand. Instead he returned her bow though his hands trembled with emotion.

The Examiner knocked discreetly on the door of the isolation room, and it creaked open. General Chammera came out, and smiled an encouraging smile at Ivan.

"My daughter waits for you. She asked to be awake so that she could greet you. Be aware that she is ashamed of her condition, but her desire to see you before you are taken again was stronger than her shame."

"General Chammera, your daughter need not be ashamed of her unfortunate condition. I would be honored to greet her regardless of any illness she might suffer. She is a proper and fine woman, and remembering her honor has given me strength all these months. With your leave, sirs, I will go in."

Ivan tried to be calm as he opened the door and went into the isolation room. It was spotlessly clean, and prepared for the operation. Lying on the operating table, covered with a white sheet and veiled, was a slender figure.

"Jenta." Ivan spoke, but his voice came out only as a hoarse whisper. He cleared his throat. "Honored wife." The prone figure stirred and struggled to sit.

"No, be still. I will wash and come over to you."

Ivan crossed to the corner of the room and quickly stripped and stepped into a shower stall . Water with some sort of antiseptic sprayed him, stinging against his already purified flesh. The water stopped and then his body was blown dry with a stream of warm air. As quickly as he could manage, and tripping over his eagerness to touch his Jenta's face, he pulled on his operating uniform and covered his hair and face with the required coverings. As he crossed the room to Jenta, he pulled on one glove, but left one hand uncovered. He wanted to touch her face and feel her skin just once.

He came close to her, and he could smell the foul odar of the fistula, but he paid no attention to it. He came closer to her and he removed her veil and looked at her face. She was thinner than she should have been and her color was not the creamy brown of his memory, but ashen. Her hair was dull with illness and her eyes were shadowed with pain and loss.

Her eyes met his, and they were full of tears. "Oh, Ivan! You are finally here. I wish I were not so horrible. I have lost our baby and I am foul."

"Hush, now. Don't fret." Ivan spoke from his deepest places. "We will mourn for her when this is over. Right now, it is important that you become well. It is important to me that you are well because I treasure you and..." his voice became thick with emotion, "and I love you. So be strong for me little Jenta."

"You love me? I have hoped you would love me for a very long time. I love you as well. I have from the moment you bled for me. I will be stronger now because I know."

Ivan took his uncovered hand and traced it down the thin curve of her face and across her lips. She loved him. Her skin was still as soft as clouds. He longed to touch her more, but he knew his duty to her was pressing.

"We will start now," he said. He pressed the preset anesthetic and she was quickly asleep. Resolutely he pulled on the other glove and walked to the instrument table. He wished for a moment that he could cut his hand again and bleed for her instead, but he could not. He lifted the sheet and positioned her body. Without knowing why, he paused and thought of the Maker of the barbarian queen. He picked up a scalpel. From his deepest places, he prayed, though he did not know why.

~ Chapter 27 ~

Minerva woke up and moaned again. Her knee throbbed and her head hurt. She turned in bed carefully, gingerly moving her sore leg over the edge and carefully standing on it. Lorn stirred, but did not wake. Good, he needed to sleep for a while. He had a long, terrible day ahead of him. It had been a long, terrible night.

The Examiners had come like a storm and had removed Sojourner like a paper slip caught in its wind. Sojourner had been compelled to go with them, trembling and only barely containing her fear. Minerva, the Chosen, and the drudge had been in shock at the swiftness of the moment. Josilyn, the drudge, dropped to her knees and sobbed.

"She will not be killed tonight..." It was the soft-spoken Lara. "He will remove her fingers, two of them, and a delegation will be sent to your country to demand surrender. There is time for you to plan."

"That is not why I am weeping. Sojourner is very delicate, very frail. She was born with an affliction all too common in the Burrows. You see, our land was destroyed by toxic warfare a thousand years ago, and our ancestors were driven underground. There were only twenty thousand left on the entire continent, and there was barely anything alive. Still, we survived and developed. Despite that, the toxins cause serious problems with our gene pool. There are so few healthy people in our land. So few that function without implants to bolster them. Sojourner is one of the most ill of those that can function. In fact, the first eight years of her life were spent without hope. It is only because of her extraordinary spirit that she has lived and become so great. Her life is amazing. Beyond all hope, she is alive and revered. She is a mother and a wife. She fills our thoughts with great images. She is God's gift to our people. To see her treated so poorly is a travesty. Having her fingers chopped off would be bad enough for you or me, but for her, it will be devastating. It may not be possible for her to be rescued tonight. I am a healer in my country, and I have worked on her before. Even if I can make her strong enough to travel on land, her implants may need a day or two to readjust so that they can tolerate flight. She is delicate and wonderful and requires special care."

Pura stepped forward and knelt beside her. "I believe you that your nation is greater than we imagined, and I believe you that Sojourner is a great woman in your country. I want to take my three little sons to your country and let them grow up to be brothers and have a real future. We need to plan now, while the eyes of the Empire are watching your Sojourner. We must plan how to help her. And us!"

Minerva stepped forward and knelt, too. Her heart was pounding in her chest. "I do not know what I want, but I do not want this. Surely there is something that can be done."

Lyla's voice crackled into the air. "There is something. I know the passages under the palace and they connect to the sewers. All of the homes are connected. The Forsaken roam the tunnels at night, and seek food in the refuse of the Empire. The ducts leading to the individual houses are numbered according to village and resident. For instance, Pura, you lived in the village of Deepvalley, like I did. Your house was three away from mine. Mine was three from the duct. There is an access by each duct for workers to enter and exit. The Examiners also use these entries to monitor whether or not too much food is being wasted. When I have needed, I have gone to Deepvalley, to the top where I would meet my father, and he would help me when he could. It was very dangerous for him, and his signs were rare. The Forsaken all survive by watching for the signs from their families in the duct work. My sign from my father was a red rag tied around a food bone. If an Examiner or a worker found it, he might think it odd, but not strange enough to investigate. He would usually assume that it was a piece of trash that had fallen out of the processing duct. It happens. Once an Examiner became suspicious about it and questioned my father, but he said it was his way of telling his wife that his meat was ill-prepared. The Examiner accepted the explanation. There is a secret network of help to the Forsaken, though it only relieves our misery for a moment. If my need were dire, I would take the rag and place it under the edge of the access cover, just barely sticking out. Every few days, my father checks to see if my need is dire." Her voice grew sad. "I imagine he will wonder after a while, why I have not shown him my color."

"Lyla," Minerva's voice cracked, "Somehow this will be used to help us. How would I know to direct someone to my home?"

"What is your village called?"

"Lord's River. There is no longer a river, but that is what it is called. I do not know where the entry to the duct would be because it is outside the village toward the street. I have never been there. I am certain that my husband or sons would know. "

"Oh. I understand that. Is there a possibility that your husband would allow you to speak about this?"

"We do not have a proper household. We hide it carefully."

Kata looked up in surprise. "Your household is a hidden one? Your husband is Lord Lorn Provo, and your household is not proper? How can that be?"

"It is not strange to come from an improper home." Jonta stood and stretched as though her back was tired. "I grew up in an improper household. My mother was a raging tyrant with the temperment of a pack of snarling dogs. My father is a man of rank in the Administration, and he commands respect from all of the men in his branch of this government. When he comes home at night, he is reduced in rank to a houseboy. I am here in the service of the Empire as a result. The Examiners gave them the choice of my mother becoming Forsaken or me being placed as a candidate for the Emperor's Chosen. My father could not even stand up to her in this, and now I am sacrificed to this place. If there is some way I can take my baby daughter and the son I carry to a distant place, I will certainly do it."

Lara brushed her wheaten hair back from her face and cuddled one of her sturdy twins. "Well, I grew up in a proper household, but I don't know if it was better than that. My father required my mother to be silent, even when she was in the women's quarter. He required silence from his daughters and strict obedience from his sons. My mother hobbled wherever she walked because of the depth of her purification. She was constantly in pain and his requirements of her were a misery to us all. She bled and suffered infections constantly. Life was like a punishment every day for her and for us, his children. Finally, my grandfather began to suspect her mistreatment, and the Examiners came. My father was purified deeply, but it did not work. He was purified again and again, but his manners did not change. Finally, he was Outcast for his treatment of his family. In gratitude, and for protection from my father's family, I was placed as a candidate for the Chosen. If there is a place where my mother can be tended and we are all safe from the caprices of my father's people, I want to go there."

"Actually, I wouldn't want to go anywhere but home." Simiat spoke thoughtfully. Her pale hair falling about her, and her blue eyes distant. "My nation rebelled against the Empire, and my father was one of the leaders of the rebellion. When the rebellion was put down, the fathers in the leadership were all required to place their eligible daughters as candidates for the Chosen. I was the unfortunate one. I just want to go home with my children where the Examiners are not as feared and our private lives are more free. There is a young man there, and although I might not ever be joined to him now, I still might catch a glimpse of him through the window. I would love to be with my mother and work in our garden in the sunshine. My girls might have the chance to choose their husbands. It was once a pleasant place to live, though I imagine it becomes more and more like this place since the rebellion."

Minerva felt a pang of discomfort. She knew the treaty well because she had written it. It had seemed a good idea at the time. 'A Chosen is required to bind the treaty.' Simiat was the hostage. She was sweet and funny, and she had been given away to an Empire she did not love.

"Enough of this." Lyla's voice rang out and startled everyone out of their private thoughts. "Minerva, if you can manage to convince your improper husband to be of help, use my color, a red rag, and dangle it down into the cover, like it is stuck under the edge. When you arrive, remove the rag so they will know you are there. If your husband is unwilling, the absence of a rag will tell them it is not safe. Josilyn, here are the directions from the palace to the place where Lord Provo lives."

"You know the way to my house?" Minerva was stunned.

Lyla laughed. "You are quite a renowned cook, Mistress. Some of the Forsaken have been at state dinners and we remember your cooking well. There are hardly ever any leftover thrown away, but ocassionally we have been lucky. Though, as of late, there have been some fairly terrible things come down your duct. Do you have a daughter that struggles to learn to cook?"

Minerva laughed, chagrined. "My Tooya is not doing well with her training at all. She would rather tell stories to the children in the creche or draw fanciful pictures on scraps of paper. She also likes to build little devices. She has no talent for cooking."

"Yes, that is true. I seem to remember bacon and orange stew. Still, I ate it. The life of the Forsaken is not one of choices. But enough of this! Write down how to get from the palace to your duct. Josilyn, write it down, it is complicated."

"We can't use paper, we will be questioned." Josilyn thought for a moment. "Mistress Minerva, write it on your thigh, no one will see it there, and you can recopy it when you get home."

Minerva sat with Josilyn, and as quickly as they could, they wrote the directions to use to guide them through the tunnels. It would be difficult, but if she had to, she was resolved to search for Sojourner herself. Lorn had to see the reason behind helping her. He would need proof.

They were just completing the directions when they heard the chime signalling the return of the Examiners. Quickly they lowered their skirts and put on their veils. They all went and stood by the walls, holding the children back and silencing them as best they could. The outer door opened and the Examiners half dragged in their prisoner. She stumbled between them using an ornate walking stick to help her keep her balance. Silently, the Examiners unfastened the poles and then the collar from her neck, then the larger of the two casually lifted her under her arms and carried her like one would a distasteful small burden, away from his body and with a disgusted expression on his face. He took her into the cell and carelessly dropped her on the cot. She collapsed in an ashen-faced heap, clutching the stick close to her with her maimed hand, and moaning miserably. The Examiner then turned and closed the door to the cell with a hard and resolute crash as if to signify its finality. He then gestured to Minerva to follow him. She had been holding back a squirming blond-haired girl, who ran and hid under a table as soon as she was released.

Minerva felt a fury rising in her. There was no reason for this type of cruelty. There was no cause for it. She longed to lash out at them and kick and scream, but she was too afraid. Instead she followed stiffly, the opaque eye-holes hiding the fury in her eyes. The Examiners walked in front of her, their backs stiff, their steps long and unyielding. Minerva had to half run to keep up with them. Her robes tangled about her legs and her veil crowded against her nose and mouth, making it difficult to breathe. She felt a stitch in her side and she gasped in great gulps of air whenever she could. The ramp leading to the cloister door seem to be too far away. Suddenly, the Examiners stopped and turned. Minerva had been concentrating on trying to keep up with them and she stumbled on her hem and fell painfully on her knee.

"Wife of Lord Provo, be advised that your husband will be included in the delegation going to the Captive's lands. Do not pack too many articles of clothing for him. He is allowed only one valise. In his absence, our order will be providing an escort for your oldest son to the market once a week to buy provisions. We caution you against extravagance in your husband's absence. Further, we are aware that your daughter, Tooya, is approaching marriagable age. During our visit recently, we became aware that her cooking is quite bad. We will require Tooya to show improvement." The Examiner that spoke looked at her intently. "Do you understand our requirements?"

Breathlessly, Minerva nodded. She stifled a whimper. Her knee throbbed.

"Do you require assistance to stand?" The second Examiner asked matter of factly. Minerva nodded. The Examiner extended his hand to her and uncertainly, Minerva placed her hand in his. His hand trembled slightly as she pulled herself up, and she heard him breathe in sharply. She looked up quickly into his face and saw him looking at her with fleeting hunger and sorrow mingled. For a moment she had a new understanding, and it made her heart weep in her. He was an Examiner, but he was a lonely man first, castrated and untouched. It became easier to understand his anger.

He released her hand slowly, as if he treasured the connection, and for a moment he looked at his hand in silence.

"Brother!" the first Examiner spoke sharply. "Be at peace."

"Yes! I know this is the price," the second mumbled. He squared his shoulders and turned away. "Try to keep pace with us, wife of Provo."

They began walking, but at a slower pace. Minerva was grateful for that, but still it took all of her energy to move up the ramp. The Examiner that had trembled at the touch of her hand was the same man that had dropped Sojourner like a bundle of soiled rags. She wanted this long, sad day to end. If he knew she was an honorable wife, would he have trembled to touch Sojourner? Minerva wanted to be home. She could not think clearly.

Finally, they reached the top of the ramp and stopped. The cloister doors were heavy and plain on this side. She leaned against the wall and rubbed her sore knee. Yes, she would definitely have to put ice on it, but it would be fine. The second Examiner opened the door a crack and peered out. "The corridor is still very full. She will need to wait until it empties more to avoid any accidental touch. Her honor must be preserved." He spoke to Minerva over his shoulder. "Wife of Provo, if you need to sit to relieve your knee, then do so. When your husband is here and the corridors are cleared, we will allow your husband to come inside the door to help you up if you cannot manage "

Minerva bowed her head, hoping he would see the gesture, and thankfully she lowered herself to the ground. The Examiner nodded. His companion spoke quietly to him for a moment, their stange high pitched voices sounded like bees humming as they conversed quietly.

The crowd that had gathered parted and the medicart was positioned. Lorn lifted Minerva as carefully as he could, grunting with the effort to not jostle her knee. Minerva gritted her teeth and held in her moans.

The man that fell on her was being held tightly by several bystanders. He was pleading with them piteously to be let go. It was an accident. His lord needed him. The witch had cast a spell. All was lost. On and on his litinay of angst poured out of him, and then he was abruptly silent. Again the crowd parted and the Emperor was there, and from what little of his face Minerva could see through her pain and opaque eye holes, his face was dark with anger and fiercesome.

"What is this? Who is disturbing my evening meal?"

The shorter Examiner stepped forward. "Sire, we returned the wife of Provo to the top of the ramp, waiting until the majority of the contigent had left. We had just allowed the wife of Provo out of the cloister doors so that her husband could take her home when this man," he pointed to the captive servant, "ran into her and injured her leg. It was already weakened from a fall on the ramp leading to the cloister, but it was merely bruised. Now, the injury will take some skill to set and mend. This is an honorable woman, that has already been established, her fault being she sings while she does her housework, as you recall."

"Let me see her knee."

There was a murmur of shock as the Examiners stepped forward and blocked Minerva from view. Minerva felt panic rise in her as the Emperor raised her skirt to her knees and examined her knee.

"Yes, I think I know what has happened. Is there a scanner?" There was a flurry of activity as a supply cart was brought. "My brothers and I became very good at tending to this type of wound during our training." He passed a scanning device over her swollen knee. "Ah! Yes! This is a simple matter."

Kalig injected her knee with some medication and the pain in her knee dulled and then subsided completely. He smiled to himself as he incised her knee and performed some type of procedure, looking at his scanner often for reference. He worked with rapid, sure hands, and he hummed in his beautiful voice as he worked. He seemed content, and sure of himself. In a short time, he was done, and he closed the wound with a stitcher and splinted her knee. He sterilized the area and lowered her skirt.

"Wife of Provo, your leg will be much better in a few days. Now, tell me, what do you have written on your thigh? I saw a hint of dark writing, and I am curious as to what it is."

Minerva felt sweat trickling down her face and blinding her.

"Father of All," she whispered, "It is a recipe. I did not want to forget the ingredients to tell your Chosen, and I was afraid I would lose a piece of paper. I did not think I would lose my leg. I guess I was wrong."

Kalig looked at her in wonder.

"Did you just make a joke to the Emperor? Brilliant!" He threw back his head and laughed. "You guess you were wrong. A recipe!" He turned to Lorn. "Sir Provo, you will be allowed to talk to your wife freely for one hour a day. Not only can she sing and cook, but she has the grace under difficult circumstances to be clever. This talent should not be wasted."

Kalig then turned to the servant being held by the onlookers.

"Explain yourself."

"Majesty," the servant blubbered, "My master, Lord Simon has taken leave of his senses. A short time ago, he suddenly grabbed his head where the captive struck him with her stick and he cried out. He began ranting about his sins and crying for forgiveness. He ran out of the palace determined to repair all of his past wrongdoings." The servant dropped his eyes. "Not that there are any of significance. I tried to stop him from running out of the palace in his distressed state and I accidentally knocked down the good wife of Lord Provo. I did not know there was an honorable woman in the corridor, or else I would have been careful to avoid touching her."

"It would have been more prudent to go to the patrols to retrieve your lord. You must not hurt an honorable wife. It is the basis of civilization to keep her tame and protected from harm. Would my brothers, the Examiners stand forward, please?"

The two Examiners stepped forward and took the servant firmly by each arm. The men in the corridor began to move away, clearly frightened. Kalig gestured to one of the guards standing nearby and took his gun. The servant began to wail and scream, pleading for mercy. Kalig took practiced aim and shot him in the knee. He returned the gun to the guard. Minerva gasped and closed her eyes. The man continued to scream. Kalig turned to Minerva.

"Wife of Provo, no one will ever hurt an honorable wife in the Empire of Light." Then he turned to the Examiners. "Take him and tend to his leg, and when he is well enough, purify him." He paused and looked deeply at the tall Examiner, and Minerva thought that he smiled a greeting to him. The Examiner slightly raised his eyebrows. This must be one of the youngest brothers. She did not want to think of these things. She felt sick.

"Minerva," Lorn whispered to her. "Let us go."

Minerva nodded, relieved, and Lorn started pushing her medicart toward the waiting transport. The sobbing, hopeless servant was also being loaded onto a medicart. Minerva felt sorry for him, and she wanted to vanish. She wanted to go back three days and just be discontent with her life instead of being embroiled in the doings of the Empire.

The ride home through the deepening night was uneventful and silent. Lorn was permitted to ride with her in the transport, but he was troubled and concerned, and only quietly sat beside her, holding her hand. That was good. She did not want to talk yet. They rode in silence, and in silence they were helped into their home. When they got inside, Lorn still was silent.

At their home, Lorn helped her off the medicart and onto a couch in the women's quarters. Their children were still up, waiting for them. There was a flurry of explanations and whispered exchanges. Tooya had found all of the listening devices, she thought, and had them in the loop box in the kitchen. Born had fixed dinner. Shin and Lonta had cleaned up, but had broken a dish. Tooya had been too bossy, and Lonta had peeked out the street windows at some boys. Lorn and Minerva accepted sympathy and handed out justice and praise as needed, and in their usual loving, quarreling flurry, the children went to their rooms to sleep. Finally, they were alone, and finally, they were safe enough to speak, though Minerva still did not want to speak out loud fearing a stray listening device.

"My love!" Minerva whispered. "You have been appointed to the delegation to the Burrows. The Examiners told me. This is what we hoped for. You will represent the Empire in a far place."

"It matters, but not as much as I thought. It will be hard for me to represent our Empire fully proud."

"What do you mean? This is what we have dreamed of ever since we heard the Blasted Lands had regrown." Minerva watched her husband carefully, wanting to hear how he felt before she told him all she was thinking.

Lorn crossed to a chair and slumped into it. His face was taut and unhappy. "Tonight I saw the leader of our Empire hack the fingers off a frail old woman. I can't be proud of that even if she is improper, or even if she were a fiend from a nightmare. I can't be proud of that," his voice trailed off into silence.

"Maybe there is more hope than you realize."

"Minerva, you did not see what I saw. I think you are the brightest and best mind in the Empire, but you do not get to see all that I see, and I haven't the words to explain it all...."

"My love, I have something to tell you. I have many things to tell you, and they might be great things. I have seen things tonight that I haven't the words to explain as well. It is not all as we thought. In the cloister, the captive demonstrated many wonderous things, and we spoke to Lyla, the Forsaken. She is safe in the Burrows. She spoke of the hidden greatness of the Burrows and its great technologies. The captive, Sojourner, was able to compromise the locks on her cell and she walked among us and we shared like sisters."

Lorn sat up straight and turned a blank look toward his wife. "What happened?"

Excitedly, she told Lorn of all that had happened to her in the cloister. She watched his face sag in disbelief and then grow intent as she talked. " She said we would be welcome in the Burrows," Minerva finished. "That it is possible for us to have a better life"

Lorn stood up and walked to the window and flicked a corner of the curtain aside to look out. When he turned around, Minerva could see the conflict playing across his expression. "How would that be possible? Sweetness, the Empire is mighty, and there is no power to stand against it. Even with great technologies, I doubt any power on Earth is mighty enough to withstand this organization"

"Husband! Listen! Let's say that we decide not to believe that the Burrows are more powerful than we imagined, and it ends up capturing us. We are lost. I say that we should listen to the captive and be prepared to believe if we see enough evidence."

Lorn rubbed his eyes tiredly. "I would love to talk to the captive, but I don't see how that is possible."

Minerva sat up painfully and leaned closer to her husband. "It is possible, Lorn. She will be here later if we allow it."

Lorn tensed and looked at her in astonishment. "What do you mean? How can she be here later if we allow it?"

Minerva raised her robe and displayed her thigh. "See this? It is a map of the sewers that run beneath the Empire. There should be an opening outside this compound that workers use. If we put a red rag underneath the edge of the cover that blocks the entrance, and we watch it for a span of time, and the rag is removed, then we will know that the captive is ready to come up and be here with us."

"Minerva, I saw the captive! She was devastated by the ceremony. When Kalig chopped off her fingers, she was ruined. She is a frail old woman. She will not be here any time soon. She may not go anywhere ever again."

"One of the drudges in the cloister is also a woman from the Burrows. She is a spy and a Healer in their communities. I know, it is shocking! She was hiding in the cloister to tend to the wounds of the captive, and she assured us that she was going to remove the captive and hide until the shield sticks are activated."

"Minerva, this is all too fantastic. What shield sticks? What is a shield stick? Why would the Chosen agree to help a renegade old woman from a backward land? I'm telling you, that if I didn't know you to be such a sensible woman, I would not listen to a word of this. We are both overtired. Let's go to bed."

"Please Lorn! Just humor me in this. Just once. Put the rag in place."

"Very well, I will, but only to humor you," his voice held an unusual edge of irritation.

Lorn got up slowly, his tiredness draped about him like a robe, and went to Minerva's workroom where she sewed. He rummaged about in her drawers, messing them about, no doubt, and soon returned with a new piece of red cloth. Minerva pressed her lips together. It would be worth a length of red cloth to prove her point. Lorn glowered at her sullenly, and without any of his usual good grace, he stalked outside.

The minutes ticked by, and then more minutes ticked by. Minerva began to feel anxious, and to make matters worse her knee began to throb as the medicine the Emperor had injected into her knee began to wear off. She gritted her teeth against the pain. Her tired body and mind began to ache with strain. The minutes stretched interminably, and Minerva felt a blackness rising in her. Something was wrong, she knew it. She felt tears begin to well up in her eyes and her throat tightened with unspoken sobs. The sounds of her house became sinister, the creaks and pops of appliances began to sound like unwelcome steps and whispered voices. She began to feel unsafe.

With a suddenness that made her yelp in surprise and fear, her front door banged open and Lorn staggered through the door, supporting a slender figure. Sojourner! Sojourner was in her home! A veiled and robed woman that Minerva assumed was Josilyn and a weathered old man followed close behind him. They closed the door quickly and Lorn helped Sojourner over to a chair. She sagged in the chair, exhausted and only barely conscious. Josilyn took off her veil and crossed to Sojourner, only nodding a greeting to Minerva, but more intent on tending Sojourner.

Lorn busied himself, closing curtains and dimming any lights that might allow someone to distinguish activity from the common courtyard of the village. He cast furtive glances at Sojourner and Josilyn, trying not to seem concerned that they were unveiled in his home. The man stood quietly by the door, obviously exhausted by what they had had to endure to get to Lord Parvo's home. Minerva lowered her veil. Perhaps he had not seen her face.

Lorn finished covering the windows and turned to the man. "I have seen you at the palace. You are a groundskeeper, or so I have believed for a number of years. Explain to me why I should not contact the palace at this moment and have you and your woman and the captive arrested?"

The elderly man straightened. "I am one of the many. I am here as one who loves his country and wants to protect it. I am Elfin, and I am a Master Gardener, one of only seven Master Gardeners. I have been evaluating the collateral damage of the Great Destruction on your soil. It is salvagable. I greet you as one who hopes for peace."

"Our soil is salvageable. Whatever do you mean? Are you a spy?"

"If that is what you want to call it. I am not nearly so glamourous. I prefer growing ornamental bushes and trees to spying. I especially enjoy growing hibiscus bushes. I will spy if necessary, though. Tonight, I suppose I am a spy. I hope to be home at the Burrows within a few days where I will pass the rest of my days being a Master Gardener."

"I don't believe you. I think this is madness and that your wife is a crazed old woman that is meddling in state affairs. I think you are both delusional and are trying to get something you do not deserve. How dare you steal the captive and drag her through the sewers? She is necessary for the success of this endeavor. Do you desire her death? Do you want the people of the Burrows to be annihilated? We have an opportunity to spare many lives if negotiations go well. She is necessary, and needs to be returned to the palace. My own wife has been duped somehow. This is madness!"

Josilyn turned from her work on Sojourner. "I need some water, please. Elfin would you mind? Also, I need my kit. You have it?"

"Yes, my love. Here is your kit." He turned to Lorn, "Might I get some water, sir?"

Lorn threw his hands up in frustration. "Through those doors and to the right. It is the kitchen area, and it has water and containers. I do not know my way around Minerva's kitchen, and I would suggest that you do not make a mess in there. She is particular about it, but she is indisposed at the moment."

Minerva watched the goings on through a fog of pain. Lorn crossed to her couch and sat down gingerly on the edge. Even though he was careful, she still gasped with pain as her leg was jostled.

"My love, I am so sorry you are suffering. What can I do for you? Tell me how to help you."

Minerva could see his concern, but the pain in her leg grew more and more intense. "I don't know! I don't know!" She sobbed.

Josilyn left Sojourner's side and crossed to where Minerva was lying. "So it is true. The Emperor repaired your knee. It is rumored he is skillful at doing such things." She pulled out a tiny scanning device and ran it across Minerva's knee. "Yes. It was the proper procedure for the level of healing in this country. Torn cartilage. Still, unnecessary if one has the proper skills. Let me see what I can do. Ah! Elfin! Thank you, dear, for the water."

"Stay away from my wife, drudge! What kind of creature are you to be in another man's house without a veil? What are you?" Lorn's voice held a note of desperation.

Josilyn sighed and stood formally. "I am one of the many. I am Josilyn, a Master Healer, one of ten Master Healers of the Burrows. I came to assess the level of medical technology and the general health of the people of the Empire. Those that serve the Empire directly are healthy, though those that are considered low estate are not nearly as well. The women are not healthy for the most part because only those that are blessed with husbands that are naturally inclined to be healers are tended properly. For instance, Lord Provo, it is rumored that you have little skill in tending to your wife, and it is through the grace of our Maker that five children were carried to term. It is a miracle she is so healthy. You are helpless right now, but I am not. I am going to help her if you will stand aside."

Lorn looked darkly at her, but Minerva understood through her agony that Josilyn could help. She grasped Lorn's sleeve and nodded to him. He glowered at Josilyn and stepped aside. "Take care, drudge!"

Josilyn ignored him with the look of one who was focused on other things. She opened her kit and took out some thin sheets of a substance. This must be the Heal all Lyla spoke about. Josilyn swabbed an antiseptic and then she adjusted her scanner and ran it across the incision. The pain dulled and then, her knee was numb. Josilyn removed the stitching the Emperor had put in her knee and then laid a piece of the Heal-all deep in her knee. Minerva felt her knee growing hot and then felt a jolt of pain even though her knee was numbed. Layer by layer, Josilyn moved sometimes pausing and getting out a small instrument and using it and sometimes just using the Heal-all. Although it seemed like it took a very long time to do the procedure, it was soon over.

Josilyn applied a type on skin covering over the incision and straightened. Minerva was tired, weary even to her soul.

"Lord Provo, your wife will need to be easy with her moving about for a few days. She will be in some pain, but it is the normal pain that tells her her boundries. Now, I will go back to tending our Storyteller. I would rather not be disturbed for a while."

Lorn looked nonplussed. Minerva understood. He was still a man of the Empire and even though their house was not strictly proper, he had served the Empire for many years. Josilyn looked over to her husband and they spoke together quietly. Elfin crossed to Lorn and stood before him respectfully, and cleared his throat.

"Sir, I need to impose on you further, but in exchange I will answer yor questions. I am going to set up a communication with the Burrows so that we might work better on the Storyteller. She is important to our country. She is the first Master Storyteller in our country for many years, and there may not be another for many years. This was a chance she was willing to take in the hopes of peace, but it has not gone well. Excuse me for a moment, please."

Elfin pulled thin threadlike wires off of his pantlegs and quickly outlined the room with them. There was a moment of static, and then he spoke.

"This is Elfin of Sand Burrow. I greet you as one of the many, a traveler in a far away place. Is there Leadership available?" Minerva wanted to sleep, but she was too interested in what was happening.

The voice that came out of the air was a woman's voice. Minerva did not recognize it, though Elfin smiled and Josilyn looked up momentarily from her work and smiled briefly. "Hail Elfin! I greet you old friend. This is Cloe. You are in a safe place?"

"We are uncertain of the loyalities of these people, though we are safe this moment. We are in the residence of a certain Lord Provo and his wife Minerva. Minerva was in the cloister with Sojourner. The escape through the sewers was arduous and draining on her. Her wound has been adequately treated, but her implants are out of balance. We have her staff, but we need some direction on the adustments that can be made. Are there Healers available to interpret the data?"

"Yes. Of course. We are all anxiously standing by!"

The Healer took the wooden staff and placed it on Sojourner's temple, the base of her ear, the back of her head and so on. At each point, she would stroke the staff as the new voice would give a string of meaningless instructions. Minerva could not keep her attention focused, and she drifted off to sleep.

— Chapter 28 —

Minerva stood and stepped away from the bed. Her knee was sore, but it was healed, she could tell. She marvelled at the smooth skin over her knee. She stopped and sniffed the air. Was someone cooking? Cooking in her kitchen? Even Born would not cook without asking first! She quickly put her robe on and without covering her face she limped into the kitchen, scolding remarks forming on her lips. It was still early, so no one should be up.

She burst into her kitchen and stopped as suddenly, stunned at what she saw. Her son, Born was sitting meekly at the counter, and the tall Examiner was at her stove, cooking breakfast food. Minerva remembered her leg was supposed to be injured, and she acted like she had hobbled painfully to the kitchen, and she leaned against the door.

"Wife of Provo," the Examiner looked up from his cooking. "You should not be up stumbling about like this. I have come to prepare a meal for your family and give your husband the rest of his instructions. You should be resting your leg. Here, sit!"

The Examiner carried a chair over to Minerva and helped her sit. His hands were gentle and yet she could feel his wiry strength.

"You know how to cook?" Her question sounded foolish in her ears and she wished she could call it back. She could be Forsaken for useless talk.

The tall Examiner's eyes smiled, but he did not. "We have no one else to cook for us. We must be self-sufficient. Some of us are excellent cooks. We do not have many luxuries, but we are well-fed and live among beautiful settings. Our lives are hard, but not intolerable or else we would be hopeless. I am known among the brothers for my cooking."

"It is very kind of you to come and help me, though my husband said he would secure a drudge to help me about the house. I would hate to be a bother to you." Minerva spoke freely before she realized she had spoken again, and again, the Examiner's eyes smiled.

"That is to be expected. I have several purposes for being here this morning, not just this. I have instructions for your husband, and I wanted to make certain you were sound and recovering. I brought you medication for your pain, though it seems you are managing it well. And I have another reason. Could I send your son to fetch his father?"

Minerva nodded and gestured to Born that she needed her veil. With a concerned look, Born left the kitchen.

"You forgot your veil in your haste to see who could be in your kitchen? You are a dedicated woman."

He looked at her carefully and then he spoke again, and he seemed afraid to speak, but his need was greater than his fear. "I will never know a woman, even in the manner of the men of the Empire. I am mutilated. Still, I hunger to see a woman and to hear her voice and I remember a small moment with my own mother before I was taken from her. I was at the palace when you sang, and it was like drinking in great gulps of cold water when thirst is plaguing you. It made me happy to hear your voice, and it made me happy to see your mother's face. It is a kind, intelligent face. Your children have names and your husband treasures you. You should be Forsaken, for your singing and the freedoms I imagine you take, but it comforts me to know you sing in your house. Ah, this is done. Let me fix you a plate. You will want my recipe, but I won't give it to you. It is my own speciality, and I alone make it."

He looked in several cabinets until he found a plate, and then he served Minerva a generous helping. She took her fork and scooped a bite. She did not know what this was, but it smelled savory. It had a crust and some sort of spiced meat and eggs mixed. She took a bite and smiled. It was delicious, but she thought she could figure out how to make it.

"You like it, then?" This time the Examiner did smile, and his smile was beautiful, and his face was young and handsome. He looked like a boyish version of Kalig when he smiled. He must be a brother to him.

Minerva looked shyly away, but she nodded and smiled again. The Examiner turned back to the stove and stirred something bubbling in a saucepan. He hummed to himself like his brother did when he was mending her knee. This is what he loved to do. He loved to cook, and his brother liked tending the sick. These were men who had been taught to be what they were not. The Examiner brought the bubbling saucepan over to Minerva and spooned something onto her plate. It was a porridge sweet with fruit, and thick with a creamy sauce. It was delicious. Almost as good as the sweet porridge that Minerva made, but she did not say so. Instead, she smiled again.

The Examiner was pleased with himself and as he turned away he smiled again. Minerva heard her husband's firm steps hurrying throught the hallway into the kitchen. He paused when he entered just long enough to hand Minerva a house veil and then he stood erect beside her.

" Greetings, Sir. My household is disordered due to the injury my honorable wife has suffered in the accident at the palace. I beg for your indulgence in our dissarray."

"It is understood that your circumstances are compromised. As long as it is contained in a short span of time. Your wife informs me you have secured a drudge for the duration of time you will be gone in service to the Empire."

"Er, um, yes. She should be arriving soon. Her husband is the one of the groundskeepers at the palace and I arranged it last night late."

"That is well and good. I will return later in the day to retrieve you for your journey. I will be travelling with you as a representative of the Law. If you have made arrangements for help for your wife, then I will be content with that. My brothers and I will accept your judgement."

"I see that my wife has managed to prepare a breakfast despite her injuries. Would you honor us with a taste? She is well known for her cooking, and this smells very wonderful."

The young man straightened and seemed pleased beyond words and Minerva smiled behind her veil. She was a well-known cook, and this young man was pleased. How could this be the same man that dropped Sojourner like a stone yesterday?

Sojourner! Somewhere in this house was a Storyteller called Sojourner. She would be somewhere unless her husband had made good his threat to notify the palace of her whereabouts. She tried not to show any emotion.

"Might I ask why we are not leaving this morning?"

"We are granting a consideration to the guide of the expedition. Captain Jarvo's wife requires a procedure that only the Captain may perform."

Lorn straightened and caught his breath. "The man must be made of sterner stuff than others to have just been purified and now to tend to his wife's needs. How will he manage travelling?"

"His father, the commander of ground forces, Commander Jarvo, will travel with us to tend to him. Captain Jarvo is a strong man, and skillful in medical techniques. He is stretched to his limits, but he is the only one of the squad that has not been compromised by the debachary of the Burrowites. Several are professing confusion about Deity, and one has gone rather mad.

After even a brief encounter with the captive, our emminent Lord Simon has exhibited signs of madness. She must be an infection to all those that encounter her. The thinking of the people of the Burrows is an infection and an outrage against reason. The Law will redeem them."

"Clear thinking benefits everyone." Lorn said, forcing his voice to sound jovial. Minerva hoped the Examiner would not hear the forced quality of his voice and question him further.

"Yes," the Examiner responded calmly. He still seemed pleased that his cooking was so well received that he was not listening to the nuances. It was a good thing.

"I must go and tend to other preparations for the journey. I will return mid-afternoon to accompany you to the transport. Make good use of your time."

"Yes, sir! I will." Lorn was thoughtful. "I will see you out."

"No need. I know my way out." The Examiner started to leave the kitchen, but he stopped at the door and turned. "Wife of Provo, get well soon...."

Minerva looked at her husband, and when she heard the front door open and close she took off her veil. "Did you send them away?"

"No, I didn't. Elfin had very compelling evidence that the Empire is compromised and we are going to be contained since the Storyteller failed to establish ties. How could she negotiate? She is just a Storyteller. This is a matter best managed by leadership. I just hope we all survive. We must be players on both sides to save ourselves and preserve the people. We must help them so they will help us."

"How is the Storyteller feeling? Will she be able to heal enough to escape?"

"The Healer is certain that she will be in a few days. Something about her implants needing time to flow or some such thing. Sometimes they are too mystical to fully understand. I suppose we need to learn if we are going to survive. I must make them understand that they are just as wrong as the Empire if they contain us beyond our disarmament. I will still go to negotiate. I wish you were allowed to go."

Minerva had a sudden thought. "Are they still listening with their devices?"

"No! This is your home and we do not listen to the private conversations of families unless we walk into the room." Sojourner commented as she walked carefully into the room, using the wall and other solid objects to help her keep her balance. "I have been hiding in the other room, but I have to tell you the smells in this kitchen have been so wonderful that I almost revealed myself to the Examiner for a bite or two. He has been cooking for quite a while."

Lorn looked stunned. "The Examiner was cooking in this kitchen? The world is an insane place!" He laughed. "I have heard that the good food the Examiners eat is one of the few things that keep them going. I would suppose they need some pleasure or they would become complete monsters. Still, I would have never imagined one cooking in your kitchen, Minerva. I actually have a hard time imagining any one daring to try without your permission."

Minerva smiled ruefully, "I know I am ferocious about my kitchen, but I have to admit this is quite good. The sweet porridge needs a bit of cinnamon, I think."

"Cinnamon? I don't know what that is." Sojourner looked interested. "We only have spices and herbs that can be grown locally. Of course, I have read about cinnamon, but it has been lost to us since the ruin of our lands."

"Well, let me give you a taste of this with a bit of cinnamon sprinkled on one side and without on the other." Minerva stood without thinking, and walked to her cupboards and busied herself preparing a plate for Sojourner. She turned with the plate and stopped at the expression on her husband's face. He was watching her with astonishment.

"You are well! The drudge is truly a healer. How can this be? I didn't expect this so soon."

Minerva smiled, "It is amazing. It is good to be up and about." Then she sobered as she looked at Sojourner. "You are not as well, yet the healer still worked on you when I fell asleep. Will you heal?"

"I am getting old and I cannot have very many more implant upgrades. I have received the best of our care, and there is not much more that can be done. The balance is delicate. When I get back to First Burrow, the healers will have to reroute many of the neural stimulants. I cannot sustain injuries without dire consequences to my nervous system. I can limp about, but I will get where I am going. Just you watch!" She took a bite of the sweet porridge with cinnamon. "Oh! My! This is wonderful. You will be able to negotiate with this, Sir Provo. I suggest you take some with you to help with your negotiations."

Lorn looked serious. "If you are serious about this, I will take all the cinnamon I can carry. I love our Empire, and I am beginning to believe it will be hurtful to ignore your warnings. I know you do not understand this, but our Empire has endured nearly a thousand years because of our beliefs and orderliness. Many may long for more freedoms, but the whole of our society is sound and strong. We became great through being united. Your society has the potential for moral chaos, which brings unrest. Although I will admit the concept of personal freedom and the opportunity to fulfill your own interests is compelling, it is too much of a risk to unfetter an entire people. I want my wife to walk unveiled if she chooses, and I want to hold her hand when we walk, but not at the expense of order. We have to sacrifice something for the greater good."

Sojourner had been eating with relish, but as she listened she slowed and leaned into her listening. She put her fork down and looked intently at Lorn, interested in his thoughts and soaking them in.

"You don't understand our culture any better than we understand yours. Our culture is built on the strength of individuals fulfilling his or her best potential. The culture evolves as we reach higher. Even still, individuals are altered in order to serve the greater good. We are from a limited gene pool, and it plagues us. We have little room in our society for those that do not function within certain norms. For instance, if an individual has a natural inclination toward an unsteady temperament, he or she is implanted and given to Handlers until he or she has developed enough of a neural capacity to function without the implants. Behaviors and inclinations are altered because it is important that every individual be useful within our limitations. We are happy, but some question if we are all truly happy because our technology alters us. It removes some of our struggle. Further, we do not have a contingency plan for those that cannot be altered. They are salvaged, and that is also a terrible thing. Still, we have great freedom within our limitations. It is like a fish that swims to its best abilities, but understands it will never fly. We need to understand each other, though. Our technology will not sustain us forever. We need fresh genes infused in our blood. We cannot take just anyone, though. We can only take those that have the latent abilities we have developed or else they will never be able to function in our culture."

"What are you saying...what latent abilities?"

"What we discovered in our long isolation is that we can utilize certain physical attributes that we all possess, but some possess in stronger quantities. The very ancient called it ch'i, or Ki, or a variety of other things. For most of human history it was treated as a mystical anomoly, or a type of evil power or something along those lines. Basically, it is simple. We all have a certain amount of electrical impulses, and some of us are more electrical than others. It is genetic. The whole world has certain magnetic and chemical components that we can interact with, but again, some more than others. It also has a spiritual componant, an element of faith, but how do we prove that to those that do not believe? It will be difficult. We can, however, prove all of these other elements of our physiology with hard science, and we will be looking for those among your population that have the physical characteristics that will make it possible for them to enhance our gene pool. Not everyone will be able to mingle with us and produce children who can use our technologies without great struggle. We don't intend to alter the Empire except to remove its threat and develop an understanding of our places. We have a need for some of your people to come and live among us and allow your children to love our children."

"Why would you tell me this? Isn't this something best kept as a secret?"

"No. If your Empire annihilates us, the land you have conquered will disintegrate and become useless. We are only in the beginning stages of truly being able to purify the damage done a thousand years ago. It is still too fragile to live on its own. It is like me. It functions, but only because it is carefully tended. It is still damaged. If we are removed, the collapse will destroy the land again, and there is no guarantee that it will not be even worse than before. We have to contain your people until they understand the fact that we must be left alone to do our work. No conquest. Understand this, Lord Provo, and we will all do better."

Lorn looked thoughtful. "I will bring cinnamon and I will bring banana chips. I imagine they are no longer available in the Burrows. We will come to terms that are acceptable."

Lorn was interrupted by the door chimes, and Born escorted in Elfin and Josilyn. Josilyn went directly to Sojourner and used her scanner on her.

"I greet you my friend." Sojourner smiled. "You must taste this porridge. It has cinnamon in it."

"I have had the pleasure of tasting cinnamon. It makes my eyes water it is so strong." Josilyn smiled. "You are much better. Your balance will be the biggest problem until we can get you home. No foot races." Sojourner smiled and swatted playfully at her. Josilyn turned to Minerva. "And how are you this morning? Are you ready to race?"

"It is a little sore, but I am getting about wonderfully well. I thank you."

"I think you are overly tired as well. You have had several hard days in a row; I'm afraid you are a bit run down. I have some supplements that you will find helpful. Just chew them up and swallow. Nothing to it."

Minerva looked at the tiny pill, and she reluctantly put it in her mouth. She chewed it and was surprised when it tasted like a strange fruit, tart and rich. Her face must have shown her surprise at the flavor.

"It is cranberry. I imagine there haven't been many of these floating about in the Empire for a thousand years or so. I understand the bogs on this continent never produced well anyway, and were lost during the upheavals. Interesting flavor, eh?" She turned to Lorn and scanned him. "Hummm. Elecrolytes are low and you have an ingrown toenail. Want me to tend to it?"

"Good Healer! I certainly appreciate this, but I have only been touched by my mother and my wife, and my personal prejudice against being touched by any other woman is too much for me to overcome. I was purified once, and the memory is still strong. My toenail is of little consequence."

Minerva looked at him askance. "Why didn't you tell me you have a sore toe? I would have tended to it."

Lorn smiled wanly. "My sweet, you are the best cook in the Empire and your are a worthy woman in more ways than I can count. I am most fortunate to have you as my wife. However, you have an ungentle hand when it comes to toes and splinters and such. I would rather endure the toe."

Minerva was miffed. Ungentle hands, indeed! He had never complained about her touches before.

"Don't be angry! Not today when I have to go away from you. This is not a terrible thing, to not want you to pry out my toenail. I would rather spend this day just talking to you and spending time preparing. I need to understand these people and have some idea of what I am to say that will guide me in my understanding. Let's not fuss about my toe."

Minerva felt her ire evaporate. He was right. There were too many things to accomplish today.

Lorn turned to Sojourner. "I think I would like to hear a story for one thing. It would be helpful to me in understanding how it is that your words have changed men of the Empire who were considered beyond corruption. Four of the squad members are professing a belief in deity that is contrary to their conditioning."

Sojourner sat up and her face shone with happiness. "Four of them? Truly? Which ones? This is wonderful!"

"Perhaps for your people, but it is terrible for them. They are being reconditioned and Purified. They have families waiting for them and it is agony for them. I will guard myself carefully while I listen."

"They are being punished for believing? I did not realize this. I thought my stories had no effect on people of the Empire. I understand that being Purified is a terrible ordeal. I thought believing would set them free. Now I don't know what story to tell you that isn't full of the wonder of believing." Sojourner's voice was full of sadness and her shoulders slumped tiredly.

"There is no way you could have known the consequences of believing in deity. It is something that many struggle with from time to time. History has shown that conflicting views about deity have been disasterous for stable societies."

"Yet, our culture is based on a belief and we cannot function without faith."

"It will be interesting to see what the next thousand years will bring to us. But, we cannot concern ourselves with this right now. Right now, I need to understand something about your thinking. Would you mind telling me a story?"

"I would be happy to tell you a story, but I am not certain what to tell! Remember our stories are not our theology. We tell them to illustrate our search, and we consider them myths and fanciful imaginings that help us understand a truth."

"Do you have a story about punishment? I want to understand your concept of justice, so tell me a story of punishment. That is what I need to hear."

Elfin, who had been silent, spoke. "Tell the story of the creature that ate up all of the colors. I love that story and would appreciate hearing it. It speaks of a type of punishment, though it is not entirely about that incarnation."

"Yes, the Color Eater is a good choice. Well then, ….

"Come and sit with me in this soft light, and I will tell you something. Look! Do you see how it shines through the curtains? See how it casts its shadows and its soft light shifts. It is like a silent dance, the light and shadow. See how the glow makes the colors of this room all seem to move to their own rhythms? Look more. Look at this bright plate. See the vibrant colors that have been fired into it? Don't they seem alive in the flickering light through the curtains? Did you know that the colors once were truly alive? Once, at the beginning of time, they were alive and beautiful beyond measure, and they became arrogant and terrible in their beauty. That is why the Color Eater was able to devour them.

"For untold ages, and time unmeasured, all of the Color Sprites had life. They were not spirits that lived like other spirits. They did not commune with the other beings, but they viewed all of creation as their canvas. They never tired of swirling themselves across the universe. It was their purpose to express themselves and all of Heaven took pleasure in their beauty.

"However, Corruption lives in the universe, and he has claimed a dark purpose for himself. For untold ages, he has tried to usurp the Maker's majesty and he has tried to control Heaven's glory. Sometimes, he has tried to overwhelm Heaven, other times he has tried to take over Heaven covertly. He has never succeeded, though at times, he has caused much sorrow. In all of his darkness, through all of his deceptions, one of the worst crimes that he has committed has been to bring ruin and death to the Color Sprites.

"From the beginning, the Color Sprites had been hard to understand. They always lived their lives with only their own purpose in mind, and they never minded what the other beings of Heaven thought of them. The other spirits in Heaven did not mind that, for the beauty of the Color Sprites was beyond description. They poured themselves across Creation, and even the most common object was constantly made beautiful. They danced across the cosmos, and melded themselves to each other and to creation in an ever-shifting array of brilliance.

"Corruption patiently ruined them.

"He began his crusade thinking to lure the self-absorbed Color Sprites to his cause with the promise of absolute freedom and dominion over the other creative spirits. It did not work. The Color Sprites did not care to dominate the other spirits. They did not care about the other spirits at all. All they wanted to do was express their inner visions. Corruption was dismayed. He had never imagined that there could be no ambition in them to rule others.

"Corruption was certain that he could use the Color Sprites, though, to unseat the Maker, and to rule Heaven. Deep in his domain, he schemed and plotted. Finally, after many years, he devised a creature out of tiny pieces of ruin and waste whose purpose was to devour Color Sprites. He reasoned that he would frighten them into submission with the Color Eater. He rode his dark, ravenous creature toward Heaven, but the Maker, who protects his creation diligently, unseated him easily, and caged the Color Eater in a far corner of space. There, it raged impotently in its hungry imprisonment.

"Corruption was livid. He became obsessed with dominating the Color Sprites and bending them to his purpose. He began stalking them, haunting their movements, searching for their weakness. The Color Sprites did not care that Corruption followed them. They did not believe that he could ruin them because their only ambition was to make every moment of their existence more beautiful than the last. At first, this frustrated Corruption, but then, he began to realize how he could use this to dominate the Color Sprites and perhaps, use them in his quest to claim Heaven as his own.

"Patiently, Corruption began to ruin the Color Sprites. Sometimes, he would gaze at their creations, not in wonder as others did, but in disappointment. He would mention that the Sprites that were here before were much more talented than this group. Then he would leave, grumbling in disgust that his time had been wasted. Sometimes, he would find small groups of sprites and praise their creations above all others. He offered opinions, he criticized details, he pretended great interest. Some Sprites began to take notice of him, and they began to value his opinions. Those that Corruption would praise became proud of his recognition of them. Those that he did not show an appreciation for acted as though they scorned his opinion.

"Patiently, Corruption nurtured the differences between the Color Sprites. Finally, after many years of deceit, some of the Color Sprites withdrew from the rest of their companions, claiming that they did not desire to work with inferior colors. Soon, other Color Sprites began to withdraw from the company of others. They began to divide into clans according to their appearance. They each claimed their own region of space, and they drew boundaries throughout the cosmos.

"The Maker was disappointed by the Color Sprites for their arrogance, and he counseled them to turn from their division. They did not listen, and in defiance, they withdrew even further from each other. They began to try to dominate each other, and they even fought with each other. Corruption and his servants constantly circulated through the different colors' encampments, spreading rumors and hearsay.

"The Maker worked tirelessly among the Color Sprites, believing that reason would convince them to reconcile themselves to each other. Many spirits secretly felt that He should force them into obedience, but the Maker believed that the glory of the universe was the individual choosing to do the best thing. In truth, many of the Color Sprites began to see that they had been foolish, and they repented of their conceit. However, the Maker did not convince them all to turn from their division.

"There were some Color Sprites that had become bound to their hatred, and they refused to let go of their war. They decided to ally themselves together to war against the Color Sprites that had made peace with Heaven. In secret haste, they brought themselves to the bound Color Eater, their thoughts clouded by their insane hatred. They loosed him from his cage thinking he would be sent to Heaven to wage war against the color sprites there.

"Faster than they could think or feel, the mindless, ravenous Color Eater devoured them all. Faster than a moment, the Color Eater sped through the universe, even to the gates of Heaven. Faster than a gasp, the Color Eater consumed the Color Sprites.

"At once, all of the colors of the universe were gone, and all of creation was plunged into bland, empty shades of gray. The Maker wept, and all of Creation wept with Him. Even Corruption was stunned by the devastation.

"The Maker is wise, and the Maker is powerful. For long days, He mourned as He considered all of the different options that he had before Him to remedy the void left by the death of the Color Sprites. Many of Heaven's spirits begged Him to resurrect the Color Sprites, or to create a new race of Color Sprites that did not serve their own purposes, but only lived to please others. The Maker chose not to do this. The Maker reminded the host of Heaven that He had woven consequences into the fabric of the universe. He would not break His own laws.

"In these long days of weeping, the Color Eater lay in a bloated stupor, unable to move, its appetite sated. There was nothing left for it to eat. The Maker regarded the Color Eater lying outside Heaven's gates, and He grew angry, and He made a decision.

"The Maker took the Color Eater around its bloated middle, and he squeezed it until it could no longer hold the lifeless Color Sprites inside. He cast it into the deepest places of space, binding it with his mightest chords. Then, He took the remains of the color sprites and he wept over them, and He made a funeral pyre for them. He cast His purest flame onto the pyre, and the Color Sprites were consumed.

"As the fire consumed them, their essence was mingled into the light that glowed from the fire. The colors were joined to the light, and when the light fell on the ashes of the Color Sprites, the ashes glowed with every hue that they had displayed in their lives. The Maker took the ashes and scattered them throughout the Universe, and whenever the light from any fire touches them, the ashes shine forth in a multitude of colors. The Maker took a bit of each color of ash and he mixed it into a multitude of shades of brown, and He colored all of the remaining spirits that color, to remind them to never become arrogant about the color of their skin.

"Then, the Maker went to the evil Color Eater, where he was bound him with unbreakable bonds in the furthest reaches of space. He made him eternally ravenous to remind the universe of the folly of creating without being a creator. There the beast rages in impotent, mindless hunger. Whatever he can suck into his yawning maw, he does, for he is always starving for the taste of the color sprites, but they are no more. He swirls and rages in space like a never satisfied, empty belly. He is a great dark hole in the universe, and he should never be forgotten.

"And the colors? They shine forth in the light, and they are hard to see in the dark. They still seem to live, though they do not. Corruption strives endlessly to call their conflict to life, and sometimes he almost succeeds. Sometimes their ashes seem to infect those that use them with a mindless arrogance, and sometimes with unreasoning division.

"Still, even in death, they are beautiful, and deep in every spirit, we long for the days that they lived and flowed across the cosmos in an ever shifting pattern of tint and hue. Watch their memory dance in this soft light. Even now, I am breathless in their presence.

Sojourner's eyes were shining with her inner vision. Minerva looked at the other Burrowites, and they were also seeing with distant eyes, caught up in the story and intent on its meaning. She looked at her husband, and he looked miserable. He drew close to her and put his arms around her, as though he needed her warmth. "How will I reach such a people as this? They are too different from us."

Minerva returned his embrace, and she opened her thoughts and she prayed to the Maker for peace.

— Chapter 29 —

Ivan leaned back in the soft seat of the transport. He drew in a shaky breath and tried again to calm his thoughts. The procedure had been difficult and complex. Jenta was weakened from her long illness and shame. Ivan felt like he had ravaged her by operating on her, though he knew he had only done what was necessary. He had been allowed to stay with her until she awoke from the procedure. Her mother had been waiting with him, silent and tense. Jenta had finally awoken, and though her mother stood back and let Ivan tend to her, he could sense her impatience to be tending her daughter.

"My good wife!" Ivan wanted to speak more intimately, but he was conscious of his mother-in-law watching. "Are you in much pain? You will honor me by allowing me to tend to your needs."

"I am thirsty!" Jenta whispered hoarsely. "Might I have a drink?"

"I can give you shaved ice. Just small amounts so that you will not get ill."

He had prepared a cup of shaved ice anticipating her needs, and he carefully spooned small bites into her mouth. He did not want his mother-in-law to see him smooth Jenta's hair away from her face, or trail his fingers across her cheek. She was so thin and pale. He never wanted to leave her again. No empire was as important as this woman. He caught himself thinking these things, and he felt guilty. Being among the heathens had changed him. The claptrap speeches of the barbarian queen had touched him after all. It made him afraid. Jenta drifted off to sleep, and he had no recourse. He had to leave. He stood uncertainly and looked at his mother-in-law.

"Honorable mother-in-law. I thank you for tending to the needs of my wife. She will recover under your care and I am grateful."

His mother-in-law gestured that she would like to speak.

"Please, speak freely," Ivan felt strange giving her permission to speak.

"I honor you for the scar on you palm, sir. I will turn away if you would like a private moment."

Her voice was like Jenta's voice with its birdsong quality. He thought of all of the women's voices he had heard over the past year, but he thought the voices of his wife and this woman were the most beautiful ones. He nodded to Jenta's mother and he knelt beside Jenta's bed. He brushed the hair off her forehead again and adjusted her cover. He knew what he did was useless, but he did not want to leave her. He picked up her hand

and held it for a moment. The palm was hard from all of her work, but the skin on the top of her hand was soft. He pressed it against his cheek, and then, conscious of his mother-in-law in the room, he laid it carefully on the cover and stood. Silently he crossed to the door and without pausing, he left.

He left, but his chest was tight with tears he would not shed. He left, but he had to clench his hands into fists and force his legs to move. He walked without seeing and he could not listen to the words being directed toward him. He felt his father take his arm and guide him and heard his father answering for him, though it was through the roaring of his own thoughts, and it did not matter what was said.

Now he was sitting in the transport, and he was leaving his home again. His father reached over to him and roughly squeezed his hand. "Steady, son. She is in good hands and is beloved by many in this family."

Ivan drew in a shaky breath. "I did not get to see my children. Are they well?"

"Of course, I did not tend to them directly, but your mother informed me of their well-being. You have a daughter, apparently, that is quite amusing and she tends to keep the whole bunch stirred up. She has been a trial to your mother, though she has also grown fond of her in a special way. Your oldest, the boy that looks so much like you? He is very fine. I have been spending some time with him. He can climb a tree in a twinkling though he cannot seem to keep his clothing clean or free of permenant damage. He is an adventurer. Your mother and I are very pleased with your children and how strong and bright they are. Your Jenta must be very beautiful because they are all better looking than you ever were!"

Ivan looked at his father in amazement. He saw his father's mouth twitch at the corners and he looked at Ivan with humor in his eyes. Ivan felt some of the tension drain out of him, and he smiled in spite of himself. "And I suppose you are happy that my mother is so beautiful because your children are such an improvement in your line? We are both lucky."

His father laughed, and despite himself, Ivan chuckled. And then without knowing why, he dissolved into tears. His father let him sob for a moment or two, seeming to know he needed to cleanse himself, and then he handed him a hankerchief and comforted him in his rough, soldier's way. "Steady, son. This will soon be over and you will not be required to leave your family for a long time. You will be free to rest until you are whole."

Ivan wiped his eyes impatiently. He had to find a way to pull himself together. He had to be done with the crumbling of his insides. He had stayed strong throughout the entire mission, clinging to the hope and clarity of the Empire. He knew the Purification would be terrible, and was prepared, it was part of the price of honor. He did not know he would have to hold his wife's well-being in his hands. In the ancient days, there were public physicians that trained to tend to any and all. The Lawgiver had decreed that that was one of the reasons women had become feral, and only a husband should tend to his wife. Certain Examiners tended to the illnesses of men, but only husband's tended to the family. Ivan knew deep in his innermost places that he should not ever have to tend to his wife like this. He would rather her become feral than to hold her heart and his at the point of a knife. He realized he had begun to question the Lawgiver, and it made him afraid.

He looked out the window at the magnificent buildings and the carefully planned gardens and parkways. The pavement gleamed under the transport, and it glided smoothly, a testament of engineering and efficiency. Yet it seemed false and unsecured.

The sun was slanting through the clouds and the shadows were growing long as the transport pulled along the dock and stopped. The ship that was going to take them back to the Burrows was much smaller and faster than the gigantic troop aircraft carrier that carried them home. This ship was beautiful and ornate, meant to impress with its wealth and speed. In a mere two days, this amazing ship would be able to cross the ocean separating the continents. Long ago, there were aircraft with the capability of crossing the oceans in hours, but the need had disappeared with the demise of the Evil Nation. Perhaps it would change when the Empire had taken control of the new lands. Soon there would be a need for magnificent aircraft as well as ships.

Ivan noticed a commotion at the foot of the gangplank, and he directed his father's attention to it. There were several men dressed as Lords in some kind of struggle with a number of men dressed in livery trying to separate them. Ivan and his father watched in amusement for a moment, but only a moment. They briskly crossed to the struggle, arriving at the same time as a tall Examiner and with rough efficiency they separated the men, and the serving men held them apart. Ivan was surprised to see who the three combatants were, Lord Simon, Lord Provo and then the third, his own Lieutenant, Lord Simon's son.

"What is the meaning of this?" The Examiner glowered at the Lords and the serving men. "Lord Provo! You are supposed to be representing the Empire on this mission. This is not a good way to begin. Lord Simon! What are you doing?"

Lord Simon pulled away from his servant. His hair was wild and his clothing was torn and soiled. His face and arms were scratched, and one of his eyes was swollen almost shut. "I have to be the one to go to the wild lands! They have put something in my head, and I have to get it out! It is in my head! I will be good, and I won't eat and I won't even ask for water! Just let me go to the wild lands and find one of their witch healers to take this thing out of my head! It is controlling me! If they take it out, I promise to never be bad again! I will not cheat or steal! I will no longer torment the Forsaken or make sport of them! I will treat them with the kindness they deserve! I will leave them alone! Just let me go! Just let me have this thing removed from my head!"

"My apologies, sir. I came to the dock to begin my duty and was attacked by Lord Simon trying to compel me to let him take my place. His son has just arrived and was trying to contain his father, as were these serving men. He is stronger than he looks."

The Examiner looked at them and thought for a moment. "He needs to be taken to the Purification center and be placed with Lieutenant Bosson. Apparently his guilt is driving him mad, and he needs to be Purified in order to begin his healing."

Lieutenant Simon stepped forward. Ivan was surprised to see his face so serious and concerned. "Sir, please, let me take him home! Let me take care of him. I am capable of helping him." He turned to Ivan. "Captain! Captain Jarvo, speak for me! Please intercede on my behalf!"

"Jarvo! Provo! The names sound the same!" Lord Simon giggled and rubbed his hands together. "What is the chance of this? Perhaps you have a connection outside of this mission. Maybe in the distant past you were related. Jarvo! Provo!"

Ivan looked at his father, and then back at Simon. In his thoughts he said, 'You are an honorable son and have served the Empire well. Sometimes we need the support of our fathers, and sometimes the support of the sons. I believe that you want to help your father, but this may be too serious for you. It may be too hard. Perhaps you may be able to help you father, but it will break your heart.' Instead he said, "Steady, man! Consider the Empire and what is best!"

Lieutenant Simon looked at Ivan with angry frustration. "Sir! He is ill and needs to be tended by his son. This will pass."

The tall Examiner stepped forward and frowned. "Lieutenant, my brothers are on their way to retrieve your father. Comply and be at peace."

The younger Simon seemed to deflate before Ivan's eyes. Ivan felt sadness for him, but he did not say anything. Instead he stood aside as the Examiners arrived and collected Lord Simon. He passed by his

Lieutenant and he put his hand on Simon's shoulder in passing, but it did not seem to matter. This had been a very long day, a long day. He wanted to be on the ship and he wanted to sleep. He wanted to have this mission over.

Ivan, his father and Lord Provo watched the Examiners leave with Lord Simon. The tall Examiner did not watch. Instead he started giving instructions to the ship's crew concerning the luggage that needed to be stowed. He looked at the men and indicated they needed to follow him on board. Ivan's leaden legs followed the Examiner, though he did not know how. He turned once and watched the transport that was taking Lord Simon to be Purified. Lieutenant Simon was still standing on the dock, watching his father's transport travelling farther away from him. His shoulders slumped, and his sadness and frustration seemed to pour out of him. Ivan turned his eyes away and his leaden legs carried him away as well.

— Chapter 30 —

Sojourner woke with a start, disoriented and sweating from her dream. It had started off so nicely. She had been with her beloved Stephan, and they had been flying together in a light plane. She was happy in her dream. Stephan's arms were around her, and they were lost in the beauty of the sky and in the joy of love shared long and well. She looked out of the clear body of the plane, and she noticed they were flying over contaminated lands, grey and foul beneath the hazy glow of a vast shield.

"Hold me tighter, my love! I don't want to fall," she breathed to Stephan, and his arms tightened around her. Even so, she began to feel the bottom of the plane dissolve and she began to feel air rushing through the bottom, blowing into the plane. "Tighter, my love! Hold me tighter!" She felt Stephan's arms tighten around her, but it did no good. "Are you holding me?" She spoke with a shaking voice.

"I am holding tighter, Sojourner! I am holding as tightly as I can! Sojourner!" Stephan's voice held a hint of panic. "Please don't fall through my arms! Please don't fall!" He was shouting in desperation as she began to slip through the dissolving plane. "Stay with me! Stay!"

"Stephan!" Sojourner shrieked as she slipped through his arms and began to plummett through the air. She clawed furiously at the air, wheeling and cartwheeling helplessly toward the hissing dangerous shield. She could see Stephan pressed against the clear sides of the light plane and see his mouth open in a soundless scream. The plane turned a lazy half circle and flew off with her husband as she fell into the shield and sank through its poisonous shell with the sickening sound of sizzling flesh. Before she hit the toxic soil, she awoke.

Shaken, she sat up and then cautiously, she stood and looked around her. She was still at Minerva's, and though she worried that she was putting her new friend in danger, she was glad to be here after her dream. She would someday invite Minerva into her home at Deep Woods Burrow. It was so different from this place. One would not even know there was a growing city underfoot because Deep Woods intruded into the environment so little. Even the outer access doors were blended into the landscape, and there was little crop cultivated topside. Mostly, the land was being restored into a deep deciduous forest with occasional meadows cut through with wet weather creeks, and pocketed by caves, and deep lakes. Long ago, this had been a place where the Native people had escaped from a forced march called the Trail of Tears, and had blended into the emmigrant population from across the seas. Stephan had dedicated his life to the restoration of the deep hills and clear streams. He had made amazing progress and had gained the recognition of being a Master Gardener. His discovery of the Acceleration Matrix had allowed the Gardeners to reclaim land in twenty years that may have taken two hundred years to reclaim. The land was beautiful and varied.

Sojourner thought about their home as she dressed for the day. She thought about the comfortable apartment festooned with growing things and welcoming soft furnishings. It was a place where friends often came for visits and her children and now her grandchildren played with their friends in the courtyard garden. Nearby, Stephan had his personal laboratory, and sometimes, Sojourner would find her way there to watch him work, lost in a problem or tenderly tending to seedlings. Through the years, she had grown more and more content to just watch him work. At first, she had wanted to help him, but she soon realized that his work was like her stories. She certainly did not appreciate him trying to tell her how a story should be written, but she craved his admiration when one was completed. She had adopted this attitude toward his work, and they were happy with it. They were separate in so many ways, yet they were not separate at all. She wanted to go home.

Unsteadily, she made her way to the kitchen. She could tell that someone was already up and busy because the smells were tantalizing. Minerva must be cooking. As she neared, she could hear the rich, sweet voice singing a song with the odd melodies of the Empire. It was beautiful.

"Come taste the nectar-
It comes from this flower!
It is sweet for the tasting!
Its sweetness is power!"

Minerva's voice trailed off as she saw Sojourner balancing her way into the kitchen.

"Don't stop. Your voice is lovely."

Minerva snorted in derision and turned back to her cooking. "I would not be in over my head if it were not for this voice. Do you know how a proper wife of the Empire became embroiled in all this intrigue? My sweet husband who as we speak is a thousand miles at sea in the Imperial Flagship, participated in one too many toasts at the Captive's Celebration, and let it slip that I could sing. The Emperor became intrugued and required a song from me. I sang a lullaby, and then Kalig required poor Chiria to sing. It did not go well."

Sojourner winced. "I heard the singing lesson! I guess a sweet voice is not a requirement for a Chosen."

"Women are not to speak without permission. I don't know that my father ever heard my mother's voice. His hand was unscarred. My mother was unlucky throughout her life."

"What does that mean, unscarred hand? Why would it be important if a man had a scar on his hand?"

Minerva looked at Sojourner in amazement, and quickly looked back at her steaming pan, "How do the men in your country spare you? Are you all purified without mercy?"

"What in the world do you mean? I have never been purified except by the searching of my own heart and by the prayers I offer. Purity isn't something imposed on someone, it comes from searching one's heart. I am purified by the Maker's mercy, my husband had nothing to do with it. I still don't understand what you mean by your father's hands were unscarred."

"He did not shed his blood to spare my mother, and her life was full of the pain of his requirements. The Chosen are all purified publically to be certain all of them are entirely proper."

"Yes, Lyla told me about it. So if a man spares his wife the ceremony, the scar will be on his hand?"

"Yes, usually along a palm line. There are not too many men with scars on their hands, but enough to have to be careful. If there were too many the Examiners would begin to suspect that wives may not be purified."

"That is not even an issue in my country. As a matter of fact, a purified woman would be treated medically to repair the damage. We consider the marriage bed a place of joy and love. I have always enjoyed a loving relationship with my husband, from the first kiss. Well, from the first conscious kiss!" Sojourner smiled.

"Your lives are very different from ours. What do you mean conscious kiss?" Minerva set a plate of food on the table and gestured for Sojourner to eat.

"My husband loved me for a very long time before I let myself return his feelings. One day he followed me into a peach grove and tried to kiss me, so I knocked him a good solid hit with my basket, and he fell off of his hoverboard and was knocked out. While he was in the hospital, his mother talked very seriously to me about his feelings. You see, I thought he was making sport of me. After talking to his mother, I realized his feelings for me were deep and good, so I leaned over and kissed him. He didn't know for a long time that I had kissed him, years and years later I told him. He thought our first kiss was after my brother's wedding under the bower of roses he had planted in the arboretum in honor of my brother's joining. It was a very nice kiss, but not the first." Sojourner smiled at Minerva. "I am assuming from your conversations that you have enjoyed a first kiss?"

Minerva smiled as she carried a plate of food to the table and sat down with her. "Yes! I had a sweet first kiss! Lorn was supposed to purify me, but instead he cut his palm. I was so amazed at my good fortune that I wept with happiness and relief. I bound up his hand and during the binding, I had the terrible fortune of my sheet falling off my bare body. Lorn stood and stared with wonder and terror on his face, then he fainted. Yes! He fainted dead away! I forgot my nakedness and did all that I could to revive him, and when he revived, he sat up and took another look at me and fainted dead away again. This time, I was very offended. I thought he found me so hideous that he could not bear the sight of me, so I let him lay! Yes! I did! This time, when he regained consciousness I made certain I was covered from head to toe in sheets. I cut a tiny hole in the sheet to peek out of, and I sat in a corner and would not eat for a day. He was beside himself, pacing silently back and forth, sometimes coming close and sometimes huddled in a far corner. I knew we had ten whole days together, and I was miserable, thinking I had been joined to a madman. Finally he came and sat down next to me. He seemed to gather up all of his courage and he said he never imagined anything so beautiful as I was, and that he was overwhelmed by the experience. He said he was certain that my beauty would make him swoon again, so I might want to reveal myself a bit more slowly next time. I still do not know why I did it, but I uncovered my foot and waggled it at him. He pretended to faint. Then I showed him my elbow, and so the game continued. No, I did not drop my sheet again until we were properly joined, but the rest of the days we spent together were filled with laughing and silliness. When it was time for us to go home, we were reluctant to part, and he pulled me close and kissed me. I felt like I would burst with happiness at the thought of being joined to such a man. It has been a good joining, some troubles, but mostly good."

"Minerva! You tell a good story! How I wish I had known you for my whole life. Before we are taken home, I would like to eat all your food and listen to you sing all day."

"Have you received word about when you will be taken?"

"Yes, we have made plans. It has been decided to leave you behind so that Lorn will not fall under suspicion for having knowledge of this. We will present him as a prisoner, and will return him with a treaty. It will be hard, but it will save your life. Perhaps in time you and your family will be able to relocate, but there are too many variables to predict what will happen. You have helped us, but you have not been disloyal.

It is hard to imagine the lives you have saved. We will be taking the Chosen and their children. It will go very badly for them if Kalig discovers the hologram in the cell where I am supposed to be."

"I suppose it will all happen in a day or two."

"No. It will be happening today. Within hours. First the lightplanes will be removing the crew from the flagship, and it will be salvaged. Then a squadron will arrive and remove all of our personnel and the number of the population that has passed our screening process and has been invited to join us. We had hoped for twenty thousand, but we have only generated contacts with five thousand. This culture is very closed, and it is hard to make contacts."

"How will this be done? Will your planes land here?"

"No, we would never put you or your family in danger. Elfin is coming to guide me through the sewers to a safe place."

"Is it possible for you to get to the sewer without being detected?"

"We will certainly try! Elfin is very clever and he is known to the patrols for wandering through the streets with his elderly wife. I will use my staff as though my legs are unsteady, which they are, and it will go well. The opening is not far from your front door. Didn't you know?"

"When I go out, I am veiled and can barely see where I am walking. I keep my eyes on my husband's very fit behind and we have devised a method of hisses to communicate. He is careful where he steps and I follow carefully. Some husbands are not careful as to how they guide their wives, but they learn quickly to guard her steps."

"What happens if he is careless?"

"If a husband abuses his wife and she is hurt by him or allowed great hurt, the Examiners step in and begin monitoring the family. If he continues being abusive, he may be outcast and his goods and life are taken from him. The family is tended by the Examiners then, and the sons are made Examiners regardless of the station of the family. The Lawgiver says that because of the tendency of sons of abusers to become abusers themselves, they must not be allowed families. It is a certainty that many wives are not treated well, but families try to keep those problems from the Examiners."

"The Examiner that was here yesterday was the same one that treated me roughly. He seems lonely for the company of a woman he respects."

"I was surprised by this as well. I have never spoken to an Examiner without it being necessary. I have heard it rumored, though, that the Examiners often search for abuses so they might outcast a man and tend to his family. I can't imagine how lonely and hopeless it might feel to know that your entire existence will be without the comfort of a family."

"Perhaps a life like this might be easier to tolerate if there was hope of an afterlife. If there was a prayer one could say for comfort...." Sojourner looked thoughtful. "I wish you believed as I do, so that we could pray for the Examiners."

"I would pray anyway, if I had the heart to do it. Who can truly stop you from praying?" Minerva said quietly. "Prayers just happen sometimes."

Sojourner smiled softly, "Well, that is a new thought to me. Prayers that just happen... " Sojourner looked at Minerva and smiled, "Someday, I hope we are neighbors."

"Mother," Tooya poked her head into the room, "What is for breakfast? Hello Mistress Storyteller." Tooya's face was wreathed in a sleepy smile. "I am glad you are still here. Are you going to tell us stories today? Do you know any more stories about your ancestor that was a storyteller?"

"You love those ancient stories. She was a colorful woman. She had a manner about her that attracted interesting events. For example, when she was a very young woman, before she married, she bought a small house on a piece of property in a rough neighborhood. It wasn't her first choice, but everyone has to start somewhere. Unluckily, her new next door neighbor was a cantankerous, hard-drinking man with a terrible temper with several brothers living on the same street that were just as bad. Soon after she moved in, the man somehow got the idea in his silly head that his property line was several feet over on my ancestor's property. He decided that the fence that separated the properties needed to be pulled out and moved. It was springtime, and rainy, as springtime tends to be in many places, and the ground was spoungy wet. That wasn't going to stop the man! No! Well, the man and his brothers fortified themselves with enough alcohol to make them brave. With their new bravery they went to stand up to the little woman next door. They drove their huge, rough work vehicle into the backyard and hooked a chain onto the fence, intending to pull the fence, posts and all, right out of the ground. They revved the big motors until they were roaring and with a mighty surge forward, they began to pull. Unfortunately for them, the fence did not budge. Instead, the wet, spongy ground sucked in the tires of the truck as they spun helplessly in the wet soil. In a twinkling, the truck was mired in the mud. The drunken men did not let up. Instead, they revved the mighty motor even higher. They tried more power. The truck sank lower in the mud. In their drunkenness and rage, they pushed and pulled and spun their mighty tires. Deeper and deeper they sank into the mud. Within an hour, the truck was buried up to its bed, and the men were sobering up to their new problem. It began to rain. The fence had not budged even a fraction.

The brothers and their friends realized they had been defeated by the unmoving fence and the spoungy wet soil. They began to dig, trying to free the truck. Days passed and the man and his brothers fumed and worked, trying futilely to free their truck. They needed the truck for their work, and every day the truck was buried, the less money they made. They all had families and responsibilities. Finally, after days of work, the men managed to free their truck. The yard was in ruins and the man's wife was inconsolable. He glowered at the fence, and he did not speak to my ancestor.

Months passed and my ancestor found her place in the neighborhood, making friends and improving her property. She would smile and wave at her neighbor.

He was morose. It was tense, but my ancestor did not let it trouble her. Finally, the man came to her and stood at her door. "Miss," he said without rancor, "I have decided to let you use my land as long as you live here. Good fences make good neighbors, after all. I don't think you can hurt my land any how."

"My ancestor smiled and did not say what she thought....'Not more than you do all by yourself." Instead, she said thank you and she lived in peace."

Tooya smiled. "I don't believe you."

Sojourner smiled back. "I didn't expect that you would."

– Chapter 30 –

Ivan felt himself being shaked awake by firm hands. He bolted up, freed from his dreams of Jenta suffering and his children crying and shying away from him because he was a stranger.

"Steady, Captain!" It was the Examiner. "I have taken the liberty of preparing you a meal because you need nourishment. I understand much has been required from you in the service of the Empire, and still the Empire's requirements are pressing. We have much to discuss, though I understand you are not completely well. Get yourself dressed and eat as much as you want to prepare yourself for your trials."

Without speaking, Ivan got out of bed, still groggy from his deep dreaming, and prepared himself for the day. He looked at his face in the mirror as he shaved, and was surprised at the new lines around his eyes and the deepening creases on his forehead and around his mouth. He did not look rested. The Examiner stood aside and watched him impassively.

Ivan sat on the edge of the bed and looked at the food on the bedside table. It looked and smelled delicious, and despite himself, he began to eat with gusto. As he ate his thoughts returned to visions of Jenta sleeping, her hair scattered about on the pillow. When he returned, he would sleep with her at night instead of sending her back to her own quarters. Sometimes, after they had shared his requirements, they both fell asleep twined together. When he would wake up, he always had sent her back to her own bed, but he wouldn't send her away anymore. He would let her use his shoulder as a pillow and he would hold her in his arms. When he returned, he would go to the women's quarter's and watch his children play. No one need know he was breaching the directives. He knew that deep in his innermost places, he would never again believe the Law was without flaw, and therefore, it was open to interpretation. Its flaw was that it did not recognize the depth of a man's heart, it only controlled his actions. He would die for the Empire, but he would kill for his family. There was a difference.

Suddenly the ship shuddered and he was jolted out of his reverie. He left his food unfinished and with a deep sense of dread growing in him, he hurried through the corridor leading to the deck. The Examiner following on his heels, he mounted the stairs two at a time and without concern for his own safety, he burst through the doors onto the deck. What he saw made him freeze in his tracks. Suspended in the sky above the flagship was an enormous, silent airship. It was not like the ancient airplanes that zoomed across the sky trailing great plumes of exhaust. Instead, it was irregularly shaped, and without sound or exhaust. It was gleaming and irridescent and floated above them like a cloud made of earth.

Ivan watched as several pieces of the craft loosened and flitted down toward them. He shook himself into action. "Man defenses! Quickly!"

As if waking from a trance, the crew began hurrying to their defensive posts. The flagship trained its guns on the floating craft and on the smaller craft that began to break away from the main body in increasing numbers. Commander Jarvo and the Examiner came on deck and Ivan saluted smartly to his father.

"Sir! We are in readiness! Your orders?"

Commander Jarvo stepped easily into his role of Commander. "Stand ready! Warning shot on my mark! Alpha gun! Fire!"

The gunner pushed the firing mechinism, but the gun did not fire.

"Beta gun! Fire!

Again the weapon was silent. One of the small bright planes landed on the deck of the flagship. The cockpit opened and a slender, tall form stepped out easily, seemingly unconcerned at the weapons being trained on her. Another plane landed and another. Tall, slender figures stepped out in unconcerned efficiency, ignoring the shouts and defensive positions forming around them. The pilots moved with almost casual confidence, positioning themselves in a strange formation for defense. Without any command or authorization, they pointed strange devices at the gunners and they slumped over their guns, their eyes rolled back in their heads and their mouths open in slack-jawed unconsciousness. The pilots then made adjustments to their devices, consulting each other and speaking in a soft, slurred language that Ivan had never heard spoken before. They then pointed their weapons at the crewmembers that had drawn weapons and with casual indifference, they acitvated their devices. The crewmembers fell heavily on the deck. Even as this was happening, more of the strange little planes were detaching from the cloud formation and darting toward the ship. They would hover above the deck momentarily and bright beams of light would slice away small bits of the ship, and then they would fly away, trailing the piece of the ship in the beam of light. As soon as one was gone, another would replace it. The pilots continued to render the crew unconscious with their strange weapons, and now, the small strange planes landed, a pilot would climb out casually of the craft, scoop up an unconscious crewman, place him in his or her craft and then soar off to join the cloud of aircraft.

Ivan, the Examiner, and his father stood helplessly for a moment, but then the Examiner moved forward, his movements sure and sinuous. He attacked the nearest pilot fiercely, slashing at her with his deadly hands and feet. Ivan and his father also attacked, though Ivan was careful to attack a man, because the memory of having to be purified was too fresh. Ivan had been very successful at hand to hand combat, and he almost felt sorry for the man he had singled out to fight. He was obviously untrained and stood without defending himself. Ivan kicked out with a strong whirling kick, intending to kill the pilot with one blow. With casual indifference, the young pilot deflected the blow and adjusted his weapon and pointed his device at Ivan. Ivan felt himself stiffen and fall though he did not lose consciousness as the crew did.

The young man stepped over to him and spoke in the language of the Empire. "I am also called Ivan, I am one of the many. We are here to defend our borders and end this conflict. I am one of the Guardians of the Great People. I will not hurt you. You will not be rendered unconscious, though you will be taken to the Burrows as a captive. I will answer your questions."

"I never saw any aircraft while I was on my mission. This is impossible. How do you know my name is Ivan? How?" Ivan struggled to move his leaden arms and legs.

"Sir, we have monitored all of your activities as your spied on our land. You have taken our beloved Master Storyteller, thinking she is the queen. Her family is anxious to have her back."

"Family? We saw no evidence of a family."

"You also saw no aircraft. Think of all the things you will discover in the next few hours. You will see evidence of many great things."

Ivan sagged against the deck. He looked over at his father and the Examiner. They were also prone and unmoving. The Examiner was raging against his inability to move and he had a livid bruise beginning to rise on his cheek. The female pilot he had fought was dishevelled and had a cut over one eye. Ivan felt a slight satisfaction when he saw that. Only a slight satisfaction. Mostly, he felt a deep frustration and grief as he looked around him. The beautiful ship was being sliced away, and the crew was being made helpless and being carried away. He felt his insides were being devoured along with the ship. The deck was cleared by the dipping, darting pilots, and the ones that landed now were going below deck and returning with sleepy crewmembers and goods. Lord Provo stumbled onto the deck clutching his clothes and a satchel with his official papers. He was struggling to maintain some element of dignity, and Ivan was thankful for his presence of mind. He was guided onto one of the airplanes and was taken into the cloud craft. Ivan wondered briefly why he had not been taken, but then he realized he and his father and the Examiner were on display to demoralize the crew. He did not know what to do. He looked at his father, and his father was staring straight ahead, trying not to show emotion. Ivan closed his eyes. He could not bear to watch this.

In less time than he could have possibly imagined, the ship was emptied and the deck was stripped. The young pilot named Ivan came and easily lifted him to a sitting and then a standing position. Jarvo was guided to a plane and was placed inside and strapped into restraints. He was humiliated and ashamed. He tried to find his father, but could not see him. He could only watch as the deck of the ship shrank into a tiny, toy sized blot on the vast ocean. The aircraft continued diving and darting at the ship until it was gone. The last little craft joined the cloud craft, and then the cloud craft began to reconfigure itself into a sleek fast arrow shaped craft. It began to move forward, slowly gathering speed and altitude. Suddenly, the airship shuddered and seemed to shiver in anticipation. It shot forward, heading at a terrifying angle upward. Ivan felt his insides dropping away, and he was thankful for the restraints as he felt a few terrifying moments of weightlessness. The craft levelled off at a very high altitude, and Ivan marvelled that he was still warm and did not need any special equipment to breathe. The ship then began to descend and Ivan was astonished to look out his window and see the coast of the New Lands. The craft levelled off again and began to hover in its cloud formation. The tiny planes, each with its own pilot and cargo began to peel away from the main ship and scatter. Ivan presumed the reason for this was to take the crew to different Burrows. He wanted to scream and weep. He had led his people wrongly, and now this crew was going to be taken prisoner. He hoped they would not be brutalized. He was the one that deserved to be punished, not them. This was his fault and he would be villified throughout history for his mistakes. His family would be Outcast. He was a man without honor. He felt himself dissolving inside. Jenta would be Forsaken. His little laughing daughter would never be happy again. They would hate him. He was lost.

His plane began to descend, but he did not feel the descent. He found himself praying to the Maker. "Please! Let there be mercy for my family! Please! Please! Please!" He began to cry and beg the unseen and unknown. He was ashamed for being so weak, but he begged the unseen and unknown to spare his Jenta the shame of his failure.

The plane landed, and the young pilot opened the passenger compartment and loosened Ivan's restraints.

Ivan found he could move his arms and legs, but he did not fight. He was defeated as he followed the young Ivan into a Burrow door. How could this hole in the ground hide these ingenious planes? The young man entered a code in a panal and the wall slid open. A vast underground city was revealed. Ivan stumbled forward, his eyes bulged in disbelief. He sank to his knees gagging and weeping in fury and painful confusion. The Burrows held cities, he was not a hero, the harlot was a wife. He vomited. The pilot gestured to a person standing nearby waiting with a cart of medical supplies. The Healer came to him and injected him with a sedative. Ivan did not know when he fell unconscious, but he was grateful that the darkness possessed him and the world went silent for a span.

— Chapter 31 —

Elfin had come and gone, and Sojourner was gone, too. Minerva restlessly wandered from room to room, straightening this and dusting that. She missed Lorn and her heart felt sick knowing that no matter what she did, the world was going to change before the end of the day. Part of her wanted to scurry about, preparing, but she realized that if she did, it would cast suspicion on Lorn. Someone would notice she had Born bring in extra rations. Someone would notice a difference in behaviors and then they would suspect Lorn had planned his part in the invasion. He would not be able to come home and she would be Forsaken. There was no way to win. She imagined sending Born to the palace with the information she had gained, but she was certain no one would believe him. He was an unproven boy.

Still, she had an idea of what was going to happen, and she had a good idea of what she could do to survive the day. She had briefed the children and they had taken her instruction in sober thoughtfulness. So much would depend on Born rising to the occasion. She wished he could be spared this responsibilty. Tooya would actually be a better choice for this type of problem solving, but Born was the eldest son, and he had no choice. All they had to do was wait for it to happen. Minerva found herself hoping the Burrows would fail.

The morning passed, and then noontime came and passed. Minerva was beginning to believe that perhaps the entire situation had blown away with the wind that was stirring the trees outside. Her hopes evaporated in an instant as the lights in her house began to flicker and then went dark. "The first step will be to disable the city..." Her house that usually hummed with the power that coursed through its veins was oddly silent. There was no soft music, the appliances in the workroom and kitchen were useless. She hoped her food would not spoil. She looked out the window, and saw that all of the lights were darkened. Men were coming out of their houses and speaking to each other, some agitated and others talking seriously like they were trying to gather information. Minerva looked at Born and gestured for him to go and join the men. He reluctantly went outside and walked to their nearest neighbor, Lord Doovan. He stood respectfully until Doovan acknowledged him. Minerva watched him carefully. Good. Born was obviously asking him the necessary questions, nervously, like a boy would be when he was suddenly in charge in his father's absence. Lord Doovan and several other men spoke seriously to Born, and Born nodded and listened. The men gestured for him to go back in the house and Lord Doovan patted him on the shoulder encouragingly. Born turned and started inside, but then he stopped and his eyes turned upward. The men had all stopped talking and their eyes were also turned to the sky.

It was more than Minerva could have imagined. It was more than Sojourner described. What had seemed improbable now filled the sky with glistening, fearsome menace. Swirling out of the clouds, seeming to swarm out of the wind were thousands of small, semi-clear aircraft. They each seemed to know exactly where they were going as they scattered throughout the city. Minerva felt like weeping. It was done, and there was no chance for a peaceful resolution. There would be no treaty that would satisfy everyone, just one that fulfilled the demands of a conqueror. She knew Sojourner spoke with great passion about how the Burrowites would not bring ruin upon them, but she did not believe that Sojourner knew everything the leaders of her country were planning. The ruin of the Evil Nation a thousand years before might be ancient history to the people of the Empire, but it was still a reality in the Burrows. Revenge was logical.

The planes swooped and darted, each intent on its own mission. Some landed in various places and citizens of the Empire would emerge from bushes and houses and hurry into the planes and vanish in a twinkling into the sky. Other planes landed by crutial defensive machinery and they simply sliced the machines into slivers and flew away with the pieces. Throughout the Empire, pieces were being carried away in what seemed an endless savaging. There seemed to be no defense that could be used, and within an hour the planes were gone. The sky above the city slowly grew opaque, sparking and hissing as hapless birds or insects flew into the growing shield and were instantly neutralized.

Minerva had understood this would happen, but it still left her in shock. The Empire was finished, and she would have to survive it along with everyone else. She hoped Lorn was not being brutalized along with the rest of the crew of the flagship. She bitterly imagined Sojourner enjoying her homecoming. She would be in her comfortable home with its amazing technologies, no doubt eating a warm meal. Her husband would be rejoicing over her and she would be clean and safe. Her children and grandchildren would be gathering, and tomorrow, her country would honor her. She should have smothered the old hag while she slept. She should never have listened to her! She would be no better off than she was right now, but at least she would not feel like a traitor.

She turned her thoughts to her own children. Somehow, she must find a way to prepare a meal.

— Chapter 32 —

Sojourner felt a stitch in her side and her knees felt weak. She felt she had been walking for her whole life.

This morning, Elfin had come for her, and dressed in the robes of a proper wife, she had trailed behind him, trying to appear as if she were going to the palace to drudge in the cloister. Elfin was known to the patrols, as was the fact that his wife drudged in the palace. Elfin and Josilyn were expected at the palace, and if they were late there would be questions asked. It was too early in the day for questions. Later it would not matter what questions were asked.

They had arrived at the palace as expected, and the fake Josilyn was sent to the cloister to wash floors. She went silently and she entered the cloister without incident. The Chosen were sitting at their breakfast, feeding the children and not speaking to each other. The tension on their faces was clear and the tension in the air was thick. When Sojourner entered they startled like a herd of deer, bounding up in fright.

"Josilyn!" Pura hissed. "There is trouble! Kalig has said that he intends to wake the captive today, and the hologram will be discovered. We are Forsaken! Our children are lost! Is there something that can be done? Help us!"

Sojourner smiled as she took her veil off. "Do not worry! It is me! I have much to tell you, but first things first! When is Kalig coming?"

"He comes before he begins his duties and again later in the afternoon. You are in time for his first visit. Hurry! We have to be prepared!" Chiria spoke in a panic.

Sojourner did not question the panic in Chiria's voice. Quickly she took off her robe and the Chosen concealed it in a closet. She entered the cell and readied herself. It was strange to her that the door to the underground passageways began in this cell. Lyla had said she was banished from the Empire through this cell. It had numerous locks under the cot in the corner. When the Chosen was Forsaken, she was forced through the trapdoor and into the sewers. It was very symbolic and painful.

Sojourner straightened her hair and then, remembering, she searched around for the discarded bandages that the Emperor had used to wrap her hand after he had savaged it. She tried not to look at her wounds, healing and clean. Josilyn had commented that Kalig had done a remarkable job in the rough way he had stopped the bleeding and had prevented infection. Of course, cauterizing the wound would make it impossible to do a regrowing, though she doubted at her age it would work anyway. She could still feel them; it was disorienting to reach for something and not be able to grasp it with her ghost fingers. She would mourn for her fingers later. She wrapped her hand in the bandages, cringing as the unclean fabric touched her hand.

The chimes sounded and she sat on the edge of the bed. There was a final opportunity to reason with Kalig, and she had to take it. The door to the cloister opened and she listened to the sounds of children squealing with pure pleasure as their father arrived. Her daughters squealed with delight when their father would return home at night. This was a universal noise. Kalig made growly monster noises and there was the sound of a wild rumpus. Sojourner's heart was stirred by the noisy play. Stephan had had many wild rumpus moments with his children. This was also a universal noise. Sojourner wondered how many fathers were playing with their children at the very same moment. She wondered how many soft words were being spoken between lovers, and how many babies were drawing in their first breaths. All of these were sounds that any human would know.

The joyous riot outside her cell slowly died down as the children began to drift into other activities. The room outside of her cell settled into a routine hum of children playing and mothers tending to them. Sojourner watched the cell door, and in a few minutes, Kalig's face appeared, framed in the barred window. For a fleeting moment, it seemed to her that he was the prisoner. The moment passed as he opened the door and stood in the doorway. He was not the father Kalig, but the Emperor as he stepped into the room. She prayed for wisdom and she stood carefully, still having to think and concentrate to keep her balance.

"Hello there, young Kalig," she began, not wanting him to gain any advantage by making an announcement. She filled her voice with a complicated mixture, part injured kindliness, part reproving elder. She must speak carefully. "I want you to know I forgive you for the difficulty you have caused me. I am willing to move past this rough beginning and discuss terms of a treaty. It will be better for us all if we begin the peace process without us having to contain your land and cull your people. I am still here to speak with you. I will not be here later."

Kalig looked at her in astonishment. "Captive, you may not speak to me! I am not here to talk to you. I am here to inform you of what will happen. Prepare yourself for the events that will take control of your existence."

"Don't you get tired of this?" She resolutely lifted her hand with the soiled wrapping. "Do you know that I have been outside the palace? My healer met me and completed the medical needs of my hand. She said you did a good job removing my fingers and cauterizing them. Would you like to see what your hatchet blow did to my hand?" Sojourner started unwrapping her hand. "I understand that you did this because you were expected to do this. I think you would rather not have chopped off my fingers." She held up her ruined hand. 'I think you are considered brutal because you do what is required quickly, but if you were given a choice, you would not cause harm to anyone."

Kalig seemed to wrestle with himself. "I forbid you to speak to me like this. Women are to be silent in the presence of men so their strange thoughts will not pollute the clarity men need to remain strong."

"Nonsense!" Sojourner barked, using the tones of discipline and reproof. "You have missed the voices you are forbidden to hear. Listen to me." She made her voice the voice of a mother speaking to a grown child and gradually, she softened it to speak to the child inside. "Kalig, the might of a nation does not come from its laws. The laws reflect the strength of its people. Look inside your own experience. What do you hunger for when you are in the silent darkness?"

"What does it matter what I want?" Kalig's voice sounded tired. "I am Kalig, forged to fulfill a specific need of a stable society. In order for society to flourish, it needs to have a place for its violence and power to be expressed with impunity. It is the Emperor's job to express the madness of his people." His voice sank and his words poured out of him like dark, sad music. "I want what I cannot have. I want to hold a woman while she sleeps... listen to her sing lullabys to my children. I want to eat dinner with my brothers. I want to gather their bones from the ditch where they were all thrown, and bury them in one of the cemeteries of the common people. I want to give them names. I want my own name...."

"It must be a terrible burden." Sojourner felt the sadness pouring out of Kalig. "I have never known such sorrow."

Kalig looked into Sojourner"s face. "How do you meet the demands of your calling? Do you have any comfort?"

"Kalig, I have no demands claiming my soul as you do. I am a storyteller. I am a simple woman and this was all a ruse to buy my people time to prepare for the Empire. I am not a queen. I am a storyteller, the Master Storyteller of my people. It was thought that I could use my talents to forge a bond between our people and avoid all of the trauma of a war or an occupation. If we can avoid the conflict and settle the differences of our people with a treaty, many lives will be spared. There is always death and loss when cultures clash. I cannot ease your suffering, but perhaps together we can spare our people from suffering. I will tell you everything. If you can spare your people the conflict it may give meaning to your suffering."

"My people are safe. It is your people that are in danger." Kalig's eyes began to grow hard again.

"I wish it were so for your sake." Sojourner crossed to him and laid her hand on his arm. He looked at her hand on him like it was an anomaly. He looked at her hand with its missing fingers and his face grew darker. "But your people are not safe. Our lightplanes are dismantling your flagship as we speak, and by nightfall your Empire will be encased in a nearly impenetrable force shield. Your powerplants will be gone. Your defenses will be compromised. By noon tomorrow, your fleet will be dismantled. Your world will be completely different by nightfall, but it doesn't have to be this way."

"I cannot believe you. I cannot. I will not. I am Kalig." He turned to leave. "Tomorrow, I will remove your hand and send it with a delegation on one of my warships. It will be a show of strength and your people will be afraid. I tell you to give you a chance to prepare yourself. I will be swift."

"Oh, Kalig. We will be swift, too." Sojourner did not have to add sorrow to her voice. She felt the sadness of the moment deep in her bones. She did not want these people to suffer. Kalig squared his shoulders and walked out of her cell without looking back. He closed the door with a decisive clang. Sojourner went to the door and watched him leave the cloister. The Chosen turned and looked at Sojourner as she left the holding cell.

"Your Kalig breaks my heart. The Empire asks too much of him." She sank into a chair and stared at the floor. The weight of the day pressed on her shoulders. She could not stop it, she would watch and wring her hands. She looked up at the Chosen through tears she did not know were falling. "Well, I cannot end this madness, but I can help you. Are you prepared to walk until your feet ache?"

Pura knelt in front of Sojourner and wiped the tears from her face with a corner of her robe. "Mistress Storyteller, I will walk my feet into nubs to spare my boys the life that awaits them. I will swim the vast ocean if I can. I want my boys to live."

Jonta crossed her hands over her swollen belly. "We have made a pact together. We will not let our children become puppets to a long dead despot."

"Yes," Chiria said. "Even if Kalig does love the

children, his loyalities are to the Empire. Even if he loves us. Even if he loves me...."

Sojourner nodded silently and without speaking, she stood and gathered her balance and strength. She went to the closet and took out the ugly black robe and put it on. Just in case. Then she turned and motioned to the Chosen. They were already preparing their escape. The babies were strapped onto their mothers in carriers and the little ones that could walk were looped together with sheets torn in strips.

Sojourner and the Chosen were speaking quietly when the door of the holding cell pushed further open and a furtive figure in rags emerged. A Forsaken. The figure cringed into view, and then another and another. Soon there were a dozen filthy ragged women standing uncertainly in the cloister, heads bowed and slumped in defeated postures. One of them gestured with a dirty wrinkled hand. "We have come to help you," she whispered hoarsely. "We have come to help you escape. We will guide you."

Sojourner felt like her heart would not survive this bludgeoning. The Forsaken offering help? She stepped forward. "I am one of the many. I am Sojourner. I honor you for your gracious offer, and I humbly accept! We have maps, but we could use guidance. How do you know of our plans?"

"We have learned over the years to listen so that we can be safe from the nobles and from the workers that make sport of us. We have learned how to find food and where to hide. We have seen strange doings over the past year. Our leader, Lyla allowed herself to be taken in the hopes that she would discover what was going on in the world. We have listened carefully to all that has been happening here. It is a just cause."

Simiat balked, "How can we trust you to lead us to the safe place?"

"Is there one here named Jonta?"

Jonta stepped forward. "I am Jonta"

The woman slowly stripped off her veil. Her ebony face was wrinkled and her hair a mass of tangle that scattered across her head. Her eyes were not defeated, though. Her eyes were like black fire glowing with anger and hope. "Do you know me?"

"Mother?" Jonta hurried forward. "You were to be spared if I became a Chosen."

Jonta's mother laughed bitterly. "No! Your father offered you as a Chosen to insure I would be Forsaken! I was not a gentle wife, but I never intended for my child to suffer because I am not proper. I will guide you to freedom because I owe you that. Maybe there will be true freedom for you."

Another Forsaken stepped forward. "Tell them. Warn them."

"Storyteller! Be warned that if you do not leave the palace with that Elfin at the regular time there will be an uproar. It seems that extra patrols are placed because of the captive. The same must leave as entered. Your way will be shorter if you travel aboveground with him. We have convinced Josilyn to stay with us to help with these little ones. She has contacted her husband. Elfin is waiting for you above. Go and pretend."

Jonta looked at her mother with tears in her eyes. "I am so sorry you have suffered. Why would father do this?"

Jonta's mother barked a laugh. "My sweet, you have a short memory if you have forgotten! If there was a woman who hated her husband, it was I! That miserable, sneaking rodent filled me with disgust from the first moment I laid eyes on him. He smelled like a wet dog and chewed with his mouth open. How he produced such a beautiful daughter is beyond me! If I hadn't come with a huge dowry, we would have starved. That nasty beast is living like a king on my dowry while your life is sold and mine is ground down. If this invasion succeeds, he will be getting a visit from me! Many of these Forsaken wish to leave, but I have a reason to stay that drives me!"

Jonta looked stunned. Her hands crossed over her swollen belly and she then reached for her small daughter. "Well, then...we should go..."

Sojourner watched the Chosen and the Forsaken file out of the cloister through the trapdoor in the holding cell with mixed feelings. It was happening and now there was no hope to turn the events off. She veiled herself and made her way to the servant's doors. Elfin was waiting for her and silently, she followed him. She did not know where they were going, but she watched Elfin's heels and listened carefully as he whispered instructions to her. Elfin had her staff, and he handed it to her so she could lean on it and keep her balance. Occasionally, they would stop and rest. The city seemed to stretch forever before them. Once a patrol stopped them and the leader asked why the wife of Elfin was walking with a stick, and Elfin said his good wife had stubbed her toe and felt it helped her walk better. He rolled his eyes and twirled his fingers around his ear.

The patrol laughed and let him pass. She would have to ask him what twirling a finger around an ear meant. It must be a very funny joke.

She tried to gauge the time. She had arrived at the cloister mid-morning and had left before the noon meal. They had walked for what seemed to be hours, but their shadows had only just begun to stretch. Elfin stopped with her in the shade of a grove of trees and they sat down. He brought out a packet of food and a flask of water and they ate, speaking quietly between bites.

"It will be about an hour before the lightplanes arrive. We will be at the shield wall shortly after it begins. We can rest for about an hour. We are somewhat concealed, though I do not feel at ease."

"Why?" Sojourner was surprised. Elfin was not one to give himself over to his fears. He was a Master Gardener, and that fact alone spoke volumes about his character. He was brave and intelligent, able to think on his feet. The fact he was here with his wife also spoke volumes about them both. Their fears were not to be taken lightly.

"Servants know more than most nobles. The patrols have been ordered to increase their presence, though we have seen that. The reason is that Kalig has decided to remove your hand this evening instead of tomorrow. He has commanded the warship be prepared to leave by nightfall, and the interior servants were preparing the Great Hall when we left. Hopefully they will not discover you are missing until we are on board the lightplanes and on our way home, but we need to be careful since the shadows are growing longer. If it is discovered you are gone before the allotted time, we may have a problem."

"We should not be resting here, then. We should press forward." Sojourner started to rise, struggling with her balance.

"Sojourner, I can see your strength is almost spent. Josilyn told me all of the things to watch for in your condition, and you need to rest for a few more minutes. We will be able to make the last few miles with the others. As a group we will be able to help you walk better. We can carry you if need be."

"Me and the babies." Sojourner laughed without joy. "It has always been like this..."

Elfin patted her hand awkwardly. "No one minds carrying you, my friend. You have brought us much happiness with your stories! When we get home, I want to hear a story about the brave traveller who overcomes great obstacles to get home."

Sojourner smiled tiredly. "I know several stories about travellers. When we get home, I will let you choose. First, I will have to insist that I be allowed to soak my feet."

Elfin smiled back, kindly. "I think I will do the same. But now, we need to move forward. Do you see that next grove of trees ahead? The ones beyond the last house? We will walk there. It is three miles."

"The land is very flat here. We will be obvious the entire way."

"Once we are past the house, we will be able to remove that terrible robe and it will not seem so difficult. You will be more comfortable then."

"Yes, when we occupy this land, we should go through and remove every black robe and burn it. That is right. Do not look shocked. I wouldn't even recycle them. Burn them to a cinder. Then, we should find every copy of the writings of the Lawgiver and burn those, too. That's right. Burn them up. No mercy to the Lawgiver and his shrouds. The world will be better off without them!"

Elfin grinned and helped Sojourner to her feet, "Come on, and we will at least rid ourselves of this black robe."

Sojourner groaned dramatically. Elfin helped her stand and regain her balance. Three miles. She could walk three miles. Elfin stepped out of the grove of trees and then Sojourner followed. One foot in front of another. She watched Elfin's feet in front of her and she counted his steps. Every time she would pass a hundred steps, she would look up to see how much closer she was to the grove of trees. At first, it seemed like the grove did not get any closer, but after a time, she began to notice the trees becoming larger, and then she could distinguish individual trees. At one point, Elfin told her she could remove the robe, and gratefully, she lifted it off her hot body and let it fall to the ground. The air rushed over her sweaty face and cooled it. She breathed in and smiled through her weariness. The air felt like God's kiss.

They walked some more and then more. The grove of trees drew closer, and Sojourner could see shadowy shapes moving in the grove. She prayed it was the Chosen and the Forsaken and not some citizen that would raise the alarm that there was an improper

Sojourner's Truth

woman loose. Mercy! That would never do. As they neared the grove, a figure left the grove and hurried to them. As it drew closer, Sojourner could see the fierce ebony features of Jonta's mother nearing and she wanted to weep for joy.

"Hurry! They have discovered that you are not in the cloister and are beginning to search!" Jonta's mother took her by her arm, and Elfin took the other arm and they helped her walk faster. Soon they were in the grove of trees, sweat pouring off their faces and breath gasping through open mouths. Sojourner's heart pounded in her chest and her joints felt like they were ready to melt. Josilyn hurried over to them and gave them drinks of water with nutrients in it. She injected them with a stimulant and then she concentrated on adjusting Sojourner's implants as best as she could.

"How do you know they are searching for us?" Elfin looked at the Forsaken, puzzled.

Jonta's mother laughed, loud and angry. "We have the palace wired, we Forsaken. They have silenced us and starved us and made us slaves to unnatural desires, but they could not take our cleverness. We will help conquer them now."

As if on cue, the air above them began to hum and buzz with activity. The lightplanes had arrived and flew over the grove like arrows newly shot.

"Come with us! Come with us and we will help you heal. We will treat you with honor and give you freedom and peace." Josilyn held her hands out toward them.

"No!" Jonta's mother looked resolved. "We are resolved to stay. We know how to live in difficulty, and we all have someone that has betrayed us. You do not want such angry creatures as the Forsaken in your gentle Burrows. Perhaps when our anger is spent. Not today."

The Forsaken gathered around Sojourner. They had all taken off their veils, and she looked into their haggard faces, infused with their own purpose and anger. Sojourner touched each cheek. She felt humbled. Josilyn stepped forward and distributed the rest of the medicines and food packets that she had in her pack. They smiled with gratitude, though their eyes were feral and angry.

"The shield wall is just a hundred yards over there. It will activate as soon as all of the lightplanes are back from their individual missions. Once it is activated, it can only be breached when wearing a special protective suit. It will be enforced for one year. During that time, we will be returning every week to affect the reordering. At any time you want to leave, be at this grove of trees and you will be taken to the Burrows. There you will not be Forsaken, but you will be called the Faithful! You will be honored." Sojourner looked at them seriously, she wanted to pierce their anger and touch them. "We will pray for you as a people. We will pray that you will find your peace of mind and rest for your torment. We will bring food for you every week and leave it here. We will bring medicine. You will not be forgotten."

Jonta's mother bowed her head, and though her eyes did not soften, her hard eyes held tears. The faces of the other Forsaken were also filled with tears as hard as diamonds. They nodded silently and then, they turned and made their way deep into the grove, blending into the shadows and disappearing into the deepening shade.

As the Forsaken faded from Sojourner's sight, she became aware of an unwelcome noise. The group fell to the ground and looked through the underbrush out into the open roadway that she and Elfin had walked not long before. In the distance she could see there were military vehicles travelling toward them slowly, with troops walking in a spread formation, searching. Standing in the lead vehicle was the unmistakable figure of Kalig. The Chosen gasped and Josilyn shushed them with a slash of her hand.

"Back to the sewer entrance! Quietly. Be ready to go in." Josilyn whispered. The Chosen began to quietly move backward, easing their sleepy children carefully along.

"They will be looking for me. I will stall them. Don't go to the sewer! You might miss the transports. I will be fine. The planes should be arriving very soon. See! There they are. Go in ones and twos. I will distract them."

As several of the Chosen slipped out the back side of the grove, running low and moving as quickly as they could with their children, Sojourner stood and leaning heavily on her staff, she stepped out of the grove and moved into the roadway.

The first lightplane touched down and one of the Chosen and her children were taken in. Sojourner walked forward. The lead vehicle sped forward, Kalig pointing at her, his mouth opened wide in an enraged scream. Another lightplane touched down and another

Chosen was taken. Sojourner walked forward. The military vehicle drew closer, Sojourner could see Kalig's face, full of hatred and fury. Two more planes left the ground with that many more Chosen and their children. Sojourner walked forward, and she stopped. The vehicle carrying Kalig roared to a stop in front of her. The Chosen were gone.

"Bring them back!" Kalig's eyes bulged with rage. "Give me my family! Bring them back now!" His face was a rigid mask of fury. "You cannot take my Chosen! You cannot take them! You cannot take my children! You cannot!"

"Your sons will grow and become fathers. Your daughters will be free. You love them enough for this. Let them go! They will bless you for it!"

"No! No! I need them!" He raised his weapon and trained it on her. "Command your planes to return them!"

"You can make the choice, Kalig. Say it, and we will negotiate with you"

"Your people cannot win. I will destroy every last creature in your pitiful nation! You cannot stand against me!"

"Oh! Kalig! How I wish for your sake that you had chosen differently."

Sojourner turned and began to walk to the waiting plane. Elfin and Josilyn were on board and they were waiting. Stephan was waiting. Her children were waiting.

"You will not do this to me!" Kalig screamed in frustration.

Sojourner heard a popping sound and felt something hit her hard in the center of her back. Did someone throw a stone at her? She turned. Kalig was sobbing in his outrage, spittle and tears mingling with his scream.

"Give them back!" He fired again.

Sojourner felt the projectile smash into her chest and tear through her. Oh! That was what was happening! She felt a deep sorrow knowing she would not see her family. There was the new story she was planning about a mercy so great that even Corruption wept when he saw it. She felt her body collapsing and the air leaving her body. She had so much left to do. She was surprised she was not overwhelmed with agony, but then she realized her implants were probably shutting down. For the first time, she was grateful for her invalid body. She felt a breeze across her face. Yes, it was like God's kiss. Her eyes began to lose their focus, but she saw the sky turn from its bright blue to a hazy grey. Then there was no breeze and all was still.

— Chapter 34 —

Ivan took Jenta's hand and together they walked to the Commons. It seemed like it had been a lifetime since he had been here. Could it have only been a year since he had hidden on the hillside, gathering misinformation and feeling superior to all? Had it only been a year since his world had spintered into shards of hopelessness?

He had been in a Healing sleep for many weeks after his capture, only occasionally swimming to the edge of consciousness. The Healers would tend to him and he knew in those moments that he was being altered. He was altered and when he was allowed to awaken, the world was changed forever. The leaders of the Burrow had gone into the Empire and had taken Jenta and his children from the complex because they were in danger of being punished for his perceived espionage. He could never go back to the empire. When he woke, she was with him, whole and anxious for him. It had been a long and hard journey and he still did not fully understand all he needed to know. In time he would know.

Tonight he would not think of his concerns. Tonight the Burrows would pay a tribute to the fallen Storyteller, Sojourner. The Storytellers had decided to give a holocast of her final contribution to their craft. The story had never been seen publically. It was a rare event because the Storytellers never revisited a telling publically, believing each event should be unique. The archives were used solely to help Storytellers learn techniques from masters of the craft. Each public telling was to be fresh, and the archives were closed to the public. Once a Storyteller had passed, his or her voice was never heard again. As a matter of fact, this viewing would be shown in every far away place, even to the furthest corner of the Empire. This was a great exception.

Ivan and Jenta were given their place in the stands. He saw Chef and Lyla. Once Chef had been an Examiner, and had been captured with Ivan. Now he was restored and joined to the woman who had one time been Forsaken. The women from the Empire still tended to cover themselves in public, even here in the Burrows. Lyla did not. There were so many differences in the world. Some would have happened whether or not Sojourner had been captured, but some were because she had been captured. It would take historians and many years to sort it all out. Lord Provo and his family filed in. He was a good man and worked hard as the ambassador. He waved at Ivan and Ivan nodded to him. His wife remained covered, though she only wore a house veil. She could not bear to have men look at her face.

Lord Provo had had a difficult job over the past year. Partly because of the turmoil the containment had caused the Empire. It had been chaos, but Kalig had risen to the occasion and had become a leader of his people. He had led his people through the Forsaken Uprising and the Examiner's Rebellion. Chiria was returned to him, but only after he agreed to marry her. The rest of the Chosen were still part of the Burrows.

His reverie was interrupted by a stirring in the front of the ampitheater. Stephen was escorted in and took a seat of honor. He moved like a very old man. His year had been terrible. He had raved like a madman and had even gone so far as to attempt to travel to the Empire to bring revenge to Kalig. There had been many troubles for him, and they only ended when Kalig travelled to the Burrows to make peace with Stephen, presenting him with the remains of his wife. It had taken its toll on him. He was joined by his daughter and her little daughter, Sojourner. Other family members joined him and sat around him like a shield. The night crept over the commons, and velvet darkness filled the corners with deep shadows.

A light illumined the stage, revealing the Leader they called Joseph. He spread his arms and the crowd quieted. "My friends, I greet you! I am one of the many, I am Joseph, a Leader of the People of the Burrows. I come to you to remember our Storyteller, Sojourner. She lived a hopeful life, a life of great triumph and meaning. She moved us to strive for deeper understanding in her life. We are moved to strive for deeper understanding in her passing. We suffer because we miss her, but we always have to be mindful she was not ours to keep. She was a blessing. Now we must let her go. I know the way she would have preferred to leave us...she would have preferred to go telling us a story. So, my friends, we honor her by giving her memory this gift. Listen now, and remember her with peace."

Joseph silently left the dais. The torches on the dais burst into flame, and a pale light began to spread out over the stage. It was time. In a twinkling the diminuative form of the Master Storyteller appeared.

"Good morning! Would you like to join me for my walk? I'm going to the market, if you want to come along. It is a fine day, isn't it? Are you well today? And your family is.....Ho! There! What is happening there? Why, it is the lame boy! And those others are mocking him!

"You there! Come here right now! You too! And you! Don't even think about running away! Shame on you! Sit! You sit now! My friend is going to get your mothers, and you will tell them what I caught you doing. Weep if you want, your tears mean nothing to me! The idea! Mocking one of the broken ones. Why you should be ashamed!

"Why is it shameful to make fun of the lame and broken? How could you ask such an impertinent question? I can't wait for your mother to get here! Your parents have neglected to teach you properly! I will tell your mother a thing or two. I'll tell you why it is shameful to make jokes at the expense of the lame and infirm, and you had better listen carefully, or I'll lose my temper entirely!

"Corruption wages an insane war against the Maker, thinking he will rule the universe. He seeks to gain our spirits by bending them and breaking them and spoiling them here on this proving ground. His intention is to keep us from our tasks or to cause us to fail. He wages a clever war. He is clever, but not wise. He has made a terrible error, and he has ruined any hope he ever had of regaining a place in Heaven.

"When this world was made and its purpose was set in motion, Corruption believed that his victory would be easily won. He thought that all of the spirits that chose to become children of this planet would be easily turned from their purpose. He does ruin some. You see, Corruption can make himself seem beguiling and attractive. He can make his manner winning and his words sound reasonable and his voice sweet. Still, more often than not, the children of Earth avoid the pitfalls that Corruption has built into the world. From the beginning, Corruption has fumed and raged in his dark realm. He has schemed and plotted, he has focused. Once long ago, he had an idea that could have destroyed us all. He decided to break a child.

"In Heaven, there was a spirit named Movement, and he was youthful and strong. He danced across the cosmos for the joy of feeling his body move. He ran when others walked. He jumped when others climbed. He was inexhaustible and rarely at rest.

"Movement was one of the first to volunteer for a chance to prove himself on Terra's troubled world. He knew in his heart that he would be faithful, and he was eager for his turn to be a human. Soon his turn came, and his task was one that he embraced. He was to be born to a tribe that lived deep in a forest, one that wrested its living from the land and only rarely saw others. He would grow, and when he was a young man, he was to rescue a hunter from a rival tribe from a wild boar. He was to return the man to his people at great personal risk. He was to fall in love with a young woman from the tribe, and with their joining, make peace between the two peoples.

"Joyfully, he allowed his task to be woven into his being. Peacefully, he embraced the deep, sleeping forgetfulness that every spirit enters when it becomes human. He entered his mother's womb. Corruption was waiting.

"Maliciously, Corruption seized the innocent Movement and twisted his back and crushed his legs in his mother's womb. He reasoned that the beasts of Earth abandon the weak, and that humans were to be woven out of the same elements as the beasts, so surely the child would be abandoned. Movement would never accomplish his task, because he would never begin it.

"Movement did not understand, for he had forgotten all of himself, but he felt the great pain of his bending. He writhed in his mother's womb until the wave of pain passed and after a long time he fell into a fretful sleep. His mother felt him moving in her, and she was happy that her baby was strong in her. No one suspected that the child had been broken.

"In Heaven, though, the Maker saw everything that happened.

"He became enraged.

"With the purity of perfect fury, the Maker enveloped all of Creation. All beings were frozen in a moment of anguish and sorrow. The Maker's eyes burned like a thousand fires and the anger on his face seemed eternal, like a carved, cold stone. Corruption saw the Maker, and for the first time he realized the futility of his rebellion. He tried to run away, but the Maker engulfed him in His outrage.

"Cowering, Corruption pleaded for mercy. "Oh! Magnificent Creator! Mercy! I see my folly! I know that I cannot conquer Heaven! I do not want to conquer Heaven! I am willing to be the lowest servant in the meanest place in the Universe! Please! Don't destroy me!"

"The Maker watched Corruption cowering in terror, and He realized His fury was too great, and He gained control of His anger. He knew in his deepest Self that His anger was complete, but He also knew He could no longer tolerate Corruption's madness.

"Destroy you!" the Maker spoke, and His voice was like deep bells and His words sounded eternal. "No! I'll not destroy you! You will live throughout this span of creation with the bargain you have made! You want to live separately from Me? So be it! I take My Spirit from you!"

"Corruption writhed in pain and terror as the Maker's life drained from him.

"You want to understand what it is to be a Creator?" The Maker's voice was like thunder. "Know the pain of creating a new type of being!"

"Corruption felt his back twisting and his legs being crushed. He screamed in agony. He felt the fabric of his being altering.

"Know the price of your cruelty," the Maker said. "Every child that you bend, you will bear the marks on your own being! It is woven in you now! Live with it!"

"Corruption lay, broken and twisted, gasping for breath. "How can this be?" he moaned in pain. "In my deepest parts, I never imagined You could be this harsh....I am ruined." He moaned.

"The Maker looked at Corruption, His visage was stern, but His eyes were filled with mercy. "It is time to stop this madness. You may return to Heaven as soon as you set the universe to rights. You have earned this pain, but I will still restore you if you choose well and make amends to all of those you have injured. This is not harsh; it is mercy and justice. "

"Corruption was consumed by his pain, and he did not listen to the Maker. Instead, he only perceived his ruin. "You are not who I imagined You to be," groaned Corruption. "I thought I understood You! I never imagined this...." he moaned as he felt the stabbing pains in his back. "I will never be able to defeat you like this! But, I will never give up! You are harsh and cruel! You deceive the universe! I alone know the depth of your evil! I will defeat You! I deserve to be God after the way You have treated me! I deserve to be the Ruler of All!"

"With great effort, Corruption struggled to his feet. In his eyes, there was the feral light of madness. He faced the Maker. "What I do is a noble thing; the way

You persecute me proves it! But I will win! I know I will! I will gain my strength back with every victory I have! You have woven balance into the Universe, and I will gain strength every time a broken child is discarded! I will gain strength every time one of Your puppets falls from its strings. They will bless me for freeing them! You think to punish me? When I gain Heaven, I will shred You without mercy! Without Mercy!"

"The Maker did not listen to Corruption's ravings because they were tiresome. He turned away from the madness of Corruption's words, and he walked away. He had better things to do.

"In the proper time the baby that had been Movement was born into this world. His mother rejected him, and his tribe abandoned him. His father and his brother carried him deep into the forest, unsuckled, un-named, unwashed. They left him inside the boundary of their enemies' hunting ground, hoping to bring calamity on their tribe.

"The Maker, Himself, stood guard over the child, and the spirits of Heaven guided help to rescue the baby. A hunter from the rival tribe followed a voice in the rustling breeze through the forest, and discovered the infant, weak and feeble. He fell on his knees and thanked his gods that he had discovered such a sign. Here was proof that his enemies were cursed! His gods had left an infant with the peculiar coloring of the enemies, yet it was twisted and unwell. This child must be the talisman that would protect them from the murderers. Tenderly, he gathered the baby into his arms, and as quickly as he could, he made his way home to his village.

"The villagers gathered around the hunter, and they rejoiced at the wondrous discovery. They named the child Luck, and the mothers took turns caring for him. When he grew big enough, the hunters would take him on their hunts, and the Maker smiled on their efforts. The tribe prospered.

"Luck was never a very strong boy, but he was lively and he had a joyful manner about him. Because the tribe embraced him, and he believed he was a gift from the gods, he never felt sorry for himself. He grew as strong as his bent back and twisted legs would allow. He would join in as the other boys played, never minding that he could not win at their games. He joined in for the joy of moving. When the other children jumped, he climbed; when they ran, he hobbled after them. When he heard music, he felt in his bones that there was a dance locked within them. Although he was easily exhausted, he rarely gave up.

"The tribe cherished his spirited love of life. The shaman said he was sent to show them that their lives were not futile. Even when Luck was naughty, the tribe believed he was a blessing to them.

"He grew into a young man. Just like every other young man in the tribe, he desired the Rites of Passage that would allow him to have a true voice in the tribe. He wanted to take a place in the decisions, he wanted a wife and children. His heart was captured by a young woman of the tribe, and he longed to achieve the same status of the other young men, so that he could marry her. She was not the most beautiful or accomplished young woman, but her heart was kind, and she was always willing to do more than her share of the work.

"The men of the tribe were reluctant for Luck to perform the Rites. They were dangerous, and even some of their best young men were hurt or killed. There were three Rites, and they were all terrible. The first was the Rite of the Warrior, and in it the young man had to endure the Walk of Fire, the Cutting of the Flesh, and the Survival of the Arrow. The second Rite was the Trial of Solitude and Hunger. The third was the Passage of the Hunter. All of the Rites had to be accomplished within a moon, or the young man had to wait for another season to try again. It was very rare for a young man to pass through the Rites the first time he attempted them, and those that failed season after season were never allowed to marry or take a place in the tribe. Very few failed completely, but it was a harsh trial to all who were brave enough to try it.

"Luck believed in his heart that he could eventually pass through the Rites, even the Walk of Fire. He practiced diligently, and trained his body to be as fit as it could be. His love for the young woman drove him forward, and his desire to be accepted as a man burned in him like an unquenchable fire. Finally, he convinced the hunters that he should be given the opportunity to take the Rites of Passage because the gods allowed him to grow into a man, and it was important for him to act like one to keep the favor of the gods. The hunters decided that they should give him aid through the Rites, though, because the gods had made him wanting and incomplete. Although Luck did not like their decision, he agreed to let them give him aid.

"Somehow, he survived the Rite of the Warrior. His feet were sorely burned, and he did not come away unhurt from the Cutting. He was wounded by the arrow, though not badly. He spent his time of Solitude and Hunger resting and treating his wounds. Although he found the pangs in his belly to be a trial, he thought continually about the young woman, and he imagined the softness of her hair, and he dreamed of the warmth of her in his arms. He never lost his resolution. Weak and tired, he survived. He had a only five days before he had to complete the Rites, and for three days he slept and ate and prepared to take his battered body into the forest to hunt.

"Too soon, it came time for Luck to face the test of the Hunter. It was decided that the hunter who had first discovered Luck would go with him into the forest. It was also decided that Luck would hunt the fierce wild boar. As he had been on many hunts and knew the way of the forest, the tribe knew that this would be the easiest part of the Rites for Luck. He would require help to carry the meat home to the tribe. The hunter was proud to have been chosen to accompany Luck, and his family deemed it a good omen.

"Hunting was a way of life for the tribe, and even young boys could bring home small game for their families. Early in the morning, the tribe sent their beloved Luck into the forest with high spirits and great hopes. The young woman stepped closer to Luck than was considered proper and whispered to him that she would be eager to feast with the tribe on the game he would bring back. Despite his wounds, Luck was filled with well-being.

"Luck and the hunter searched all morning for sign of the boar, and when the sun was high in the sky they were relieved to find a trace of prints that were not more than a day old. Deeper and deeper into the forest they tracked. They traveled warily, as they could tell they were coming close to the boundaries of their hunting ground. The sun was slanting through the trees when they finally spotted their prey. The hunter stayed back, watching with pride as much as he could with the evening sun in his eyes as Luck sighted his arrow onto the boar. Luck carefully drew a bead on the boar and let forth his shot. Unfortunately, the beast moved forward, and the arrow did not kill the animal, instead, it sank deeply into his haunch. The boar started and spun about in outraged pain. The first person it saw was the hunter, and instinctively, it charged Luck's friend. Because the sun was in the hunter's eyes, he did not run away from the wounded, crazed animal. Instead, the boar charged the hunter, knocking him over and ravaging him with fearsome swiftness.

"As quickly as his bent body would allow, Luck came to the aid of his friend. Desperately, he used his spear to finish killing the boar, pushing the dead beast off of his own rescuer. The hunter was sorely wounded with deep gashes in his legs and side. He was moaning in pain and his eyes were full of fear. Luck knew the ways of the forest, and he quickly found the things he would need to help his friend stay alive until he could get him back to the village. As best he could, he covered his friends wounds with willow bark and the moss that the shaman used to treat wounds. He bound them tightly, and he tried to lift his friend. Unfortunately, he was too weakened from the Rites to lift the hunter, so he lashed limbs together with vines and made a litter to drag his friend to the village.

"The willow bark had helped the hunter control his pain. He begged Luck to prepare the boar to take back to the tribe. The tribe needed the food, and Luck deserved to be a man of the tribe. They could not travel at night, and he may be fitter to travel in the morning. Please, he pleaded, rest and food tonight...a fire, these healing plants...rest and food... Promise.

"Luck prepared a fire, and soon, he had the magical parts of the boar roasting over the fire. He prepared the heart, the liver, the kidneys. He did not know how they helped the sick, but these were the magical parts that the shaman used to heal the sick. Although he was weary, he prepared the meat, and with great care, he fed his wounded friend.

"Through the long night, Luck tended to the fire, and to his friend, the hunter. He felt a deep weariness in his bones and in his soul, and he longed to sleep. The hunter slept fitfully, and when morning came at last, he seemed to be much weaker than he was the night before. Luck cursed himself for not trying to get the hunter back to the village the night before, and he began the long, arduous journey back to their home.

"All through the terrible morning, Luck pulled the litter through the forest. The hunter was feverish and barely conscience. He murmured fitfully, groaning with pain every time Luck hit a stone or root. He fell silent. Luck stopped briefly and turned and looked back at his mentor and friend. His pale face was drawn and silent. Luck's heart skipped a beat, and he turned with great resolution toward his village. Luck strained against his load, pulling with all of his strength and all of his heart. Sweat poured down his face and down his shoulders, and his weary body was wracked with pain. He longed to leave the meat from his kill behind, but he had promised the hunter that he would bring his kill back to the tribe so they would have food. He had promised the hunter he would complete his Rites. He had promised...he was so tired....

"He battled to pull his load, his twisted back aching, his hobbling legs tripping. He could tell he was getting closer to the village, he could see the river that his village was near ahead of him. The sun was high in the sky, and he knew he could be there when the sun was slanting at his back if he could keep his broken body moving. He felt like his heart would burst in his chest, and his breath was like fire in his weary lungs. His legs quivered and shook with every painful step.

"From deep in the shadowed forest, there were those that had been watching Luck struggle with his burden, and they had been following him. From early in the morning, two hunters from the tribe of the Others had been shadowing Luck. At first, their intention had been to ambush them and take the meat back to their own tribe. Their tribe was hungry, and when they saw that their enemies had a kill and that one of them was wounded, they decided to take the kill, and murder their rivals. It would be a glorious morning. Then, as they drew closer, they noticed Luck's broken body, and they became afraid.

"It is the Broken Child!" exclaimed one. "He has lived!"

"Our tribe has been cursed ever since he was left to die in this forest. We have been hungry and our trials have been terrible since the child was left. We cannot kill him, or the gods will utterly destroy us!" added the other hunter.

"Let us follow them. Perhaps we can mend our curse. Perhaps there is hope for us."

"The hunters agreed to follow, though they did not know what they could accomplish. As they followed, they saw that Luck struggled beyond his limits, and their hearts were stirred, and they were ashamed of what their tribe had done, and they were proud of the great determination and heart that Luck displayed. They prayed to their gods that Luck would accomplish his task, hoping that their prayers would bring forgiveness to their tribe. They prayed, and then they caught their breaths as Luck stumbled and fell and did not rise.

"Get up, Broken Child!" whispered the first hunter hoarsely.

"Redeem us!" wept the other.

"If we help them, their tribe may think we have done this, and they will kill us. There will be war."

"We cannot let our lost brother die like this! We can remove the curse from us if we help them. We have to take the chance!"

"The first hunter nodded his head silently, and the two hunters left their hiding places and moved cautiously to the unconsciouses men. Carefully, they turned Luck over, and their hearts were pierced with the weariness etched into his young face. A small trickle of blood issued from the corner of Luck's mouth, and his bent body was cold and clammy to the touch. The other man felt of fire, and his wounds were puckered and livid with heat. Tenderly, the hunters lifted Luck onto the litter, thinking the heat from the hunter would be helpful to Luck. They divided the meat, and bound it onto their backs, thinking that it would appease their gods if they returned all to their rivals. They bent to their loads, and they began pulling the litter toward the village.

"It did not take long for them to find the village, they were young and strong, and their minds were unclouded with pain. They found the village, and they entered it without a thought for their own safety. They pulled the litter into the center of the village, not looking to the left or the right. They believed in their hearts that their own village would prosper if the two men were brought home, though they were certain that they would be killed.

"They carefully lowered the litters to the ground, and they put the carcass of the boar on the ground, too. The villagers began to gather, slowly at first, then in a great outpouring. The hunters were terrified. They cowered in fear. They did not know the village had so many people. The hunters were taken by some very stern men to a hut, and they were pushed inside, and the door was barred. They did not know what their fate would be.

"Outside, the medicine man was called, and Luck and the hunter were taken to the Healing Place. The medicine man and his helpers began to tend to the wounds of the hunter and to the illness of Luck. The elders of the tribe went to the men and questioned the hunters.

They were astonished when they found out that Luck had been born to their rivals, and that they had chosen to abandon him like the beasts abandoned their weak. The hunters hung their heads, their voices full of shame and regret.

"Our people have paid dearly for our smallness of heart. Our tribe is now cursed. When we saw our brother was grown, we were afraid."

"We watched him, and we followed, and we were proud of him and his greatness of spirit. We know he is blest by the gods."

"We ask that you spare us..."

"We want to be forgiven..."

"The elders looked at each other, and they understood each other.

"The eldest of them stood, and said, "We have learned mercy, and so have you."

"Another stood. "We thank you for your help."

"Another stood. "Join us in our prayers for our hunters. Come and pray."

"Together, they went to pray. Like one tribe, they danced when the hunter's fever broke, and he sat up and ate the strong broth his wife prepared for him.

"Like one tribe, they prayed for Luck, and they wept like lost children when he died.

"Luck's broken body was given to the Earth, and his people mourned. The young woman was bereft, for she loved Luck. One of the hunters from Luck's mother's tribe felt his heart stirred by her devotion, and he resolved in his heart that he would try to be worthy of her. Perhaps there was room in her heart for another....

"Luck's body was returned to the Earth, and his spirit returned to Heaven. As he came back into himself, and he remembered all of who he was, he buried his head in his hands and he wept for sorrow, remembering the life he left. He felt a hand on his shoulder, and he looked up into the Maker's face.

"You have done well, Movement. All of Heaven awaits to celebrate your homecoming!"

"But Maker! I failed! I did not marry the young woman...she was so lovely...There is not peace between our tribes. I belong to Corruption. I have failed." He dropped his eyes.

"Do you want to serve Corruption?" asked the Maker gently.

"No!" replied Movement.

"Then come home, child."

"But what of Corruption?" Movement asked, his voice still thick with unshed tears.

"The Maker's eyes flashed with a deep fire, and He looked afar at the twisted being that cringed at the edge of the universe. "He has no claim over you," said the Maker, and the weaving of the universe encompassed his words. "Come home!"

"And so it happened. Movement stretched out his arms and embraced the great rush of dance and speed that he loved. The young hunter from Luck's tribe married the young woman, for her heart had room to love. There was peace between the tribes.

"Corruption has never stopped breaking children, though. It is dangerous for him to do so, because for every life that is victorious, he bears the injustice of their breaking on his own body. However, for every broken child that is neglected or forgotten, he gains a measure of his strength back. Every taunt makes him stronger, every abandonment makes him more whole. There have been times on this troubled orb when Corruption has become almost whole. There are times when he is diminished, a shadow of his former self.

That is why it is important to remember compassion. That is why ....Ah! here come your mothers. Yes, they are angry. It seems they understand, and have taught you something. All of you! Sit up straight! Tell the truth, and things will go better for you."

The holo-image became still, hands outstretched, face alight with the captured moment of Sojourner's inner fire.

Ivan breathed in deeply. The air smelled sweet, like honeysuckles and roses. The velvet night lay about him like a deep, soft blanket. Ivan looked out in the gathering night through eyes clouded with tears for the lost Storyteller and for his part in her pain. On the dais, the image of the Storyteller was bright and clear, standing in silent stillness, capturing the moment as was her habit. For a moment, Ivan felt his connection to all of those that felt the same pain. His eyes could no longer hold his tears, and they spilled over in a hot rush. He looked away for a moment to regain his composure, and when he looked back to the dais, the image of Sojourner flickered once, and faded. The torches went dark; only the moon and stars shone in the deep night sky.

About the Author

Katherine D. Bennett is a teacher and the author of a number of children's stories published on CD's. She and her family live in the rural Midwest where she teaches in the public school system.

Printed in the United States
35739LVS00001B/2